BROOKLYN CUPID

LEXI RAY

BROOKLYN CUPID

LEXI RAY

Brooklyn Cupid

Editing: Tracy Liebchen

Proofing: Mary / On Pointe Digital Services

❀ Created with Vellum

PLAYLIST

Rules—KCPK
TWO SUGARS—Tai Verdes
Sexy Villain—Remi Wolf
Out of My League—Fitz and The Tantrums
Love To Love You Baby - Single Edit—Donna Summer
She—Harry Styles
Empire State Of Mind—JAY-Z, Alicia Keys
I Don't Care—Kyson Facer, Jada Facer
Don't Take The Money—Bleachers
Inside And Out—Feist
Ever Since New York—Harry Styles
Honesty—Pink Sweat$
RUNAWAY—OneRepublic
Wings—Birdy
The Man—The Killers
About You—G Flip
golden hour—JVKE
My God (feat. Weyes Blood)—The Killers, Weyes Blood, Lucius

You can find the playlist on Spotify

1

JACE

Dumbo neighborhood,
Brooklyn,
New York City

"*HE IS FORTY FEET AWAY... THIRTY-FIVE...*" ROEY'S VOICE IN MY earpiece is like an AI countdown.

"I have him," I whisper, my heart starting to thud. But my hands are steady on the dart rifle. A gun has become my arm's extension in the last few years.

For a split second, a passing yellow cab blocks my scope, then the reticle is back on the short dark silhouette of our target, Anatolyi Reznik. Walking hurriedly on the other side of the street from the office building I'm in, he nervously looks around, scanning the dark street like he can sense Roey and Miller shadowing him.

I got this.

"*Thirty feet. He's suspicious.*"

There's a loud banging on the third floor above me.

Freaking Brooklyn. It's midnight on a Wednesday, but apparently, New York City never sleeps.

"*Don't fuck it up, Shooter.*"

This is our highest-paid job yet, and I reel in anticipation over the walking five-million dollars in my view, about to be sedated. That is besides the fact that we beat the Brexton Recovery bounty hunters who lost this assignment half a year ago. Assholes can suck it this time.

"Twenty feet. No passersby."

I breathe steadily, the reticle of my scope moving with the hurried figure of the crypto-currency mastermind who screwed some very important people for a lot of money.

"Ten feet. Yellow cab is coming. Hold it."

The cab pulls to a stop, completely blurring my scope vision as Reznik disappears behind it.

"Wait."

Through the open window that holds my dart rifle, I hear voices by the cab, one of them female and overly excited. Then the cab pulls away, clearing my scope vision with—

No, not Reznik. A pink fur coat envelopes him in an embrace.

"Who is this?" I murmur in annoyance, studying the bulky fashion coat that looks like it's been ripped off a unicorn.

The long blonde hair, slender legs, and stilettos belong to a young girl. She blocks Reznik as she chats him up, her fairytale princess laughter echoing through the empty street of Dumbo, the trendy Brooklyn neighborhood that overlooks the East River and Manhattan on the other side of it.

"Wait. It's someone he knows."

Odd.

This must be the reason he left his bodyguards by the subway. Somehow, the meeting with this girl is special.

This is the trickiest assignment I've had in a year of working for Roey.

Six months ago, Reznik sent three trackers who located him to a hospital after poking them with a nerve-agent-poisoned needle embedded in his wrist bracelet. We don't want to take the chance of grabbing him bare-handed. So sedating him with a dart was the go-to choice.

A loud bark jerks both the blondie and Reznik's heads to the left. A lone white dog walks up to them, and the girl gets down on her haunches.

"Oh, look at you, sweetie," she coos, stretching her hand to the dog. "Are you lost?"

Her sugary voice is distracting. But in the position she is in, Reznik's figure looms right above her.

"I have a clear shot," I say.

"Go for it. We'll deal with the girl later."

This is what I did for four years overseas. While guys my age went to college, hung out with girls, and partied, I spent my time with my eye on the scope. A job is a job. I was the best at it, didn't know better, and was running from my shitty orphan childhood.

But the girl distracts me.

No women or children—my heart gives an uneasy thud at the thought.

"Got you," I murmur, focusing on Reznik, and squeeze the trigger at the precise moment the dog barks and the blondie in pink jerks to her feet.

"Fuck!" I exhale, horror washing over me.

The girl stumbles. Reznik asks her something, then looks around and takes off with the speed of light, his hurried footsteps fading into the night.

"Dammit!" I curse. "Roey, I shot the girl! Reznik's on the run."

We can't chase him for fear of being injected with poison. The five million dollars we almost had in our hands is slipping away.

"Fuck!" Roey yells into my earpiece, his breathing strained as he starts running.

The girl stumbles toward the side of the building and slumps against the brick facade, the sedative working almost instantly.

I can't believe this!

I couldn't possibly have missed him!

Not tonight!

Three months of work!

Five million dollars!

No women or children.

The blondie topples over onto the pavement like a rag doll.

2

JACE

"What do we do?" I exhale in panic.

"Okay, listen, she knows him. We need to know how. She's our only chance to find him again. Get the fuck down here."

Two shadows, Roey and Miller, wearing black hoodies and baseball hats, hurry up to the girl's body on the ground.

I set the rifle down on the floor, and in seconds, I'm down the stairs, out of the building, and trotting across the street.

No people in sight. No cars. Thank God!

Roey already picked her up and is holding her motionless body in his arms.

Miller rubs his face with both hands, murmuring on repeat, "Goddammit."

"I don't know what happened," I apologize. "The freaking dog barked. She jumped up."

There's another bark to the left—the white dog that looks like a pit bull stares at us from the distance.

"Come on." Roey motions and starts walking.

"Where are you taking her?"

"That we have to figure out."

We round the corner like three thieves with the pink-blonde baggage in Roey's arms. The street opens into a park that overlooks the East River and both the Brooklyn and Manhattan Bridges.

Carefully, Roey sets the girl down on a park bench and exhales, fixing his baseball hat with both hands.

"Well, we fucked it up," he says, scanning the empty park as we stand under the streetlight.

This is a weird twist. I study the pretty young girl who looks like she just stepped off a Barbie magazine, and guilt twists my stomach.

"Okay." Roey sets his hands on his hips. "Here's the plan. You"—he gives me a backward nod—"are staying with her until she comes to. Give that sedative about half an hour."

"Me?" He must be crazy. "Not a chance. *You* are the lady's man."

"Jace, we don't need a lady's man right now. You look more trustworthy. When she comes to, you help her out. Sweet talk her. I'll guide you"—he taps his earpiece—"until you find out how she knows Reznik. Considering the guy lays low for months, it's a miracle that someone *does* know him around here."

"Miller is a better candidate," I argue.

"Well, *you* fucked up the shot, Jace."

I grunt, shame washing over me. Roey knows I never miss. So he's angry at the fact that the five-million-dollar bounty is dissipating faster than smoke in the wind.

"You fucked it up, so fix it, Shooter," he says more bitterly.

"Roey—"

"Sit down." He pushes me onto the bench next to the blondie, grabs my arm, and slings it around her shoulders, her head lolling onto her chest. "Put on your glasses."

"Ugh. Can we just—"

"Jace! Put on your fucking glasses!" he barks. "We don't have time for your insecurities."

Reluctantly, I take the glasses out of my pocket. They are black-rimmed fakes, for camouflage, which *gives me a nerdy vibe,* as per Roey.

He snatches my baseball hat and slicks my hair. "Perfect," he murmurs, working me like I'm a puppet.

"Now what?"

"Now we split. Stay put. We're going to pick up your gun and stay around the corner."

By the time I take a deep breath, Roey and Miller are gone, and I scan the empty park.

I'm soaked with sweat under my hoodie despite the chilly April night. The scent of the girl's flowery perfume tickles my nostrils, and—

The white dog sits at a distance and stares—unmistakably, even in the dim streetlights—at me. Or her? Is it *her* dog? Nah. He has no collar. His one eye sparkles, reflecting the streetlight, making it look like he's winking at me.

My heart is pounding. This night is taking a strange turn.

"How's the hot date, lover-boy?" Roey's voice in my earpiece jerks me out of my thoughts. *"While you are chilling, check her purse."*

Right.

The dollface with perfectly outlined eyebrows, long lashes, and full lips is peaceful. Unlike me. I feel like a criminal when I reach for her silver clutch that matches her stilettos and the buttons on her huge pink fur coat.

A lipstick. A phone with bunny ears—definitely a girly type. Money. Credit cards. ID—bingo!

"Got it," I say.

"Spill."

"Her name is Lucy Moor."

Roey snorts in my earpiece. *"There are worse names."*

"Twenty-one." Only three years younger than me. "Resides in Virginia."

"Wonder what she's doing in New York. A tourist? Any indication?"

I pick up her phone—no password. Her home screen is an image of a teddy bear with a spray paint can in its paw. The picture folder is full of recent shots from outings with people. She is a party girl, by the looks of it. I keep scrolling through hundreds of photographs —people, places, parties, more parties, art, more art, dozens of pictures of feet. The hell?

I pause on one of the party pictures and check the date—six months ago.

"It looks like Miss Lucy Moor currently resides in New York," I say. "All her pictures going back at least half a year are from here."

"Any naked shots?"

"Creep." I close the folder.

Roey laughs, and then Miller's monotonous voice is in my

earpiece, guiding me to his security website with her phone browser. I type in the code, activate the ghost tracker, and close it.

Now, we have full access to all the info on her phone. Our methods are not always legal, but neither are most of our targets. Lucy Moor might just be Reznik's secret accomplice. The most innocent faces often hide dark intentions. You learn this serving in a war.

I shoot the shit with Roey for some time until Lucy Moor stirs.

"Okay, Jace, you're on."

3

JACE

THE GIRL FROWNS AT ME WHEN SHE SLOWLY SITS UP, SHAKING HER HEAD like she can shake off the buzz, then fixes her hair and looks around, confused.

"W-what's happening?"

My pulse surges as her eyes meet mine. They are a lovely shade of blue and slightly unfocused, warm and calm like an ocean. Her voice is sweet but cautious, and something shifts in my chest at the sound of it.

"I was walking by," I say, already feeling my guts twisting—I don't like this particularly shady situation. Or schmoozing a pretty girl. Or lying while looking into her naive eyes. "You were talking to a gentleman, then started going down, like fainted, I don't know." I'm losing my train of thought as I gaze into her mesmerizing eyes. "And the man took off. I tried to call him over, but he just ran."

She frowns, checks her pockets, then picks up her clutch.

"Ran, huh?" she murmurs, checking its contents—making sure nothing is stolen?—then looks around.

"Yeah," I say, my heart nervously pumping. "You know him?"

"Diadia Tolia? Yeah…" Her gaze pauses on the dog, her features softening into a smile. "Ran, huh?" she repeats absently. I know she's still disoriented from the sedative.

"Diadia means uncle in Russian. They must be close. Tell her to call him," Roey instructs me.

8

"Yeah, kinda weird. Wanna call him?"

She shakes her head again, turning her gaze to me, her pretty puffy lips parted. "I don't… No, no." A cute frown etches her fore-head. "Who are *you*?"

She gives me an up-and-down look that's more curious than suspicious.

I get up, ruffling my hair in unease. "Was walking by, just picked you up, brought you here, was gonna call 911, but then you woke up."

"Perfect."

"How long was I out?"

"Half—"

"Two minutes," Roey corrects me. Thank God for this man.

"Two minutes," I say.

"Huh."

Doesn't look like she believes me, and I feel even more like a scumbag, wanting to yank the stupid glasses off my face. They create a barrier from the beautiful eyes in front of me, the ones I want to bring closer and get lost in.

I take a deep breath. "I'm not leaving you here by yourself," I say with as much confidence as I can master. "It's late. If you pass out again… Have you been drinking?"

"Good, good."

She nods. "Yeah, but…"

"Want me to call someone?"

"No, I live right here. I'll just walk."

"You're not walking by yourself. There are bad guys on the streets at this time of night."

She stares at me.

Shit.

Roey chuckles in my earpiece.

"I'll walk you to the door," I say, motioning in a vague direction. Suddenly, I feel protective of her. I want to make sure she gets home safe.

I help her up, and we make small talk as we walk.

"What's your name?" she asks.

"Jace Reed."

"You kidding me, Shooter?"

9

I shouldn't have said my real name, but Lucy Moor's voice is hypnotic, and without thinking, I tell her that I reside in Costa Mesa, California, and that I'm in New York for work, renting an Airbnb in Southern Brooklyn. Which is true. That's where we anchored for the last several months tracking Reznik. It's close to Brighton Beach where he was spotted last.

Lucy Moor is not shy and way too trusting. She has a soft sweet voice and contagious laughter. Also, gorgeous legs which are not so stable—blame the sedative for that—and the highest heels I've ever seen that reflect the streetlights like disco balls.

I offer my arm for stability, still feeling like a dick, and she wraps her hand around it, leaning on me just slightly. I want to carry her in my arms as an apology for what I just did to her.

She's breathtakingly beautiful when she smiles. I'm sure she has many admirers, rich fancy guys, a whole city of them. Probably a fancy-ass boyfriend, too.

We pause only five streets away from the park at the doors to Goldsling Towers.

I look up, scanning the building that holds seven-figure condos with a view of Manhattan across the East River.

"You live here?" I muse.

"Yeah, for now." She shrugs and looks up, too.

"Rich girl, huh? Maybe Reznik did share the loot. Invite yourself in."

"Well, let me just tell the concierge to check on you," I say.

Her smile grows. "Jace Reed, a gentleman, huh? And here I thought you were a night-stalker."

"You are. And she already calls you by your name, lucky bastard."

I'm sure it's the sedative plus whatever booze she had that makes her happy and flirty as she leads me past the doorman and the polite concierge inside.

I don't halt even for a second. "I'm delivering you right to your door," I say as I confidently walk her toward the elevator. I need more time with her.

"Damn, Jace, smooth. Invite yourself for a drink."

Lucy Moor giggles drunkenly as she stumbles into the elevator and presses the eleventh-floor button, then returns her cute smile to me. Her eyes study my unimpressive black outfit. "You are..."

I'm...working, yep, but I wish this wasn't how we met.

"Sweet," she says.

You have no idea…

Her quick laughter travels through my skin and lodges in my heart. She's out of my league, and being in her presence gives me an instant crush.

She opens the door to her condo, and… *wow!* I pause in the doorway, startled.

Floor-to-ceiling windows line one wall of a huge living room with an open-concept kitchen at the back, giving way to a terrace and a magnificent view of the night Manhattan skyline.

A slick white living room set and a coffee table sit on a square plush carpet right in the center like it's an appetizer on a giant dish at a fancy restaurant.

The rest of the space is filled with things that visually don't fit in —an easel with a blank canvas and over a dozen canvases propped against the walls, trays with paints and brushes everywhere.

"Pardon the mess. I'm an artist, so…" Lucy doesn't move away from the entrance but leans on the wall, her head slightly cocked as she stares at the window. "I never get tired of this view," she murmurs with a dreamy sigh.

I thought she'd be a supermodel or something of the sort. But she's an artist—the thought is a relief of sorts, though I shouldn't care what she does for a living. Unless, of course, she funnels cryptocurrency through offshore accounts for Reznik. She's an assignment. With luminous blue eyes and cute coral lips that I shouldn't be staring at.

"Is this your place?" I ask.

"Yeah. I mean, no. I rent it. I mean…" She sighs and tosses her clutch onto the shoe rack, her movements slow and lazy. "I house-sit it for friends. Or people I know."

"That's too many variables. She's bluffing." Roey voice in my earpiece startles me. I forgot all about him.

"You stay here by yourself?" I probe.

"Yeah, for now." She raises her hands above her head, stretching. Yeah, she's tipsy alright. And beautiful, like a dream. "Though one of the bedrooms will be rented out soon."

"Fishy."

"Who's the renter?"

"She's house-sitting and renting one of the rooms. Our girl is a hustler. So hustle along."

Lucy Moor exhales heavily and slowly kicks off her shoes, immediately dropping lower. I like her even better when she's shorter, barely reaching my chin.

"I haven't found one." Slowly, she takes off her pink coat, revealing a black strapless minidress with costume jewelry. "It has to be someone reliable." She carelessly tosses it onto the shoe rack as well. "It's hard to find a good person these days."

She looks so much smaller and delicate without that huge fur, and I can't take my eyes off her.

"I have a feeling our Lucy Moor has more tricks up her sleeve. Reel her in!" Roey's voice brings my eyes back to her face.

"Well, listen," she says softly, turning to me and sucking her bottom lip in with an apologetic look. "I need to rest."

"Sure, yeah. Sorry." I back out of her place and step into the hallway, feeling slightly disappointed—I don't want to part.

She smiles, batting her eyelashes. At me?

"Goodbye, Jace Reed, and thank you," she says in a flirty voice, sagging against the door as she slowly closes it.

"She likes you, and we just lost her."

"Fuck off," I murmur, walking down the hall to the elevator, feeling like the hallway is already a notch dimmer without her smile.

"Fuck! Jace, hold up! Hold up, hold up! Turn around!"

"Why?" My forefinger pauses over the elevator button.

"I said turn the fuck around! How did I not think of it? Brilliant! Go back!"

Yessir.

Just the thought of seeing that pretty girl again makes me nervous as hell. But my heart is ecstatic. It pounds harder than on my first service trip to Yemen when I was eighteen.

I stop by the door I just walked out of and knock, my hoodie practically steaming from me sweating.

The door opens to reveal Lucy Moor again with her lovely smile, in that same black strapless minidress, with impossibly long legs and bare feet. She looks surprised but somewhat curious.

"Jace? You there?" Roey's warning voice pulls me out of my stupor and forces me to smile at her.

I know what Roey's about to say, and it's bad, bad, bad. These blue eyes are trouble. I can sense it. My heart does too, pounding wildly.

Lucy Moor, you weren't supposed to happen, I say to myself, lost in her luminous gaze, when I repeat Roey's words in my earpiece:

"How much is that room for rent?"

4

LU

I'm still in bed when my phone rings, and Greg, the concierge from downstairs, announces, "Miss Moor, you have a visitor."

"A visitor?"

I rub my eyes, trying to get rid of the slight grogginess that I've never had even during the worst hangovers. The morning sunlight is unusually razor-sharp.

"Mr. Jace Reed," the concierge says. "The gentleman says you are expecting him."

I wake up in an instant.

Right, my savior from the night before.

"Let him up, please. Thank you, Greg!"

Well, last night, I definitely had one too many before meeting Uncle.

He and Mom used to be close. Uncle used to come to visit every several months, on holidays, then once a year, until he disappeared when I started the university three years ago.

He called me out of the blue just yesterday and wanted to meet up, said he was in New York.

"Huh. I haven't talked to him in years," Mom said when I called her. "Never told him you left Virginia."

Well, if he's on social media, he'd find me easily because my face is all over it.

But Uncle disappeared again. I called him when I got home, but his number was disconnected.

Thank god for the hot Dark Knight, Jace Reed.

Renting the extra bedroom to a stranger might've been a hasty decision, but it's too late.

I throw on a pair of sweatpants and a loose T-shirt over a sports bra, then tie my messy hair into a bun on top of my head and practice a friendly yet stern face in the mirror. My new roommate should know that I was out of character last night, but I'll be a strict landlord.

Landlord, right.

Renting a room that doesn't belong to me in the first place is shady. But my best friend, Becky, okayed it with the owners.

I try to remember what Jace Reed told me about himself last night. He's twenty-four, an Ohio native, and currently resides in Costa Mesa, California. Occupation—automotive equipment salesman.

The doorbell rings, and my heartbeat spikes as I trot to the door then pause and take a deep breath.

I am a mess, with no makeup and bed hair, but I didn't expect Mr. Savior to show up so early. Noon seems like a good time when you are drinking the night before. Your hangover the next day has a different opinion.

Maybe this was a bad idea.

The thought spins in my head, pumping my blood with anxiety as I open the door, and my heart halts at the sight of Jace Reed in my doorway.

Brown hair, close cut, slightly outgrown on the top, handsome face, black-rimmed glasses.

"Hey," he says softly.

Hey.

I glance at the same black jeans and a hoodie he wore yesterday.

"I'm Jace, remember?" he says hesitantly, his eyes warm and curious.

A silly laugh escapes me when I realize I didn't respond. "Yeah, come in."

He holds my gaze for a moment, and his eyes the color of burnt amber widen just slightly in some sort of recognition like he knows me from somewhere else and I'm supposed to remember him. But he drops his gaze right away, a confused frown on his forehead like he's mistaken.

He's almost a head taller than me, hands in his pockets when he steps in. His presence fills the room. That's what made me agree to rent a room to him yesterday—he made me feel safe.

"Feeling better today?" he asks with a softness in his voice that's in contrast with his strong body and dark clothes.

"Yeah." I smile at my feet. "Last night was…" I try to choose the right word. "Peculiar," I say at the same time he says, "Interesting."

We both chuckle, then say, "Yeah," at the same time, grin, and glance at each other.

He looks away, but I keep my eyes on him. His smile changes his face, rendering it in the most humble and heart-warming way.

He looks like a good guy.

So do most serial killers, I hear Becky's voice in my head.

"So…" I say, feeling awkward and giddy at once.

"So, it's three thousand a month, right?" Jace finishes my sentence.

"Yes."

Three thousand for a room is not a lot, considering it's the luxury Goldsling Towers overlooking the East River.

"Cheaper than doing Airbnb," Jace reasons with a shy smile, the same as last night when he came back to ask about the room. He didn't mind the cash arrangement or an extra month's deposit. "And I'll be in and out of the city for the next several months. Here."

He pulls a bank envelope with cash out of his pocket and hands it to me.

"Wow. That's quick," I say, staring at it. "Well…" I guess there's no backing away from this. "Thank you," I say at the same time he says, "Thank you."

We both stifle a chuckle, and Jace wipes the corner of his mouth with his thumb, hiding his smile.

"You didn't even hear the rules yet," I say, feeling unusually at ease.

"I'm good with rules."

"Yeah?" I meet his gaze, and holy hell, his smiling eyes are brighter, sparklier, and lock with mine a little longer.

"No parties," I say.

"I don't party."

"Unless you run it by me, that is," I correct, trying not to sound like a bitch. "No smoking inside. I don't like smoke."

"I quit," he responds right away as his smile grows a little.

"Please, leave your shoes at the door. I don't have a cleaning lady. And, well, cleaning is part of living here."

"Yes, ma'am." He nods, his smile widening.

Yes, ma'am, huh?

It makes me smile too, and for a moment, we just gaze at each other, and I forget that we met only the night before. He feels so… familiar. Like we've been friends for a while. The unease I felt when I opened the door to him just minutes ago is gone.

He's quiet and polite and seems trustworthy. At least those black-rimmed glasses do. So does the polite way he talks, almost apologetically, like he's intruding.

"Pardon the mess," I say, noticing him glance around. "I'll clean up and move the easel and the canvases to my room. I'm getting ready for a solo exhibit, so…"

"No worries. I'm not fussy," he reassures me. "Need help? Looks heavy." He nods toward the easel. "Looks like a dozen artists are working here."

I chuckle. "No, just me. So, when are you ready to move in?"

He shrugs. "Today?"

I laugh, then quiet as I realize he's not joking and notice the blush coloring his cheeks.

"Sure," I say, stifling an amused chuckle. "That works. But don't you need to bring stuff? The room is fully furnished, but—"

"I just have my clothes. I'll be fine. If that's alright with you." He looks down at his feet as he says the last words like he's uncomfortable.

"Absolutely. Phew, this was easier than I thought."

He raises his smiling eyes to me again. "What *did* you think?"

I shrug.

"So, should we clean this up?" He nods to the living room.

Oh, I love this guy already. "I can do it later," I argue.

"Two pairs of hands are better than one," he says.

Only half an hour later, we've moved most of my stuff into my bedroom, and Jace's phone dings.

"So, I'm coming back this evening," he says as he texts, and I hand him the key to the condo.

Our eyes snap to the key then to each other.

"See you, roommate," I say.

He grins. "Yeah, roommate," he echoes, and when he leaves, the butterflies in my stomach are having an orgy.

I have Jace's phone number and the picture of his ID. His info is at the front desk downstairs. This feels... like a relationship. I'm being silly, of course.

I call Becky.

"B, I have a roommate!" I announce excitedly but with slight nervousness, because Becky always insists on giving an opinion about everything I do *before* I do it. Usually, I listen. But this whole roommate thing happened too fast.

"Who is she?"

"It's a he."

"What? Lu! Someone you know?"

"I just met him last night."

"Girl, what the fuck?"

Becky starts lecturing me, and my mood falls.

She might be right. I do get excited about new things easily before I give myself time to think them over. I generally like people while Becky is suspicious of everyone.

That's Becky, my best friend. Coincidentally, also my agent.

"Alright, I wanna meet this Jace Reed," she says. "I'll give you my unbiased opinion and make sure you're safe, considering you met him on the street. If I sense anything shady, you are kicking him out."

"I took a picture of his driver's license, though I couldn't find anything about him online."

"Yeah, suspicious. You are too trusting, Lu."

He *looks* trustful, I want to argue. But that's Becky—meticulous and organized, also with a maternal attitude toward me despite being only a few years older.

18

"By the way, I need to see more paintings for your upcoming exhibition."

"I'm on it, B. I just have too many things going on."

"Don't you always?"

Thank God for Becky. She hooked me up with the gallery. She'll take a percentage of my art sales. She's also trying to get me to publish a book. My Story Den spicy romance stories are getting more popular, and the bounties and commissions I get from the increasing views are getting higher.

"You need to up your writing game, Lu."

Yeah, that, too.

If art is supposed to be my big ticket, writing is my bread and butter. Or at least bread, generic and on sale.

"Lu, spicy romance is the queen these days. But you need to create an unforgettable character that sticks. A good story to go with it. Chemistry."

"I know, B," I huff in frustration.

Erotica shorts are not even my thing, but I've read enough of those and started writing while I was in college, trying to make extra cash. I have a small following, but my stories are no different from the gazillion other ones out there.

"I know you have it in you, Lu. Your *Beautiful Vice* mafia romance about Konstantin and Eva is a huge step up. So rinse and repeat, but up the game, dial up the smut, and use all that richness of colors you are so good with in painting. You know what I mean? Writing needs color. Get it?"

"I get it."

Becky is not an artist, but she has a vision for things.

"Your stories are like Twinkies. And you need to create your own recipe for a Red Velvet Cake."

"Right."

"With chocolate truffle layers."

"Ha!"

"Then I'll get you an editor, proofreader, formatter, cover designer, and we get it published. You have four hundred thousand followers on your social media, but they don't know that you write, because you are embarrassed of your smutty stories."

Right. My following is only for my art. My stories are a dark secret for a totally different audience.

"If we do it right, we can both make big money, Lu."

I listen. Becky is business-savvy. There were times in college when she hustled, experimenting with different ways to make money on different platforms. "Testing the market," she called it. Like the pictures of her feet that she sold on some shady website to the fetish patrons who paid thousands for them. Or the photos she took of the highly controversial local graffiti and sold to the top street apparel brands.

Becky comes from money, but she has a brilliant mind and is trying to hit a goldmine on her own.

"Me and Tito might swing by. Meanwhile, think about that book idea, Lu. And get more info on your shady roommate."

I laugh. "He's not shady, B."

"Yet to be determined."

She hangs up, and a sudden thought strikes me.

No way…

I go over every detail of Jace being in my condo and shake my head in disbelief.

Jace gave me the rent money, agreed to all the rules, helped me move things, and said he'll officially move in tonight.

But during all that, I forgot the most important thing—to show him his room.

And he never asked…

5

JACE

"The bug is in," I say reluctantly as Roey, Miller, and I sit around the coffee table in the Sheepshead Bay apartment.

I installed the bug in the living room lamp in case Reznik shows up. Did it while Lucy went to her room to get me the key to the condo. Felt like a dick about it, too.

"We need a bug in her bedroom, too," Roey says indifferently like spying on people is a new normal.

I already feel shady as fuck for Miller going through her personal info.

"Not a chance," I argue. "We can't... It's..."

Illegal, yes, but we use a lot of this stuff with high-stake criminals. *Not* people like Lucy. Does that make *me* a criminal?

"I'm moving in tonight," I say, my body instantly tense.

It shouldn't be a big deal, yet I feel awkward—no, correction —*weird* as hell about becoming roommates with a girl.

Roey nods, satisfaction written all over his face. "Good. Good. So here's the brief intel on our Lucy."

I haven't even moved into Goldsling Towers yet, but she's *our* Lucy. I like the sound of it.

"Twenty-one years old. Virginia native. Summa cum laude high school graduate. Virginia Tech. Art major. Honor society. Dropped out. An only child. Mother—Belarusian, naturalized citizen, an accountant. Father—American, cable installation. *Lucy Moor*, her verified online profile, has four hundred thousand followers. Artist and portraitist. Four speeding tickets in Virginia. $45,000 student loan debt—paid off. $4,300 in a bank account. Bone marrow donor. Single. 5'4. Blue eyes."

Nice to meet you, Lucy Moor.

I mull over the info as Roey answers a phone call, disappears into the bedroom, then comes back.

"That was Seth Gordon," he announces when he hangs up. "I told him we were on Reznik's trail. Told him Reznik was meeting up with a young woman, but we lost him, so we are tracking *her* instead. He didn't want the details, just said to get things done."

"We're on it." Miller nods.

My phone beeps.

Amon/Brexton Recovery: Nothing makes my day like your failure, Shooter.

The Brexton Recovery bounty firm is our biggest rival. I met Amon nine months ago when we worked on the same assignment for the Chicago Syndicate. Nice guy but less than subtle in his work ethic and cocky as fuck.

I smirk. "Amon from Brexton. Our employer must've told them we lost the target."

Roey snorts. "Tell the Brexton douchebags to fuck off." He slumps on the couch next to me. "So, we have a short gig in Atlantic City next week. But I might just take Miller and fly in another guy of mine so you can stay in Brooklyn and get every detail about our Lucy."

"I don't understand why we are so fixated on her," I say.

"Because Reznik didn't pop up on the scene until he arranged a meeting with her. Somehow, she's important to him. So prepare to spend some time with her."

"Doing what exactly?" I try to sound indifferent but I'm excited. Lucy Moor draws me in like a magnet.

"Hustling, Jace, hustling. There's a lot of money at stake here. Get Lucy drunk and talking."

"I'll look suspicious," I say, hating the word *hustling* when it comes to a girl.

"Then don't look suspicious. We can't just say, '*Sweetheart, your mom's friend is wanted by a construction mogul for over a billion dollars he stole from him. Plus, Diadia fucking Tolia carries a deadly nerve agent with him at all times. Want part of the reward for giving intel on him?*'" Roey sucks his teeth. "Not gonna work. But if we are lucky, Reznik gets in touch with her again, and we'll be on him. So work your magic."

"I don't have any magic."

"Then find it, Jace! Be a player for once."

"She's out of his league," murmurs Miller, who rarely gives any input besides work-related stuff, his nose always in the computer.

"Nuh-huh. Bullshit." Roey shakes his head. "Kill that thought right there. There's no such thing as someone being out of your league."

Miller snorts, and so do I.

Easy for Roey to say. Roey with his macho-attitude, over six-foot frame, and *dark smoldering eyes that can fuck your soul and make it climax*, as per his many dates, could've charmed a devil. He can be a lumberjack, a hardcore military guy, a romantic with flowers, dressed in all-white yacht club apparel, depending on what girl he's trying to get into his bed. I saw him do a Painting & Wine class with a teacher and five of her girlfriends just because she said she didn't go for anyone who doesn't appreciate art, so Roey took an art course to prove that he was a humble man.

"Drill this into your head, Jace," he says, pointing his phone at me. "No one is out of your league. The two reasons you might feel that way are one, you are just running with fantasies without actually having clear intentions about a person, and two, you are not ready to put in the amount of work necessary to woo that person."

I chuckle. Everything is a military plan for Roey. His invasions can be either a gentle negotiation or a plain ambush. He applies *The Art of War* to his tactics with women with astounding professionalism.

"Speaking of your current accommodation," he continues, "your main goal is to spend as much time around Lucy as possible. I still want you here every day to keep you up to date with other assignments. But consider rooming with Lucy as a vacation while trying to get intel."

Every time I'm around Lucy, I know—I just fucking know—surviving her proximity will be anything but easy. Especially when I need to get her talking and there are several lies I have to keep to myself. But mostly because I've always had good intuition. And my gut feeling is telling me she's going to be the cause of something big in my life, but I don't know whether it's a good thing or not.

Once upon a time, Monica was something I wanted with all my heart.

Once upon a time, I wanted to serve my country.

Sometimes the things you want the most bring you hell.

But as soon as I pack a duffle bag and head for the F-train, my heart sings a happy song.

I've watched enough movies to know that this is what it feels like when you go to a summer camp as a kid, to a prom with your crush as a teen, or on a dream road trip with your best friends in college.

Growing up an orphan in a group home, I've never had those experiences. But heading to Dumbo feels like I'm setting on an adventure. And my partner? The Brooklyn "It Girl," beautiful Lucy Moor.

I should pay more attention to the warnings in my head. Instead, I feel like I won the trip of a lifetime.

6

LU

A BARK SNAPS MY HEAD IN THE DIRECTION OF A CORNER STORE TWO blocks from Goldsling Towers.

There's that cute dog again. A pit bull, I think.

"Huh," I muse.

The sight of him briefly brings back the memory of the night I was picked up by my new roommate.

In the daylight, the dog looks so lonely and unclean that my heart aches at the sight.

"Hey, cutie." I smile, walking up to him, then sit on my haunches and stretch my hand out to pet him.

He sniffs my yellow boots, then my green pants, licking my knee, and then my hand.

"You like colors, huh? Can't see them but can smell them," I tease him.

He has one blue eye. The other one is gouged out but properly healed. It makes his furrowed brows look even more precious. There's no collar on him.

I click my tongue to lure him into the store and ask Nick, the cashier, about him.

"I see him now and then." He shrugs. "No, no owner. I should call the local Animal Care Center."

"I'll take him in for now and put an ad," I announce hurriedly, already excited about the new project. "You are stuck with me, little muffin," I coo to the dog.

When I walk out, he follows me like I'm a rescuer, hurrying on his short legs. I smile, crossing the street and talking to him so he doesn't lag behind.

Light pink inside his ears. A brown mouth and nose. He is so stinking cute that I want—no, *need*—to paint him.

"He's coming with me," I inform the Goldsling Towers' doorman and the concierge as the dog loyally follows me into the elevator.

"What shall I call you for now?" I ask him twenty minutes later as I give him a bath with my peach-scented shampoo.

He likes my touch and closes his one eye as I rub his ears.

"Pushkin. Yeah, that's it!"

Not sure Russia's most beloved poet with a less than desirable reputation would've appreciated a dog being called by his name. But now I have a cute reminder of my Eastern-European heritage in my house.

"Hi, Pushkin," I whisper as I rub the foam into him, splashing him with warm water and running my hand through his slick coat. "Poor thing." I study his gouged eye. "Who did this to you, you cute muffin?"

I'll take care of him. How can I not when he looks so adorable with puffs of shampoo foam around his head and cutely sneezes like a baby?

Then his ears prick. A tiny growl escapes his throat as his head snaps toward the bathroom door.

"What is it, cutie?"

I hear the jangling of the keys—Jace.

"That's my roommate," I tell him.

But Pushkin doesn't relax until the noise in the living room is gone.

I dry him off and take him to the kitchen.

"Welcome to your new home, cutie. At least for a day or two until I find out where you came from," I say as Pushkin sniffs my feet. I open the fridge to see what I can possibly find for him to eat. "You must be hungry, huh?"

I scan the Russian food in the fridge that he probably won't be a fan of. Except... Moscow salami—that's a thought.

He growls angrily, and I turn to see Jace freeze at the door to his room.

"We have another roommate!" I announce with a smile, though Pushkin growls again. *Not so much into Jace, huh?*

Jace is a handsome guy. Without those glasses that give him a too-serious look, he'd actually be hot. Maybe even hotter without the usual bulky hoodie that hides his strong body.

"Where did he come from?" Jace asks as he stares at Pushkin like he sees a ghost.

Pushkin responds with another growl.

"I took him in," I say. "He's lost I guess. I'll try to find his owners. Meanwhile, meet Pushkin."

"Pushkin?"

"Yeah, like the Russian poet."

I glance at my new roommate and catch his eyes on me. Every time our eyes meet, my heartbeat spikes, my lips hitch in an uncontrollable smile, and hope flickers for just a second that Jace will sit down and chat with me, tell me more about him, and ask me about myself.

He doesn't.

His glances are quick like he's stealing them. He moved in only two days ago and feels like a guest, while I want to talk more and make him feel at ease.

Pushkin keeps growling.

Jace playfully narrows his eyes on him, his lips curling into a little smile—Jace is daring Pushkin, and Pushkin goes off in loud barking.

"Pushkin! Stop!" I shout, laughing, but he backs off with a vicious growl as Jace starts slowly walking past him and the kitchen island.

"I'm gonna go get some groceries," Jace says without looking at me.

That means he's planning on spending more time at the condo.

"See you!" I say enthusiastically.

I'm excited about my new roommate.

Pushkin—not so much. He watches Jace like a hawk with his one eye. I should do something about his gouged eye. But right now, Pushkin is gonna get his first taste of Eastern European cold cuts. If he likes them, I might just keep him.

The last week brought two cuties to my condo. One of them is already eating out of my palm. The other one is a mystery, but I'm determined to learn more about Jace. From an artistic point of view, he is a perfect model. I want to paint him. What else can an artist wish for but a live-in model?

Pushkin follows me to my room, his pink tongue licking the remains of the salami off his nose.

I need to write. I need to start a new painting. Becky found me another client. They want a full-body portrait in a Gothic style. I need to do another teddy bear painting for my solo exhibition.

Work, work, work.

Only a year in New York, and my life is fireworks. My online following is growing. I have my first solo exhibit scheduled in two months. I keep diligently writing romance stories online, amassing enough views to make money through in-app ads. I've been living in a luxury apartment that I house-sit for Becky's clients who moved to Europe indefinitely.

And I paint, getting involved in every project possible, including the Williamsburg community wall competition that I won and went viral.

And I dress up and go out and smile and dance and meet new people because Becky says that networking is more important than talent. I say luck is more important than networking. But without talent, I wouldn't have ended up in New York. So, thank you, talent and Becky and possibly luck.

New York is wonderful!

And so, so, so exhausting.

There are days when I feel like a hamster in a wheel. Like I'm running with no direction, and everyone is passing me, but I can't keep up. So I run harder. I love it and hate it and can't live without it.

I turn on the French Kiwi Juice on my speaker for the mood. With all the art supplies, my room is crowded. The floor is covered with plastic so I don't ruin the parquet. Paint jars and tubes are everywhere. I don't have a place to store them or the money to rent a studio or even buy proper storage furniture.

Pushkin lies down by my bed and watches me.

"That's what I do, little man," I tell him as I pick up brushes and set them into a jar with water on the small table next to a big easel with a blank canvas.

This is my domain—colors, textures, sounds. I get lost in this for hours. Pushkin is the audience I never had, and he breaks the solitude that usually comes with my work.

Writing is the opposite. It's all words and a tangle of thoughts, but once you get the story going, you interact with your characters, talk to them, and suddenly the world you created becomes very real, making a home in your head with all its dramas and shenanigans.

Art is external.

Writing is internal.

It's the balance I so often need in my life.

So while the music trickles through the speakers and Pushkin watches, I set the blank canvas up on an easel and a sketch next to it and start mapping out the new painting with a pencil.

By evening, the rough sketch of the gothic portrait is ready. It's a big piece, and the clients already sent their photos.

But I need a break. Switching activities is the cure for burnout, and, boy, do I have a handful.

The next on my to-do list is brainstorming a new romantic novel.

I lie on my bed with the open laptop in front of me, trying to come up with a decent idea, but my brain hits a dry spell. I've been staring at the ceiling for half an hour when I hear the click of the key in the front door, and Pushkin rises to his feet, growling.

I have the instant urge to run out of my room and strike up a conversation with Jace. My mood goes from sulky to cheerful in seconds, and I catch myself smiling, listening to the footsteps in the living room.

There's a handsome guy in my house. A salesman. Is he?

They say one's eyes are a window to one's soul. Jace's eyes are floor to ceiling, wide open, and genuinely reflect all of his emotions. They are in his careful glances at me. And his overly fascinated gaze when he thinks I'm not looking. And the warmth when he smiles.

The playfulness when he makes faces at Pushkin—I caught that a couple of times.

Jace is a perfect—

Oh…

I hold on to the vague thought that flickers in the back of my mind.

Oh, oh, oh…

I try to catch it by the tail before it gets away.

Yes!

A smile splits my face.

I have it!

Right here!

Under my nose!

Yes!

Jace was literally a Good Samaritan when he saved me on the street. But there's a mystery about him.

So, why not Jace?

I pull my computer toward me and start typing everything I can think of with my excited Jace-infused brain.

I'll observe him, copy his habits and behavior, which will make it so much easier to build a believable character. He'll never know.

The words have never spilled easier.

"A mysterious roommate. An instant attraction. Dark secrets that turn her life upside down," I type like mad.

Yes, yes, and yes!

I kick my feet in the air in excitement.

Jace Reed, welcome to my writing world!

7

JACE

Being in Goldsling Towers feels like a dream. The luxury condo. The shady assignment. Lucy Moor…

My breath hitches in my throat when she walks out of her room in the morning.

She doesn't notice me sitting on the edge of the living room couch and texting.

Good job, I tell myself for wearing the stupid glasses—gotta keep the humble appearance, right?

Without makeup, Lucy's brows and lashes are light. She's a natural blonde, floating like an angel between the living room and the kitchen, wearing only a T-shirt that barely covers her butt.

Fuck my life.

My body stiffens, my eyes glued to her as I'm lost for words.

Yep, this is my roommate.

Lucy in the daytime is even more charming, her hair pulled into a thick braid.

I'm not really shy around pretty girls, just not sociable. But none ever made me feel like someone is slowly pulling the rug from under my feet.

I catch a peek of candy-blue booty shorts barely visible under her T-shirt and exhale in relief, then curse at the fact that I was watching her butt.

This is going to be complicated.

I clear my throat, and she finally notices me.

"Jace!" Her bright-blue eyes widen in delight.

She's the friendliest person I've ever met and the most humble pretty girl. No, not just pretty. She's like a fairy in a fantasy movie. A princess, maybe.

"Hey there," I say, managing a smile and fixing the stupid glasses that keep sliding down my nose.

She grins. "How's life, roomie? Do you like the place?"

Her voice is like a caress.

"It's great, thank you."

"You don't spend much time here. This view alone"—she nods toward the windows—"is worth it."

Her eyes eat me up in a subtle and friendly but obvious way. I think she likes me.

"How's everything?" I ask just to hear her voice again. I really need to up my chatting game if I want to get to know her better.

"I started a new project," she says with an eager smile. "Two."

I cock a brow at her, and she laughs, making me grin in return. Our eyes meet, and god damn, I'm melting under her gaze, about to turn into a puddle on this white couch.

A low growl from the doorway to her room makes us turn in that direction.

"Hey, cute muffin," she coos, walking toward the evil dog who obviously thinks I'm a stranger in this house.

Well, I moved in first.

He turned out to be a stray.

The twist? Lucy picked him up and brought him home.

"You are at it again?" she asks him, kneeling and patting the little fucker. "Jace lives here."

Like I said, I was first.

The weird part? The dog has one eye. So he looks like he's winking all the time.

The downside? That shithead hates me. He blissfully closes his one eye when Lucy strokes him but instantly growls when I rise from the couch.

Jealous much?

I have a feeling anyone who gets close to Lucy falls under her spell. I already am, stealing glances at her long bare legs and the cute braid dangling down her back. She'll be my undoing if I keep spending time around her.

Lucy turns to see me grab the keys from the kitchen island. "Leaving?"

I think I see disappointment on her face.

"Yeah, work," I say.

"See you tonight!" she says with a big smile that leaves goose-bumps on my skin.

I already can't wait for tonight.

This is a shakeup that I never saw coming—becoming Lucy's roommate. She's an artist, an influencer, and a dozen other things, as I found out online. Yep, I already found her social profile. I feel like I moved in with a celebrity.

And with a white monster, who cocks his head as I open the front door.

I purposefully narrow my eyes at him and bare my teeth.

He barks.

I chuckle, shutting the front door behind me and heading for a meeting with Roey.

8

JACE

Compared to the luxury condo, the Sheepshead Bay apartment feels like a dingy cave. It smells of tobacco and grilled food. Books lie open, spines up—Roey is a compulsive reader. He picked up reading while on deployment.

"To keep my brain in check," he explained to me once.

He smokes with his head sticking out of the window to the fire escape. I crave a cigarette, too, but I quit.

Roey Torres and I met overseas in the service. In fact, he was my captain. Almost ten years older than me, he retired from the service several years ago and has been in the bounty-hunting business ever since.

Currently, the main team is Roey, Miller, and I.

Roey is the mastermind and the big boss.

I am the hands-on kinda guy, literally, since no one can beat me in distance shooting with a sniper rifle except for expert snipers.

Danny Miller is our IT guy and rarely does fieldwork. His connections include DMV workers, police personnel, hackers, and dark web guys, which gives him access to a lot more info than regular private investigators.

Miller summarizes the surveillance report from the night we lost Reznik.

"The surveillance team picked up Reznik on Dumbo cameras

before he went into the subway. As per the MTA cameras, he took the F-train that goes to Brighton Beach. Then we lost him. But he's in Brighton, I'm sure."

Hence the reason we anchored in the Sheepshead Bay neighborhood next door. That's beside the fact that our main connection for weapons and tracking devices, Sergei Kolchak, lives in Brighton. He is the one who manages the surveillance team in Ukraine, a hundred IT guys who survey public cameras and devices they access through their own connections and use face recognition to track people. It's cheap labor but it's getting expensive for 24-hour surveillance for several months already.

Roey, Miller, and I finally settle around the coffee table, loaded with takeout food. Roey is slurping on *mastava* soup and I dig into *lulya kebab* from a small Uzbek joint in Brighton.

The one thing I appreciate about Southern Brooklyn, Brighton Beach specifically, is the amazing food. Uzbek, Kazakh, Georgian, Tajik, Kyrgyz—you spy an unusual word on a restaurant sign, chances are it's the name of a country or a region in Eurasia you didn't know existed.

Belarus—I knew that one. Best gymnasts and tractors in the world, beautiful lakes, and the last surviving dictatorship in Europe. Now Lucy Moor, whose mother is Belarusian. Suddenly, I want to know everything about the potato country.

Lucy's mother, Iryna Moor, formerly Iryna Vaitovich, used to reside in Brighton Beach until twenty-one years ago when she moved to Virginia.

"Reznik is Ukrainian and used to reside in Brighton, too," Roey says. "Maybe it's some old Eastern European bonding."

"Do you think Iryna Moor has something to do with this cryptocurrency scam?" I ask.

"I'd say no. He did have a silent female partner, but she's supposedly overseas and filthy rich by now. Miller is running Lucy's mother's records, but I think it's just a coincidence. The Moors are not rich. You can tell they are tight about money, so obviously, Reznik didn't share his loot."

That is, the one and a half billion dollars he swindled his investors out of, including the fifty-million investment from his former partner and now our employer, Seth Gordon, the construction mogul.

Reznik is wanted by the FBI for his participation in a large-scale virtual coin fraud scheme. A year ago, he was charged in the United States District Court with multiple counts of fraud and money laundering. The FBI reward for any info is $100,000. Seth Gordon's bounty is five million. Yeah, exactly. The government can suck it. That's why they can't catch their most wanted for decades.

And us?

Right, just lost him. Because of a cute blonde girl who might be our only chance to locate him again.

We don't have any active jobs yet. Usually, they are last minute and urgent. So right now, we're chilling.

The difference? Roey and Miller are stuck in this small apartment. Me? I'm residing in Goldsling Towers.

"Try to learn her daily routine," Roey says, bringing up Lucy again. "You just never know when Reznik might contact her again. Become her best friend so she tells you where she goes and who she talks to."

"What if Reznik doesn't contact her again?" I ask. "Maybe he got spooked and won't take another chance."

"Then consider it a paid vacation."

"For how long?"

Roey licks the kebab sauce off his fingers. "We are here until we get something. One month? Two? Who knows. But when we get him, it'll be the biggest paycheck we've ever had."

"And I'll retire," says Miller.

"The fuck you will," Roey rasps with a chuckle. "But if this works out, we'll get the biggest contracts from all the needy screwed-over rich people out there."

I nod on reflex, but my mind is stuck on the "two months." Two months with Lucy Moor. Maybe even more!

"Why are you smiling?" Roey asks, and I raise my eyes to see him smirk at me. I didn't notice I was. He gently punches my shoulder. "We get to wait it out here, in this hole. You get to room with the hottest girl in Brooklyn. Is your dick hard? Yeah?" He pinches my cheek.

"Fuck off, Torres." I slap his hand away but notice his envious stare as I leave the apartment.

"Jace?" He stops me when I'm almost out the door. "Take your gun and keep it in your apartment. Maybe Diadia fucking Tolia will show up out of nowhere."

Right.

But as soon as I leave, my thoughts are already about Lucy.

Something has to be done about that dog monster who hates me. The failure with Reznik wasn't even my fault. The dog is the real villain here.

On the way to Goldsling Towers, I stop by a grocery store and buy the biggest meatiest bone they have. Also a bag of dog food, a squeaky toy, peanut butter, and bacon treats.

My backpack has a gun and dog snacks. Life is an adventure.

I tense as I ride the elevator to the condo, my heart pounding as I put the key in the door.

Every encounter with Lucy sets me on the verge of a nervous breakdown. God, I need to get my shit together. No girl has had this effect on me.

The apartment is quiet when I walk in, and I pause for a moment in the doorway, gazing out the window.

Lucy was right—you don't get used to the view. I stand for a hot moment staring at the skyline behind the floor-to-ceiling windows.

Lucy is not home, and my heartbeat chills the fuck down when I finally stir and close the door.

A growl comes from behind the kitchen island. I can't see the white monster, but he's plotting to kill me, I know it.

Carefully, I set my backpack down on the floor and lower myself to my haunches.

"All right, shithead, game on," I murmur, unwrapping the meaty bribe. "Come here, you monster," I coo then repeatedly click my tongue.

Here he is, stepping from behind the kitchen island.

An idiotic chuckle escapes my throat—he's wearing an eye patch.

"Seriously?" I can't hold back a goofy grin.

Pushkin is a ridiculous sight—a one-eyed dog with a pirate patch with a skull and crossbones. Lucy is creative, I'll give her that.

His good eye glares at me for just a second then drops to the bone. He slowly comes up, sniffs it, licks it, then straightens up and stares at me like I offended him.

I shift, immediately evoking a growl from him as he rears.

"Not a gourmet-kinda-guy, huh?" Despite the fact that he lives in a Goldsling luxury condo and sleeps on the parquet floor. "Fine."

Carefully, I rip the dog food package next, take several pebbles of dog food, and toss them toward Pushkin's paws.

He sniffs at them then cocks his head at me.

"Picky," I murmur not a bit disheartened. "Alright. Next one."

I tear the package with bacon bits, noticing Pushkin sniffing the air.

"You like that? Yeah?" I toss one bacon bit toward his front paws, and his pink tongue immediately licks it off.

"Bacon, huh? You are a dude, for sure. There." I toss another one toward him, and it disappears in Pushkin's mouth as he eagerly lifts his head, moves closer to me, and stares at the package in my hand.

I shake it, spreading the smell, gloating at the sight of the furry pirate taking slow steps toward me.

"Caaah-mon, shithead," I tease him, shake several bits into my hand, and lower it to the floor.

In a minute, the white monster cleans off my palm and fingers with his tongue, then nuzzles my other hand that holds the package, and I stifle a victorious chuckle.

"Friends, yeah?" I get up and stick several bacon bits in my pocket. I'll drive this dog insane. "Say a word for me to Lucy, will ya?"

Mission number one is accomplished.

Pushkin stares at me lovingly as I take my backpack to my room, shutting the door in his face. He whimpers, and I see a shadow under the door as he lowers himself to the floor and sniffs the air in the door gap, wanting more of that bacon.

He is sneaky, I feel it in my gut. So I don't want him to see me take a gun out of my backpack and tuck it under my mattress.

There's one more thing I need to do because it bothers me.

I walk out of my room and don't even look at the pirate guy as I walk by, shaking the bacon bits in my pocket.

The soft clacking of Pushkin's claws against the parquet makes me grin. Pushkin is now my bitch.

I walk to the lamp and take the bug I planted there the other day out.

I've made up my mind. Spying on Lucy is out of the question.

9

LU

My morning starts with the jingle of the keys in the hallway and the front door softly closing.

Jace.

I bury myself into the blanket cocoon, knowing that an hour later, the door will open again.

Jace gets up at dawn and goes for what I assume is a jog. I am yet to get up early enough to see if he wears glasses when he jogs. Or his black hoodie.

Usually, when I'm up, Jace is already gone.

Every morning, I make myself coffee and grits for breakfast, then take Pushkin out.

I took a picture of Pushkin with the pirate patch, made a quick flyer in Photoshop about him being lost, put my email address on it, and printed ten copies to post on the streets and at the local convenience store.

A week later, I receive an email, "I think your dog is Dogo Argentino, not a pit bull." The only other emails I've gotten were the ones asking if I want to sell the pirate dog.

"No way, Jose," I murmur, deleting yet another email with such a proposal and glance at Pushkin. "Looks like you are mine for right now, cutie."

He likes watching me paint. Likes my choice of music, too, most of it, except the Australian didgeridoo.

I move the gothic canvas I'm working on against the wall. It's seven by four feet, so the easel just makes it complicated. I put on socks so my feet don't stick to the clear plastic covering the floor. The little paint spots don't wash off, but I love them. Colors are the essence of life.

I work through lunch and into the late afternoon when Becky texts.

Becky: We are on our way.

She doesn't ask, just lets me know.

My neck aches from craning it for too long at the canvas when I finally put the brushes and the mixing tray aside and wash my hands.

The doorbell rings.

"Where is he?" Becky tosses her sunglasses onto the coffee table and kicks off her high-heeled boots then flings herself onto the couch.

My friend Tito follows.

"Not home," I say with a smile.

They've been dying to meet Jace just so they can discuss the conspiracy theories about what he does and who he is.

Becky and Tito are the most stylish people I know and are often assumed to be a couple. Except Tito is not into women. He's Becky's best friend and, soon after I moved to New York, became mine, too. His family comes from Mexico and old money. But just like Becky, he wants to be independent and makes big bucks at a pharmaceutical company.

Dark hair styled to one side, hazel eyes, and a chiseled aristocratic face, Tito leads with his body and overly expressive gestures. He's handsome and doesn't come across as gay, and women swoon over him just as easily as men.

I can tell Tito is curious about my roommate and can't hide his disappointment when I say my roommate is not home.

I make tea and a plate of assorted Russian cookies, also a plate with *chebureks*—deep-fried meat-filled turnovers—and *pirozhkis* with meat and cabbage.

I usually shop at Eastern European markets in Brighton. I don't have my mom's cooking here in New York, but Brighton Beach is gourmet heaven.

Becky asks for Russian chocolate candies. She loves picking at the colorful wrappers.

"They are all different colors and sizes and patterns, and they make no sense," she says as she bites down on a vodka-filled chocolate, grunts in satisfaction, and rummages through the others. She'll eat the entire bowl of them by the time she leaves.

The door lock clicks, and Jace appears in the doorway.

"Oh, there you are, Mr. Dark Knight!" Becky says cheerily, cocking her head and brazenly studying Jace.

"Stop," I whisper to her and smile at Jace. Yep, a black hoodie, jeans, and glasses—his usual outfit. "Hey, Jace! Come meet my friends!"

Pushkin springs up to his feet and trots toward Jace.

This is strange. The first several days, Pushkin couldn't stand Jace, barked and cornered him like he was an enemy. Suddenly, one day, Pushkin follows him around like Jace is his best friend.

Becky waves at Jace with her fingers.

Tito's eyes narrow in curiosity as Jace comes over and takes a seat on the couch, an awkward smile on his face.

"Jace, try these," I say and pass him a plate with a chicken-stuffed *cheburek*.

He eats quietly, answering Becky's questions.

"California, huh? You surf?" she asks.

Jace shakes his head with a soft smile. "Only moved there a year ago, after the service."

"Service?" Becky gives me a puzzled look.

He nods. "Yes, I was… um… in the army."

"So, you know how to throw a punch or two?"

"Something like that." He smiles and rubs his neck, seemingly uncomfortable like he just spilled a secret.

That's new. Maybe I can run his name in the service database. His great physical form makes sense now, and I suddenly want him to shed his clothes to see what he looks like naked.

Jesus, Lu, calm down.

Note to self—crank up the heat in the apartment.

"So, who do you hang out with here in the city?" Becky can be relentless with questions, especially when she's fishing for info.

"Work guys. My friend, Roey." He goes suddenly quiet.

I bet Roey dresses in sweatpants and hoodies and wears glasses, too.

"So, Roey is a local?" Becky pushes on.

"No, he's my roommate from Costa Mesa." Jace wipes the corner of his bottom lip with his thumb and doesn't look up.

"Oh, but he's here, in New York?"

She'll drive Jace insane.

He looks almost curious when he lifts his eyes to Becky. There's this genuine kindness about him, in the way he doesn't react to Becky's provocation, which is her weapon.

"I started working for him after the service," Jace explains. "He's in and out of the city for work."

Becky keeps interrogating Jace.

He answers patiently. His calm confidence is magnetic, making me stare as I forget myself.

He's definitely hot-cute. His dark-amber eyes catch the light and acquire specks of warm caramel. I wish his glasses didn't hide them so much.

Becky asks about his hobbies, and Jace stalls for a moment like he's trying to figure out how much to share.

"I'm taking online classes in building construction and carpentry."

Becky's eyebrow hitches in surprise. "Car-pen-try?"

"Natural material carpentry and self-sustaining spaces."

"For what?"

"I want to build a self-sustaining jungle resort in the tropics."

Becky looks at me like he said he wants to be a unicorn then turns to him. "And live like a recluse, or what?"

Jace smiles mysteriously.

"Leave him alone," I snap at her. "Tea, Jace?"

"No, thank you."

He collects our empty plates and walks to the open kitchen.

Pushkin follows him.

"He's cute," Becky whispers as Jace washes the plates, then excuses himself when his phone rings and disappears into his room.

"If he wasn't so quiet, he'd be hot. It's in the attitude. Also in those glasses. He's probably boring and considerate in bed."

"B! What the hell?"

"I mean, just a theory. What do you think, Tito?"

Tito shrugs, elegantly swinging one leg over the other. "The quiet ones are the freakiest."

There goes their usual guessing game, though they are better at it when they drink, occasionally getting so wrapped up in it that they pick up one-night stands for each other.

I roll my eyes. "He's not your type, B."

"Oh, God, no! I'm just playing with the idea. Does he have a girlfriend?"

"I didn't ask."

"Maybe he has a boyfriend." Tito cocks a brow. "Whether he does or not, let me know."

Becky doesn't let go of her favorite guessing game. "I bet his parents are blue-collar, maybe even avid church-goers. He seems very polite and well-mannered. Also, army—he went there because his parents are proud Americans, and discipline is in their blood."

"Entrepreneurs, family business, maybe," Tito counteracts. "An only child, private school, worked since early years, probably in the family business. Hence, good work ethics and manners. Army was a rebellion. Maybe, against his father, who is a patriarch and had Jace under his thumb his whole life. That's why he wants to run away to the jungle."

Becky narrows her eyes on the door to Jace's room. "Hey, invite him out with us sometime."

I frown. "Why?"

Becky is never friendly with strangers unless it's a hot guy she might be interested in for a night or... networking, right.

"Why not? Maybe he's cool when he's drunk. Tito will tell you for sure if your roommate is gay. And if he is, Tito will be delighted. Right, Tito?"

Tito's lips stretch in a playful smile. "I like him. Something about him is..." He makes this inarticulate sound, "Mmm," like he's tasting a new pastry. "I'm telling you. He's a walking surprise. I called it. He's a hottie. In a different outfit, maybe without the glasses, maybe with a different job. Remember I said that."

This is getting awkward.

I still don't know much about the guy who has the keys to my apartment. I checked out his room the other day. Of course, I did. Nothing but a duffle bag, his clothes neatly stacked in two drawers, and several pieces hanging in the closet, including a suit. I've yet to find out what Jace Reed looks like in a suit. Probably like a banker.

"Where do you hide those candies?" Becky asks, abruptly getting up and walking to the kitchen.

She finished the bowl, I knew it. How the girl who eats that many sweets manages to stay in great shape is a mystery. Even with the five-hour-a-week workouts like Becky has with her personal trainer.

"In the upper cupboard," I tell her.

"I want the ones filled with prunes and cream and covered in chocolate." She opens the cupboard but can't reach the top shelf.

"Grab the stool—" I prompt.

She shuts me up with a wave of her hand and places it on her hip.

"Hey, Jace!" she shouts as Tito and I exchange amused glances.

That's Becky, hustling people, studying them, gauging their reactions and behavior. That's why she's so good as a talent scout, though she should've been an FBI profiler.

Jace's head appears in the cracked door of his room.

"Sweetie, can you get that for me?" Becky pleads in a too-friendly tone, motioning to the cupboard. "You are taller than any of us."

Jace effortlessly reaches for the top shelf but can't see the contents, feeling the shelf with his hand.

Tito leans back into the couch and cocks his head, eyeing Jace in the kitchen like he can see through clothes.

"A little bit to the left, Jace," he prompts. "Nope, to the right. Just an inch."

He's so enjoying this teasing and evidently has an eye on Jace even though he just met my roommate.

Becky's big eyes snap up at me.

"What?" I mouth, then drop my eyes to Jace's mid-section that Becky is motioning to.

I crane my neck to have a better look at Jace, who is partially blocked by the kitchen island, and do a startled double take.

His hoodie has ridden up and exposes a sliver of skin just above his sweatpants. Covered in tattoos.

Huh?

"Thanks, sweetie," Becky blurts when Jace finally gets the candy bag, then watches him until he disappears into his room.

She turns to meet my eyes in surprise with a did-you-just-see-that look.

"Your nerdy roommate is tattooed. How about that?" Becky whispers like she just discovered a secret when she comes back to the couch. "I mean, every mouse these days gets inked, but his were in color and solid all the way. And not the amateur stuff."

I'm intrigued. "Army?" And because my creative brain never rests, it's already spinning the info for my new book.

"Ask him to show you his tattoos sometime," Tito says. "You can tell a lot about a man by the tattoos he has."

They eventually drag me to my room to see the gothic portrait I'm working on. But their voices drown in my thoughts that are all about my roommate. With tattoos. And glasses. And kind eyes that occasionally pause on mine with an intensity that makes me burn from the inside.

I don't know what draws me to Jace. I barely know him. But he has stories. I feel it. I see it in his eyes. I want to know them all.

And when Becky and Tito leave, I put an empty canvas on the easel and paint Jace's eyes.

10

JACE

THEY CALL HER LU. SO IN MY MIND, I CALL HER LU, TOO. A WEEK later, I know quite a bit about her.

She is obsessed with Eastern European food. She almost never takes a cab because she wants to save money. Fridays and Saturdays are going out nights while weeknights are for galleries and work. Her favorite movie is *Knockin' on Heaven's Door*, the German one, which I've yet to see. Her favorite food is anything pickled. She loves colors and constantly listens to music.

A lot of this info comes from hearing her loud conversations on the phone as she paints all through the day, often late into the night.

Lu is a sweetheart. Also a workaholic, a ray of sunshine, a late sleeper, a coffee drinker, a walking mess at home, but also a bombshell in outrageous outfits and scandalously high heels when she goes out. She is friendly, considerate, and talented.

Okay, so I might've gotten carried away. But Lu is simply delightful.

And she makes me hella self-aware.

This is a new world for me—bright colors, sweet scents, and a merry-go-round attitude. The last year was the happiest in my life—having a job I love, friends, Roey, and living five minutes from the beach in sunny California, thousands of miles away from the dusty military camps I'm used to and an eternity from the loneliness of growing up in a group home.

And then Lu came into my life, and the world suddenly acquired so many colors and sounds that I can't help staring around, trying to process them all.

Lu is open and good-hearted.

Her friends, on the other hand, are protective and invasive.

There's Becky, who during our first acquaintance, studied me scrupulously like I was a felon. Becky-type girls are why I stick to my 'voluntary celibacy,' as Roey calls it. She reminds me of Monica, my high school crush and a traitor.

Then there's Tito, who dresses like a suburban GQ—loafers, colorful pants, and cashmere V-necks, and has a habit of drumming his fingers on his thigh. He loves Sam Smith and Pino Grigio, and, judging by the way his gaze slithered over my body, he was trying to figure out whether he had a chance with me.

Wrong door, buddy.

I still can't believe this is my life, at Goldsling Towers, though it's only been a week.

The weather is warming up, and suddenly it's too hot in the condo. I feel like I'm sweating all the time, but I don't want to wear short sleeves and expose my body in front of Lu to avoid any questions. And I keep those damn glasses on, annoyed and feeling like a scammer.

It's hard to keep a distance when Lu is so touchy-touchy with people and with me when I'm around. Her touch is distracting and the heat that goes through my body every time we randomly bump into each other here and there is killing me every day.

I get home one day to hear the music blasting from Lu's room. Her head pops out of her room as if she's been waiting for me, and right away there's a grin on her face.

"Hey." I smile, taking off my shoes, my heart fluttering at the sight of her. "How's the art going?"

She lights up. "Wanna see?"

It's the first time she's offered, though I've seen some of her stuff online.

"Can I?" I ask, trying not to sound too eager.

She laughs, comes out of her room, and takes me by the wrist. "I insist!"

With a playful spark in her eyes, she starts pulling me toward her room.

Her hand holding mine is smudged with blue paint. And so is a strand of her blonde hair.

Touching. See? Her body language around others is very informal. Around me it's intimate. At least, in my head.

"You keep asking me what sort of art I do," she says as she pulls me into her room. "Ta-da!"

Her room is a mess. The carpet is rolled up against one wall. A wardrobe is pushed into one corner, and a big bed is against the window. Clear plastic covers most of the floor like she's about to dispose of a dead body. Cans, bottles, and jars of paint are everywhere. Mixing pallets litter the floor. Canvases, small and large, are stacked against the walls—Lu has no sense of order.

I take it all in, trying to think about anything but her hand still wrapped around my wrist.

Then she lets go, and I take a deep breath.

"I'm preparing for an exhibit at a gallery on Broad Street. It'll be my first solo exhibition," she says proudly.

She pulls a drape off a five-by-four feet canvas against the wall, and I come face to face with a giant blindfolded teddy bear.

Huh…

"What's this?"

"The theme is Childhood Interrupted, teddy bears in a social context—war, hunger, child labor, trafficking. This one is called *Marred*." I notice dirty hands creeping up to the bear from all sides. "And this"—she takes her phone from a nightstand and shows me another canvas—a teddy bear sitting among—

"Grass?" I murmur.

"Sugar cane," she corrects. There are chocolate wrappers everywhere. Children in torn clothes curiously crouch around the toy. "Child labor in Africa, used by chocolate corporations."

Wow, she is not all bubbles and pink.

"These are already at the gallery," she says and shows me another one.

It's a teddy bear in a dilapidated building, dust and gray rubble in the background, a sniper's target on its head.

"War zones," she says.

49

I don't like this one. A nasty feeling gathers in my stomach.

No women or children...

The teddy bears in Lu's paintings are all in bright colors while the background and other objects are in dark pastels outlined with black ink.

It's another flashback to my life overseas, and my smile fades.

"I get occasional orders for styled portraits," Lu continues.

"What's that?"

"When people want their portraits but, say, dressed like royals, or in luxury setting, or superhero-themed, or Da Vinci style. Like this one."

She points at the giant canvas with barely any paint but sketched in details—dramatic sky and ravens over a gothic castle, a couple in lavish outfits at the front.

"*Modern Gothic*," she announces. "It's a play on Wood's *American Gothic*."

"I don't know much about art," I say apologetically.

"We'll change that." She nods cheerfully.

Yes, let's change that. "Can't you just photoshop it?" I ask.

She laughs. "Sure! But then it's easy. This"—she gracefully points at it with an open palm—"is fine art, Jace."

I feel stupid. Of course, it is.

I look around, wondering how she sleeps here amidst all this mess, the strong smell of paint, and stacks and stacks of gallery-wrapped canvases. There's a clear path to the bathroom and the walk-in closet. The rest of the floor is a battlefield.

"Can I see those?" I ask, nodding at the stacks covered by drapes, wanting to see every single bit of her imagination. But to my disappointment, she waves me off. "You need shelves for your art stuff," I murmur, looking around. Or ten shelves—there's so much stuff.

"That would be helpful, but it's an extra expense." Her smile is almost apologetic.

She is a brilliant artist, yet, it doesn't give her enough income. Pity.

"I write, too," she says quieter. "It brings in extra cash."

"Oh, yeah?" I sort of knew that. Miller said she has a profile on an online writing platform, but I never got to check it out. "What do you write?"

She squints at me. "Spicy romance stories." Her lips stretch in a grin.

Oh.

"Spicy?" I cock an eyebrow, trying not to look away when our eyes meet.

"Like, explicit." She cocks a brow, mimicking me.

"Like *Fifty Shades of Grey*?"

She laughs. She constantly laughs, and I can't get enough. Every time I make her laugh, I feel like there's another tiny bond between us.

"Something like that," she murmurs as she studies the room like she's new here, but I can tell she's shy. "Minus S&M," she adds, biting her lower lip.

I think I just made her blush.

"Can I read them?" I ask.

She gives me a reproachful stare. "That's a no."

"What's your pen name?" I tease.

"*Big* no, Jace Reed." She laughs again, blushes, licks her lips, and looks away.

"So you like writing that kind of stuff?"

I want to get in her head and see what my cute roommate cooks up in her mind.

"Well, it's money. I get paid by how much time readers spend on my profile reading and how many ads get viewed in the meantime. So I advertise my stories on one of my social profiles."

"The art one?"

She flicks a surprised glance at me.

Yeah, I gave myself away. Yeah, I checked her out online. Correction, I do it every day. Correction, twice a day, excited about every update.

"No, a different one. It's too explicit to be mixed up with my art. I'm not a fan of the stories I write, but…"

But? Now I'm even more curious.

Lu wraps her arms around her waist like she is uncomfortable talking about it.

"So, why don't you write what you want?" I suggest.

"It doesn't sell. I'm starting a new story that might be a little more complex." She bites her lip to hide a smile.

What was that, Lu?

She blushes again and starts walking around, putting the drapes over the canvases she just bared for me, avoiding looking at me.

"The new story will be from the heart," she says.

"But still spicy?" I tease her, every cell in my body flaring up at the word.

She squints at me, wrinkling her nose. "Yeah."

"Smut from the heart."

She laughs, throwing her head back, and pretends to throw her phone at me.

"I do other things, too," she confesses.

Like hustling rent.

"Wanna strike big, huh?"

"I want to make a sinful amount of money and blind people with my awesomeness," she explains with a smile but, I figure, with total truthfulness.

Lu already blinds me with her mere presence in my life. I need sunglasses around her so I don't look so in awe. And also so I can stare at her cute butt and gorgeous legs. Her laughter is as adorable as her oversized shirt hanging off her shoulder, making me want to kiss her bare skin. And booty shorts. Don't even get me started on those.

The more time I spend talking to her, the more I want to know her. And definitely read those stories she writes.

So as soon as I leave her room, I text Miller.

Me: I need to know Lucy Moor's pen name on the writing platform she uses. Thanks, man.

My heart beats wildly when, only a minute later, my phone beeps with a message notification.

Danny Miller: It's Story Den. Her pen name is @MidnightLu.

11

JACE

I don't feel bad about snooping around on the Story Den, or SD. I might become Lu's fan. She needs to grow her fanbase, right? I'm in.

I create a reader's profile and type her pen name in the search field.

Her avatar is a flower. No face—smart.

She's published forty-six episodes in the last three years, has over 19,000 followers, and 132 patrons—super-fans, I guess?

This should be interesting.

I go to her most recent and most-read series, *Beautiful Vice*.

#Enemiestolovers, the tag says, and I'm giddy like I'm about to unwrap a Christmas present.

The beginning is fast-paced. Lu writes action. Cool.

The story is simple but somewhat brutal. This Russian Bratva guy, Konstantin Orlov, kills a rival and takes his daughter as a debt payment, saying she'll be his wife. Obviously, he's not picky, though she's extremely beautiful. He whisks her away to Irkutsk, Russia, and locks her in his country estate.

#Morallygrey seems to be the trending color among romance readers. And the guy, Konstantin Orlov, is "darker than the deepest pits of hell," as his captive, Eva, describes.

He's obviously an exception among the grumpy-serial-killer-looking Russian guys, because he's extremely hot, and so are his two brothers and five bodyguards. All GQ.

Lu must know that Russian Bratva is thug culture at best. But alright, this is fiction. And—I chuckle because the story is quite entertaining—Konstantin went to Oxford University. This must've happened somewhere between him killing dozens of people and blowing up rival mafia syndicates overseas. He must really need a bachelor's degree for that. Could've bribed the Oxford University dean since he's the richest and most powerful man in the world—and that, my friends, is public knowledge.

My brain is on fire.

Lu! Help me out here!

What? Is? This?

But then we get closer acquainted with the female lead, Eva, who our brutal Konstantin calls *"katsiónak,"* which means kitten in Russian. Cute.

Eva is a harmless sunshine, extremely horny, drop-dead gorgeous and has a master's degree, which I have a feeling will be irrelevant in this story.

And *katsiónak* grows claws one chapter at a time.

My kidnapper and future husband leans on the doorframe, tonguing his cheek, arms folded across his broad chest. His eyes, hypnotic yet cold and dark, narrow on me.

"Oh, yeah, sweetheart? Tell me again how much you hate me."

The vase I throw at him shatters into pieces against the wall, only a few feet from his head.

Yet he doesn't move. The corner of his gorgeous mouth curls into a smirk. It's his reflex to everything I do around him, mostly getting angry.

There are dozens of reasons for my hate.

He burned down my house, killed my father, took me captive. And now, has stripped me naked and studies me like a rare specimen with sardonic amusement and that low raspy murmur, "I own you, Eva. You are mine. Mine to play with. Mine to torment. Mine to break."

That murmur crawls under my skin, sending shivers down my spine.

But my body has a mind of its own, tingling under his scorching eyes, twisting on the inside at the approving gaze that lazily trails over my bare body that silently whimpers with the unknown before arousal.

"I hate you," I hiss, despising myself for such a reaction. "If I'm meant to plunge into the darkness of your bloody kingdom and this God-forsaken snow cavern, I'll make sure you regret the day you laid your eyes on me."

His arrogant brow cocks at my words.

He pushes off the doorframe and takes slow steps toward me, the vase shards crackling under his boots.

Every cell in my body lights at his proximity.

He stops right in front of me, lifts his hand, and brushes my bare nipples with the back of his fingers, eliciting goosebumps I can't hide.

His smirk deepens—the beast notices everything.

"You think what happened in the last days is darkness, Eva? You haven't felt it yet. It's only just creeping up to your feet. But when it touches you"—his hand slides lower, much lower—"oh, *katsiónak*, when it *does* touch you"—his fingers slide between my legs, grazing my sensitive folds as he brings his gorgeous lips to my ear—"you might never want to go back to light."

They say those who have nothing to lose are the most fearless.

I've been stripped of everything that was ever dear to me.

I won't give up so easily.

If I go down, I'm dragging my soon-to-be husband with me, all the way to hell.

He thinks he is my punishment. But I'll make him my kryptonite, growing stronger every day until I have the power to destroy him.

This beautiful beast.

The head of the Bratva mafia.

Konstantin Orlov.

I stand naked in front of him, weak from his touch and the sweet invasion of his fingers, my mind simmering with rage but my body craving more of him.

Hate is a weapon. And I'll fight with everything I've got until he's dead.

My hands ball into fists. "You think the scariest shade of darkness is pitch black, Konstantin? You'll learn that the worst of it is red, bright red, the color of your blood, and the color of the blazing fire I'm going to burn you in until you turn to ash."

His chuckle is sinister.

"Are fires red in America? Because in Russia, they are orange-yellow. Welcome to my Motherland."

He brings his fingers that were just stroking me between my legs to his mouth and licks them, one by one, his full lips sucking them dry, his steel gaze locked with mine.

"So sweet, my future wife." His whisper sends chills over my bare skin, all the way down to my burning core. "I'm looking forward to watching us burn together, *katsiónak*."

The end of the third chapter makes me look forward to the next one.

Wow.

Lu is actually a good writer. Her language is poetic and the banter between the characters is fantastic.

I read on, and two more chapters in, I'm invested in Konstantin and Eva's story, though Eva is way too mouthy, and Konstantin needs to tame it down and learn to listen. He also needs to learn that shooting another man's kneecap is not a solution to his newly found excessive jealousy.

Then the smut kicks in. With a bang, literally.

The fire from the explosion flares behind us as Konstantin sets me on the hood of his LaFerrari Aperta.

Why someone would have a sports car in Siberia in the winter is puzzling, but I read on.

He opens my chinchilla fur coat and pushes my legs apart, kneeling between them, the flickers of the blaze dancing in his smoldering eyes.

"You are not a good listener, Eva, are you? Look what you made me do."

I can't look behind me because all I want lately is to look into

his onyx eyes. Especially when they are so close. When they take my breath away.

Emotions bubble inside me, the lust I never knew, the craving for the man I hate, the need to touch him, feeling invincible when I do as if his power is contagious.

Kryptonite...

Would you want it if it came from the person you loathe?

Is it loathing when you want him so much?

Is it simple want when you feel the world fall apart when he steps out of sight?

The air burns between us.

He knows what I'm thinking. I know he does.

The sparkle in his eyes is dangerous but, oh, so irresistible, when he pulls my panties to the side, leans in, and drags his tongue along my soaked folds, making me whimper with need.

Oooh-kaaay.

My eyes widen as I read on.

Apparently, Lu likes tattooed guys. And #alphaholes. Also... wait, big dicks. Yep. *Wow, Lu.* And guys who obsessively smoke or walk around with a cigarette between their lips and blow up buildings and kill people for no particular reason.

Wait, Lu doesn't like smoking. Maybe that's just what readers like.

I skim the next paragraph.

He grunts when my hand wraps around his erection, big and heavy.

"You are going to take every inch of me, Eva," he rasps. "Every inch I give you."

"I can't, Konstantin. You are too big."

"Oh, yes, you can, *katsiónak*. And you will. You'll do it like a good girl. Because you are my wife. You are mine. And I take care of what's mine. Look at you, dripping already. So wet for me. You were made for me. And so was your pus—"

I have to look away and exhale like I can unread what I just read. I'm cold, then suddenly sweating and burning up.

I mean, I've read a romance like this before. But I can't picture Lu with her innocent blue eyes and sunshine smile writing, **"You are doing so well, my wife, my little whore. I want to see you come on my co—"**

Fucking hell!

I slam the laptop lid shut, my heart pounding.

She writes *that*?

I roll onto my stomach and bury my face in the pillow in disbelief. Yet my erection strains my sweatpants, and I instinctively push my hips into the mattress.

Interesting.

Apparently, my body doesn't get the message from my brain. I'm not a prude. Occasionally, I watch porn. Who doesn't? But a visual is one thing. This... this... it's like reading porn subtitles.

And this is Lu we're talking about. Does she actually like this in real life?

If it weren't for certain words in the story, I wouldn't have believed she wrote that.

But it's right there.

"Cute muffin"—that's what Eva called her cat that burned in the house Konstantin set on fire.

Lu calls Pushkin that all the time.

And Konstantin... Well, the dude is psycho, arrogant and possessive, but I have a feeling he'll be redeemed at the end.

Calm down, Jace. It's just a made-up story.

I roll onto my back and exhale, trying to cool down.

Okay, okay, okay. So, there's *Fifty Shades*.

Yeah, *that* book.

Now, hear me out.

Cole Bergen got a package from the States on his birthday when we served overseas. His buddy sent him *Fifty Shades of Grey*.

"What the hell is this?" he mused.

That glorious day, we got introduced to Christian and Anastasia.

To say that the book became the most sought out item at the garrison would be an understatement. We read the book out loud by bonfires and in the bunkers, laughing and cheering and secretly having wet dreams about the story. We might not have remembered each other's birthdays, but soon, we knew by heart parts of the book that very quickly acquired crinkled corners, sticky pages, and fingerprints of half of the garrison.

There are all shades of deprivation at war, and that romance was a window into a different world. A world that made us forget that we could be shot the next day. That our families and loved ones were far away and some of us didn't have any. That our lives were cheap, but we signed up for it, and that was our job.

Cole Bergen was blown up a year later during a raid. We burned the book at a bonfire afterward, drinking to oblivion, cheering to Cole, laughing, joking, remembering, then sitting silently for the rest of the night and swallowing tears that never showed on our faces but burned our throats—something that becomes a habit in the service.

Yeah, *Fifty Shades* was a fairytale while reality for some of us was just not that bright.

Now, my roommate is Lucy Moor. She is the reality with a kind voice and contagious laughter.

And a *filthy fucking mind.*

I'm not a reader, but—

Lu, you are addictive.

She's not a plotter, but her words make me hard.

Positive emotions, I remind myself.

Real-life application, my mind smirks.

I'll second that, my dick agrees.

I'll just read one more chapter.

For research.

Just one.

I take a deep breath and open my computer again.

12

JACE

I GET UP AT SIX, AS USUAL. PUSHUPS, PLANKS, AND PULL-UPS, HANGING from the door frame of the walk-in closet. Goldsling Towers has a gym, but I don't want to get too comfortable here. Plus I'm used to a simple military routine.

There's one exception now. I work out twice as hard, trying to sweat Lu's spicy stories out of my body.

Her proximity tests my sanity. Every glance at her reminds me of her not-so-sweet writing, and I wonder if I can keep from quoting it by accident.

Like the following evening when I catch her in the foyer of the building as I come home.

Lu strides out of the elevator wearing high-heeled boots, a short polka-dot jumpsuit, and a blue faux fur coat, light enough for the middle of May.

"Wow," I greet her, my heart swelling at the sight but also from the disappointment that she'll be gone all night. "Venus in Fur, huh?"

Her jaw falls open, eyes widening. "Jace! Well-read, huh?"

She's gaping at me, and I try to act cool.

The only reason I know the name of that book is because Roey once tried to educate me on the origins of S&M, a pure coincidence that makes Lu stare at me like I'm a perv. Or, maybe, an expert in old-school erotica.

When Lu is home, nothing matches. Polkadot sweatpants, t-shirts with cute animals or crazy art, tanks, oversized long sleeves that hang off one shoulder, leggings, or shorts. Short, short shorts...

Lu's going-out clothes are perfectly matched and styled, including her nail polish, her hair flat-ironed, sometimes pulled up into a high ponytail.

She bats her eyelashes at me, and I want to fold like origami, stalk her to wherever she's going just to be in her presence all night, in the world where she *is*.

"Hey, can I ask you for a favor?" she shouts to me across the hall before exiting the building.

"Anything."

"Can you walk Pushkin tomorrow morning, please?" Her innocent blue eyes are so hesitant like there's a chance I could say no. "It might be a late night, and I—"

"Done," I respond.

There's absolutely nothing I won't do for her. Even if her requests were as bold as those of the characters in her books.

No such luck.

"Thanks, Jace! You are the best!"

I love the way she says my name, softer than other words like it's special.

I get back to the empty apartment and meet Pushkin's sad eye, the werewolf-style eye patch making me smile. He already misses her too.

So, being a good roommate just like she asked, I take Pushkin with me for a jog the next morning.

He needs a boot camp. His lazy ass gives up after only three minutes of my usual jogging routine along the river. Even bacon bits can't force him to make another step.

The white pirate is gonna learn discipline. I'm now planning on turning him into Usain Bolt.

His purple waistcoat with yellow paw prints and the ridiculous pirate patch stops two female joggers, who flock to me like I have a cute baby I need help with.

"Oh! My! God!" they coo around him for ten minutes, and the shithead blissfully closes his eye at their touch, then leers at me as they make small talk with me.

When we get back to the condo, I run into my room, pull off my hoodie, and exhale in relief.

It's fucking hot in this apartment. I should probably talk to Lu about that. I still refuse to wear T-shirts to avoid questions about my tattoos.

A quick lukewarm shower helps to cool down my mind, my body, and certain parts that get restless now and then at the memories of Lu's spicy stories. I'm her patron on SD now, and my first generous donation will hopefully make her life easier.

I put on sweatpants and a thin long-sleeved sports shirt, then remember the glasses, put on those stupid things, and walk to the kitchen.

Lu is up, surprisingly early, cutely yawning as she pads toward the kitchen for the coffee that I made earlier.

She's wearing a short string dress with daisies. Her frizzy hair is done into a braid that hangs down her back. No makeup. She looks sleepy and so deliciously natural.

I steal a quick glance at her long bare legs.

Yes, definitely delicious.

She's beautiful in a homey way. Not the wham-glam-flash-warning Lu when she goes out, but I-like-to-bake-bread-and-don't-care-about-the-paint-smudges-on-my-skin Lu.

"Coffee?" She smiles at me.

"Sure." That's a first. I already had a cup, but I'm craving her presence.

"How do you like it? Tell me, so I can get it down."

"I'll do it."

"You are my roommate, and I like having you here." She's already hustling by the espresso machine. "Trust me, in a month, I'll know what you wear, how loud you snore"—I don't, I want to argue—"what time you get up and go to bed, how long before my voice starts driving you crazy."

She laughs, her laughter making my heart flutter.

"And the other way around," I murmur, smiling.

"What other way?" She looks at me in question.

"I mean… I'll know what you wear, what time you go to bed… I mean."

I'm not blushing. Nope. Not fucking happening. That sounded

creepy as hell. Why do girls get to say these things so easily and we guys have to make sure they don't sound like innuendos?

"Oh, yeah!" Lu laughs again. "Right. Here."

She passes me a coffee with the perfect amount of cream and sugar. I can get used to this, a girl making me coffee in the morning.

"Hey, I'm making grits and toast. Want some?" She doesn't even look at me like I already agreed.

I'm usually out of the condo by this time. We don't interact much in the morning. I hate grits since the army. So I argue. "I don't want to bother—"

"I'd love to!" Lu chirps and takes two bowls out of the cupboard. "I love eating healthy in the morning because then I can stuff my face with delicious unhealthy food the rest of the day. It's a balance."

She's a balance between my happiness at being around her and the aching anticipation when I'm not, looking forward to the moment when we are in the same space.

Beautiful, talented, and a cook.

I instantly relax, my heart snapping into a soothing rhythm.

Lu talks for both of us, and I like it, both her voice and the way she rubs the sole of her bare foot on the arch of the other while she's making breakfast. For *me*. I feel giddy like a teen on a first date.

There's a smudge of paint on her hands.

"Did you paint this morning?" I ask, watching her hustle and feeling awkward standing at the island like a prince being waited on.

"Last night when I got home. Sometimes I can't sleep. And I like working late when the rest of the world is asleep."

My Midnight Lu.

Pushkin comes up from behind me. With a longing huff, he drops to the floor next to me and sets his head on my bare foot.

"He likes you." Lu smiles. "No one claimed him yet, so he's ours." She drops to her haunches and gives him a tiny treat. "Yeah, cute muffin?"

The tea kettle whistles loudly, and she pours water into the bowls with grits, while I'm stuck on the word *ours*.

That's Lu—trusting and humble. There's a reason I stayed away at first like I knew that she's this magic potion I'll want more of after just one taste.

"Sit." She nods to the kitchen island.

She moves around effortlessly and gestures freely, every movement fluid and easy. She's invasively friendly in a sweet kind of way, and when she passes me a bowl of grits, I tell myself it's a one-time thing, and I can definitely survive them if Lu makes them for me. *Especially* when she sits down next to me and talks about art and her new portrait order as my whole body tenses at her proximity.

"Hey, Lucy, I was wondering—"

"Call me Lu, please," she interrupts. "All my friends do."

I am a friend, and not just in my mind. Good. *We'll be friends, Lu. For now.*

All the best relationships start with friendship. Konstantin wouldn't agree. He went all ape-shit when Eva called him that. "Do all your friends know what you taste like?" he asked. But his Oxford degree didn't make him a good psychologist, because I can tell you for sure that by the end of the book, Eva was his best friend. He just didn't know it, because his alpha personality took a liking to calling her his little slut.

I finished the book, yep. It sucked me in.

And I'm all for friendship.

I forget what I wanted to ask and steal glances at Lu's hands, delicate and with bright yellow nail polish that has paint smudges around the cuticles.

This breakfast moment affects me in a strange melancholic way.

I've never had a family. My roommates were orphan kids like me in a group home, then soldiers. Roey is my best friend and the closest to what would be an older brother. I had a girlfriend for a brief time which wasn't anything to write home about.

Lu is now my friend and feels like the morning sunshine after the coldest night. And God, do I want to wake up in that sunshine every day!

Everything feels surreal. The view of the Manhattan skyline glistening in the sun. The scent of burnt toast and strong coffee. Lu and her paint smudges. Her chatter and the flirty, "Let's hang out. We can watch a movie one night."

I want another day like this, with awful grits and wonderful Lu.

Yes, I want a movie night with her. I'm not used to people wanting me around in this easy unconditional way.

Friends are a rarity. When you grow up knowing even your parents didn't want you, you appreciate genuine interest.

Lu is genuine.

And this might be my favorite morning of all time.

13

JACE

It's shopping time. For the first time in a long time, I'm shopping for a present. For a girl. In a home improvement store.

A set of shelves—check. A set of small drawers on wheels—check. A handful of artists' basics that I Googled online—mixing palettes, palette knives, rags.

Next, I stop at a decor store and buy a designer wood art supply cabinet and a stackable folding bookshelf. Thank god for a rental truck I borrowed from Roey.

Traffic is a given in Brooklyn, even at two in the afternoon. I get stuck on BQE, but Lu is worth it. I'm excited like I've bought myself a present I've been dreaming about for years.

I haul my loot to Goldsling Towers through the hallway to the elevator past the concierge who raises his brows. He likes me. I made sure of that. My glasses really do the trick. So does Pushkin with his pink leash. But I learned that our concierge, Greg, likes fine cognac. So at Roey's advice, I got him Armenian stuff. Yeah, there's a fine line between bribes and gifts.

"Renovating?" Greg asks on my third walk through the hallway.
Making Lu happy.
"Something like that," I answer with a broad smile.

Up in the condo, I take off my shirt, because the condo is empty and hot as hell, and spend the next hour building a giant shelf for

Lu's paints and brushes then assemble the smaller cart and the cabinet.

I might've gotten carried away, I realize when I'm done, as I stand in the center of her room and look at the new furniture.

I hope this makes her happy. I want to see her smile.

Back in my room, I simmer in anticipation of seeing Lu's reaction.

Curiosity is a bitch, and so is my obsessed mind.

Restless, I open Story Den again.

I'm not reading this for the substance. I want to see what crazy fantasies her artsy mind conjures. Besides big boys and tight wet… Yeah, those.

I decided to treat her stories like a manual. Some learn by practicing. I'm good with theory.

Spider pose.

Golden Arch.

Prince Albert's piercing.

I Google every new term and make notes.

I enjoyed *Beautiful Vice.* Eva fell in love with Konstantin. Konstantin went down on his knees in front of her in the presence of the entire Bratva clan, asking for her forgiveness. They renewed their vows. He cut her skin to remove her birth control implant because he wanted five children but didn't trust doctors and, well, no one was allowed to touch Eva but him. He bought her an entire freaking town in France, because he already bought her a tropical island in Chapter Seven as an apology for missing a dinner date because he was torturing a guy who dared touch her hair during a gala. Chivalry is not dead. And, of course, it was HEA, as they say in the romance world, happily ever after.

Lu, you officially won me over to the smutty side of literature.

This is the only novel-sized work under @MidnightLu. The rest are erotic shorts.

I open them one by one and skim the barely existent plot, focusing on the hot scenes.

My body flares up at the words like there's hot air seeping into my pores.

He thrusts inside me, and I whimper at the slight pain and the pleasure that intertwine into a scorching fire, burning within me.

Is that how it feels for girls?

"I'm gonna make you come, little fawn."

Little fawn? This must be a popular mountain recluse romance genre.

"So many times, you can't walk afterward."

The dude is gonna hurt her.
I flip to the next story, searching for the raunchy scenes, looking for anything slightly more realistic.

"Nuh-uh. Tsk-tsk. No hands, kitten."

Katsiónak! I must have a *Beautiful Vice* hangover because I instantly like this guy.

"You are so wet for me, petal."

Petal? How does Lu come up with those nicknames?

"You are too big."
   "Take me like the good little whore that you are. All of it."

Dude, tame it down.

"There you are," he growls, and I scream in ecstasy, hot tears spilling down my cheeks as his hips snap against mine as he pounds away.

He impaled her, that's it. And she's crying.

"Real men don't need assistance when they eat."

This one is a sex Terminator.

"That's what I call a meal."

He's fucking intense.

His mouth takes as much of me in as it can and bites down—

Enough.

My erection is heavy, almost hurting as it strains my jeans. Those stories spin in my head, and I rub myself through the fabric, trying to calm down.

This is way out of my comfort zone, but I can learn what women like, what *Lu* likes. She might be writing this to please the readers, but I've been to war and know how to observe and look for patterns.

There's certainly a pattern in her writing, the little words and scenes that get repeated here and there, the ones that Lu enjoys writing. I need to pay more attention.

Research, I remind myself.

So, what do I do? Start reading everything @MidnightLu wrote so far.

14

JACE

"JACE!" LU SHOUTS FROM HER ROOM, AND I RUSH IN, MY PULSE IN MY gut, afraid she might not like the new furniture I got her.

Her smile is from ear to ear. My instant relief makes me feel like I just got resuscitated. But before I can say a word, Lu flings herself at me, wrapping her arms around my neck.

"Thank you," she whispers, her hot breath grazing my skin.

The smell of her peach shampoo tickles my nostrils and chases it with goosebumps. She feels so much smaller and fragile in my arms, but when she pulls away, it's as if a warm blanket was yanked off me. She has so much heat for such a small human.

A mist of tears shines in her eyes. Yep, it's official—I made a girl cry.

"Jace..." She bites her bottom lip, her beautiful blue eyes pools of water. "You are amazing."

And an asshole for spying on her, I want to add. Also for secretly reading her stories.

She goes around the room, touching the shelves and checking the new drawers. There's impatience in her movements as if she wants to immediately rearrange her room but doesn't want to seem too eager.

I should probably leave, but I can't tear my eyes off her.

Lu is this little marvel who combines sass and graceful feminism, #smuttyromance narratives and wholehearted glee about the new shelves. Also, the genuine care when she makes cute colorful outfits for Pushkin. And makes breakfasts for me.

I love her quirky childish streak that makes her sing in the shower, occasionally so loud that I can hear it behind closed doors. Or when she lies on her stomach on her bed, writing on the computer as she wiggles her toes in those adorable colorful socks that she changes every day.

"*You* are amazing, Lu," I say, trying hard not to look flustered at her display of affection.

"And you...you..."

She takes a little breath to say something but stalls, her eyes locking with mine for a little too long.

Long enough for my heart to do a flip and my mind to finish that sentence the way I want to.

Long enough for me to want to touch her again, feel her skin, taste her lips, and inhale her scent.

When you grow up in a group home, you get used to pulling, tugging, and occasional beatings. The *careless* touch. Not the affectionate one of a mother, a sister, or a loved one.

The silence between us lasts seconds, but it changes everything and makes me aware of how much my body yearns for her.

I know Lu feels it too.

She flinches. There's a flicker of surprise in her gaze. A little frown like she just saw me in a different light.

And then it's gone. She smiles widely and says quietly, "You are incredible."

That's it.

One minute, one word, one glance, and I make up my mind—I want to be her man. And not a short-term fling. I want a deep connection, intimacy, making love, making plans, planning the future, imagining a future together.

Everything changes in my mind though we carry on as usual.

Roommates. *Friends*—the word makes me smile.

I spend the rest of the day studying online and sigh in disappointment when Lu leaves in the evening. She doesn't come back until after midnight, and when the door to her room closes, I go out onto the terrace and watch the sparkling night downtown across the river, feeling inexplicably happy that Lu is home.

Back in my room, I fall asleep with the same feeling in my chest and wake up to the thought of her. Always do. The only thing that mars my happiness is the thought that my feelings are one-sided and soon, this will all end.

It makes every day special. Including my little white monster.

Pushkin's morning runs with me are now a daily thing. My shithead actually *runs*. Practice makes perfect. He's getting into shape and becoming a local celebrity with his fashion outfits and eye patches.

I stick around the house in the mornings too, wanting more of Lu and soaking in every detail about her.

Breakfasts and coffee together become a routine, considering Lu gets up much earlier lately.

I do ask her about her uncle.

She shrugs. "He's disappeared again. I hadn't seen him in years until that night I passed out on the street and met you. I can't get ahold of him either."

That's bad news. Not because we are back to square one, but because Roey might pull me out of the condo and back to the Sheepshead Bay apartment, though I'm not ready to move out.

I tell him that, too.

"Reznik might just reappear in Lu's life again," I say, trying to sound convincing. "I'm staying there for now. If there's a chance of running into him at her place, we have to take it. It's a five-million-dollar chance, right?"

I avoid eye contact with Roey, because he senses something is going on with me.

But because he's my best friend, I end up telling him a gazillion things about Lu.

"She was so happy to make grits for me," I say. "I couldn't bear seeing her sad if I said no to them." I smile as I meet his gaze. "What?"

Roey stares at me with a puzzled look, then sticks a cigarette between his lips. "I see where this is going."

I feel awkward as if I got caught doing something dirty.

Roey lights the cigarette, exhales a cloud of smoke out the open window, and says, "Bacon."

"What?" I'm confused.

"Everything tastes better with bacon. Buy bacon so you can survive her grits."

Noted.

I do.

The more time Lu and I spend together, the more she gets in my head and makes a home there.

As she promised, she educates me about art, sits me down on the couch one day, takes a seat next to me, and shows me art albums.

"*Nude Descending a Staircase.*" She points at one image.

Alright, we're starting with a weird one.

And then dozens more follow.

Picasso—I like this guy. Modernism reminds me of her friend Becky's outfits on her social media. Pollock, Rothko, Warhol, Basquiat. I won't remember all the names, but that's not even the point. Lu would be disappointed that I'm way more excited about her bare knees brushing against my jeans than the actual prominent artists as she explains to me different art movements.

"Can we make this a daily class?" I ask. "This art thing?"

I chuckle when she catches me glancing at her legs right up against my thigh, and she laughs. "Sure."

Turns out, the weird Eastern European foods beat the crazy art.

"Is there any food you don't like?" she asks with a mischievous glint in her eyes.

"Not really."

She grins. "Brain? Liver? Anything?"

"I tried all of that. Really good."

"Wanna be adventurous?"

With food or...?

She giggles. Lu's giggle is like an unsolicited smutty image from her spicy stories.

"Okay, okay. It's a layered Russian salad." She pulls a carry-out container with Cyrillic letters on it out of the fridge. "It's from a Ukrainian deli in Brighton."

"It's suspiciously pink," I say when she pops the lid and carefully cuts off a chunk of a cake-looking mass.

"Open your mouth," she orders, bringing a forkful to my lips.

I like her in charge but give her an exaggerated side-eye as I take a forkful of the salad and try to discern the flavors.

"Not bad." I try really hard to figure out the components. "Vegetables. Mayo..."

"Uh-huh." Her smile grows bigger.

"Something salty mixed in."

"Yes! It's marinated herring! Wow, you like it, Jace! It's called Herring Under Fur."

The last word is not a good visual. I clear my throat. "The word *fur* should never be used for a dish."

She produces a trill of laughter. "Want another bite?"

Marinated herring, boiled vegetables, boiled egg, and sweet mayo—my chest suppresses the bile, because our likes and dislikes are often psychological, and *fur* just ruined it.

"I'm good." I smile, then excuse myself, and spend a minute in the bathroom gagging.

15

JACE

Another month in Goldsling Towers is coming up, so I give Lu rent money, and she lights up like a Christmas tree.

"Thank you, Jace!"

There's so much gratitude in her voice that I feel bad. I've noticed she tries to save money. But all the clothes she has!

"It's mostly from thrift stores," she explains with a blush when I ask. Is she embarrassed? "B gives me some of her outfits. She has tons. She doesn't care. I have to keep up appearances at galleries and on my social media. If it were up to me, I'd walk around the city in jeans, sneakers, and oversized shirts. I used to, back in Virginia."

I want to kiss that rosy color of her cheeks.

Fuck, I'm obsessing. The night I met her, I knew, I just knew I'd fall head over heels.

Yep, it's happening.

When I came back from the service, I lived day by day, traveling the world for several months, trying to feel normal and blend in, all the while mentally struggling to adjust.

Then Roey pulled me out of the claws of depression and brought me into his bounty business.

It got easier to breathe. The California sun and ocean took my mind off the desert memories. Roey became like a big brother, always around, always there for me despite his own issues. To say that Roey feels like an entire family in one person is not an exaggeration.

Now there's Lu, who makes me forget what it was like before her.

I've been neglecting my online course lately. Roey and I plan on going to Thailand when we finish the Reznik job. It will be a nice vacation. Roey's agenda is to investigate a runaway bounty in Bangkok. Mine is to search for plots of land for my dream project. I'd never been interested in construction until I watched a video of an indigenous woman building a villa out of bamboo and jungle materials by hand. I want to try it, hence me taking online courses in carpentry.

I should be studying but my mood is more mischievous.

I've read all of Lu's stories multiple times. So, out of curiosity, I roam through other authors on SD.

Roey calls, and I can't say a word because I'm laughing.

"Your pirate dog is causing a scene?" he muses.

"No. Just hanging out on Story Den. These authors have creativity, I tell you. Listen to this—*Practical Cock-Tease,* a step-brother romance."

Roey chuckles. "Our Lucy wrote that?"

"No, a random title. *My Sweet Widow: A Mafia Romance,*" I continue. "I assume, she's a widow after she's his wife and before she's his mistress."

"You sound like you know all the genres."

I do. *"My Vicious Yoga Instructor,"* I name another one.

"And how he ruined my upward-facing dog," Roey adds, and we both start cackling.

"Wait, wait. There. *Midnight Cocks,* a reverse harem small ranch romance."

Roey roars with laughter, then pauses. "Wait, what the hell is reverse harem?"

"That's, well, like a harem, but one girl and… Yeah, it's a thing."

"And two guys?"

"Well, no, that's technically menage, which is three people. Reverse harem is one girl and at least three guys."

"At *least*? How the fuck is that fair to the guys?"

"Men are not the target reading audience."

"You sound like an expert."

"Well, I've been researching."

When he hangs up, I lie in my bed and think about Lu.

She left for the rest of the night, and it makes me melancholic, makes me wanna go out on the terrace and smoke out the loneliness that lodges inside me in her absence.

The next morning, I walk out of my room and see Lu standing by the window, staring at the Manhattan skyline in the distance, with a coffee mug in her hand, in rainbow socks and a long T-shirt, Pushkin by her feet.

He lifts his head at me, but I press my forefinger to my lips in a silent "shh," pull my phone out of my jeans, and quietly snap a quick picture of her. I have several by now, the stolen shots that I stare at when I feel like seeing her but she's not around.

I recently learned that Lu is not always sunshine and smiles. There are days when she's quiet. Too quiet. No music, no singing, no cooing to Pushkin. Her phone beeps in her room but remains unanswered.

Like today.

"Morning," I say, uneasy at the silence.

Lu turns around with a smile that doesn't reach her eyes. "Morning."

"What's wrong?"

She's not herself.

"Just... Just tired." Her smile flickers on and off as she walks over to the kitchen. "Grits?"

I nod, watching her smile widen and her shoulders straighten up. She's a natural caretaker and enjoys doing things for others.

And then she makes us coffee, grits, and bacon. Thank God for bacon!

"Maybe you should take a break from work," I say, trying to figure out her mood.

"I can't. I have an exhibition coming up. And orders. And I need money."

"Everyone needs a break."

She shakes her head. "I'm good at what I do, Jace. That's what I got. I don't want a nine-to-five job. I want to work until four in the morning if I feel like it. Or have breakfast on a terrace at noon. And have music playing all the time, and paint, and…"

It becomes too much, I get it, and she has to press the brakes.

"And I'm trying to save for a rainy day, so if anything happens, I can rely on myself," she finishes softly as she effortlessly prepares us breakfast. Multitasking is her forte.

There's a strange melancholy in the way she says, "Rainy day," like she knows what those are, and maybe she does—that's part of Lu I am yet to learn.

I wish she didn't have rainy days, and when she does, I want to cover them and make her smile and tuck her under a warm blanket on the couch and watch a movie and tell her, "Lu, don't worry about a thing. I'm right here."

My heart clenches at the need to wrap my arms around her and make her feel okay.

I ask her about Virginia, her family, and her university years. And as we eat, she talks, falling into the usual Lu-rhythm, filling the air with her sweet voice.

"So tonight," she says when I clean the dishes and she sits on the high stool and swings her rainbow-socked feet, "we are going to a bar. B, Tito, and I. Wanna come?"

Her words make my eyes snap to meet hers. "Me?"

I stall like she's asking me to marry her, but already feeling excited like it's an actual date, which it isn't.

Lu is gorgeous and magnetic. It's an effort not to stare at her. Give me a beer, and I'll be openly gawking. Do we want that scenario? Or a worse one—me getting drunk and spilling the truth about how we met. Or Becky coaxing it out of me.

I've met Lu's crew several times by now. People use phones these days to meet up. Well, not Lu's friends, who occasionally pop in without calling. Apparently, because Lu is notorious for ignoring her phone.

"I need to discuss work, but you are avoiding me!" Becky complained a week ago when she stormed into the condo unannounced, eyeing me like I'm keeping Lu away from her.

Tito dropped by when Lu wasn't home the other day. That was a bold move. And intentional, I sensed, when he asked if I wanted to do lunch.

So when Lu invites me to a bar, I know I should come up with an excuse not to go. Becky will interrogate me. Tito will try to get me into his bed.

"Come with us!" Lu insists, waiting for my reply. "It'll be fun. Well, with you there. You'll make sure B doesn't drag me to yet another club or party. I'm so tired of those. But she doesn't take no for an answer. Networking, she calls it."

This is a bad idea. "Sure," I say and already feel stressed out at the thought.

What should I wear?

Should I drink?

"Can I bring a friend?" Roey can handle any interrogations and play in his league if he's so adamant about extracting the info.

Lu's smile flickers off. "A girl?"

"No, my, um, colleague."

Her smile widens again. "Sure!"

Did I see relief on her face?

Oh, Lu.

If only she knew that there are no other girls. All I think about is her.

16

JACE

"Getting close to your target is a bad idea," Roey argues with me over the phone when I tell him we are going to a bar with Lu and her crew.

"We're trying to get info," I counteract. "*Find the magic*, remember? You have plenty, so work it." I'm insistent, to my own surprise. "Otherwise, we might never find Reznik." That last bit is a little too pessimistic.

"We'll find Reznik," Roey responds with bitterness.

He's not used to losing bounties. There was only one, who fled to Thailand, and Roey didn't have connections there. Hence the reason he wants to go there—to see if he can track the guy.

"I want to get to know Lu better," I say, disheartened.

"Oh, you are doing that alright. With your hand wrapped around your dick."

Fuck off.

I should've kept my mouth shut about the smutty stories Lu writes online. Roey will forever tease me now.

Roey insists on educating me on sex. I mean, he was the first to teach me cooking, laundry, banking, and social media. I was twenty-two, back from deployment. Most people know these things before they reach puberty. But most people are not the property of the state, growing up with limited resources.

Roey's favorite topic is women. When he has one drink too many, he's unstoppable.

"Twenty percent of women can come during regular sex, that's statistics," he said once.

My eyebrows hitched. "One in five?"

"Yep. They are complicated creatures. Most need some sort of additional stimulation."

This type of talk humored me more than intrigued me. I'm sure it's less complicated than he said. "So it's better to learn to cover—"

"All the bases, yes. Jace, bedding chicks is not so different from combat. You suck—you lose. Practice makes perfect."

"I'm great with theory," I joked.

"Uh-huh. Better hope you are as skilled in bed from the start as you are with hitting targets."

Except now, hitting the perfect sniper score seems much easier than figuring out how to charm Lu.

Roey doesn't make it easy either, always taunting me with her. "Are you working your stick every night reading Miss Moor's diaries?"

"Cut it out," I grunt, though Roey is the only one I'm comfortable discussing my not-so-stellar sexual achievements or the lack thereof.

"You can rope her in slowly. Show her your shark tattoo."

"Seriously, Roey..."

"She'll be impressed. Girls on the beach usually are."

I shake my head in annoyance. "It's a stupid tattoo."

"It wasn't when you got it, ancient meaning and all. Hey, here's an idea. You might be a virgin, but you are hung. I don't know how it was back in school, but you sure are not gonna disappoint a girl these days. Visually, that is."

"Shut up."

He often jokes about the incident with Monica, which, years later, got much easier to discuss.

"You don't even have to do much, buddy. Just get it out and show—"

"Dude!" He knows how to wind me up.

"Come to think about it, you'll probably rip her apart with that thing. Not all women like big guys."

I curse under my breath, but Roey's enjoying this too much. "Lucy will paint all over it. It's art."

"Torres, knock it off!" I'm so ready to strangle him.

"Hey, does she only do paintings?"

I'm glad we're changing the topic. "Think so. Why?"

"Maybe she does casting. She could totally take your Moby-Dick—"

"I hate you," I blurt out.

He roars with laughter but quickly agrees to come over to the bar in Williamsburg Lu invited us to.

And I feel like I'm going to the most important meeting of my life.

A good impression is the key, so I open my closet.

I have several outfits for different occasions. An expensive black suit and several dress shirts that I barely ever wear except for meetings with important clients. Casual button-ups, mostly black. Hoodies, black. Jeans. Sweatpants. Dress shoes, HeyDudes, sneakers and Converses, and a pair of work boots for dirty jobs.

Shit. There's nothing in this closet to impress Lu. For once, I wish I had some swanky clothes.

So, black it is, a long-sleeved cashmere sweater and jeans. Tito will approve.

I stand in front of the mirror, fixing my hair with gel and failing. It's growing out of the crew-cut style, and I don't know how to handle it. I've always had a buzz cut. Property of the state doesn't have many choices or say in what they want to do. Neither do servicemen.

I'm nervous. More nervous than the first weeks in the army. I almost didn't make it back then. After years in a group home and bullying, I wanted to be a Superman, that quiet guy who doesn't stick out but can kick everyone's ass.

Well, the first month in boot camp almost killed me.

But don't underestimate the kid who always wanted to prove his worth. It took me four years of service to get to where I am. Another year to have more money in my bank account than most guys my age who went to college and have great careers. Thanks to Roey and… yeah, my "sales" job.

The self-imposed celibacy, as Roey calls it? Well, it's another mountain to conquer. I'll get to it. I'm not worried. I am patient. I'm an observer. I'm a good learner. With Lu? I feel like all those years of tempering myself were meant to conquer the girl of my dreams.

So here I come.

17

JACE

THE BAR IS PACKED. THE NOISE DROWNS THE LOUD BEATING OF MY heart as I push my way through the large crowded space of tall bar tables with stools, armchairs around coffee tables, and bookcases.

I've never been to a bar that looks like the living room of a Gothic mansion. But this is Williamsburg, a trendy Brooklyn neighborhood. Every place here tries to top the neighbors and the overpriced rivals in Manhattan.

I'm diligently wearing my glasses. I don't know how you get used to the damn things. Despite the fake lenses, the world feels warped, and the awkward frame keeps sliding down my nose, irritating the shit out of me. But Roey insists that they make me look more trustworthy. So I keep wearing them.

I spot Lu and her friends at one of the bar tables, and my heart flutters madly just at the sight of her. She's wearing a jeweled jacket and dress shorts that match her red stilettos. Fashionable, as always.

"Hey, stranger!" she exclaims and greets me with a big hug and a kiss on my cheek like I'm her close friend.

A quick trip to the bar, and I get beers for Lu and myself.

Yep, she's a beer kinda girl—who would've known?

Lu, you are winning my heart one day at a time.

"You look like a sophisticated banker," Tito says as I greet him and Becky at the table.

I assume it's a compliment, though Becky's condescending gaze says she's not impressed. This girl needs to cool it.

Tito looks different tonight. Jewelry on his wrists, a pendant around his neck pointing super-low south down his open chest, clad in a low-cut fashion jumper. I don't remember any girl in my life who's given me more heated glances than Tito. Not glances, no—he's eating me up like Pac-Man.

"How's your day, Jace? Your job?" Becky asks, starting the interrogation.

Tito flirts.

Becky inspects me.

Lu just smiles and sways to the music. She loves music. I love watching her. If only I didn't constantly feel Becky's eyes on me or get bombarded with her questions. They are *all* curious about me. It's teamwork, I realize.

Becky narrows her eyes on me like she's trying to uncover my secret. *Good luck.*

"So, sweetie, tell us more about yourself."

Here we go again. I'm still waiting for Roey to show up—he can deflect her attention.

"Ohio born," I say, though I've already told her this the last time at the condo. "Four years in the army. Now, California. Sales." I try to be concise for the dozenth time.

Tito arches a brow. "How was the army?"

I shrug. "Is there a way to answer that question in one sentence?"

"Where are your parents? Ohio?"

I didn't want to bring it up, but now there's no point in lying. "I don't have any. I grew up in the system."

There's a strange silence for a moment, and I smile at Lu, though there's so much pity in her eyes that I regret bringing this up.

"Sorry," she says.

"Property of the state, huh?" Tito murmurs, his gaze on me softening.

"It's alright." I chuckle. "Many people lose their parents. I just didn't have any."

I think even Becky eased back on her bitchiness.

This is not a sensitive topic for me. Most people don't get upset about not having a sibling. Some of us don't have parents, and we don't know what it's like to have them. I never used my past as a pity card, but obviously, some people think it is.

"Girlfriend?" Becky's eyes study me over the rim of her Martini glass as she takes a sip.

"No."

"Boyfriend?" Of course, the question comes from Tito.

"No."

His eyes narrow on me with that seductive glint as he drawls, "You don't try, you don't know."

I hold his gaze for a moment, trying to hold back laughter. His flirting is endearing. "No," I mouth. I need another beer ASAP.

"So, Tito, what do you do?" I ask, changing the topic. I know quite a bit about Lu. I know Becky is a talent scout and an entrepreneur, with a double major in business management and arts administration.

Tito is a mystery. I like him. His overly seductive gazes don't make me uneasy, I'm not sensitive like that. I could've been friends with him if his thoughts about me didn't involve sex, and I'm pretty sure they do.

Becky slides her arm around Tito's shoulders. "He's the brain of our little circle."

Tito lifts his chin with what looks like a proud look on his face.

"Chromatography," he says.

I take a gulp of beer and frown. I know what that is, but I'm not sure I heard it right. Tito? Really?

Becky is narrowing her eyes at me in triumph.

Tito's lips curl in a smirk.

"You do chemical analysis?" I ask, and their faces fall in an instant. "You work in a lab? What company?"

He's startled that he didn't throw me off with the chemical term. He would've if I didn't have a buddy in the army who wanted to go to college for chromatography, so I know all about it.

"Analytical chemist," Tito explains, seemingly impressed with my knowledge. "I work in research and development for a pharmaceutical company that specializes in cancer research."

"Wow. I would've never guessed," I murmur, and judging by the slightly irritated flash in Tito's gaze, that was the wrong comment.

"What *was* your guess?" he asks, a little too hostile. "Wait, wait, wait for it"—his lips curl in a mocking smirk—"fashion designer? Stylist? Hairdresser?"

I shake my head with an embarrassed smile. He is right, a hundred fucking percent.

"Because I'm queer?" he insists.

"I didn't mean it like that," I apologize.

"Maybe I have a chihuahua, too? Or a cat? And like nail polish?" He widens his eyes at me in mock surprise.

"Sorry, I made an assumption."

"You think?"

Easy, tiger.

Lu cuts in. "Jesus, Tito, what's with you tonight?"

"Assumptions can be insulting, Jace," Tito continues.

I feel like a dick. It's just he never talked about his work, and I've never met anyone who does cutting-edge medical research in their mid-twenties.

I'm about to ask him about his work when he nods toward Becky.

"You'd never guess looking at our Becky that she used to sell pictures of her feet online."

"Oh, gaaawd," Becky drawls, and Tito barks out a laugh.

I stare at Becky for a moment before I catch myself. Suddenly, the pictures of feet on Lu's phone make sense.

"How did that go?" I ask, hiding a smile. Becky is not as straight as an arrow as she comes across at first.

She doesn't even flinch. "Profitable if done right."

Fucking Becky—this girl probably beats Roey in the crazy shit she's into. Where the hell *is* Roey?

"I made some good cash," she explains nonchalantly. "It just got weird after a while. There's no future potential besides an overwhelming number of creepy messages. That was in my college years, anyway."

She amuses me. She's like a hand grenade without a safety switch. Totally Roey's specialty.

"People actually pay for that?" I ask. "For the pictures of... your feet?"

"Yup." Becky exhales with a hint of annoyance.

Lu nods, smiling.

"Yeah," Tito echoes.

Becky goes on. "Foot fetish is extremely common. One in seven has fantasized about feet. Five percent have a full fetish. Also, part of the brain that's responsible for sexual arousal is next to the one that processes foot sensations."

She's got the stats down. And this group, as per my observation, is definitely open to conversations about all things kinky. No wonder Lu writes smut.

Tito cheers to me with a Martini in his hand. "So it's safe to say that having a foot massage can get one horny."

"Good to know," I murmur, chasing the info with a gulp of beer, trying not to ogle Lu who just licked the foam off the rim of her beer glass and is leaning on the table, which pushes her breasts up. She's such a tease, and she doesn't even know it.

"Jace, wanna go for a foot massage?" Tito is a heavy hitter, and his irritation earlier might just be from not getting the answers he wants from me.

I stare him dead in the eyes.

His smile widens.

So does mine.

"No," I mouth. He's in denial. "But thank you."

And sure enough, now all I think about is massaging Lu's feet. She often walks around our condo barefoot, and her nail polish matches the one on her toes.

Our condo—since when? I'm appropriating Lu quicker than the third beer makes its way into my bloodstream.

And that beer... It makes my fantasies go wild. All I want is to drag Lu onto my lap and kiss the hell out of her sweet coral lips.

18

JACE

"You must come here often," I say after another group who crowds Lu to say hi leaves.

Every time I talk to Lu, Becky cuts in. She definitely likes to be the center of attention and is overly protective of her friends.

"Every month or so," Becky explains. "Lu is a celebrity in Williamsburg. She did the art piece for the community center garden in the fall that went viral."

A tall skinny guy in a worn-out sweater with overly long sleeves, despite the warm May weather, puts his hands as if in prayer and bows to Lu. She laughs, and he wraps his arm around her to take a selfie, then bows again and nervously wipes his mouth.

We all watch them as they chat.

"He's into her," Tito says. "So awkward, though. A celebrity crush. He's probably a virgin and has wet dreams about her."

That remark reminds me of how I felt about Monica when I was a teen, and I tense.

"Nah." Becky narrows her eyes on the guy, dissecting his movements. "There are no guy virgins in their mid-twenties unless there's something wrong with them or they live in the mountains. Or! Are voluntarily/involuntarily celibate. That's a special breed."

Is it now?

I want to hear more. Apparently, I'm a breed.

Tito waves her off. "You'd be surprised. I've met a couple. Occasionally, they are asexual, not into anything at all. Nothing wrong with virgins. I'd teach him things." He cocks his head, studying the guy.

Becky snorts, and Lu ditches the "special breed" guy and slides back into her seat.

"Oh, I'd get him all wild," Tito carries on, leaning back in his chair, and I have a feeling by the charged glance at me that he's selling himself. "Newbies are the most enthusiastic in bed."

Becky turns her unblinking gaze to me. "What do you think, Jace?"

She says it so slowly, without taking her eyes off me, like she's waiting for me to spill some important information about myself.

I shrug indifferently, though I'm tense as fuck on the inside. "Not everyone is a pushy alpha."

Where's Roey?

Becky raises her eyebrows in surprise, and I freeze—I just used the words from Lu's stories.

And the fucking guy comes back. He puts his sweater-sleeved hand on Lu's cheek, whispers something in her ear, and I want to rip his hand off her.

She gently pushes him away with an awkward smile. "No, thank you."

"See?" Tito says when the guy bugs off. "Looks like he wants to take our Lu for a wild ride."

"Stop, Tito," Lu says, waving him off.

"If he's a virgin, he might be a fun ride," Tito carries on.

"What?" She frowns, confused.

"Oh, nothing. We were just playing a guessing game," he says. "Oh, that's cute." I meet his eyes. "Jace, you are blushing."

My entire body just got ten degrees hotter. My glasses are fogging up. I take them off and rub my eyes. I hate those damn things.

Lu asks me to help her with the drinks. She likes beer, the choice of drink that doesn't fit with her high heels, blonde hair, and jeweled jacket. My kinda girl. I mean, yeah, assumptions. Tito is right, we are all full of those.

"I think Tito got a little too sensitive over his job," Lu explains, leaning over to me so I can hear her over the loud music as we wait for our drinks at the bar. "He hates when people assume he is a boy toy whereas he won the Medical Innovation Award in college at the age of eighteen."

"Wow."

"And he really likes you, so he went off earlier. He won't stop teasing you until he either gets what he wants or gets a clear rejection."

"I'm not into guys," I say.

"Good to know," she blurts out, then bites down on her smile and looks away.

Oh, shit. Is she interested?

"And"—she grabs the two Martinis as I pick up our beers—"you look really good without those glasses."

She gives me a flirty glance and a smile and walks off, and I follow on weak knees, wanting to pick her up, carry her home, and kiss the hell out of her.

Home... That word again. We share a home, and this makes my fantasies even wilder.

Those glasses are really my weakness because when we reach our table, they are on Becky.

Fucking Becky.

She cocks her head at me with a cold smile, her eyes narrowing dangerously through the fake lenses.

Shit.

"I like your glasses, Jace," she drawls.

Maybe, this outing was a mistake.

Slowly, as if putting on a show, Becky takes them off and winks at me. Soon, my fake glasses will be public knowledge. And because the beer is making me careless, I put them in my back pocket, not a bit worried that they might crack.

Fuck those things.

Yep, I'm getting tipsy.

Becky smiles knowingly into her Martini.

Lu steals flirty glances at me.

And Tito openly stares at me with his fuck-me eyes.

I need to stop drinking. It makes me bold, and Lu being so close is my personal inferno.

One of her spicy stories comes to mind, and in a second, there's no stopping my thoughts that flicker in fast succession—a dark corner, her coral lips, my tongue, her slender legs, my hands, her thighs…

"Dreaming?" Tito's voice snaps my gaze away from studying Lu's hands.

He has no idea. Neither does Lu.

Maybe Becky. That girl is a human lie detector, though she keeps a lot of things to herself. I'm sure she uses them against people. Maybe I'm just too wary. She really does remind me of Monica.

Fucking Monica…

My experience with Monica was what put me off about the dating game.

There are always firsts.

We never remember our first steps or words. We *do* sometimes remember our first day at school, the first big party, or our first friend. But we *always* remember our first big humiliation. Especially when it's public. When you are seventeen. When it's with the girl you are in love with. When she makes you feel special and offers that "first time," and you can barely contain the excitement when you are making out with her in an empty school gym. It should click in your head that it's not the best place for your "first time," though a group home doesn't have many romantic options. But hormones don't rationalize. Not even when she asks you to lose all your clothes while she's still dressed.

Hell, her hands on you are the best feeling ever. She's the only person who touched you *there*.

And then comes her laughter, devilish and not so friendly anymore, followed by the outside noises, footsteps, then muffled laughter in the room where it was supposed to be just the two of you.

You finally notice faces in the windows and cellphones clicking pictures while she picks up your clothes and runs off. And there's no way to cover your naked body or fight the humiliation and horror when you realize that dozens of people are filming you, and the girl of your dreams is gone.

Sometimes, being seventeen sucks.

Occasionally, it's the first time you die on the inside.

19

LU

WHERE DID HE JUST GO?

I was studying Jace's smile that makes him so handsome when it faded, giving way to a haunted look in his eyes.

He stares at his beer in silence.

I can't stop stealing glances at him. His sleeves are pushed up, the sweater tightly hugging his muscles. And, oh, does he have a nice body. Without glasses, he's hot in a subtle way that makes my eyes latch onto him, trying to figure out what hides under that calm surface.

It's always the quiet ones...

Becky's words make so much sense. She's experienced, and I'm not. Well, not really. Not by a mile.

An orphan... I can't get the word out of my mind. Why didn't Jace ever mention that? How does it feel to grow up without a family?

I grab my phone and start writing in my notepad app. My tipsy brain often comes up with the best lines, and if I don't write them down, they'll be swallowed by the next morning's hangover.

My screen lights up with a message.

Chad: Hey, doll, missing you tonight. What are you doing?

It's Friday night, so of course he's drinking and probably looking for a hook up. After our swift one-month dating and breakup, he's still looking for a second chance.

Another message comes.

Then another.

Irritated, I finally respond.

Me: Out with friends.

Chad: Where?

"Who's texting you?" Becky asks, annoyed and curious.

"Ugh, it's Chad."

Becky rolls her eyes. "He's horny. Please, don't tell him where we are."

Jace shifts in his seat. "You have a boyfriend?"

I meet his searching gaze, etched with what I think is disappointment. His eyes are so much more intense without those glasses like he's looking through me.

Tito breaks my stupor. "She doesn't. It's her ex. He wants her back and wants to tap her because he didn't get to, and it's driving him insane."

I smile, slightly embarrassed at the truth, and Jace's expression softens. "Oh."

Is that relief on his face?

Tito saves me. "That's what happens. Men can't get what they want, and they turn into jerks."

"Shitty men," Jace says.

Yes, thank you!

Suddenly, I want to kiss his lips, sit on his lap, and have his strong hands on my body. I'd let him do a lot more than Chad ever did.

The thought startles me.

Sheesh.

I need to cool it.

Becky and Tito start playing the guessing game, picking a person in the crowd and creating a background story. Usually men. *Mostly* men. While I sit and wish I was alone with Jace.

"Oh! There's a fine catch. B! Pay attention!" Tito spots someone by the door, and we all look in that direction.

Becky lifts her chin, narrowing her eyes at the target. "Delicious. A bad boy."

Tito nods. "Yes, a hundred percent. Though a little older than you. Mid-thirties."

"Maybe early thirties. I don't mind vintage. Construction?"

"Nuh-uh. Too stylish and clean, despite his five-o'clock shadow."

"An entrepreneur."

Tito shakes his head. "Too rough around the edges. And too handsome. Guys like that either don't have a brain or use it for something more edgy."

"Harsh," Jace says, grinning as he's staring at the guy fighting his way through the crowd. "Edgy, huh?"

"Maybe a cop," Becky says with a glint in her eyes that's a cue she's found a new prey for tonight.

"A professional athlete. A boxer, maybe," Tito suggests.

"Single," Becky guesses.

"Divorced," Tito snaps. "Baby mama is a psycho. And even hotter than him."

"He came to hunt. Oh, yeah, baby." Becky is interested.

"Oh, no," I murmur and lean over to Jace. "They do this all the time. Sometimes, they place bets. Trust me, it gets suspenseful. Looks like Becky found a new target. If he's single, watch her. She'll mess with the guy just to win a bet with Tito."

Jace raises his eyebrows in amusement. "They have bets, huh?"

"Yep."

"Hey, Tito." Jace gives him a backward nod. "I bet the guy is single, does sales, and he'll be ready to take Becky home within five minutes, without her even trying."

Both Becky and Tito burst out laughing.

Becky cocks a brow. "Jace Reed, you have a gambling streak in you. Who would've known?"

Tito leans over the table, bringing his face close to Jace's. "It's a bet. Which part?"

"All three," Jace says. "If I'm wrong about any of those, I lose."

"Fierce." Tito's eyes light up. "What's the bet?"

"A beer."

Tito falls back onto his chair. "Yawn."

"Breakfast," Jace retorts right away.

Tito sits up straight. "In bed?"

"Sure." Jace grins.

"Hey!" I protest. Not fair.

Jace laughs freely, and I'm startled for a moment.

His laugh... Wow... It's a weapon. My skin tingles at the soft low sound, so beautiful I want to paint it, just like every other bit of him. His body. His smile. His voice, dreams, and thoughts.

Jace's laughter quiets, and his hand slides to the small of my back as he leans over.

My body right away tenses and leans into him as if there's some gravity between us.

Jace has never been so straightforward. He's never touched me like this before.

His hot murmur grazes my cheek. "Don't worry. Tito's idea of breakfast in bed is a little over the top. I win—he's serving *you* breakfast in bed."

I laugh in response. "And if *he* wins?"

"He won't."

"I heard that," Tito says. "But it's a deal anyway." He shakes Jace's hand.

I turn to look at the stranger and frown. "I think he's looking over here."

Becky frowns too though straightens up and elegantly picks up her cocktail. "I think so."

Yep, totally Becky's type. Handsome, tall, and confident. Leather jacket slung over his broad shoulders, a white T, black jeans, and dress shoes.

His casual gaze sweeps around the bar like he owns the place before it stops on our table as he gets closer. But he's not looking at Becky or me. He is—

I turn to look at Jace. The guy approaching is looking at *Jace*?

Mr. Handsome walks up to our table and stops between me and Becky like he belongs here.

Jace grins. "This is my friend, Roey."

20

LU

BECKY'S JAW FALLS OPEN, EYEBROWS LIFTING AS SHE LOSES HER USUAL cool for a moment. "*This* is your *friend?*"

She's surprised, and so am I.

Tito is gawking, murmuring, "Jace, you just cheated on a bet."

Mr. Handsome, aka Roey, is a little older than Jace and has a totally different vibe. Birds of a feather, they say, but these two don't have anything in common except for their bodies, which are well-muscled and not in a gym way.

Roey turns to study Becky way too openly, up and down.

Oh, no, B, he's such a player and a ten. Jace is totally winning this bet.

Jace can't stop smiling. "Tito, you lost."

"You cheated," Tito murmurs.

"I didn't. There was no stipulation."

"Stipulation?" Tito hisses. "Really?"

Jace winks at him.

Wow, Jace is sexy when he winks. Can I paint a wink and its energy?

I narrow my eyes at Jace in fake spite. "You cheater."

He winks at me, and I think my panties start melting at that wink.

The new guy watches everyone with amusement and not an

97

ounce of confusion. He's totally in his element and gives Jace a backward nod. "Are you going to introduce us?"

Jace is not in a hurry to do so as if he wants his friend to take charge.

"You are Becky, I assume." Roey aims his sexy half-smile at Becky first.

Yep, Becky is screwed. The fact that she's slightly flustered is amusing.

"Yes." Becky stretches her hand out to Roey for a shake with fake reluctance, like she's bothered, though I know she's collecting herself. All three of us are.

"This is Lu," Jace says.

Roey's hand is big, but his handshake is gentle.

"Nice to meet you, Lu."

The way he looks at me is different from the charged gaze he was giving Becky a second ago. It's almost cold. Professional?

Tito shifts in his seat. "I'm Tito, just in case. I'm here, too." He waves, leering at Roey, until Roey stretches his hand across the table, which leaves Tito no choice but to shake it.

Becky flicks a strand of her hair, elegantly taking a sip of her Martini and motioning with her eyes to Roey. "Sweetie, take a seat."

He slowly turns to face her, slightly towering over her. The bar is packed. There's barely any room to stand.

"There are no chairs." He smiles and adds, "Sweetie."

"It's just a little hard to breathe when there's so much of you"— she waves around—"in my personal space."

Roey's lips stretch in a gorgeous smile. "Already taking your breath away, huh?"

I stifle a chuckle.

Her eyes flash at him with indignation, and she gives him an up-and-down look with a cocked brow.

"Wanna sit on my lap?" he offers.

Oh, he's way more straightforward than Becky. Yep, Jace won.

"In your dreams," she blurts.

"Careful there. I make my dreams come true."

He grins at her, and I'm surprised she doesn't roll her eyes. But I swear I hear a sound—his skin sizzling as Becky burns him with her stare.

He smiles, turning away from her, and taps the table. "Drinks?"

After taking Tito and Jace's orders, he walks off.

Jace smiles into his empty glass.

Tito grins at Becky. "What a stud, huh?"

She stares at Jace as if waiting for an explanation of how Roey is possibly his friend.

Roey comes back with the drinks, setting one down in front of Becky too.

She cocks her head. "I didn't tell you what I drink."

He shrugs. "The bartender did."

I like this guy. Anyone who can knock the air out of Becky has my respect.

"What do you do, Roey?" I ask.

He cheers me with his beer. "Sales."

"Like Jace?"

"Yeah," he drawls. "Like Jace."

Becky snorts.

They gotta be the hottest sales team I know, and while we talk, mostly Jace and Roey, exchanging jokes, completely at ease with each other, I can't help thinking that they are also the most unlikely salespeople I've ever met.

We are getting drunker. Becky is weirdly quiet, looking around and avoiding Roey. People start pushing against us. This place is suffocatingly crowded.

A tall bulky guy bumps into Tito, who puts his palm against his back and says, "Sweetie, another step and you'll be on my lap."

The guy shakes his hand off and gives Tito a stare, then murmurs, "Faggot."

"Watch your mouth!" Becky snaps and gets into a short spat with him while Roey and Jace exchange glances. Jace's eyes narrow in a slightly vicious glare, something I've never seen in him.

"Hey, hey! Cool it!" Roey finally snaps at the guy and straightens up, his chin raised in an intimidating manner.

Becky jumps off her chair and motions for the guy to back off.

"Okay," she exhales in irritation, "one more drink, and we are leaving. It's suffocating here."

Jace moves out of his seat. "I'll get 'em."

But Becky stops him with a curt, "Girl talk. You hold the fort," and we fight through the crowd toward the bar.

"So, Roey, huh?" I tease her.

Becky rolls her eyes. "He's a—hashtag—alpha hole."

"Maybe just confident. Your type."

"Hell, no. Way too cocky. He'd probably be good in bed, though. If he kept his mouth shut."

She is a talent scout and has an eye for creative minds, also for hot guys, good food, and new ventures. And, oh, does she know how to read people.

It takes forever to place the order with the bartender in the packed bar, and as we carry the drinks to our table, there's a commotion in the crowd.

People crane their necks over others' shoulders, to where our table is. When we approach, the table next to ours is a mess like it was shaken, drinks spilled, glasses everywhere. Both the guy who made a slur at Tito and his buddy are crouching on the ground as everyone throws startled glances at Jace and Roey, who are on their feet next to them.

"What happened?" I ask in shock.

Roey rolls his shoulders. "Nothing. They ran into the table, and it got a little messy. The guy is drunk."

"Serves them right," I murmur, turning to Jace.

There's an edge in him, sharp gaze, clenched teeth, not a trace of the usual sweetness. It's eerie but sexy.

And Tito is staring at me with raised eyebrows and a startled look on his face.

A bouncer and another man are making their way to us. "I need to ask you to leave," the man says—the owner, I've seen him before.

Becky throws her hands in the air. "Wait, what?"

"Fighting is against the rules in this place. Both parties are leaving."

"We are not at fault!" She turns to Tito. "What the hell?"

Tito is being all diplomatic. "The guys were making remarks, and—"

"That might be so," the owner cuts him off, "but your friends started the fight."

Some girl buts in, "And knocked the two jerks out like ninjas."

"What?" I frown in confusion, drinks still in my hands. I missed what happened, but Jace is definitely not the fighting type. Roey, maybe.

Becky still protests. Tito still stares at me like I missed the biggest show ever.

Jace takes the drinks out of my hands and sets them down then nods toward the exit. "It's just a misunderstanding. Let's leave."

I hear, "Solar plexus," and "Navy Seals," and "Two strike-outs," as we walk out. Being escorted out by the bouncer is slightly embarrassing. This is *our* place, and being kicked out is a first.

"I'm never coming here again. Jerks," Becky hisses.

Outside, Roey lights a cigarette as we try to figure out where to go next. Becky is still fuming.

A tipsy guy walks out of the bar and studies us with a vague smile.

"Are they, like, professionals?" he asks me and nods toward Roey and Jace.

"What are you talking about?"

"Cause that was"—the guy widens his eyes and nods drunkenly —"an A-class five-second knockout."

The guy is drunk, obviously. He stumbles toward Roey, and I'm about to ask him to leave us alone when he points to Roey's chest. "Hey, man, thank you for your service."

My gaze drops to the dog tag over Roey's T-shirt, and he nods and tucks the tag underneath.

I think I'm more confused than ever.

21

JACE

BARHOPPING THE OTHER NIGHT WAS THE MOST FUN I'VE HAD IN A while.

Except for the first bar when Roey caused a scene, dragging me into it, though the homophobic assholes deserved it, and it felt good to not hold back for once.

I can't stand bullies, hate seeing people shriveling into themselves like Tito did after the insult for a fleeting moment. That used to be me as a teenager.

Thank God Lu and Becky didn't see how things went down. Tito might spill, and I couldn't help but notice his admiring looks at me for the rest of the night. I wish Lu looked at me like that.

Lu at home is a total cutie-pie—sweatpants and a white tank top. Today, we are cleaning our condo.

Pushkin is splayed on the parquet floor in his purple bib-overalls and an eye patch with a yellow smiley face. He refuses to move even when I push him with a steam mop.

I'm not wearing glasses anymore—fuck them—and catch Lu often casting puzzled glances at me.

"How do you say shithead in Russian?" I ask her, mopping around Pushkin. I like when she talks, so I make her talk all the time.

She laughs. "*Дурачина*[1]."

I gently push Pushkin's body across the floor of the wide space between the living room and the kitchen island as I repeat, "*Du-ra-tshí-na*," and Lu burst out in laughter.

"Unbelievable." I shake my head at Pushkin, who thinks I'm playing with him and, in his turn, plays dead or really enjoys the steam mop action.

"I can teach you Russian, if you want," Lu offers.

"What about Belarusian?"

"Sure, but Russian is more popular."

"Are they different?"

"Yeah, like Spanish and Portuguese. My mom speaks both. I only know some words in Belarusian and Ukrainian, but I'm fluent in Russian because my grandma barely spoke English."

"How do you say"—I pause because I'm fishing for the obvious and no, not the curse words—"love?"

"*Любовь*[2]," she replies slowly.

"Liu-bóv'," I repeat several times.

"How do you say 'head over heels'?" I ask. If I learn another language, it's gonna be something I can use later. Hopefully, with her.

Lu's gaze latches on to me. "*По уши*[3]."

"Páw-ou-shi," I repeat. "Sounds Chinese."

She bursts out laughing then makes sure I pronounce it right as I repeat it several times, holding her gaze.

"Though in Russian," she explains as her smile grows, "it means *up to one's ears*."

This time, I laugh loudly, catching her surprised gaze at me. "Are you messing with me?"

"Nope." She grins.

"Seriously?"

"Seriously."

"You serious." I stare at her in distrust. "You literally say in Russian, 'he fell up to his ears in love'?"

"Yep."

"Crazy language."

"Not any crazier than head over heels. Like what does that even mean?"

"Means he's so in love he loses his mind and falls over and tumbles."

"So doesn't make sense."

"So does."

I keep saying *he*, and we keep making love jokes, and my heart by this point is bigger than my chest.

I finish steaming the floors and move Pushkin like roadkill to Lu's feet. "Here, your dog might need cleaning, too."

She puts her hands on her hips, so adorable in her white tank and sweatpants, and cocks her head at me. "You mean *our* dog, Jace." She gives me a playful glare. "I think he followed *you* that night we met, so he's *ours*. And since he loves you so, why don't *you* clean him?"

Our dog.

My heart sings.

I'm falling for her. No, it *already* happened. Days ago, weeks. When I heard her sing in the shower for the first time? When she made me grits? When I saw those paint smudges on her face? When she picked up our crippled Pushkin from the street and made the first pirate patch for him? Or the very night I shot her?

Don't know. But I fell over and tumbled up to the eleventh floor of Goldsling Towers that night, and now I'm up to my ears in love, and my brain doesn't even count, because around her, I don't think, I feel.

Attraction is like a bonfire. The more you feed it, the brighter it burns.

The way Lu looks at me is different now, intense, making my breath catch. It's a look with a hint of a promise. Of what? I'm not sure. Hopefully us. Maybe in the future she can playfully call me *du-ra-tshi-na* and I can tell her that I'm in love with her up to my ears.

"Jace! I'm taking you out for dinner. My treat!" she announces when we're done cleaning. "Please, tell me you don't have to go to some sales meetings!"

Thai food is not a date, but I can't help feeling like we are sliding into a close friend zone as we sit in a small joint on Front Street and share shrimp soba noodles and a salmon roll.

"We share it so we can try it all," Lu says.

And I want to share *myself* with her. I wanna be her friend, then best friend, then lover, soulmate, boyfriend, husband—Jesus, my mind spins out of control—because in my opinion, that's how the strongest bonds form.

They say women are obsessive with relationships and commitment. I'll tell you that I'm already imagining what our kids would look like, if they'd look like her or me, and how many we'd have. Yep. The thought is brief but powerful, and I stuff my face with soba noodles just to bring myself back down to earth.

Lu is wearing wide pants, an oversized blue sweater, and a headband sprinkled with little cherries. She's so adorable.

"Stand by that cherry blossom tree," I tell her on the way home.

She throws her hands up in the air and lifts one leg, her mouth wide open in laughter as cherry petals fall on her.

I snap a picture for my Lu collection.

We take Pushkin for a walk in Main Street Park.

"Oh, hiiiiii!"

We turn around to see one of the joggers I run into in the morning.

"I was wondering who makes all these cute clothes for our Pushkin! You must be Jace's girl, then." She walks up with her hand outstretched to Lu for a handshake. "I'm Amber. I see your boyfriend jogging in the mornings all the time."

The word stuns me. I'm about to tell the lady that we are not an item, but Lu laughs. "I'm Lu."

"Your dog is adorable. Especially when he jogs with Jace. *You* two are so adorable."

We are adorable together, Lu.

I smile all the way back to the condo.

Lu notices. "Your jogger really likes us."

"Uh-huh." I know which part of the conversation she's thinking about but doesn't mention.

"Jace, you are blushing," she says.

I can't. Fucking. Help it!

Lu elbows me and laughs through her nose, but I keep my eyes everywhere but her because I'm turning red up to the tips of my ears.

"Yeah, adorable…" she sneers.

This is Lu—half-American, half-Belarusian, and a hundred percent tease.

"Sssso adorable," she whispers under her breath and giggles.

"I have some work to do," she announces when we get back home. "That crazy dark academia portrait, ravens, skulls, a dominatrix, and a dark lord."

"Sounds crowded."

"Yeah. It's a lot of money, too."

I go to my room but leave the door open, getting on my phone and reading about Thailand and its construction laws and regulations.

Thailand is a dream. Maybe Lu will want to visit. Maybe, she'll be part of my dreams. To make that a reality, I have to take the online classes I've been slacking on.

Hours later, it's past midnight. I should go to bed, but as usual, I can't sleep.

Besides Lu being a constant in my life and in this apartment, it's the past that often snaps me back into the dark like a slingshot.

Occasionally, when I wake up, I still think I'm back in Yemen. I feel the heat against my skin. Hear the crunching of the rubble under my boots. Hear the hollow gunshots in the distance. Smell the smoke and sweat.

It's too quiet and dark in my room at night. Even with the open door, I can't hear any sounds from Lu's room. And when she's not tangible, I feel even more lost.

Restless, I grab my cigarette pack and walk out into the living room.

There's a sliver of light coming from under Lu's door, music trickling from behind it. I have the urge to go in there and watch her paint.

Instead, I walk out onto the terrace, lean on the railing, and stare at the night skyline while I twist a cigarette between my fingers.

During moments like this, I want a cigarette badly. Not the actual nicotine—I cut that out quickly. I want to feel the sharp smoke scorching my lungs, close my eyes, and remember the dusty silence pierced with occasional gunshots. Weirdly, no matter how much you run from your past and the horrible memories, they are part of who you are and the thread that connects to your present.

My memories are tame, only occasionally showing claws, hitting a bit too hard on certain nights.

It's always the same scene. A shot punches the air, echoing with the thud of my heart. The target in the scope falls silently. That's the perk of a long-distance shot—your weapon has a sound, but death is quiet, like a silent movie. Those two sounds are forever etched into my mind—the shot and the thud of my heart.

I stare at the East River drowning in darkness, sprinkled with the shiny reflections of the Manhattan lights.

I listen to the city noise, the distant sirens and the honking.

I look at the lit-up windows and try to figure out what kind of lives people live in them, what they do, what makes them happy, if they *are* happy.

I like crowds and traffic, bright signs and flashy displays. Also, the ocean, fairs, and concerts. They help drown out the memories of loneliness.

I bring the cigarette to my nose and inhale.

A very distant memory flashes in my mind. One guy in boot camp holding me down to the ground, another fisting my hair, yanking my head up, the third one shoving a cigarette in my mouth and making me chew it as he hisses, "Show us how tough you are, orphan pussy."

That was before I learned how to fight back.

I stick the cigarette back in the pack. This used to be a painkiller, but recently, I don't need it. Lu laces every minute of my life with her voice and laughter and blue eyes. Just thinking about her brings a smile to my lips. It's Pavlov's reflex. Just like Pushkin, I'd let her do anything she wants to me, as long as I get to be by her side.

I finally step back into the living room and hear a noise coming from Lu's room. She's talking to someone, and I tiptoe in the dark toward her door.

"You have beautiful eyes," she says in a low seductive voice.

I turn around, searching in the dark for Pushkin, who lies by the window. No, she's not talking to him.

"Do you like what you see?" Her voice behind the door is even lower this time, and my heart tightens with jealousy.

Who is he, Lu?

No way. She doesn't have a guy. Not that I know of.

I press my forehead to her door and close my eyes, trying to suppress the slight ache in my heart. I want to go back to the terrace to have that damn cigarette.

"This is all for you. All of me," she says barely audibly.

Lu, baby, there can't be anyone else but me.

I can't handle the thought, and I feel bad for eavesdropping, so I'm about to step back when—

I hear my name.

It can't be. I'm hallucinating.

But I hear it again, the soft, "Jace," on an exhale.

My heart gives out a loud thud.

She's dreaming about *me*?

Or is @MidnightLu working?

Or is she…

"Yes, Jace," she says softly.

I hold my breath, waiting for more.

But Lu goes quiet. The only sound coming from her room now is soft music while my heart pounds so hard that it sounds like it's knocking on her door.

Maybe, I'm hearing things, projecting out what's not there.

Before I get caught creeping behind her door, I step back and keep backing away until I reach my room.

And because I can't get Lu out of my mind, I go inside and release my tension as I re-read her stories.

---

1. *"Дурачина."* — *(Russian)* "Shithead."
2. *"Любовь."* — *(Russian)* "Love."
3. *"По уши."* — *(Russian)* "Up to {one's} ears."

22

LU

JOHN TEMPLE IS THE TEMPORARY PROJECT NAME FOR THE NEW NOVEL I started days ago. It's a dark roommate romance with mafia vibes, nothing like what I've written before.

I think out the chapters carefully and work on my wording. More importantly, I write down my thoughts about Jace. They find their way into the new chapters, and I catch myself writing Jace instead of John Temple, every mistake resonating in my heart with a subtle feeling that I shouldn't be writing about a real person.

But I can't help it. The new novel feels like my diary. Jace is the easiest inspiration I've ever had. Come to think of it, he's the only real person who's inspired my stories or my paintings.

The paintings, yeah.

Last night, I stayed up and painted his portrait, a quick impressionist one with large brushstrokes and barely any details, except for his eyes, the old Jace—with a hoodie and glasses on.

I'm yet to paint his new look. He stopped wearing glasses, and I can't stop looking at him. At times, his eyes burn me with so much intensity that my chest tightens. There's a mystery under his sweet appearance that calls to me, like the lucky number you wait to scratch off on a lottery ticket.

Last night, I set one of his portraits in front of my bed, studied it for some time, and, for the first time, fantasized about Jace. His hands. The way he touched me in the bar. The way my body drew tight when his hot whisper grazed my cheek. The way his gaze heated up when we rode the cab home from the bar, and we couldn't look away from each other as the street lights slid across the darkness. How much I wanted him to kiss me. How much I craved his touch.

I should be ashamed of what I did in front of his portrait last night.

I got carried away.

Too loud.

Too hot.

Too wet.

And too quick...

But his gaze was so realistic on the portrait that the fantasies about him spun in my head and wouldn't go away until they found release.

And here we are. Jace is now my bedroom secret.

Today, I get up super early. I want to make breakfast for him. This has become my favorite part of the day—waking up to Jace at home.

I pour myself a steaming cup of coffee and listen to the sound of the running tap in his bathroom, then close my eyes and imagine what he's doing, what he's wearing, what he looks like naked.

My fantasies spin in my mind, lacing with the ones from the night before, until the cup in my hands tilts, spilling the coffee onto my wrist.

"Ouch!" I yelp and drop the cup onto the floor, the hot splashes and glass pieces going everywhere.

The door to Jace's room swings open.

"What happened?" he asks as he rushes to the kitchen. "Shit. Don't move."

I raise my eyes at him, and my heart...stops.

I once watched the famous time-lapse video of a Monarch butterfly emerging out of its cocoon. It's amazing and beautiful and is only a minute and a half long.

What I see right now has the same effect, except the scene cuts right away from what I knew about Jace to *now* as he stands in all his half-naked glory.

He examines the mess, grabs a paper towel, and bends over to wipe the floor by the fridge, checking for glass.

"Okay, step away from the glass over there by the fridge. Let me clean up. You could cut your feet on the glass."

I don't answer and just keep staring at him.

Wow.

He's wearing only sweatpants. No glasses, no shirt. I could tell before that his body was toned. He works out and jogs.

Except *this* body—oh, hell—should be on the *Sports Illustrated* magazine cover.

But that's not what has me gawking.

His entire front torso is tattooed.

"Lu?"

As he straightens up, my gaze slides from the V of his dog tag hanging between the perfect pectorals to the midsection covered in intricate tribal designs, down, down…

"Lu?"

I raise my eyes to meet his.

His are tense with worry. "Take one step to stand over there, please."

He helps me to step onto the dry tile. I stare at his hand holding mine like it belongs to someone else, someone else's perfect inked body.

"Don't move."

I can't even talk, startled by the sight.

He takes another paper towel and starts wiping the floor in front of me, and I stand frozen in my place and stare.

Holy moly, his back is tattooed, too.

Who *is* this guy? A salesman, right? Right?! Anyone can get tattoos. But an office guy his age doesn't have a reason to get professional art plastered all over his body.

When he's done cleaning and throws the glass pieces into the trashcan, he straightens up, and I still gawk with my mouth open.

Oh. My. God.

My gaze is licking him up like candy.

"These are…intense," I manage to say, trying to fight my shock. "Did you get them done while in the service?"

"Traveling in Asia."

He traveled overseas—that's new.

He ruffles his hair. "I'll make you another coffee," he says and takes two cups out of the cupboard.

"Where did you get them?" I don't want coffee. I want to study him, catalog all these images, take pictures of him, paint him, like this—only in his sweatpants, maybe without them.

Heat creeps up my cheeks as I think about it.

"It's needlework," he answers. "Done by an indigenous shaman."

"Like old-school?" My jaw drops in shock. I've never seen that type of tattoo. "Did it hurt a lot?"

"Define *a lot*." A soft chuckle escapes him.

Right.

"The color was added afterward the traditional way," he explains with his back to me as he pours coffee.

Does he have any more surprises?

"Don't move," I order as I step toward him to study his tattoos closer.

Without thinking, I bring my hand to his back and trail my forefinger along what looks like a tribal pattern forming into a panther.

His muscles twitch.

"Birds," I murmur, tracing another shape. "Mythological creatures."

"They are all symbolic," he explains.

I need to know more. Later. After I'm done pawing him.

Every time my fingertips touch his skin, his muscles tense up. His skin is covered in goosebumps, and my face has the silliest half-smile. There's heat radiating from him, and my body responds, burning from the inside.

"You're a walking piece of art, Jace," I murmur.

He chuckles, turning around, and his bare chest is right in front of me, his burning gaze locked with mine as he passes me the coffee mug.

On reflex, I take it and take a step back, studying him again.

There's only a foot between us. A foot that separates me from this gorgeous human. A foot that's hundreds of miles between how I perceived Jace before and now.

My gaze slides down to his midsection, then trails lower.

"Oh," I whisper, pausing on a shark tattoo disappearing into his sweatpants that hang dangerously low on his hips.

"It's a shark," I state the obvious. "I want to see but..." I lick my lips. "That would be inappropriate, right?"

I don't lift my eyes, just stare at the shark tattoo, feeling my cheeks heat up.

"Right," Jace whispers.

"But..."

"Lu?"

"But I'm an artist. And that's art. I like art. Do you have those tattoos down there too?"

I'm not elaborating on *there.* Hips, legs, and wherever this shark's "nest" is. My heart pounds at the thought, my face on fire.

"Lu," he whispers with a warning.

I'm fixated on the shark teeth that peek from behind the waistband of his sweatpants.

"I like sharks," I whisper and make a slight movement to touch his abdomen but then catch myself as I see him suck in his stomach.

"Lu?" he repeats.

I raise my eyes to meet Jace's.

He is achingly beautiful, pure male energy radiating from him. I paint emotions and people's energies. I can feel it but can't describe it. Not yet. I'll find the way. In the next chapter of my novel.

I try to smile, my entire body blushing.

"Gonna go put on a shirt, okay?" he says softly.

I nod as he passes by, our hands brushing, and I turn right away to catch the last sight of his glorious tattooed back before he disappears into his room.

"Grits?" I ask, a half-smile stuck on my lips.

"Sure!" he says from his room.

My quiet roommate is a naked God.

And the silly grits are the last thing on my mind.

23

LU

"Covered in tattoos," I tell Becky as we walk through the Broad Street gallery, working out the placement of my paintings during the upcoming show.

She cocks a brow. "No shit?"

"B, indigenous tattoos! Done with needles and stuff." I skip the detail about the shark.

"Holy shit." She chuckles. "Maybe he was some bad-ass salesman overseas. His glasses are fake, by the way. Oh, and did you hear Tito's story from the other night? Roey knocked out that one rude guy who made a slur at Tito, and Jace did a solar plexus strike to the other guy. So..."

My mind goes blank.

"Your roommate is a salesman with fighting skills," Becky says in a tone that's much less condescending than it used to be. "Army?"

"I suppose."

"Should I be worried? He might be just like your ex."

I'm not sure I can even call Chad my ex. We never crossed a certain line. I didn't feel like it. I dated him because he was insistent. Except, "I always get what I want," sounds sexy when you are drinking with a gorgeous intimidating wealthy guy. But not when, two weeks later, he's trying to undress you and doesn't get a hint when you say no.

"Jace is nothing like Chad," I argue.

Becky doesn't buy it. "Sure. Jace goes overseas and spends weeks getting needle tattoos. Do you know how painful that is? How long it takes? He might be a nut job."

Her bitterness is unmistakable.

"You don't like him, do you?" My heart falls at the thought. She's my best friend, and usually, I value her opinion.

"I never said that. I do like him."

"Liar."

"I do. I actually do, Lu. You know what I don't like?" Her gaze narrows. "Lies. Can't fucking stand them. I don't like secrets either. And I have a feeling Jace has a handful."

When we're done, I take a train to Brighton Beach, which is way too far to go grocery shopping, but I'm excited to have my fridge stocked with yummy Eastern-European food as well as the candy that Becky eats with the speed of light.

Stepping off the train, I'm surrounded by Cyrillic letters on every sign, which instantly reminds me of Mom.

When I came to Brighton Beach for the first time, every little story Mom told me came alive. Her hanging out on the beach in the summer, taking strolls on the boardwalk, feeding seagulls, and ignoring the stern, overly open stares of the older immigrants who crowd the many benches. Fake designer logos and excessive bling in clothes shops. Foods from every corner of the former USSR and pastry sellers out on the streets. Crowds of smoking men with mug-shot faces and women of all ages in dresses and high heels outside restaurants at night. The overwhelming number of parties and the loud music in cars. The notorious double-parking. Eastern-European flags on license plates.

"Come back to the USSR," Mom calls the seven blocks under the elevated train tracks that drip all year round and the trains that deafen passersby. "And no one parties like the Hispanics and Eastern Europeans, trust me."

I wish Mom came here more often. She came half a year ago, spent two days partying with her friends in Sokoloff, the popular restaurant on the Brighton boardwalk, and flew back. I asked her to come for my exhibit, but Dad is having hand surgery, so it's not happening.

My parents don't exactly have money to splurge. They lost their jobs during the pandemic. My biological father offered to pay for my university and the dorms and anything else I wanted. But I want to make it on my own. It's not out of bitterness, no. I don't even know my biological father very well, despite having met up with him a bunch of times when I learned about him.

It's not his fault my mom never told him she was pregnant, then married my dad who adopted me, then chose not to tell me or my biological father until I was eighteen.

"Why?" I shouted when she told me several years ago.

"Because you *have* a father. Mike *is* your father. And I wanted you to be an adult to know the facts." Her accent got heavier when she got bitter. So did her smoking.

"*Facts*, she says. That's not fair!" I shouted. "I had the right to know!"

"See? Grownup and still can't take it like one. Baby, take time thinking it over instead of shouting."

Easy for her to say. Mom has the patience of a partisan and the calm of a python. She is impossible to argue with.

My dad is impossible not to love, especially when he wrapped me in a hug that day and said, "You've always been mine. The rest is just a biological detail."

And that biological detail turned out to be a handsome man on the heavy side with a family of his own. I wouldn't care much, but strange unease and curiosity fill me knowing that that man's DNA runs in my body, that I was made out of his flesh, or a sperm, an accidental particle—whatever.

Bags with food from a Ukrainian deli make my arms hurt as I struggle like a hag lady back toward the subway station. I could've taken a cab, but that's extra money I don't need to spend, considering I just spent a fortune on candy for Becky.

Then there comes a text.

Father #2: Hey, kiddo. How is everything?

My bio dad. *Dad*—I struggle to call him that. Father is more appropriate like there's an emotional difference in the words. Having two dads is strange.

I'm about to text back when my eyes catch a familiar figure across the street. My heart thumps in my chest in surprise—Jace, talking to a man.

Jace? In Brighton?

They shake hands and split.

I'm about to call Jace's name, but he's walking away too fast. So I hurriedly cross the road toward his companion who stands smoking at the curb, typing something on his phone.

"Excuse me," I say with the widest smile I can pull off.

He's in his fifties, dressed in a plaid shirt and jeans, gold watch and necklace. His hostile expression is definitely an Eastern-European trademark, with no hint of friendliness when he raises his cold eyes to me.

"You know Jace Reed?" I ask with as much friendliness as I can muster.

His eyes narrow slightly. "What about him?"

The heavy Eastern-European accent is unmistakable. Russian, though he could be from any of the post-Soviet countries that speak it.

"I just saw you talking," I admit. "We are meeting up in ten minutes," I lie, "but he doesn't have many friends in the city, so I just wanted to say hi."

The guy stares at me unblinkingly. "You know him?"

"He's my boyfriend." I lie again and start blushing right away, changing the bags from one hand to another to disguise it.

"Boyfriend, you say?"

His eyes quickly drop to my bags that have the Ukrainian deli logo, then my outfit. There's only one word for it—he's profiling me like a true Eastern European.

"He's only been in the city for a few months, but yeah." I don't know why I lied. "*А вы как с ним знакомы?*[1]" I ask in Russian.

His face lights up instantly in amusement. "*Откуда?*[2]" I think that curve of his lips is a smile.

"*Мама из Беларуси.*[3]" I shrug.

"*Красавица. Сразу видно наша.*[4]"

He nods in approval, and I laugh, making him smile as he puffs out the cigarette smoke.

"So how do you know Jace?" I insist, switching to English because my Russian is rusty.

"Work."

A train passes above us with roaring loudness. It's the trademark of Brighton, as well as the water and oil dripping from the tracks, spotting Brighton Beach Avenue with permanent puddles.

I wait until the train is gone and smile at the guy, who flicks the cigarette onto the road and is about to turn.

"You are his client?"

He chuckles. "He is *mine*."

"Oh?"

He squints at me. "He told you what he does?"

Automotive equipment sales, right? He's never once said he does business in Brighton.

"Yeah. What a job, huh?"

The man tsks. "With his record, he could be working in an elite unit overseas. This is a much better pay, I guess. But hey, good catch."

He winks and cackles.

I fake a laugh, but I don't understand the meaning of what he said.

"Take care." He turns to leave then turns back to me. "Forgot to tell him. The BNVD-51s will take an extra two weeks. *Передашь?*[5]"

"Sure!"

"*Ну давай, красавица!*[6]"

He leaves, and I drop the bags and dial Jace.

"Jace! You still in Brighton?"

There's a pause on the other end of the line, then his cautious voice, "Hey, Lu. How do you know?"

I laugh, mostly because I'm suddenly nervous.

"I just saw you a minute ago! I'm here shopping. Wanna meet up? I'm on Brighton 4, ocean side."

"I'll be right there."

I'm excited about the surprise meeting, then open Google search and type in "BNVD-51."

My breath hitches when I scan the search results. There are no variations for what the code stands for, absolutely none, all the results bringing the same thing—military-grade night vision goggles.

I raise my eyes from my phone, my heart pounding, my stomach twisting as I see Jace, wearing jeans and a T-shirt, walking toward me through the crowd, his smile wide.

Elite unit, the Russian man's words echo in my head.

Salesman, my ass.

---

1. *"А вы как с ним знакомы?"* — *(Russian)* "How do you know him?"
2. *"Откуда?"* — *(Russian)* "Where from?"
3. *"Мама из Беларуси."* — *(Russian)* "Mom is from Belarus."
4. *"Красавица. Сразу видно наша."* — *(Russian)* "Pretty one. I can tell ours."
5. *"Передашь?"* — *(Russian)* "Pass it on?"
6. *"Ну давай, красавица!"* — *(Russian)* "So long, pretty one!"

24

LU

I CAN'T MAKE SENSE OF WHAT I LEARNED ABOUT JACE, BUT I KEEP MY mouth shut and my eyes on him.

We have lunch at a small Uzbek joint in Brighton, and Jace says he's going home too. But instead of taking the train, he calls a car service.

"It'll be so much quicker by train," I tell him. "It's traffic time. We'll get stuck for more than an hour if we take a cab."

"So we'll spend more time together."

He smiles mysteriously and winks.

And my heart winks.

But despite the excitement, an eerie feeling settles inside me at the thought that one of the plot twists in my new novel just came true.

I'm falling deeper for Jace. I'm not sure it's a good thing, but I can't help it.

He's ingrained in my daily life. I'm attuned to his moods. And I feel him pulling back. His cautious glances when we first met have turned into open stares. Yet, he doesn't make any moves on me. Doesn't flirt much.

When we get home, I go to my room to work. And I can't get the encounter in Brighton out of my mind.

Does Jace sell military equipment? Is that even legal?

Suddenly the memories of his tattooed body return like a flood, the conversation with the Russian guy. *"You know what he does?"*

My heartbeat spikes at the sound of Jace's every footstep in the living room, at his low but gentle voice, "Hey, little dude," as he plays with Pushkin who's in love with him.

I have to write this down. I *need* to write.

I know I'm obsessing, but I'm an artist, and artists thrive on blurring the line between reality and the imaginary world.

I already have ten chapters of the new book written. Characters, backgrounds, and future twists are all mapped out. My male lead, John Temple, is an accountant who rents a room from an artist, Emily Aberdeen. Except she doesn't know that they met before or that he's using her to track his enemy. And he's not an accountant at all but an undercover agent, hiding guns in his room, shadowing her every footstep, all the while falling in love with her as he watches her on camera. And she is falling in love with him, painting him obsessively, both of them hiding their feelings until the night he comes into her room, the night that sets their feelings free but also spills the secrets, and everything changes...

My fingers fly over the keyboard as I type another chapter.

Often, the loudest people don't have anything meaningful to say.

Often, the quietest ones have the best stories.

I am yet to hear John's stories. There's a dark side to him. It's in his eyes that lock with mine and make my every cell come alive. In his occasional touches, so mundane during the day when we bump into each other in the apartment.

Until night falls. And in my mind, those touches acquire a different meaning, lacing with my fantasies and making my body burn with a sweet desire that leaves me sleepless at night.

Loud people can take you by storm and hold you hostage. And when they leave, you feel relieved, replenishing the energy they stole from you.

It's the quiet ones who get under your skin, burrowing deeper, day by day, leaving traces of themselves like the night dew. When they leave, they leave you wanting more, craving their presence like a drug.

Some people are vampires. Others are givers.

John is both. He gives me so much—feelings, inspiration, himself. But what he'll take in return might leave me hollow.

Once I learn his every secret.

Once he's gone.

Maybe there's a reason he has a shark tattoo. You can admire sharks from afar but never get close. I sensed it the first time I met him.

But how can I stay away when I want him so much closer?

Today my MC, John Temple, acquired a new nickname, Sharki.

I fall on my back on the bed and grin at the ceiling.

God, I love when I'm inspired and full of ideas. I feel invincible. Everything is coming along great in this novel. Everything but the spicy scenes.

For the first time, my writing is not about sex, and I'm puzzled.

Even more so about my actual roommate.

25

LU

THE DOORBELL RINGS.

Tito, as always, shows up unannounced. He's grumpy and sucks at hiding his emotions.

"What happened?" I ask, letting him in.

"I need a drinking buddy." He plops on the couch.

"Trouble with work?"

"With Jamie."

That's his ex he's been on and off with for two years, madly in love but not being able to deal with the fact that Jamie's workplace is less than gay-friendly, hence the fighting and breakups.

"I don't want to go out tonight," I say, wrinkling my nose in apology. My new story pumps my blood with excitement, and I need to keep writing.

Tito doesn't seem discouraged by my answer. "Is Jace home?"

Jealousy pounces its claws at me. "Oh, I see."

Just then, Jace steps out of his room, and my heart does a cartwheel.

He's wearing a long-sleeved shirt and shorts that go down below his knees. Just an extra patch of exposed skin makes Jace even more delicious.

And Tito is trying to steal him away.

Not a chance.

He has a crush on Jace.

I have a crush on Jace—there, I said it.

So does Pushkin.

I've never met a guy who's so quiet and elusive yet manages to get everyone under his spell.

"I don't really feel like going out," Jace says with a sympathetic gaze when Tito suggests bar-hopping, and Tito exhales through his puffed lips in frustration. "But hey, how about a drinking night at home? Here?"

Tito sits up like a ninja and points his forefingers like guns at Jace. "Jace! Buddy! I fucking love you!" Then he turns to me. "You're in?"

"Yes!" I exclaim, failing to hide my excitement, and catch Jace's smiling glance at me.

An evening with my two favorite guys? Yes, please. My book boyfriend is right here, ready to get drunk.

"And Jace picks the music so we don't fight about it!" I say because we always do.

"Deal!" the two of them say at the same time.

While Tito and Jace run to the liquor store, I arrange plates of appetizers.

"How much do I owe you?" I ask Tito when they come back.

Tito exhales in annoyance. "You ask me again, and I won't talk to you anymore."

I smile playfully. "Then you won't have that one sweet person you can always come to unannounced when you need a drinking buddy."

Tito's lips hitch in a cocky smile. "I'll just call Jace."

"Oh, you traitor!"

Jace grins. God, he's beautiful when he smiles.

And his choice of music is a surprise—disco.

"Old school, I like it," Tito says with his mouth full of the Georgian cheese pastry he snatched from the kitchen.

We settle on the couch around the coffee table loaded with plates of appetizers and do a round of vodka shots, the way my mom has done with her friends for as long as I can remember.

"Lemon or pickles afterward. Or sauerkraut," Tito explains to Jace. "It's the way the Eastern Europeans drink."

"I've trained you well, my friend," I say to Tito.

Jace is amused at every little detail—the taste of pickled green tomatoes, the cod liver pate, then nods approvingly at the Olivier salad. "Better than Herring Under Fur."

Tito bursts out in laughter. "She got you with that one, huh?"

Jace grins at me.

I feel high on happiness like life is so good and is only gonna get better.

I pour us shots again.

Tito is a beautiful human when he's happy. Also flirty as hell when he's tipsy and a red flag when he's drunk.

"Oh, and"—he gives Jace a meaningful stare—"whoever pours shots serves the entire evening. No change of hands. And this lady right here"—he nods at me—"has a craaaaaazy hand."

Jace gives him a confused look. "What does that mean?"

"Apparently, every person has a certain energy that projects on the booze effect."

Jace chuckles. "Never heard of such a thing."

It does sound crazy, but I've spent years around my mom's crazy friends who have all sorts of superstitions and rituals and keep a calendar with every day denoting some sort of holiday. Astronaut's Day, Einstein's Birthday, Lazarus Saturday, International Tiger Day…

I open my phone and search the calendar. "It's Border Guards Day today," I announce.

"See? Eastern Europeans are crazy. *Good* crazy," Tito says and we cheer, "*Búdzem!*"

"It means, 'We will,' or 'To our future,'" I explain to Jace.

"To our future," he repeats softly, locking eyes with me.

We throw back the shots, chase them with soda, then lemon, then another five minutes of appetizers, another round of shots, all the while talking louder over the music, laughing when Tito brings up Roey and Becky.

Tito is not Roey's fan, despite Roey standing up for him at the bar in Williamsburg and partying for hours together after that.

"There's that hypersexual energy around him," Tito explains. "Like he's gonna whip his dick out and hypnotize you like those snake charmers."

I laugh so hard, I can't sit straight and hold my stomach as I lean on Jace.

Jace points his forefinger at Tito. "Women say he can."

Tito shakes his head. "I'm serious. He's all muscles and swagger but with a rough biker attitude and slutty glint in his eyes."

"Oh?" I muse. "A little harsh."

"He acts like he's Adonis's mafia brother but lacks sophistication. Unlike our Jace here." He picks up a shot glass and cheers to Jace.

Our Jace.

I like that.

My Jace sounds even better. He has no idea what I do to him in my novel.

I'm tipsy, yes, and I feel so *so* happy.

Pushkin partakes too, sniffing at the sardine sandwich, licking it, and turning away. He huffs disappointedly and plops on the floor by Jace's feet, who takes pity on the little guy and gives him a slice of Moscow salami.

Tito steps out to the terrace to smoke.

I turn up the music, and it's "Get Down Tonight" by KC.

"Dance-dance-dance!" Tito shouts, sliding back into the living room and to the center of the room in slick disco moves.

He's a spectacular dancer, confident and magnetic.

I run to my room and come back with a furry scarf, pink heart glasses, a yellow hat. We share the props and do selfies and laugh and throw back another round of shots.

Jace wrinkles his nose afterward and exhales loudly like he's exhausted.

"I'm not kidding you," Tito shouts, noticing. "Her hand is crazy. Trust me, tomorrow you'll be questioning everything that happened tonight."

It's a promise, I hope.

Jace meets my eyes, and I wink at him.

26

LU

THREE HOURS LATER, IT'S DARK, AND WE ARE WASTED.

The blanket of Manhattan lights shimmers under the opaque dark sky, and I realize it's the best little party I've had in this place. I feel like flying, getting undressed, hugging the world, kissing Jace, and dancing and painting and writing and drinking more—all at the same time.

I dart out onto the terrace, lean over the railing, and shout, "Heeeeeeeey!" at the top of my voice, because I can't hold back euphoria.

Suddenly, strong arms appear behind my knees and around my back, and Jace picks me up into his arms like I'm a feather.

"Crazy girl, we'll have a visit from angry neighbors," he says with laughter rather than reproach as he carries me back.

I want to tell him that I want to make out with him, and him carrying me in his arms is ridiculously romantic.

But we're already in the living room. "That's The Way I Like It" is blasting. I'm back on my feet, and Jace is not touching me anymore. But he's dancing, and—oh, my God—he is a great dancer, his movements tame but rhythmic and sexy.

"Shots!" I yell.

We do another round. I don't know what time it is. I don't care. We are drunk.

And we are back to dancing.

Jace points his forefinger at Tito. "You owe me breakfast in bed."

I've never seen Jace so relaxed and easygoing. Drunk, obviously.

Tito dances up to him with the seductiveness of a feline during mating season. "I'll deliver."

"How about you deliver it to Lu?"

"What's Lu got to do with it?" He dances against Jace like Magic Mike at warm-up.

"We didn't specify the bet. I want my breakfast served to Lu." Jace cocks a brow. But he doesn't know how persistent Tito can be when he wants something.

"Coward," Tito blurts with a smile. "Jace, why don't we cut the bullshit?" Here it comes. "Can I take you home?" He slides his hands on Jace's chest.

Jace veers away, dances up behind me, takes both my hands in his, and points them like guns at Tito. "No."

I burst out in laughter at Jace's diplomatic handling of Tito's flirting. Also to hide the fact that my body heats up at his touch.

His hands slide around my waist, and I cover them with mine.

Yes!

Tito doesn't give up, glancing at us touching. He can seduce a straight homophobic guy if he tries hard enough.

"You need a hand? I have gentle hands. Skillful too."

Jace's arms tighten around my waist. "Not my jam."

We sway to the music, and *I* wanna be his jam so badly. His. Whatever he wants. Yes, my roommate is hot and drunk, but he's not shy with me anymore.

Viva alcohol!

Jace's hips swing to the music against mine. He leans to press his nose to my neck, sending goosebumps down my body, and inhales.

"You smell so good," he murmurs.

So do you.

Tito's eyes narrow at us. "Jace, I wanna see your tattoos. Rumor has it you have a shark tattoo."

I spin around and meet Jace's playful gaze.

"Come on, Jace!" I cheer. "Shirt! Off! Shirt! Off!"

Tito joins in. We squeal in unison when Jace reaches behind his back and pulls his shirt off, then starts swinging it above his head and rolling his hips to the music.

Whoa!

Both Tito and I gawk, walk up, and start touching him.

Tito is eating him up with his eyes. He's shameless when he's drunk.

I'm playing along like it's Tito's idea though my head spins at the touch, at the subtle scent of Jace's deodorant, his bare torso so close to me.

"Jace, baby," Tito drawls, sliding his one hand to the shark tattoo.

I slap it away. "Back off! Jace is mine!" I laugh, though I'd love to let my hand travel the path of that sneaky shark.

"Oh! Since when?"

"He's my roommate."

"Well, then," Tito says bitterly and purposefully places his hand on Jace's chest.

Any other guy would've pushed him away. But not Jace. Nor does he care about Tito's hands, because Jace's eyes are on me.

I lean over to Tito. "Back off," I hiss, playfully narrowing my eyes at him, and lean in to press my cheek to Jace's shoulder. "Mine."

Jace dances out of Tito's touch, steps behind me, and wraps his arms around my waist, pressing me close. "Mine," he whispers in my ear.

It's not the booze that makes me dizzy. It's Jace. His strong body I want to caress. His lips planting a little kiss on my cheek.

"Fine!" Tito throws his hands in the air, grabs my phone from the table, and changes the song.

"Promises" by Sam Smith comes on, Tito's favorite song.

I hum along to the soft seductive tunes.

"Jace, you might have to fight this guy off," I joke as Tito lifts his hands and swings his hips, dancing his way to us.

Jace lets go and turns me around. Locks his gaze with mine.

He likes me. And I... Oh, I'd love to kiss him.

I don't know if he can see all of this in my gaze, but his fingers start stroking my back. His hand comes up to my face and slowly tucks a loose strand of my hair behind my ear.

Then he leans over, his lips touching my ear when he whispers, "Lu, I love the way you dance."

This evening smells like love, tastes like it, and feels incredible. So does his shirtless body so close that his shark is pressed against my midsection.

My Sharki.

My Jace, my tipsy brain whispers as I hold my breath and turn my head just a little so our lips are only inches away. We sway to the music, so close that if I stood on my tiptoes I could kiss him.

The I-can-give-you-everything-tonight tune is spinning in my head.

"Did I tell you that you are amazing?" he whispers.

His fingers gently stroke my chin, tipping it up.

"Show me," I dare him, keeping his gaze and sliding my hands up his bare torso, then down.

His lips inch lower, hitching in a little smile. His eyes drop to my mouth.

The doorbell rings.

Dammit!

It rings again, and Jace and I pull apart. Our eyes are locked but the distance between us is growing.

"Neighbors complaining about the music, I bet," Tito sighs.

But when I swing the door open, ready to apologize and go back to Jace, Roey towers on the other side.

"Roey!"

I fling at him to give him a hug, laughing, then drag him inside.

"Come-come-come!" I motion enthusiastically. The more the merrier. "What are you drinking? We are having a disco party!"

"It took forever to talk your concierge downstairs into letting me up," he says, walking in.

My tipsy brain doesn't yet realize that there must be a reason for him showing up.

Jace sings to the music as he dances up toward Roey.

"You don't answer your phone," Roey says, nods to Tito, and studies half-naked Jace up and down.

His serious tone sobers me up since he still didn't tell me what he wants to drink.

"We are flying to California tonight," he announces.

I open my mouth to protest, then turn to look at Jace.

The music carries on, but Jace stops and widens his arms at a loss. "I'm... I'm drunk and—"

"Then sober up, get ready, and let's go," Roey cuts him off, then turns to meet my stare. "Sorry, Lu."

So much for the party and I-give-you-everything-tonight dance.

27

JACE

"JACE IS MINE."

I smile like a fool, even though I feel miserable with a black coffee in my hand as Roey and I take a cab to JFK.

Sobering up after being yanked out of a great party sucks.

Even more so when we stand in line through the security check-in for the red-eye flight, and I can't focus on anything Roey says about our current case because I get a message from Lu.

Lu: Your work sucks! Tito is drunk. He's staying over. I'm cleaning. Pushkin is sleeping by the door to your room.

A sad emoji follows. Then a picture of her and Tito on the couch, heads hanging low, pouting.

Laughter escapes me, but my heart clenches with so much disappointment that I feel like quitting my job.

It's booze, I know, the abrupt cut off of the dopamine and serotonin.

Me: I'll be back soon.

Lu: Can't wait.

Lu: Hurry up!

Me: Tito owes you breakfast in bed. Remind him.

Unknown: Your buddy, Mr. I'm-Rambo-with-fuck-me-eyes, didn't take our Miss Becky home. So technically, you lost the bet.

I laugh. So, Lu gave Tito my number.

Me: He was ready, trust me. Her loss. And yours. You owe Lu breakfast.

I follow the message with a devil emoji.

Tito: I'll wait for you to come back. We'll have it together. The three of us.

A winking emoji follows.
The guy never gives up. I laugh and forward the message to Lu.

Lu: Ignore him. You are mine, Jace Reed. Can you just come home soon? Pleeeeease?

Boom!
My heart slams in my chest, and I drink half a cup of my third coffee in one gulp to make sure I'm almost sober and I didn't just dream it up.

Lu is drunk. Tomorrow, it'll be forgotten. Yet I can't stop staring at the messages and start typing the response, **Miss you already.**

Then correct it.

Me: Miss you guys already.

I wish *I* could serve her breakfast in bed, and other things…
Inevitably, a scene from *Beautiful Vice* comes to mind.

"I love breakfast in bed," Konstantin grunts, slowly pulling the sheet off my naked body. "Spread your legs for me, wife."

Bro…

I absolutely can't get hard while I'm going through the security checkpoint.

But everything I read written by Lu I reenact with *us* in my mind. I feel this urge for her. It's in every cell like she's the source of gravity.

My phone dings, but it's not a message, it's a notification from SD—I'm officially @MidnightLu's patron. And this app is officially gonna send me to a loony bin with my obsession for Lu.

I tap my feet impatiently as we get scanned at the checkpoint, then pull my phone out and click the red notification bubble.

"You are obsessing," Roey says as we start walking to our gate.

No argument here. I almost trot down the airport jetway, wanting to plant my ass in my seat and check the SD, a smile of anticipation on my lips.

@MidnightLu:

Hi, guys, I'm writing a new romance. Yes, it will come in chapters. It's quite different from my previous works, but I think you'll fall in love with the main character. It's a slow burn that turns into a blaze in the second half. So, be prepared!

Expect the first chapter to drop any time soon!

The blurb and the intro are below!

Muah!

Lu is upping the spice. Interesting. I eagerly dive into the blurb.

What do you do when a hot stranger saves your life one night?

You let him walk you home.

You find out he is an accountant.

He looks hotter than sin and vaguely familiar, though you can't place his face and can't help feeling he's hiding something.

What do you do when he says he's new to the city and is looking for a room?

You tell him that you have a room for rent.

So, here we are.

John Temple is now my roommate. And in a short time, he becomes my close friend, my muse, and my obsession.

But I am a good girl. I don't cross forbidden lines. And I don't chase the hot guy who seems to pull back every time sparks fly between us.

He's so close yet so far.

Until he isn't.

Until the night he knocks on my bedroom door, and I let him in.

The night he closes the torturous inches between us, I realize that my body is as addicted to him as my mind, and my heart follows.

But soon, I learn his dark secrets, and my world spins on its axis.

I shouldn't have opened the door that night.

I shouldn't have taken him in as my roommate.

Because good-hearted quiet accountants don't carry guns. Nor do they make people disappear.

His secrets come from *my* past. And I might be his next target.

John Temple already won my heart.

But it's too late when I realize he only did it to ruin me.

I might be going mad, but this sounds vaguely familiar. I swallow hard at the name of the new novel, *Sharki*.

This is just a coincidence, I tell myself.

A fucking coincidence.

I jump to the intro where the main heroine tells the story of how John Temple saved her from an attacker on the street one dark night. My stomach turns at the words.

As promised, John comes back the next day.

In the daylight, he looks different. A little older than me, with dark eyes, messy hair, and glasses.

Wait a second…

His hoodie and jeans are black. An unlit cigarette hangs between his full lips. His dark gaze pierces me as he stands in the hallway of my apartment and doesn't even look around like he's not interested in the room he's about to rent. Like he came here *for me*.

Why does it make me nervous?

Why do I like it so much?

"Rent is $3000," I tell him.

"Deal."

Oh, man…

I close my eyes and recall our conversation when I rented my room. I repeat it in my head, open my eyes, and read the next line.

"No parties. No smoking inside. I don't like smoke."

Yep, that one.

My heart stalls for a moment.

"Deal."

"Please, take off your shoes—"

"—by the door. I don't have a cleaning lady"—I remember every fucking word she said.

"I hope we get along," I say.

A tiny smile curves his lips. "We'll get along just fine, Miss Aberdeen."

He tosses his bag onto the floor.

"And cleaning is part of the deal," I say, glancing at the bag.

"Yes, ma'am." He finally looks around. "Is it always so hot here?"

Since you got here, yes.

Our eyes meet.

He reaches behind him and pulls his hoodie over his head.

His T-shirt underneath rides up, giving me a clear view of his abdomen, and I gape, as the shirt slides back down, hiding it right away.

"Is everything all right?"

His voice pulls me out of my momentary shock that comes back when I glance at his arms.

Tattoos are snaking up his biceps and disappearing under the T-shirt sleeves, part of the tattoo peeking above his collar.

His gaze is probing when I meet his eyes.

"So..." I say in a weak voice.

"Yes, Miss Aberdeen?" His smile widens, making me blush.

I've never looked suggestively at Lu, have I?
No. This is not me. This is pure John Temple.
Phew.

"I go by Emily, or you can call me Em."

"Em it is."

His voice is like a caress. Do all accountants sound so comforting in a seductive sort of way?

I know him from somewhere, though I can't quite place it. The sight of him gives me goosebumps. His gaze is too prying like he's waiting for me to recognize him.

"Have we met before?" I ask, confused.

There's an itch inside my memory that I can't scratch. That sparkle in his smoldering eyes—I remember it. But how?

His lips twitch in a tiny smile like he's about to tell me. "Have we?" He raises a brow.

"Never mind."

I know that everything in this apartment changes starting today. We won't be just roommates. I don't know how I know it or what will happen but it's a subtle feeling you get when you know your fate just walked in through the door.

I've never felt anyone's presence so powerfully. Every cell of mine comes alive as I show him his new place. *Our* place.

"I'm in the city for several months only," he explains.

I nod. "Sure." But my inner voice whispers, *"No, you're not."* And my heart smiles.

Soon, we'll get to know each other better.

But right now, I know three things about John Temple.

He's an accountant.

He's my new roommate.

And he has a tattoo of a shark on his abdomen.

Well, hello, Sharki.

I look up from the phone and feel myself sweat.
My heart is raging against my chest.

Am I freaking dreaming?

I just found out Lu's secret: she writes about me.

No, there's no mistake. Except the story is dark, and I only pray Lu's intuition is not that great, and I'm not a villain in her eyes.

But her feelings? Can it be?

There are too many variables in this story, but one thing is clear: I've just become a—wait for it—book boyfriend.

28

JACE

I was eighteen and fresh out of the system when I went into boot camp, and, after a year of extensive training, I was deployed overseas.

With my unprecedented shooting record in boot camp, I could bypass the years in service and enlist in a sniper school right away. I stalled, despite the pressure from the higher-ups and the rumors about me being a prodigy marksman.

Deployment wasn't what I signed up for but I got it anyway. My shooting talent was a curse of sorts, yet a job. Besides taking down important targets, I'd like to think I saved many of my buddies' lives. Including Roey's, who was my Company Commander.

That's how we bonded.

He retired from the service while I was still overseas.

"You don't want to get the sniper qualification? I get it," he said before shipping off home. "Then get out of this shit, Jace. War is an addiction of the worst kind. It'll mess you up."

It messed *him* up all right. In his early thirties, he still tries to fight his PTSD, but drinking is a shitty way of doing it.

"You complete your four years, get back to the States, and call me," he said.

That I did.

In a way, Roey saved me when he brought me in to work with

him and taught me all I needed to know about bounty hunting. The technicalities, the ethics, the discipline.

Roey's career in bounty hunting didn't start in the traditional way. He never did jail bond jobs, tracking those who skipped bail. Correction, he did two, helping his old army buddy. But in both cases, the guys were on the FBI's most wanted list, so there was an extra bounty besides the bond award.

His specialty is those on the darker side of the law or those who go against the powerful and wealthy, and the clients choose not to involve law enforcement.

"We are not punishers," he explained. "None of the macho-I'm-gonna-knock-your-teeth-out-and-snap-your-neck bullshit. Targets' personalities and priors are none of our business. Our job is to seek out and deliver valuable people who broke the law or royally screwed others."

There are quick jobs—debtors, usually, as well as runaway wives or teenagers of the wealthy. Dealing with rich people's personal problems is easy.

There are medium-heat jobs, usually involving smart and dangerous people who know where to hide and how to clean their tracks. Fighting skills are more useful than weapons. Miller's IT skills and connections help to do the jobs that regular private investigators can't.

And there are high-risk jobs. Mafia, contractors, debtors of the worst kind, with priors and violent records. We hardly ever resort to using weapons. We treat people right, unlike our biggest rivals from Brexton Recovery. But occasionally, things get tricky.

That's where I come in.

I shoot forty-forty, a natural born, they say. I'm nothing like the Canadian sniper of Joint Task Force 2 who, several years ago, beat the world record and shot the target at a staggering 2.2 miles. The bullet flew for ten seconds. No matter how good your scope is, that's some insane trajectory math that takes into consideration the weapon, the distance, and the wind.

I never came close, not even when I shot our target's car tire from the roof of a ten-story building 0.8 miles away during my first bounty job with Roey a year ago.

Roey high-fived me. He'd seen me do trickier stuff overseas.

On hearing that it was a twenty-three-year-old former military shooter who aced the shot, the captured target licked his lips and stared at me with curiosity. "When I'm out of jail, kid, come work for me."

He died in jail. Not that I wanted to work for the Chicago Syndicate's most wanted man, anyway.

In my current job, my skills are meant to damage and incapacitate. Mostly, inanimate objects. I prefer the peaceful way, as is the case with Reznik.

La Jolla is sunny. The fresh Pacific breeze and the waves crashing against the rocky South Californian beach are a distraction from the noisy, fumes-and-traffic-packed streets of New York.

The La Jolla job turned out to be pretty easy.

The client—Mrs. Kubinsky, a pretty gallerist and a divorcee in her forties with more money than God himself.

The target—her twenty-six-year-old stud of a boyfriend who ghosted her, swiping on his way out a USB with the sensitive clients' info he was intending to sell to the black market art dealers.

The run-away boyfriend was pretty clever. He got a burner phone and used cash. My guess is he was screwing with Mrs. Kubinsky and buying more time. Obviously, there was some personal revenge. His mistake was logging into his social media. Typical. IP addresses are easy to track. The approximate location was then sent to the Eastern European surveillance team, and since the young gigolo never thought of wearing a disguise, face recognition picked him up on public cameras in no time. That's where we got him—eating tacos at a Taqueria in East LA. To think that tacos can ruin one's life…

Fifty grand to locate him and bring him in with the precious USB was pennies to Mrs. Kubinsky, but the glee on her face when we did was priceless.

I love bagging assholes.

What she does with him and how she sets flames to his future is her business.

Ours is done as we sit on the patio of her nine-million-dollar oceanfront villa and sip coffee, going over the final bill.

"I'll recommend you if any of my friends ever need this sort of job," Mrs. Kubinsky says, elegantly crossing her bare legs as she fixes her luscious dark hair and sunglasses.

The view of the Pacific is beautiful, and I love the warm sun in contrast to the cool breeze.

Soon, we are leaving, following Mrs. Kubinsky through a bright minimalistic living room that doesn't have much decor besides several giant paintings.

"Is that a modern variation of *Nude Descending a Staircase*?" I ask, pointing at one of the pieces I vaguely recognize. Lu would be proud her educational sessions with me didn't go in vain.

Mrs. Kubinsky turns her startled eyes to me. "Well, well! You are into art, Mr. Reed?"

"My friend is an artist in Brooklyn. She's really good."

"What sort of art?"

We are not supposed to get friendly with clients. With some exceptions. Like Roey hooking up with a wealthy widow in La Crosse, Wisconsin five months ago. "Not friendly, it was a follow-up," he dismissed my reproach later.

And I can't help myself. I'm boasting about Lu like she's my wife. I pull out my phone and proudly show Mrs. Kubinsky a couple of Lu's teddy bear works.

"That's a very clever concept," Mrs. Kubinsky says without much enthusiasm. I assume she sees hundreds of new artists a month. "And her style is refreshing, though not something I would pick for representation. You have my card, Mr. Reed. Get her to email me. Maybe I can connect her with someone up her alley."

Afterward, I drag Roey to Windansea Beach. This happens every time we are home or between jobs. Roey enjoys the beach but mostly the potential of hookups and surfing. Granted, he grew up on the West Coast and is a fantastic surfer.

Me, I love water in any form or size.

SoCal has been my home for over a year. But the drastic change of scenery after months in New York makes it feel like Lu is far away, and I don't like it.

I send her a picture of Roey and me on the beach.

Lu: Hotties! I wish I was there with you!

My heart melts just a little more. There won't be much left of it but a puddle at Lu's feet if I continue in this manner.

"Distracted, buddy?" Roey asks. "Wanna go to Goldsling Towers? Looks like work is the last thing on your mind."

"It's not like that."

"I'm not blind. Or a twenty-four-year-old virgin."

Here we go.

"Listen, you need advice—ask. You need some pointers, I'm here."

"What are you talking about?"

"About you finally meeting a girl you might give longer than a two-week chance. And so will your dick."

"She's an assignment, right?" I probe him, though I hate that word.

"Don't be coy with me. I was hoping you'd keep your head cool around her. Obviously, it's not working. You're fucking falling like a heavy rock off a cliff. So, there are two ways to do this. You toughen up and finish what we started and we're out. Or—"

I hold my breath because Roey is the only person in my life who I trust to give me an advice.

"Or you figure out if the girl feels the same way about you as you do about her. For that, you need to make a move."

I will. As soon as I get back.

I'm not in denial about what's happening to me, just trying to curb my feelings. For the first time in my life, I feel like a happy puppy off the leash, and there's a wide field in front of me instead of a kennel, and as I take the first leap, I'm anticipating the run, and I dash toward the open space, and she... she is the whole open world in front of me I want to get lost in.

Lu, you are my goddamn universe.

I'd give up California for her. For the first time, I want to anchor. And my heart already did. In apartment 1101 at Goldsling Towers, Brooklyn, New York, with wonderful Lu who makes amazing art, writes spicy stories, and adopted a one-eyed pit bull.

29

JACE

Lu: What time are you coming back tonight?

Me: Late afternoon.

LU RESPONDS WITH A CELEBRATION EMOJI, AND MY HEART SINGS, threatening to break out of my ribcage and jump out of the plane onto the JFK airport landing strip.

The first thing we do when we get back to the city is drop our equipment at the Sheepshead Bay apartment.

Roey orders takeout. There are three things he loves the most: women, food, and danger. Not necessarily in that order.

Today, it's *pel'meni*, Russian dumplings, though I was hoping to have lunch with Lu.

Miller gives a brief report on Reznik from the surveillance team.

Roey twists his fork between his fingers like he used to do with a knife back in the day. And he's having a rum and coke, way too early, which means he's about to slide into another binge.

I see all the signs. I've spent plenty of time with Roey, and I feel bad leaving him on his own when he might need moral support though he hates anyone around when he goes into relapse.

But I can't bear another hour without Lu.

Every message from her makes my heart thud with the sound of a gong.

Lu: We are having a party at the condo tonight. A lot of people. It's the first week of summer. Hurry up!

Shit. I was hoping for some alone time with Lu.

Lu: Does Roey want to come?

"Not my scene," Roey says when I pass the invite from Lu. "*You get drunk and get into action.*"

"What action?"

"Several weeks ago, I'd say, try to get the intel. Now, you should get your personal game going."

I hate when he talks like this. Even more so the possibility of telling Lu what I do for a living and how we met her. Deep down, I think it'll ruin things, and I want just a little more time with her.

Two hours later, I'm at Goldsling Towers.

Becky and Tito are already there. The music is pumping. The terrace doors are open, and there's a small crowd out there.

Lu emerges from the terrace in a white summer dress with a red belt and matching red platform sandals.

"Hi," she says softly as she wraps me into a tight hug.

My heart whimpers, "Hi," at her closeness and the smell of her perfume. The red lipstick in contrast with her blonde hair in a high ponytail makes her look like a Hollywood starlet.

"Red and white, huh?" I smile, noticing she has the matching red nail polish.

"Homage to my mom's friends back home," she explains, which has something to do with the opposition movement back in Belarus. How she keeps up with all the world events is a mystery to me.

You can tell Pushkin is adopted. He doesn't have Lu's party genes in him, growls and barks when new people arrive, and runs to hide behind the furniture when someone attempts to take a picture with him.

So, I take him to my room and give him bacon treats.

"Sorry, buddy. You'll have to stay here for a while," I say, rubbing behind his ears and playing with him for a bit.

He has a little silver heart hanging off his neck that says *Pushkin*. That's new.

"Look at us," I say, "Now we both have dog tags." He licks my hand and raises his adorable pitiful eye at me. "Be good, yeah?"

Good thinking, I tell myself when, two hours later, the condo and the terrace are packed with people. And no one takes their fucking shoes off or throws away their empty plastic cups. Guess who's doing the cleaning tomorrow?

For a while, it's loud laughter and chatter, rock music and Lu walking around, introducing people.

I can't take my eyes off her. Her smile lights up my heart even when it's meant for others. Like I've been walking aimlessly through life for the longest time, and a voice suddenly said, "Stop, stop, stop. Look, it's her."

Lu is sunshine on a gloomy day, and when I see her after the trip, something in my heart clicks into place. She is it for me. I just need to figure out my course of action.

Her eyes meet mine across the room, her smile flickering shyly. I might die if that smile ever touches my lips.

Jace is mine.

I gulp the third beer and exhale in relief when Tito comes over and makes small talk.

I really shouldn't be drinking so much. The more I drink, the more I'm aware of Lu. Something between us changed after the disco night. And I'm patiently waiting for the next chapter of *Sharki* to confirm my suspicions.

Becky saunters over. She's straight as an arrow, speaks her mind, and would probably make for a horrible spy.

"Are you gonna make a move?" she asks me, her eyes glistening from booze.

I fake confusion.

She rolls her eyes. "Or you just gonna stare at Lu from afar all night?"

Yes, for now.

"Seriously, Jace..." She swings her glass, scanning the room and looking bored. "Where's your friend?"

That was a quick change of topic, probably the whole point of her approaching me.

"You like Roey?" I smile.

"Not my type."

Liar. "Should've invited him if you wanted to see him."

"Not interested. Just curious. And you are a little too late."

She nods at the guy who just came in, looking like he takes gym, fashion, and arrogance too far.

"Who's that?"

"That, my friend, is Chad." Sounds like a frat name. "Lu's ex." Oh, shit. "He'll make a move. She'll cave in. He's an asshole. She's too nice."

I don't like this talk.

Becky leans over to murmur in my ear, "Remember, you don't play, you let others score."

I'm pretty sure Becky has scored so much in her life that she should be in a hall of fame. But for the first time, I think she might be rooting for me, though I don't know why.

She's gone, and I study the gym-buff tattooed Chad, who's a little taller and bulkier than me and dressed in a shirt and jeans that are a tad too tight.

Lu laughs at something he says. I wish she didn't. I wish his hand wasn't on her waist. She tries to avoid it, but it inevitably comes back to touch her. My eyes are glued to it touching her shoulder, then sliding to the small of her back. Another beer and I'll throw him off the terrace.

I can't stand guys like this—arrogant, flashy, and pawing at everything they can get their hands on like they want to mark their territory. A frat boy, all muscle, no brain, probably a hundred female numbers in his phone, a gold necklace the size of a tire chain, tattoos —and he flaunts them too.

Is that where she got the inspiration for her stories before?

The possibility of it makes my blood boil.

Lu looks slightly uncomfortable, turns to meet my eyes, and motions for me to come over.

"This is Jace, my roommate," she introduces us.

"Chad," he says nonchalantly, throwing an up-and-down glance at me, and pats me on the shoulder overly strongly. "What's up, roomie?"

Roomie…

I know this type. A natural-born bully. There were plenty in my group home, the ones who took pictures of me during what was supposed to be my first romantic experience. Then in the service.

Oh, there's a hierarchy of bullies in the army. I was a weak link at first. It took time to get physically strong and good at my job to earn respect. That is, besides taking part in many fistfights and having a couple of my bones broken until I learned to swing my fists faster than Jean Claude Van Damme.

Chad doesn't deserve Lu. Not even to breathe around her like he's doing right now, standing dangerously close to her while she bends slightly backward to avoid his proximity.

I excuse myself and walk out onto the terrace.

Lu follows, and Chad goes after her.

I am a nice guy. I am a fucking *quiet* guy, remember? Respectful, too. Patience is a virtue, especially when it's learned through dealing with those who test it on a daily basis.

This guy—I see Chad taking Lu aside and telling her something, stepping into her slowly, making her back away uncomfortably—stops at nothing to get what he wants.

It's already dark outside, music booming, and no one is paying attention to them.

Except me. *All* of my attention is on Lu.

Lu presses her palm against Chad's chest. She fucking touches *him*, not me. But her touch is not gentle, it's defensive. She pushes past him and starts walking away when Chad grabs her by the arm.

You are fucking done.

I set my beer down, push off the railing, and stomp toward them.

"Lu, sweetheart, don't be like that," Chad hisses as Lu tries to move away, but he yanks her toward him.

"Get your hands off her," I say, halting next to him, trying not to snap and head-butt the motherfucker.

His grip loosens as his head snaps in my direction and he gives me a calculating up-and-down stare. "What did you say, roomie?"

"Jace, it's alright," Lu murmurs, looking suddenly scared. For me? *Oh, Lu...*

It's *not* alright, neither is she, the usual light in her eyes extinguished. My vision darkens as anger ripples through my nerves.

"You heard me," I say to Chad, locking eyes with him.

I don't want to fight, not here, not in public. I want this fucking douche to disappear.

So when he lets go of Lu and fists the front of my shirt, I don't respond.

Keep calm, I tell myself.

I've made it my mantra for so many years. In the group home— avoiding the humiliation. In the service—avoiding breaking others.

"Mind your fucking business," Chad snaps, giving me a mocking smirk and pushing me away.

I clench my jaw. "You need to leave."

"Listen, nerdy boy, go back to your room and play Dungeons & Dragons."

"Chad!" Lu shouts. "Leave, please!"

Now everyone is looking, the chatter around dying out.

I fucking hate attention, but I've been here, done this, stood up to guys like this too many times in my life.

Yet, years later, unnecessary arrogance still gets to me.

"You heard her," I say as calmly as I can, blood pumping between my ears. "I don't think she wants you to come back—"

The punch comes so fast that I stumble backward, the crowd oohs, and a shriek comes from Lu.

I didn't expect this. I figured even jerks like him would have the decency to keep it civil during a party.

Wrong.

Motherfucker…

My face is on fire. My head is dizzy with anger.

But I wipe my cheek with the back of my hand and raise my eyebrows at the douchebag.

You're dead.

"Jace…" Lu takes a step toward me, but my eyes are on Chad, who only smirks cockily.

"What, no response, roomie?" He spreads his arms with a sneer. "Lost your cool?"

I don't care how I look right now. I don't even register Lu's hand on me, only him—the smug face and a sleazy smirk, like so many who made me who I am.

"Wanna say something to me, roomie?" he taunts.

Everyone is staring, but that's something I'm used to.

Becky sweeps in, puffing her chest against his. "Get out, Chad," she hisses, pointing to the terrace doors.

"I'll escort you out," I say coldly.

Lu stops me. "I'll do it."

I shake my head, my eyes on him as I gently take her by the shoulder. "Stay here. We'll be fine."

"Oh yeah?" Chad makes an ugly face then turns to Lu. "We'll be fine, sweetheart. See you later."

He walks out, and I follow, my eyes burning into his back while dozens of eyes are on me.

Here we go again.

You can't rid this world of scum. But you can learn to stand up to them.

30

LU

Jace and Chad walk out, and I feel my stomach turn.

Jace has taken a punch…

Freaking Chad!

I knew he was a fake charmer when I met him. Swift and galant. A player but funny and sweet. At first, that is.

Becky profiled him right away and called him a peacock with a rough streak. But I liked the way he poured compliments on me, drove fast on the highways, didn't give a shit about cops or security at posh places, and double parked, but hardly ever tipped—red flag, as Becky said.

The third time I told him I wasn't ready for sex, things went sour.

"So, you like being waited on but won't fuck me?"

I dumped him. Or he dumped me. Doesn't even matter, because I didn't want him after that.

He texts now and then. I try not to respond. I assume he found out about the party from someone's social media post.

Fine, I could handle his company for a minute, but I won't forgive him for punching Jace.

Jace doesn't know what he is up against. Jace is too nice, too polite. And I feel so freaking bad about what happened that when the two walk out the door, my heart starts racing in a panic attack.

I bite my lip, trying to hold back tears and anger.

Becky walks up to me. "So much for army training. Your room-mate is not good with punches. Go check and make sure Chad doesn't beat him to a pulp in the hallway."

Right. I should. God, I wish I'd never had this stupid party.

I dart out of the condo and toward the elevator, approaching the corner when I hear the words.

"I don't want you to come here or bother Lu anymore." That's Jace's voice.

Oh, God, Jace, you don't wanna do this with him.

I stop and peek from behind the corner.

They are in the elevator hallway, and Chad takes slow steps toward Jace. There's an ugly smirk on his face as he cracks his fingers.

"Oh, I see, roomie," Chad sneers. "You still trying to tell me what to do, huh? You have a thing for our Lu?"

Our Lu. Asshole.

"She was never yours and never will be," Jace says coldly.

Chad blurts out a chuckle. "Wanna get in her pants? Guess what, she likes tough guys."

I hate Chad's voice. Or the fact that after a month of dating with no sex, he called me *weird*. No, that wasn't what irritated me. It was the word *frigid* he used with his buddies behind my back.

Jerk.

Chad steps into Jace. "You came out here so that no one sees you being punched again, roomie?"

"If your brain is too slow, I'll repeat. I don't want to see your face here again."

Huh?

My ears perk up at the words.

Jace's voice is cold and dark, making shivers run down my spine at the unexpectedness of it. Like there's a switch inside him.

He doesn't budge when Chad stands chest-to-chest with him.

Jace is surprisingly calm when he says, "I see you set foot in this building or anywhere close to Lu, I'll make sure you can never walk again. Understood?"

I frown in disbelief at his untimely courage.

Chad breaks out in laughter. "That's it, roomie," he says, slowly fisting the front of Jace's shirt.

It happens fast.

Jace does a quick circular movement, pushing Chad's hands apart, then does a stomach punch, chases it with an elbow in Chad's face—bam, bam, bam—so quick and with such surgical precision that my mouth drops as I watch Chad stumble back, a startled look on his face.

He lunges at Jace, but Jace ducks.

Punch.

Knee strike.

He spins Chad like a puppet and, in a blink of an eye, has him pressed against the wall with seemingly no effort.

My heart is about to jump out of my chest.

"You are not a good listener, are you?" Jace says with mockery and a hint of danger in his voice. He didn't even flinch doing this.

What's happening?

My throat is dry, my eyes widening at the sight. I don't recognize Jace's voice, nor do I make a connection between the Jace I know and the Jace who effortlessly holds Chad like a rag doll against the wall.

With a strained angry grunt, Chad pushes off the wall into Jace and turns, swinging his arm in a punch. A punch that Jace deflects then knees him in the gut, grabs the hair on the back of his head, and smashes his face into the wall.

I stifle a shocked squeak.

"Sit down, buddy," Jace says, taking a step away as Chad slides down the wall onto the floor. "Take a break. I can take five like you and still have an even heartbeat afterward."

I gape in disbelief.

"Tell me you won't show up again or ever text Lu, and I'll let you go with minimum damage." Jace cracks his neck like this is just a warmup.

Chad roars and lunges at him from the floor, but Jace steps aside, catches him by the scruff, and smashes him against the wall again.

"I need to hear it, big boy," Jace taunts, towering over Chad.

Chad grunts, sliding up the wall and slumping against it. "Fuck you," he hisses with a bloody snarl and makes a move at Jace.

Jace knees him again, then grabs him by the wrist, twists his arm, making Chad scream in pain, and pushes him toward the elevator.

"The only reason you are standing is because I need you to get the fuck out of this building." Jace's voice is eerily calm as he presses the elevator button. "But I still didn't hear you."

He does something to Chad's arm to make him wail in pain as his knees buckle.

"Alright! Alright! Fucking alright!" Chad pleads.

Jace hauls him up and shoves him into the elevator. "I see you here again, bud, and I'll peel your tattoos off your skin. Lu's *roomie*" —Jace chuckles, freaking chuckles!—"is a little too protective of her."

The door of my condo opens, filling up the hallway with loud music.

I step back behind the wall, out of Jace's sight, my heart racing.

A couple stumbles out of my place, laughing, and I smile at them though my knees are trembling. I swallow hard again and again, dizzy and confused, backing away toward my condo as my brain tries to process what I just saw.

I run inside, right away assaulted by the loud music and Becky, who grabs my arm. "Is everything fine?"

Is it?

"I'm not sure," I murmur, staring at her.

"Lu! Where's Jace?" She looks worried.

"Oh."

Right. I need a drink, a cigarette, a cold shower, and maybe a nap to sober up and make sure I'm not hallucinating. "He's great."

Jace is great.

I stare around aimlessly, confusion mixing with admiration and a speck of fear inside me. I'm not sure I know who Jace is at all.

Heads turn when he walks back into the condo. The *usual* Jace, with a soft glint in his eyes and a kind smile as he ruffles his hair and looks around.

I walk on weak legs toward him.

"Are you alright?" I study his face and his bruised cheekbone. "I'm sorry for that guy. And thank you for sticking up for me."

His smile flickers wider. "He left. He's a dick, huh? Why were you with him?"

"Bored." I laugh nervously. "I don't know really. I *wasn't* really with him."

Now I feel embarrassed to be even associated with Chad.

Jace nods, and I can't take my eyes off him.

I like him with a bruised cheekbone. He's sexy and dangerous. And though I feel bad for him getting punched, I can't help but feel proud at knowing it was for me. What he did by the elevator is incomprehensible.

Sometimes it takes weeks to get to know someone. All it took was one punch. I want to know Jace better. Know where he learned to fight like that.

"Come here." I nod for him to follow, take him to the kitchen, and sit him down on the stool.

Tito sweeps in and jumps up to sit on the counter.

"Got a bit roughed up, huh?" he asks.

"Go away," I snap, wanting a minute with Jace.

Jace doesn't say a word. Not to Tito. Not to me when I wrap cubes of ice in a kitchen towel and walk up to him.

His Adam's apple bobs when I nudge between his knees and take his chin between my fingers, tilting it slightly up. He flinches when I press the ice towel to his bruised cheek, then raises his eyes to meet mine.

Power is contagious. Especially when it's so mundane, knowing you are better than the loud assholes who beat themselves in the chest at every corner.

In my stories, power is always in your face. In Jace, it lingers under the surface, and he uses it quietly, in secret, which makes it so much more intriguing.

Our faces are inches from each other. Suddenly I'm aware of my bare legs brushing against his jeans. His hands shift to his thighs, brushing against my bare flesh. I lean into him, knowing that he feels it too, the tension, the burn between us. His hands just kicked Chad's ass, and I really want them on me.

I admire him so much right now that it makes my anger flare up —the anger of him not kicking Chad's ass in front of everyone to see, because I want to blast it to the entire world.

I don't take my fingers off his chin, loving every second of this contact, the way we breathe deeply, almost in sync.

The room disappears as we both gaze at each other, and one thought, one tiny realization makes my heart beat wildly—this is the first time Jace is gazing at me without looking away. Maybe alcohol is to blame, but there's confidence in his gaze like he just fought off a rival and knows what he wants—me.

Our eyes stay locked, and in my mind, we are kissing, confessing our feelings, running scenarios in our heads of what can happen next.

I shift and suddenly feel his touch, his hands on my thighs, still but so hot, holding me gently in place.

The air burns between us.

I can feel it.

We *both* feel it and know what's happening.

I let my lips curl in a tiny smile. So does he. It's a silent yes, to what—neither of us know yet.

I love his eyes. Love what I see in them. I wish I could see deep enough to know where he comes from and what made him so quiet and withdrawn yet full of that inner power that he doesn't put on display.

There's one more thing I'm realizing, and it's making my heart beat wildly. I'm falling, falling, falling for him, and I'm only hoping that there'll come a moment when he catches me.

"Jesus, Lu, you gonna freeze his face!"

Tito's voice snaps me out of my trance, and I blink fast, suddenly feeling awkward.

Jace gently takes my wrist and, with a soft smile, pulls my hand away from his face.

"That's good, I think. Thank you," he says as Tito jumps off the counter and pushes a drink into his hand.

And I step away from the chair, trying to shake off the momentary desire to pull Jace into my room and let him touch me anywhere he wants.

31

JACE

My body is used to years of pain and physical abuse. But it can't handle Lu's proximity.

I'm on my fourth beer, but I can't shake off the scene in my head —her standing between my knees, holding the ice to my cheek while my body burns, wanting to mold with hers.

Tito drags me to the couch in the living room. I think he's trying to comfort me right now. That's sweet.

The couch barely has any room among a dozen people anchored around the coffee table. But a redhead named Erin scoots over and pats the miserable one foot of empty space next to her.

"Jace! So, you are Lu's roommate. I've heard a lot."

I doubt that. But she probably saw me get punched, feels bad, and might be a sucker for a charity case.

Fucking Chad.

I'm not a violent guy, but he put his hand on Lu, and God, did it feel good to let go by the elevator. I had to hold back not to knock his teeth out.

And she dated that peacock?

He kissed her?

Tried to—

Fuck, alright. I'm jealous. Guilty.

Deep breaths, Jace.

The reason I didn't touch that prick in front of everyone is because I didn't want to come across as exactly the type he is. Nor did I want to cause a scene. Or ruin the party. Or scare off Lu.

So now I'm annoyed. One, at everyone's pitying glances at me. Two, at the redhead, Erin, who leans onto me with her big breasts, saying something about California and how she loves LA.

Her voice drones on as my eyes find Lu with a friend by the open doors to the terrace.

The music is blasting. The cigarette smoke from the terrace filters into the room that smells like perfumes, incense, wine, liquor, and sexual tension. There are over four dozen people here, dancing and hooking up.

Lu throws glances at me, then at Erin, and laughs loudly at some joke, too loudly, but her eyes are not happy.

Erin's voice is too close to my ear. "So, what are your plans for tonight, Jace?"

Oh, I get it. She's a wanna-get-lost-together-tonight type. And that's fine, but not my thing. And that's the reason I feel comfortable around pushy girls—they have no effect on me. Not like Lu, who makes every hair on my body stand on edge just at her mere touch.

I turn to Erin, and her eyes slide to my lips intentionally slowly, her hand creeping to my thigh.

"I don't think our plans for tonight align," I say, then I look at Lu again.

Her gaze flickers to my lap, then to Erin. She tosses her head and bites her lip—I can sense her irritation—and she walks unsteadily out onto the terrace.

"Excuse me," I tell Erin and get up, feeling relieved as her hand slides off my lap.

I lose my beer and follow Lu.

The terrace is packed with dozens of people chatting and laughing in the warm summer air laced with smoke.

And Lu is in the very far corner, by herself, leaning against the railing and—

Lighting a cigarette.

Oh, shit.

She takes a drag and exhales theatrically, then stifles a choke.

Lu doesn't like tobacco. And she never stands alone at parties.

But right now, her arm is wrapped around her waist in a defensive pose.

"Lu?"

I approach and stop behind her, watching her turn. My eyes narrow on her cigarette.

"It's a great party, isn't it?" She tries to smile, but it's the least genuine smile I've ever seen.

"What's wrong?"

"Why do you think something is wrong?"

"Try again."

She doesn't look at me but smiles, oh, so fake. Takes another quick drag.

"You are smoking, Lu. You don't smoke."

"Erin seems to like you," she says.

So, it's about Erin?

"What does you smoking have to do with Erin?" Everything, I know.

She tosses her head. "I don't mind you hooking up, Jace. Just not in my house. Please."

Oh, great. "*I'm* hooking up?" I hold back a smile.

"It's rude. I like you living here, but if you're going to hook up, go to her place. I don't need to hear you—"

"What are you talking about?"

"Erin is not that nice. She's a bitch, actually." Lu's voice is irritated and unusually snappy. "Flirt with someone else."

She's tipsy, the cigarette sloppily hanging between her fingers.

"Lu? I wasn't flirting with her. *She* was flirting with *me.*"

"Yeah, well, have some respect for this house."

Gently, I take the cigarette out of her fingers and drop it onto the floor.

Lu's so close, unbearably close, and I want her even closer. She's gazing away, biting her lower lip.

"Lu? What's happening?"

She shakes her head.

"Look at me, please," I ask.

And now she does. She raises her eyes at me. Her eyelids flutter like she has a hard time keeping her gaze locked with mine.

Her eyes are fire. There's hurt in them like I just betrayed her.

And anger, I think. But also something that reminds me of those spicy episodes she writes, that unmistakable surge of energy.

"Did you get jealous?" I ask softly. That's a bold question.

She flinches at the words. "Yes," she whispers way too quickly.

That's all I need, and I step in closer, my heart thumping hard like it's sending an SOS signal.

"How jealous?" I ask almost in a whisper, raise my hand to her face, and gently run the back of my fingers along her cheek.

Her lips part slightly in a tiny gasp. Her face is only inches away. She doesn't break eye contact, and I pray she won't because I'm afraid to lose whatever is happening right now and I need to see that she is too.

"Very jealous," she whispers.

I lean in and kiss her.

A tiny little kiss. No tongue. Just our lips touching for a second.

When I slowly pull away, Lu's lips follow mine just an inch, like she doesn't want to let go.

And I kiss her again.

As soon as our lips fuse together, I know nothing ever compared to this, to the way my heart booms in my chest and every cell surges toward her. I have to restrain myself from attacking her when I take her face between my palms and deepen the kiss.

I kissed her so many times in my mind. But this is so much more.

When I sweep my tongue between her lips, they part so quickly, and her tongue darts out to meet mine, the velvety touch of it driving me over the edge.

I pull away just for a second, and she gasps like she needs air. Or me. More of me. And I need more of her.

I take her lips again, promising myself not to pull away unless Armageddon comes.

I slide my hands down to her waist and pull her toward me as I latch onto her lips. Her tongue tangles with mine, and the world around us falls away.

Kissing Lu is magical. Opening her lips, sliding my tongue in, drowning in the sensation is like being pulled away by a warm tender current. I want to get lost in her, *with* her. Her slender arms wrap around my neck, and I pull her closer, deepening the kiss, stepping into her until she's pressed against the wall.

I've never felt like this—like our bodies melt into each other. I want to kiss every part of her, peel her clothes off, and kiss every exposed inch.

But we are surrounded by people—the vague realization lingers in the back of my mind—so I keep it decent, keep control. I'm trained to keep cool, but it's getting harder by the second with Lu in my arms.

I hug her closer, trying to wrap myself around her.

She's so small in my arms.

She's not going anywhere.

She's mine right now.

So is this kiss.

So are her lips.

So is the smell of her perfume, the faint trace of paint, and the taste of wine. Even the tobacco, the hint of it so edgy and so unlike Lu but yet so familiar that it makes my mind go wild. Her smell fills my head and I'm free-falling.

All mine.

"Jace," she breathes out in the brief moment she breaks the kiss.

"Yes, Lu?" I breathe into her mouth and kiss the corner of it, then plant little kisses on her face.

I want to look into her eyes to see the emotions in them, but it's torture to pull away from her.

Her hands sink into my hair, pulling me closer. "Don't go yet," she whispers.

"Not a chance."

She has no idea. My heart swells. It grows tentacles that wrap around her. My mind starts spinning, chanting, "*Mine, mine, mine.*"

She gently fists my hair to hold me in place as her lips find mine again.

She's chaos. She's madness. She's everything I'm not. And she's everything I didn't know I needed.

32

JACE

THE COMMOTION BREAKS US APART, AND FOR A MOMENT, WE DON'T move, high on the kiss, smiles chasing each other.

Lu's hands are on my chest, mine stroking her back. Our faces are inches apart, and our eyes search each other's as if to make sure this is real.

"I'm leaving!"

The loud voice is Becky's, and I know it's a message for Lu. Becky didn't interrupt us—that's a miracle.

I don't know how much time passed while we kissed. Five minutes? Half an hour?

"I should probably go say goodbye to her," Lu says and bites her lip.

I hate the thought of letting her go. I need just another second with her. So I lean in and kiss her softly on the cheek, then bring my lips to her ear, whispering, "Go," and kiss her earlobe, making her giggle.

She takes a step away, grinning at me. My hands fall off her, and I groan inwardly—I'm hard, and it's unbearably hard to let her go.

"B!" Lu shouts after Becky and disappears behind the terrace doors.

Only now do I notice that it's not as noisy. There are fewer people on the terrace. The music is quieter inside. People are picking up their purses and jackets and laugh, hugging Lu goodbye.

Tito's ass is on the kitchen island as he takes sloppy sips from a margarita glass.

"A neighbor came knocking, asked to take it down a notch," he tells me when I come over. "It's midnight. Who sleeps so early on a Saturday?"

Midnight? Wow. I exhale loudly and ruffle my hair, keeping Lu in my peripheral as I start picking up empty bottles and cups.

In half an hour, it's only me, Lu, and Tito, and I finish washing the dishes.

Pushkin is out of my room and walks around sniffing everything.

Lu doesn't meet my eyes as she chats with drunk Tito on the couch. But there's a smile on her lips, a vague beautiful smile that I hope is meant for me.

"Lu," Tito whines as he slides down to lie on her lap. "I'm gonna crash here."

My heart sinks. That means no alone time with Lu. No good-night kiss. No, *"Can I put you to bed, Lu, and kiss the hell out of you so you fall asleep with my taste on your lips?"*

"Hey, guys," Tito says dreamily as Lu plays with his hair. "After your exhibit, Lu, we are all going to my house in Long Island."

"You have a house in Long Island?" I ask from the kitchen.

"In the Hamptons," Lu clarifies and ruffles his hair.

It should be me with my head on her lap, and her lips on mine.

"Jace? You are coming," Tito states.

I smile. I know all about making plans while drunk.

"Nothing funny," he adds. "It's my parents' vacation home. Huge. You and Lu will love it. She hasn't been there yet."

He says "you and Lu" like we are an item.

"Yes!" Lu exclaims and turns toward me. "Jace, say yes!"

Our eyes lock, and I feel like I'm committing to something else, something that Long Island and a vacation trip have nothing to do with. And I get to see her in a bikini every day? Sign me up.

"Yes," I say with a smile though I want to shout it at the top of my lungs.

Lu jumps off the couch and trots into her room, then comes back with a piece of paper and a pen. Scribbling something real fast, she gives it to Tito.

He laughs. "Oh, God. Again?"

He signs it—what the hell?—and Lu makes her way to me, slaps the paper on the kitchen counter, and puts her hands on her waist. "Signature, Mr. Reed."

I lean on my fists on the counter to take a look.

The most uneven and barely readable handwriting I've ever seen —even her writing is chaos—states that Tito, Lu, and I spend a weekend in July in the Hamptons.

Silly, but it makes me grin.

"She does it all the time, Jace!" Tito shouts from the couch. "If you sign, you have to deliver. It's a serious matter, trust me."

I raise my eyes to Lu.

She tries to project that mischievous playful attitude, but her eyes are burning like they did back on the terrace before I kissed her.

Without breaking eye contact, I pick up a pen. Yes, I want to be bound to her by promises and a silly drunken contract.

"If you sign," she says, flinching, "you'd have to come back here even if you move out and return to California."

Boom! My heart does that weird thing again where it thuds and then halts for a moment.

No, this is not silly. She wants to know that even if I leave, I'll come back to her. That even if something happens before that, she has a reason to call me and say, "Hey, Jace, you promised."

I don't need a reason.

I sign.

I feel like I'll always find my way to her. And I'm not sure I want to part at all.

I push the paper toward her. "Sign." Because she didn't yet.

Without looking away from me, she takes the paper and goes for the pen that I hold out. Her fingers brush against mine because I hold it so that there's no other way.

We both hold it together for a moment, our eyes locked.

"If you sign," I say quietly, "you'll have to make sure I make it."

Her playfulness is gone. She nods, whispering barely audibly, "I will," and signs.

And the dim living room becomes this happy hopeful bubble that I don't want to leave unless I leave with Lu.

Tito starts singing, "Magic In The Hamptons," and holly hell does he have a sexy voice.

Everything going on seems so sexed up. And I can't stop staring at Lu's bare feet, now that she got rid of her boots, as she walks to her room.

She comes back with a blanket and a pillow for Tito.

"Good night, guys! Love you!" she says before disappearing into her room again.

Love you...

The door to her room shuts. I can't see her but still smell her on my skin, taste her on my lips, remember her luminous eyes, her soft, "I will," to something, to the future, to me.

It's maddening.

She's a sweet ghost, and I'm stuck with a very real drunk Tito, who stops singing and starts blabbering about life and Jamie, and that I'll make a better domestic partner than him because I take care of people and things.

"Jamie is a lucky bastard to have a guy like you," I tell Tito. "You are comparing everyone to him, you know that?"

That's how I know that Jamie is the real deal, despite Tito being a playboy, and Jamie being in the closet.

"Everyone always inevitably finds the way out," I murmur as I go out to the terrace and pick up cigarette butts and empty cans.

When I'm back in the living room, Tito is splayed on his back, in only a white tank and boxers, one arm and leg hanging off the couch.

"Good night. See you in the morning," I say, tying up the last garbage bag and setting it by the front door.

Tito grunts or moans—not sure what that sound means.

"Want some water?" I ask.

"Pickle juice."

"What?"

Tito laughs drunkenly.

"Don't ask. It's a Be-la-ru-si-an thing," he slurs like he's trying to pronounce *Worcestershire sauce*. "There's a pickle jar with Cyrillic letters in the fridge."

The whole content of the fridge is Cyrillic letters, but I find the pickle jar and pour the liquid into a glass. I've never fallen faster in love with all things weird like I did in apartment 1101 of Goldsling Towers.

"Awesome for hangovers. Lu taught me," Tito explains, drinking it as I'm about to turn around. "This couch sucks, Jace. Can I sleep in your bed?"

Tito is such a smooth-talker that I can't hold back a chuckle.

"That's a no. Nice try though. Anything else, sweetheart?" I tease him, walking away.

"I'm gonna be super nice! I'll stay on my side, on the very edge. Jace, I promise!" he begs louder as I reach my room.

"There's no *your* side on my bed, Tito."

"This couch—"

"Tito." I turn and give him a reproachful stare. "Goodnight."

"Ugh." He exhales in what sounds like frustration. "I guess she won."

I guess he's talking about Lu. But she won a long time ago.

As I close the door to my room, Tito's drunk murmur is the last thing I hear. "But I do have such skillful hands."

33

JACE

L̥u, T̥ito, and I have breakfast on the terrace.

Tito is hungover, and so is Lu.

I got up early, as usual, went downstairs to get creamer and eggs, made coffee, cooked breakfast, and took it out onto the terrace while Lu and Tito soaked up the June sunlight.

"I like coffee in bed," Tito says, lighting a cigarette. "Jace, if you ever need a new roommate, I have a spare room."

Lu smiles, and I can't help but glance at her smiling lips—the lips that kiss so well that I spent an hour last night obsessing over the memories.

I'm on my way to Sheepshead Bay when I get a text from Roey.

Roey: We have a job down South.

Me: When?

Roey: Starting today.

Me: What do you mean today?

It's like he's trying to sabotage my every perfect day with Lu.

Roey: I already booked the tickets. Get your ass here.

Fuck!

We can't, I wanna say. We just got back, I want to argue. I have plans with Lu.

But, oh, yes, we can, and we do fly to Florida in the afternoon without me even getting a chance to say goodbye to Lu.

I feel like I'm living a double life. Some of my clothes are at Goldsling Towers. Some at Sheepshead Bay. And the rest are in California. That's three lives, actually.

Lu: What time are you gonna be home tonight? Wanna have dinner? I'll cook))

Fuck! Out of all days... I want to smash my phone against the wall in frustration.

Me: I'm heading to Florida, Lu. It's an unexpected work trip I just found out about. Sorry...

She doesn't respond, and my heart sinks.

I'm an asshole.

But when we land at the West Palm Beach airport, my phone dings with a message.

Lu: When are you coming back?

Me: Should be back in a week.

Me: Dinner then? Please?

I send a gif with puppy eyes and hold my breath, waiting for a reply.

Lu: Do I need to have you sign another contract to make sure you don't flake on me?

I laugh, and Roey cocks his head at me, killing my smile.

Our hotel room feels like a prison cell. But so does everything else without Lu lately.

Four more guys from Roey's temporary team meet us there. Roey opens his computer as we are about to go over our target.

This time it's a rising R&B star who broke the charts with his new album yet has a hefty debt with the Cubans in Miami and successfully ditches them.

"With the popularity came a bodyguard escort of six people," Roey explains, showing me the portfolio of the guy and his entourage. "A little excessive, but so is his paranoia."

I always wondered why people who have money often don't pay their debts until they get fucked.

Apparently, the Cubans don't want to make too much noise, and, turns out, that's the only way they deal with debtors.

So here we are, tracking the R&B star to Miami and about to execute the plan of—

"Very quiet and sophisticated interception," Roey explains. "The most important part of it relies on you, Jace. As per Miller's intel, the guy is going to a party in a mansion in Southwest Ranches, about fifteen miles northwest of Miami. It's a quieter area, and that's where we are doing a stakeout, on a deserted stretch two miles east of the mansion. Your part, Jace? You'll need to incapacitate four escort vehicles within twenty seconds. The vehicle our guy is in will be further intercepted by us. We get the guy, we deliver him to the client, and that's it. It should be a swift clean job." Roey studies me for a moment. "That is if you execute the precise shots at the car tires."

"Got it." I nod.

"That means all your focus has to be on those shots."

"Got it, Roey."

"*All* your focus."

What the fuck is he staring at me like that for? Like I'm about to fail.

The operation is tomorrow, and we discuss the plan in detail, while all I can think about is if we get done tomorrow, I'm going to see Lu much sooner than I thought.

"You are too deep in," Roey snaps when the rest of the guys go back to their rooms.

"What are you talking about?"

"Lucy."

"Why would you say that?"

He turns to lock eyes with me. "Because I know you, Jace. What are you thinking?"

"What do you mean?"

"Don't dance around. It's a serious question. Is she just a fling?"

I don't answer. She's not. But one drunk kiss from her is not an indication that she feels anything close to how I do. Granted, she doesn't yet know my story.

"So, you'll be alright leaving New York as soon as we sort out Reznik?"

No, I won't. But I don't know what to tell him. I don't even know what to tell Lu. Besides the fact that I'm head over heels in love with her.

"What does Lu have to do with anything?" I ask quieter, knowing that I can't fool Roey by answering his question with a question.

"Fucking everything!" Roey barks suddenly. "And you need to do something about it so you can do your fucking job!"

He exhales in obvious frustration, and I stare at him in shock. Roey hardly ever loses his temper.

"Miller searched all her records and emails. Reznik hasn't contacted her since the night we lost him. You obviously didn't get any info. The only reason you are still in Goldsling Towers"—Roey stares at me with the anger that makes me feel guilty—"is because I know you care about the girl, and I want you to be happy."

"The rent is not a work expense anymore. I understand that. I'll pay for it, Roey. But I'm not moving out yet. I'm not."

I understand, I fucking do, that I've been neglecting my job. But I discovered something that's more important than my job or anything else in my life, ever—Lu—and I'm not letting her go.

"It's all over your face, Shooter," Roey says a little calmer this time. "We are going over a target that will earn us a lot of money, but I see a dreamy look on your face. And I fucking hope that you don't have that look when you are in a hideout with a rifle tomorrow. We don't need another screwed operation."

Blood thumps in my head at the words. He's talking about the night I missed Reznik. And he's angry I'm not paying due attention to my job. No matter how pissed his tone makes me, Roey is right.

"Everything will work fine tomorrow," I say quieter.

Tomorrow is going to be a busy day. I will *not* fuck up.

Roey goes to the mini bar and makes himself a drink.

My heart sinks. Roey might have binges he can't control, but he never drinks before an operation.

Except today.

Shit.

And me?

It's a fucking addiction because in order to calm my nerves and frustration, I think of Lu. And as soon as Roey turns on the TV, my thoughts are back in New York.

34

JACE

I've read all of Lu's stories multiple times now. Reading lets me explore Lu's brain. There's psychology behind creation and a choice of words. And there are definitely personal preferences in one's writing.

Like oral. Lu likes oral. A lot of oral. Yup.

I usually read her stuff alone, because my dick really likes it too and gets too excited. One day, I might need this. Hopefully, for Lu. And not just in my dreams.

I open SD and see a notification.

Two new chapters from the author you follow are live!

I click on the link, and in a minute, I'm lost in Em and John's story.

It started with his eyes.

You don't always realize what turns simple attraction into more. What starts keeping you up at night. What unravels and torments you with want.

The first time, I painted only his eyes.

Then his face, the dark loose strands of his hair falling over his forehead.

Then his silhouette against the city skyline.

Now, I paint John obsessively, every day, carefully bringing his intense gaze out on the canvas.

During the day, I spend a lot of time on details.

At night, I paint him in large careless strokes, adding darker overtones, brighter red for his lips.

I paint his tattoos, though I didn't get a chance to study them yet, except the shark one.

When I miss him, I pull the covers off his portraits and set them around the room, almost a dozen of them by now. And I sit in his presence, wanting to talk to his portraits, imagining it's him, but knowing it's too crazy even for a creative person like me.

I hold my breath. I think my heart stopped beating at the words, but then it resumes, wildly and loudly like it just got more oxygen to pump.

She does *what*?

His eyes are everywhere. *He* is everywhere. His voice is in my head.

"Miss Aberdeen."

"Call me Em."

"Em it is."

The tiny smile that curves his full lips—I want it on mine. His eyes—closer. His scent—on me.

He's gone for the day, and I'm in his room. I walk into his bathroom and inhale the scent of his body wash, close my eyes, and imagine him taking a shower.

I know every part of his daily routine, the small details, the food he likes, the toothpaste he uses, the dark aggressive music he listens to, and how meticulously he folds his shirts in the drawer.

There's a cigarette pack on his nightstand. He hasn't touched it since he moved in.

His room is spotless. His laundry basket is almost empty. He takes care of his things. Unlike me. I know a lot about John on the surface, just not his mind.

Did Lu go into my room?

I lie on his bed and imagine what it'd be like to be in it with him, naked. Closing my eyes, I inhale his familiar scent. The scent is so very real. I wish I could paint it, dark, maybe blueish-gray, with warm streaks and specks of amber.

I glide my hand along my torso, wishing it were his.

Smiling, I breathe him in.

My other hand slides under his pillow and bumps against something cold.

Something that doesn't belong in a bed or under a pillow.

Something that shouldn't even be in the apartment. Or owned by an accountant.

I rise, move the pillow aside, and stare at the object that doesn't make sense.

A gun…

Fuck…

My mind starts spinning.

I never put the gun away, I realize. It's not under my pillow but under my mattress. Still…

My stomach turning in unease, I keep reading.

John says he works as an accountant at a big firm. But I went to the office building he mentioned, to his company's front desk. There is no person by his name working for them.

Phew. Maybe it's just her wild imagination?

My eyes dart along the chapter.

Damn, Em thinks her roommate is a secret agent, but that seems only to intrigue her more.

And her attraction deepens.

Lust is contagious. Fantasies are a drug. I'm addicted, and my biggest drug is the guy who lives fifty feet across from my room.

When he's there, I can hear him. Or in the kitchen, opening the fridge at night. Padding to the terrace. Talking on the phone.

Stopping by my door at night…

My breath hitches when I hear his soft footsteps behind it.

174

I lie in my bed, catching every sound, imagining what it would be like if he just walked in and saw me like this.

Naked.

Soaking my sheets with my longing.

With my hand between my legs as I think about him.

God fucking help me!

Is everything about this new character gonna look and sound like me?

I don't know what's happening, I'm not a writer, but you don't attach sexual fantasies to a person you don't like romantically, right?

I could ask Roey, but his answer is always the same—we are just smart animals but with the same needs and instincts.

He is a lady's man, a hump-her-then-dump-her guy, the charmer, the live-like-it's-your-last-day guy. Granted, serving at war will drill the latter into your brain. He believes sex is a physical necessity, and if he were to die, he'd happily do that buried in some hottie.

Me, I believe sex is a special intimate connection. And I've never had anyone special in my life.

So, there. I'm not embarrassed about being inexperienced with women. Experience can give one confidence and certain validation, sure, but doesn't change who one is.

So I keep reading. I pay attention to the plot, but it's the main character's thoughts and feelings that I reread, every line in the book resonating with my heart.

And Lu's voice is in my head, soft and intimate as I read on:

In my room, he's everywhere. A dozen canvases bear his face.

Tonight, when I strip to the music, I strip for him, putting on a show, seductively sliding my hands up and down my body.

There's an added edge this time, my body more tense as I think about the gun under his pillow, about his real job that he hides from me, and other secrets that he harbors.

Danger is seductive.

The thoughts make me bold.

I shed my clothes, swinging to the low music, pushing my panties down to my hips, and turning around, showing myself off to his portrait.

When I'm finally naked, I lie down and shamelessly spread my legs for him.

He's looking. His eyes on the canvas are locked with mine. So real, yet not. The ache of wanting him is killing me, and so is the hope that maybe he wants the same.

Sometimes, during the day, John narrows his heated gaze on me, sending goosebumps down my skin like he knows what I do behind locked doors.

I want to show him what I do.

But we are not there yet.

So I lock eyes with the painted version of him and let my hands drift down my naked body. My fingers slide between my legs, rubbing the aching flesh, opening it for his gaze as I try to sedate the burning at the thought of what he would do to me if he were here.

If he knew my dirty little secret, how unhinged I am for him, would he make me his?

This can't go on.

It'll ruin me.

But I've been doing it for weeks. Pretending to be good by day and being a deviant by night.

"Yes, Jace. It's all for you. All yours," I whisper, a moan escaping me as I slowly bring myself closer to climax.

A soft knock on my bedroom door jolts me to sit upright.

"Em?" It's *his* voice.

My stomach twists in panic as I look at the painting of him in front of my bed and myself, naked.

"Just a second!"

Holy shit!

I stab the "continue" button, but there's a message:

Looking forward to the next chapter?

Fuck!

I exhale in frustration, only now noticing my labored breathing.

"You alright, buddy?" Roey asks from his bed. "Are you reading Lu's masterpieces?"

"Maybe," I blurt and absently stare around.

Am I losing my mind and dreaming this shit up?

Then something stops me dead in my tracks as my mind goes over the chapter.

Jace.

Can't be…

I open the app again and scroll through the last chapter.

Yes! Fuck, here it is!

"Yes, Jace. It's all for you. All yours."

I stare at it in disbelief.

Lu, baby! You got carried away!

I grin at the sight of my name. I wish I could tell her. Her readers will notice.

I do a screenshot and hope there comes a day when I can tease Lu about it.

Her stories unhinge my imagination. I wonder if she's bare down there or has a little landing strip. A classic bikini, maybe?

Fuck, I shouldn't be thinking that far ahead, but I can't help it. I've never felt like this. And this novel is unlike anything she's written before. Emotions drip off the page. Yet there hasn't been a single spicy scene yet. Maybe, Lu is not into it in real life.

"Do women like smut?" I ask Roey.

He chuckles. I just gave myself away, but I don't care.

"What, you think our Lu is an exception? Women are not that much different from men, generally speaking. I mean in terms of sexuality."

"Bullshit. Porn is mostly for men."

"Wrong."

"All right. But most girls are not into porn, or crude stuff, or one-night stands."

"And plenty of guys aren't either. Have you met yourself?"

Right.

"Generally, women are not as straightforward and open about it as men," Roey explains.

"Yeah. But—"

"You know what your problem is, Jace?" His voice is sharp

again. It's the drinking, I know. "You are overthinking. Everything. All the time. Especially with girls. Instead of just letting go."

"Well, maybe I like to think."

"Well, maybe Lu will like your dick better than your brain."

That's classic Roey Torres.

"Maybe I want her to like me first before—"

"Maybe you are asexual," Roey cuts me off and throws his head back with a heavy exhale. "Maybe you like the idea of sex but are not interested in the real thing. You might just be a dreamer. Embrace it."

He's easy to talk to despite his one-sided view on relationships. But he's wrong. It's not like I didn't want women. Just not any specific one.

Until Lu.

My imagination is so *not* asexual that I'm wondering if I'm a suppressed sex freak after all. Because my fantasies about Lu are much wilder than what she writes about.

I make a mental note.

One, Lu thinks about me. And her thoughts are far from tame.

Two, Lu paints me? Does she or is it just a story? I have to find out.

Three, I promise myself that if—scratch that, *when*—Lu and I are close, I will blow her mind in bed.

35

JACE

Bam!

Bam!

Bam!

Bam!

Four shots.

Four tires blown.

Four black SUVs on an empty country highway skid in different directions and halt.

Another one speeds forward with a roar.

I get Roey's voice in my earpiece, *"Guys, get ready to intercept. In four, three, two, one, go!"*

My job is done as I keep an eye on the bodyguards who frantically scramble for their guns around the SUVs on the side of the road.

The behind-the-scene shouts in my earpiece quiet after a minute, and Roey's calm voice announces, *"Got him."*

They intercepted the target's SUV up the road as planned. The job is done in record time and with a swiftness that makes my chest swell in satisfaction.

I love shooting. Just not at people. And I do enjoy the sight of a target being delivered to a client.

Justice is not always legal, but hey, neither is war.

We book earlier flights to JFK.

I take a cab straight to Dumbo—I want to surprise Lu.

The doorman smiles at me, though I'm more aware of the two tall buff guys in sunglasses who stand across the street from the entrance.

The concierge greets me with unusual enthusiasm. "Mr. Reed! You have a guest!"

A guest?

"A guest for Miss Moor. A gentleman."

It'd better not be fucking Chad, because I'll throw him off the eleventh floor.

I hear voices behind the apartment door as I approach and Lu's soft laughter as I insert my key in the lock.

When I step into the living room, I freeze.

A five-million-dollar face is staring at me from the couch. Reznik.

His expression is a cold mask with a fake smile as he rises from the couch, his tall bulky figure too slow like he's a predator about to attack.

Lu flings to her feet and darts toward me, then stops, embarrassed at her eagerness.

My heart thunders as my brain tries to figure out what to do.

"Diadia Tolia, this is Jace, my roommate," she announces.

His unblinking stare stays locked with mine as I manage a polite smile.

"Roommate?" There's no surprise in his question.

"He comes and goes," Lu jokes with a nervous chuckle.

His eyes on me are like icicles.

Does he know what I do? Did he spy on this condo? He's a smart man with many resources to get the right intel.

"Anatolyi," he says, taking slow steps toward me and stretching his hand for a shake.

I glance at it, then back at him.

Is he wearing the infamous bracelet?

If he knows who I am, is this a trap?

I fake a smile and raise both hands in front of me. "Sorry, my hands are dirty. I'm Jace. Nice to meet you."

He lowers his hand slowly, nodding a little, his lips curling into a smirk like he knows I'm lying.

"You are a family friend, right?" I ask, dropping my backpack on the floor.

My mind is reeling, trying to figure out what to do and how to act. I should've put my gun under the sink. Or by the door. But it's in the bedroom. Fuck!

"Yes."

"Come visit us more often. Lu misses her home," I lie.

He nods, his eyes following my every movement. "Sure."

"We could do dinner. Wanna stay for dinner?" I need to keep him here for a little longer so I can alert Roey.

"Not today." His eyes glisten with what looks like acknowledgment. He senses something.

My heart pounding, I keep thinking about my gun. I could hold him at gunpoint while I call Roey. But then there's Lu. I can't show her this side of me, nor can I possibly put her in any danger.

"Would you like some Russian cookies to go?" she asks him with her sunshine smile.

Lu, if only you knew...

"*Да нет. Я ж на Брайтоне. Маме привет, да?*[1]" The fucker speaks in Russian, like it's a code.

"You'll call me again?" Lu is too nice.

And now my full attention is on how close she is to him and his hands. She reaches for him—to hug him, I guess—and my entire body screams in alert as I'm ready to tackle him in case he attempts something stupid with her.

But Reznik is too swift. He moves in my direction and bends to pick up the duffle bag from next to the shoe rack.

What's in that fucking bag?

"Gotta run," he says, and in a moment, he's out the door, leaving me with a reeling mind and Lu with a disappointed look on her face.

"That's the guy you talked to on the street the night we met," I tell her.

"Uncle Tolia, yeah."

"What did he want?"

There are tea cups on the coffee table and plates with pastries.

"He stopped by unannounced. Strange, really. I was going—"

"I need to grab something from the convenience store," I cut her off. "I'll be right back."

In a flash of a second, I'm out and slam the door of the emergency exit, trotting down the stairs and dialing Roey.

"Reznik is in Goldsling Towers. Leaving right now. Get the surveillance crew on the condo cameras and every intersection in Dumbo."

"Follow him!" Roey snaps.

"I'm running downstairs as we speak, but he knows my face and that I'm Lu's roommate. I don't have my gun on me."

"Don't fucking lose him! I'm on it!"

He hangs up as I reach the third floor when the exit door suddenly swings open, slamming into me and knocking me down.

I roll onto the floor.

"Mister Reed, isn't it?" the familiar voice rasps.

I'm about to kick back at Reznik's shadow looming over me when something heavy collides with my head, and I sink into darkness.

I'm not sure how long I've been out when the ringing of the phone brings me back.

My head throbs and spins when I start rising from the floor, and I grunt, pressing at the wound. My fingers get slippery with blood.

Fuck.

I pick up Roey's call.

"We didn't catch him, Jace. He never left the building. The guys are on it. You alright?"

I grunt, getting up. "He knocked me out."

"Jace, what's happening?"

I shake my head, fighting the dizziness. "He knew I would follow him. And he knew my last name. I don't think Lu told him, so—"

"He knows we are trying to trace him."

"Yea. Fuck..." I check the time of the last phone call—I've only been out for five minutes.

"It's alright," Roey says with disappointment. "Shit. We'll study the footage again, but chances are, he changed clothes and went out the back entrance of the Towers. The motherfucker is too clever. Are you sure you're okay? He didn't try anything..."

"I'm fine."

Back at the condo, Lu meets me with a worried expression.

"What happened, Jace?"

"I fell."

She doesn't believe me, glances at my empty hands but, without another word, sits me down and cleans my wound with peroxide.

Maybe I should get injured more often so I can feel her hands on me again. My disappointment washes away as I relax under her touch.

"What was your friend saying?" I ask.

"Uncle? Nothing much. He came to apologize for disappearing that night. Said he got a phone call and left abruptly, not knowing that I wasn't feeling well."

Bullshit.

"He's not my uncle actually."

I know that. "No?" Here I am, trying to get intel. Such an asshole.

"He's my mom's friend of over twenty years since she used to live in Brighton. He used to come visit all the time. Why are you so interested in him?"

"Just another friend of yours. It's nice to know people who are close to you."

When she steps away from me and gazes down at me with tenderness, I feel like a dick again for trying to weasel the info out of her.

My phone beeps with a message.

Roey: Lost him and his bodyguards. The surveillance team will need several hours to track back the public cameras in Dumbo. We'll get him.

I'm trying to calm my nerves, because ten minutes ago, I freaked out for a difference reason—afraid Reznik would do something to Lu.

And now I'm worried about the fact that all these lies will eventually drive Lu away from me.

---

1. *"Да нет. Я ж на Брайтоне. Маме привет, да?"* — (Russian) "Nah. I'm in Brighton. Say hi to Mom, yeah?"

36

LU

HE'S BACK!

And he's...injured.

I'm not sure what just happened. Uncle took off abruptly. Jace followed and came back with empty hands and an injury—obviously, he didn't make it to the convenience store.

But the suspicious thoughts quickly dissipate.

I've missed him. Even being silent, he fills this giant place with soothing comfort.

"It was boring her without you," I say, studying him as he texts.

"Was it?" He raises his eyes from the cell phone, smiling softly as he rubs the corner of his lips with his thumb. "Hey, I have something for you."

He gives me a small jewelry box.

"For me?" I smile like a goof as I pull the little golden bowtie and open the lid to find a pair of gold earrings with tiny pink stones that form hearts.

"Jace!"

He gets on his knees to play with Pushkin, who wears a blue patch with a yellow smiley face and excitedly sticks out his pink tongue to lick Jace's hands.

Jace shrugs, not looking at me. "Saw it in one of the shops in West Palm, figured it would match your famous pink coat. Roey dragged me there."

"Roey, huh?" I can't help but grin. "Hey, Jace?"

He lifts his eyes to me.

"Roey is into jewelry shops?"

His lips hitch in a smile, his eyes on Pushkin again, who splays on the floor while Jace rubs his tummy. Pushkin is a lucky bastard, stealing Jace's attention from me.

"Okay," I say, twisting the box in my hands, "I gotta paint for some time, but... Dinner tonight?"

"That'd be nice," Jace says, still not looking at me but playing with Pushkin too enthusiastically.

"Then a movie?" Finally, I'll have him to myself.

"Yeah. Wanna watch a movie?" he asks Pushkin, making him growl.

"Hey, Jace?" I grin when he raises his eyes at me. "I wasn't asking Pushkin."

I walk to my room, leaving the door open, grinning the whole time, and knowing—sensing—that Jace is watching me.

I'm not nosy, just curious. The jewelry box has a logo, so I quickly Google it.

Celebrities' favorite jewelry designer.

I go on the website and find similar earrings.

$3,500, gold with pink garnets.

So, Jace has money. Sure not from the automotive equipment sales.

Among all things that make me happy, Jace has become number one, beating my friends, my art, and my writing. Well, maybe not the latter, but considering my new novel started as a character study, it's Jace again.

He'd thought I was a creep if he knew what I do in secret. That I went out past dawn several times to watch him jog with Pushkin and took pictures that I painted afterward. That he left the door to his room open one afternoon, and I watched him taking a nap. That I study him when he makes food in the kitchen, the way he uses his hands, how he moves, wipes his mouth with his thumb, ruffles his hair, and leans on his fists on the counter. Dozens of little things that make Jace.

And then came the kiss during the party. That kiss, one single kiss, haunts me with such intensity that it's ripping me apart, making me write, write, write.

I'm slipping.

I should blame my editor for overlooking the latest typo. But I only saw it when I read a comment after the last chapter, "**Who the hell is Jace???**"

I freaked out at first, thinking someone I knew found my writing profile, until I reread the chapter.

Sure thing—instead of John, one line said Jace, and I almost had a heart attack while waiting for the corrected version to re-upload. Several thousand people had read it by then. I hope not many noticed. I hope I'm not losing my mind, but I'm only lying to myself.

I go into the bathroom, turn on the water, and call Becky.

My thoughts are a mess, and I need to vent.

"B, you think Jace likes me?" I ask right off the bat.

"I think Jace has a crush on you. I *know* that. You obviously don't notice how he looks at you."

"How does he look at me?"

"Like he's lived in a dungeon and just saw sunshine for the first time."

I laugh. "Seriously, B."

"Have you watched those videos where colorblind people see colors for the first time?"

"Yeah."

"Like that. Like he's trying to get used to the new world but it doesn't stop fascinating him."

"Really?" My heart warms. "Why won't he make a move then?"

I can't stop thinking about our kiss, though we act like it never happened.

"He doesn't live in the city. This is temporary, remember?"

"What does that have to do with anything?"

"Well, besides being shady as fuck and hiding things from you, which, to be fair, are none of anyone's business, he seems like a good guy. I think he's just too nice to use you for a quick shag. There's a slight chance he's a serial killer, too."

"Ew, B!"

"He fits the type. White male between twenty-four and thirty-four, quiet, intelligent, likable."

"Stop."

"He probably just doesn't want to take advantage of you for a month or two and bounce. But if you get a chance, I gotta admit, Tito was right."

"About?"

"He's probably dirty in bed. It's always the quiet ones."

"Staaaahp," I plead with a grin.

"He buys groceries, cleans, inspires your art. Builds shelves for you. Brings presents. Like, jeez, girl, pour some sugar on me."

I'm so giddy, I close my eyes and repeat her words in my head.

Becky carries on. "He doesn't come across as a hit-and-run type of guy. Unlike his friend, Rrrroey."

Just the way she says it, with extra bitterness, so unlike Becky, means Roey must've gotten under her skin. Good. Becky needs a shakeup now and then.

"I don't know, B..." I murmur and sigh.

"Lu, listen." Becky suddenly sounds too serious, and it must have something to do with work. "I read your new series on Story Den."

There's an awkward silence.

Becky usually asks me what I work on. I usually tell her. But I didn't tell her about the *Sharki* novel. I knew the moment she read the new stuff she'd know where it all comes from.

"Do you want to tell me what's going on with you and Jace? You, specifically?"

I don't know what to tell her. Nothing is going on anywhere but my head.

"I don't know, B," I say softly.

There's silence again. Becky is usually pushy, but not this time.

"We'll talk later," she says. "And Lu? The new story... I love it. Keep it up."

I walk back into the bedroom and pull a drape off one of the smaller paintings of Jace.

It's a colorful impressionist sketch of him shirtless, the New York skyline behind him as he's wiping his mouth with the back of his hand and looking at the viewer.

It's so alive. So him.

I stroke his face with my finger, feeling suddenly too emotional.

Because he's home.
Home has acquired a different meaning lately.

37

LU

I press "PUBLISH," and my heart does a cartwheel as my newest chapters get uploaded to Story Den.

I've never felt so vulnerable. There's too much of me in it, too much of Jace. A lot of made-up stuff, but at its core, it's a story of falling in love, and I write it on the same timeline with my feelings.

The readers' response makes it worth it. My followers have tripled. I get dozens of messages every day.

Even now, as soon as the chapters go live, I look at the stats on my dashboard. Twenty-five people are currently reading them.

I knock on Jace's door. "Hey."

He opens it in sweatpants and a T-shirt that hugs his biceps, vines of tattoos peeking out from under it.

"Dinner? Wanna keep me company while I cook?"

I feel at peace being in the same personal space with him. But the feeling is laced with slight excitement at his closeness.

It's an oxymoron, but that's how he makes me feel—cold and hot, calm like I'm with my best friend and slightly nervous like I'm on a date, safe like I'm with a powerful man and edgy like I'm about to discover some secrets I don't want to know. There are a lot of things Jace doesn't tell me, and it strangely reminds me of the plot twists in my novel.

"Baked chicken with onion and garlic in a mayo-sriracha marinade," I tell Jace as he follows me into the kitchen. "Boiled potatoes and a vegetable salad on the side. Sounds good?"

"Anything you make sounds good," he says as he takes a seat at the kitchen island and watches me.

He asks me about Eastern-European food and the differences in Russian, Belarusian, Polish, and Ukrainian cooking. I tell him what I know, then ask him about his favorite food while I'm making dinner.

"Anything, really. I like trying new things. I never got to eat anything different from what they served in the group home. Not even fast food. And the army didn't have many choices. Believe it or not, I spent my first allowance on food. And silly things, like movies and books and gadgets. The first time I went to a movie theatre, I was seventeen. The first fast food—same, both courtesy of Ruth, our janitor at the group home, who took several of us to a movie and then bought lunch. So I like it all."

I can't imagine what it's like to consider a movie theatre trip special or fast food a treat. I curse at myself, wishing I'd cooked something more elaborate.

An hour later, Jace takes the plates and bowls of food out to the terrace as I follow with glasses of water and a bowl of food for Pushkin.

"It's dinner à trois[1]," Jace announces as we sit down at the table, and Pushkin's bowl dings against the floor as he chows down his food.

The sun is setting over Manhattan, coloring the East River with an orange-pink glow. The buildings across the river drown in luminous colors. This feels like a date.

I try to start conversations, but they don't go anywhere. There's this subtle tension between Jace and me. Every time I look at him, his lips remind me of our kiss days ago. And he keeps his eyes down, unusually quiet, occasionally leaning down to fix the bowl with dog food that Pushkin keeps pushing all over the place.

We finish dinner without much talk.

"Did you like the food?" I ask. "It's my mom's favorite dish."

"Yes. It's the best chicken I've ever had."

"Noooo. You are so flattering me."

"I'm not. And the best boiled potatoes. And salad. And…"

"The best water."

We laugh.

"There's this recipe I want to try. Beef Stroganoff. My mom cooks it, but it's time-consuming. You'll be my guinea pig, trying all the new dishes."

Jace smiles, staring down at his plate. "Thank you for cooking."

"My pleasure. It's nice to have someone to cook for. B is not a big stay-at-home person. Neither is Tito. They'd rather go to restaurants."

I keep talking, only after some time noticing that Jace sits motionless, his eyes on the plate.

I go quiet.

Did I say something to upset him?

The distant sounds of the traffic from the street reach even up here. A police siren somewhere far, screeching brakes, and honking. The breeze is nice, and it feels like we're sitting on top of the world.

The sun is setting, the orange and pink glares dancing along the steel railing and the windows of the nearby buildings. The dark blue-gray of the eastern sky is pushing the pinks to the west.

I should paint New York like this—the concrete jungle drowning in liquid orange.

"I've been in this city for over a year and never had a rooftop dinner," I say quietly, gazing at Manhattan in the distance. "Until now. Until you, Jace. I never loved this city so much either."

Until you.

Jace lifts his eyes to Manhattan Bridge. "You know, besides Roey and my army buddies, no one has ever cooked dinner for me," he says quietly with so much sadness in his voice that my heart clenches with tenderness.

I study his hair, his face, and the sharp edge of his jaw that seems to soften when he smiles. I've painted it so many times, I know his face by heart.

Feelings surge through me.

Jace takes my breath away, especially in moments like this. Not when he's happy or dangerous or dancing, but when he's quiet like this, when his strength lingers on the surface. The strength of someone who grew up on his own, who knows the value of things, appreciates others' kindness, learned to carry on in life without complaints no matter what happens because there never was anyone to complain to.

"You know, I learned what it's like to have friends from movies," he says quietly.

He tells me about the group home he lived in and why he enlisted in the army as soon as he turned eighteen. And I let him talk about his past, because he rarely does and because I want to know everything about him.

"The army was a better option than anything I knew," he explains. "I didn't have a family, a place to go, or a particular career in mind. I needed a direction."

"Why a group home? Were you a bad kid?"

"Not at all. Just shitty luck, I guess." He shrugs. "I wasn't exactly the A-team either. And I wanted to be. And not a bully but the guy who saves the world, you know."

He smiles, but it's not a happy smile, and he doesn't look at me but stares at his plate again.

This is the first time I see him so vulnerable.

I don't know what to say to make him feel better, so I say the silliest thing that comes to mind.

"I'd cook every day if you saved me from Becky and Tito and the outings they drag me to." An awkward chuckle escapes me. "I'll cook tomorrow if you are home," I add softly.

"It's… Thank you." A smile flickers on Jace's lips, but he wipes it off with his thumb—a gesture that I learned means he's shy or uneasy.

Truth is, I never had anyone to share quiet evenings like this. This is New York City. Everyone feels obliged to keep up with the trendy events and go to the busiest places. Missing out is the biggest fear. Staying at home on weekends is a crime. But for the first time, I feel like being a criminal and breaking the city rules.

I steal a glance at Jace.

Something's wrong.

"Hey, do you want more potatoes? Salad? I can—"

"One second." Jace rises from his chair so abruptly that I stall in surprise as I watch him walk inside.

Pushkin follows him for several feet then turns and cocks his head at me.

Five minutes later, Jace comes back, the hair around his face damp, his eyes unusually sparkly. He gives me a strained smile as he picks up our plates.

"This was super nice, thanks, Lu," he says as if nothing happened. "Wanna watch a movie?"

Pushkin puts his head on my lap, and I pat him, then lean over to plant a little kiss on his nose. "Wanna watch a movie, buddy?"

"Hey, Lu?"

I raise my eyes to Jace, whose playfulness is back. "I wasn't asking him."

Touché.

His lips start spreading in a smile, and my heart suddenly feels too big for my chest.

Jace cleans the dishes.

I put the leftovers in the fridge.

By the time we're done, the sun has set, and I don't turn on the light, the glow from the TV illuminating the living room. The curtains and the door to the terrace are wide open, showing off the skyline sparkling with skyscrapers' lights.

"*Knockin' On Heaven's Door*," I announce, putting on my favorite movie. "With Til Schweiger and Jan Liefers. About two guys who run away from a hospital for the terminally ill and chase their dream."

"What's their dream?" Jace asks, settling on the couch, his back against the pillow on the side arm, legs on the couch, one leg bent at the knee propped against the back.

I quickly take in his pose as I perch on the opposite side of the couch.

"The dream is to see the ocean," I explain. "Because both guys are about to die. And '*Because,*'" I imitate Til Schweiger's voice though I'm bad at it, "'*that's all they talk about in heaven — the ocean.*'"

I laugh as I toss the remote control onto the table.

"I like the ocean," Jace murmurs.

Pushkin puts his front paws on the couch against Jace's leg, ready to jump in.

"Look at you, brat," I taunt Pushkin. "Getting all the attention and all the best spots."

"That's because no one else is taking it."

What?

I turn to Jace.

Gently, he pushes Pushkin away. "Off you go, *duratshina*." Then he lifts his eyes to meet mine and pats the couch between his legs, summoning me toward him.

My heartbeat spikes.

I shift on the couch and settle between his legs and lean with my back against his chest.

I can't relax. We've never done this before. Never cuddled. Never mentioned the kiss at the party.

Jace shifts, making more room for me, and I lean back, bending my bare leg and leaning it against his.

I wish he wore shorts too so I could feel his skin. I don't know what to do with my hands until his arms wrap around my waist, and I finally rest my hands on his.

I hope he doesn't feel my heart beating madly and pray no one calls or knocks on the door and breaks us apart.

The movie starts, but I have a hard time paying attention to it. I'm too aware of Jace's arms around me, and I'm afraid to move. It's easy to flirt when feelings aren't involved. When they are, you question everything. Every little move is significant. And me stroking Jace's hand with my thumb feels more outrageous than what my fictional characters do in bed.

I feel him breathing. *Feel* him, period. His heart is beating against mine, and it's so loud. His closeness is unbearable, but I shift to sink deeper against him.

He pulls his hand from under mine, and I curse for being too straightforward. But his fingers brush my cheek, then gently take my chin and turn my face up so I have nowhere to look but him.

He has the kindest eyes I've ever seen and the sexiest twinkle. Two in one. And those gorgeous lips that kiss so well.

"I can't stop thinking about you, Lu."

He leans in, and his lips touch mine in a soft kiss just like the night of the party.

"I've been thinking about kissing you for days," he whispers against my lips.

Me too, I want to say, but before I do, his mouth takes mine, and I forget about the words and only *feel*. Him. His lips opening mine.

His tongue brushing softly against mine. His arm around my waist tightening.

I'm not letting him go this time. I'll hold him kiss-hostage for so long that he'll have to fight me off.

So when he pulls away, I turn to my side in his arms so I can cup his face.

"I love kissing you," he says, his gaze like a caress.

"Can you kiss me more often?"

"Absolutely."

He kisses my smile, softly and gently.

I don't know what he wants. Maybe Becky was right, and he's just too nice to use me for a month or two or however long we have.

But I'm not as nice. I'll take one month. I'll take two. I'll take a chance of having a broken heart if only I can have more of him right now.

We kiss for what seems like the entire movie. And whisper-talk. And kiss again. His hands constantly move, stroke, caress like he's trying to figure out the many ways he can hold me in his arms.

When the movie is over, I don't want to let him go.

"Do we have to stop?" I whisper.

Jace chuckles. "No."

"Good."

He lowers his knee and shifts, pushing me to the side, against the back of the couch, until I'm wedged between the cushions and him.

"I can kiss you for hours, Lu baby," Jace whispers.

And he does.

---

1. *à trois* — *(French)* for three persons

38

JACE

THERE IS NO CHANCE I CAN SLEEP.

I fucking broke down during dinner. What I said was the truth. Lu is the first girl who cooked dinner for me. So it felt awkward at first. But then it dawned on me that Lu did it because she cared, that I was amidst something special that might never repeat.

And the desperation of wanting it to got the best of me.

That was what made the lump in my throat choke me up and hide in the fucking bathroom until I could breathe and talk again.

I'm grateful to be acknowledged and taken care of. But even more so to be gifted with a person like her.

This is the strangest thing about life. You have money, friends, a good job, and future plans. And when you are running on a Brooklyn street with a dart rifle, chasing a fugitive, you don't even know that the girl getting out of a random cab is your dream girl. You still have no clue when you shoot her by accident.

A prodigy sniper missing a shot for the first time in years—that's gotta be a serious sign.

But you still snooze when she smiles at you, and there's a shift in you, like you just stepped into an unknown territory. Your heart does an excited flip when she laughs and says you are cute, but you're still clueless. And only weeks later, when you know her by heart like you've been best friends since childhood, do you realize that this is it, her, *the one*.

I'm so fucking in love. I crave touching her and being touched, something most people take for granted. I crave the casualness of doing it every day, something I never experienced as an orphan.

I dream. I want a happily ever after, want a cute little apartment, or a villa on a Thai island, with a huge studio where Lu can paint without being afraid to ruin the floors. Paint on the walls, ceilings if she so chooses to, or my body. I'll take paint. And her. All of her.

I want to kiss her again. So bad it hurts. Every cell of my body is alive, sensing her across several walls and two doors as I lie on my bed and stare at the ceiling.

Her scent is in my nostrils. Flowery soap and paint. I want to bottle it.

I lick my lips, trying to trap her taste.

I think I'm going insane.

She's probably in bed, in her underwear and a T-shirt. Or pajamas? I would've given a million bucks just to be next to her, watch her sleep, and study her up close when she's unaware.

I just didn't have the fucking audacity to say, *"Hey, Lu, I'm crazy about you. Can I sleep in your bed? Nothing funny, I just feel like I'll fall apart if I don't watch you breathe. Never mind my creepy stare all through the night, or my boner that won't go away."*

Instead, I was a gentleman.

I'm in a New York State of mind—that's what they call it. They say every city has a heart. New York's is Brooklyn. Brooklyn is her. And my heart is where she is.

I wish I lived in this city. I wish I had a chance for something more than just a hookup.

I wish, I wish, I wish.

There are so many wishes, and one is clear as day—I want Lu. With me. Next to me. In my life.

She deserves better than a guy who lied his way into her house. She lets people into her life so easily. And here I am, just like that shady John Temple who Em is falling in love with.

But then I realize that I can't let this get away. I want to kiss her every morning when she gets up and make her coffee and learn how to cook so I can make dinners for her. I don't want her to worry about money, I have plenty. I want her to create beautiful art, and I want to inspire her to write unforgettable characters.

There's this constant wanting with her.

I need a distraction, and my favorite one lately is *Sharki*.

@MidnightLu released the new chapter earlier today, but before I got a chance to read it, she invited me for dinner.

Story Den it is.

My heart pumps nervously as I start reading about Em and John being attacked in their apartment. Em doesn't believe it's a coincidence. I'm sure it's not. It has to do with her past that's slowly being revealed through John's conversations she eavesdropped on.

I don't care about the plot anymore. I want more of Em and John together, more of her feelings.

And @MidnightLu delivers.

The attack earlier today left me shaken, but all my thoughts are about John.

We were being attacked, but I couldn't take my eyes off him. Accountants don't fight like this. They don't disarm five guys in minutes and beat them to a pulp.

I lie in bed, trying to calm my nerves. And all I can think of is John's hands cupping my face after he got rid of the thugs, his soft whisper, "It's alright. It's alright, baby. It's alright."

Baby.

He's never called me that.

I should be trying to sleep, but the sure way to release my tension—the *only* way lately—is to give in to my fantasies about John with my fingers sinking into the wet heat between my legs.

I wish he were here.

"Yes, John. Right there. Please," I whisper as I stroke myself.

I'm lost in my thoughts about him, my body steaming under the blanket, my fingers feverishly rubbing out the ache, when a barely audible sound that doesn't belong in my room makes my eyes snap open in the dark.

I gasp in momentary panic at the large shadow by the bed.

"Easy," the low voice calms me. John's.

The moonlight is so bright that I can see his sparkling eyes on me, a tiny smile on his lips, and the razor-sharp reflection of the moonlight on his dog tag. The tattoos covering his glorious shirtless body are like black vines.

He is only in his boxers.

He's here.

He sets his knee on the bed, the mattress dipping, and slowly tugs the blanket off me, uncovering my bare legs and thighs and my hand, clutching my shirt between them.

His gaze drops to my hand, then up my body, his large body looming over me as I lie vulnerable and exposed.

"Were you thinking about me, Em?" he drawls.

My breath hitches. "N-no?"

"No? That's disappointing. Then I'm in the wrong place."

But he doesn't move.

"I was," I whisper, swallowing hard and burning with shame.

He leans onto his hands. "You were? I hoped so. And were your naughty fingers touching yourself when you thought of me?"

He crawls between my legs, and I open them wider, inviting him in, letting go of my shirt that starts riding up, letting him know that I'm not wearing panties.

John's eyes dip to between my legs. "Show me how you missed me, Em," he drawls. "Bring your pretty fingers back to where they were and play with yourself. Don't be shy, baby. I want you as enthusiastic as you are when your door is locked."

He knows!

"Why would you think I did that?" I murmur as his fingers reach the strap of my shirt and pull it down, exposing my breasts.

"Because you smell like sex, Em." He pulls the other strap down, tugging my shirt down to my waist. "And I want you to smell like sex *and* me."

His face dips, and he places a soft kiss on my nipple, then flicks his tongue against it, setting my body on edge.

His fingers slide to the hem of my shirt and push it up as he lowers his head and kisses my stomach, then kisses lower, lower still, until his lips are exactly where my hand was just minutes ago.

"Would you like my lips right here? That little nub is calling my name. I think it's time we made a closer acquaintance, baby."

He pauses.

I hold my breath.

"I need you to answer, Em."

"Yes," I whisper.

"I can't hear you, Em."

"Yes," I say louder.

"I've been dreaming about this for a long time, Em."

His fingers tease me open and I moan at the first contact of his tongue against my core.

I stab the *"continue"* button, but this is it.

Stay tuned for the next episode!

I stay hard.

Holy shit!

My mind is a mess, and I look around like I got caught reading this in public.

Does she actually want me to sneak in on her at night?

I read the latest comments.

"Give me some Sharki."

"Love!"

"I need the next chapter. NOW!"

"I love how quiet and shy he is during the day and like a total alpha at night."

Yeah, women love alphas.

"You can't see someone's eyes in the moonlight. This is 8th-grade writing."

"Sharki is becoming my favorite book boyfriend!"

"What idiot would have a shark tattoo on his crotch..." "Ikr?"

"And then what? WHAT HAPPENS NEXT??? Next chapter OR ELSE..."

There are 1,431 comments and 15,000 reads in just several hours.

Is this for freaking real?

And I'm not talking about the highest reading score she's had in the three years she's been writing or the number of comments but the stark similarities between this Sharki and me. Down to every tattoo. Down to every piece of my clothes. What I do. How I talk. Unlike Konstantin in *Beautiful Vice*, John Temple feels real.

I go back to the previous chapter and see that my name was corrected to John.

Good.

But I still have the screenshot on my phone, and I double check it to make sure I didn't dream it up.

I have cold sweat and hot sweat. I'm dizzy, yet my body is rigid.

One thing is certain—I have a boner the size of the Empire State Building and harder than a diamond.

So, I do the most obvious thing. I reread the chapter with my hand in my sweatpants, obsessively trying to get Lu out of my system. At least, this way.

And I have an agenda. When Lu is not home, I need to get into her room to check if what she writes about in her stories is true.

That's when my phone dings with a notification.

A new chapter from @MidnightLu is here!

So she's not asleep and just uploaded another chapter.

RIP my sanity.

I swallow hard and read on.

39

LU

I AM SICK. MY EYES ARE RED SLITS. MY HEAD THROBS. DESPITE THE high temperatures outside, I'm chilly, so I throw on a pair of leggings and a hoodie with bunny ears. They are my comfort clothes.

It's raining outside. The living room and open kitchen are dim.

Jace is already pouring me coffee. "You okay?"

"I'm sick."

And judging by the way he looks, so is he.

"We both are, huh?" I smile at him weakly, wanting to wrap my arms around his neck and kiss him.

"I'm alright." He smiles. "Grits? With bacon?"

I shake my head. "I think I need to lie down."

"You need cold medicine." And he's already mixing an effervescent for me.

"You too," I say.

"Already took it. Trust me, you learn very quickly in the army that you don't get to call in sick."

"Ugh." I slump over the kitchen island, feeling like my head will fall off. "I need to work."

"You are taking a day off, Lu."

I shake my head. "I can't take days off. I have so much work."

But it's not the ache in my every muscle or the pounding head that makes me disappointed but the fact that last night felt magical, and now I feel like we are back to being roommates.

"You need food, trust me. You'll feel better," Jace says, and for the first time, he's making me breakfast as I sip Alka-Seltzer like it's an exotic cocktail—I love bubbles.

There's always a distance between us the next day after we get too close, and I don't know how to make it disappear.

When he's done cooking, he sets a plate with grits, eggs, and bacon strips in front of me. "Have some food."

I nod and force it inside me, spoon by spoon.

Jace sits down on the stool next to me and stares at his coffee cup.

Rain drums against the terrace railing outside. Clouds are heavy, weighing down on the city. I want to get cocooned in this apartment with Jace.

"Tell me more about you," I ask him, wanting to hear his voice.

I don't know what triggers those short confessions out of him, but I'm eager to listen.

He starts talking.

About growing up with dozens of kids who never went home because there was none.

The bruises from bullies and no one to confide in.

The janitor, Ruth, who was the closest person he had to a mother.

The girl he fell in love with only to find out he was a bet.

The children's cruelty, the harshest kind, because it blooms like a rotten flower in those who were never loved.

The boot camp that broke him at first but then made him stronger.

The army that saved him but also gave him the worst nightmares.

About meeting Roey.

The *Fifty Shades of Grey*—I laugh, then hold back tears, because learning about love from books has got to be the loneliest thing ever.

I learn about the months after him leaving the army, traveling to the cities on his bucket list, getting high in the Himalayans, getting tattoos, seeing the ocean for the first time, going to the zoo, going on a first date to a small fair. Doing all the things that normal people do before turning sixteen, but he was twenty-three and trying to catch up. And he's still catching up. And a girl, his roommate—me!—makes him breakfast for the first time in his life.

Jace laughs when he brings this up, and I fight a lump in my throat, staring at the stupid grits and hoping my tears don't drop into them.

His voice is low and soft as he sits hunched over the kitchen island and studies his hands that stroke the coffee cup as he talks. My heart aches for him, but he's smiling like he got blessed with the very little he got in his life.

"It'll take years to catch up and a lifetime to correct the karma or whatever it is that gave me... my strange childhood," he says. "But I'm happy. I think I broke the vicious cycle." He finally raises his smiling eyes at me. "Some people never do. Some people are born into everything they can possibly wish for and turn out for the worst."

How can he look so nonchalant while I feel like folding into myself?

My grits are cold.

My heart is hot.

I want to make him breakfast and lunch and dinner. Every day. And I want to touch him again.

I get off the chair and wrap my arms around him, giving him the tightest hug.

He might be fine, but *I* need a moment. I'm spoiled by things I take for granted—family, happy childhood, good education. Jace is so strong that I feel ashamed about ever complaining.

"Promise me something, Jace," I whisper, trying to steady my voice.

His hands cover mine. "Yes, Lu. Anything."

I want to record his whisper so I can hear his tender voice when I'm lonely.

"When you leave, when your work is done"—my chest shakes in a sob—"wherever you are, when you feel like talking or just being with someone, you call me."

He chuckles, his muscled body shaking against mine. "Sounds good."

"We'll stay in touch, won't we? Can we?"

I pull away so I can see a yes in his eyes. They are so close, the tenderness in them makes my knees weak.

"Absolutely," he whispers.

And that's where Becky was right and I was wrong. I wanted a chance with him, however short. And short I got. But now I want more, so much more, falling so fast, feeling so weak at the thought of losing him, that I bite into my lower lip to keep back a sob.

"Maybe, I won't leave," Jace says, studying my face.

My heartbeat spikes to incredible heights.

"Please, don't," I whisper.

My eyes drop to his lips. His to mine.

"Come here." He pulls me into him and kisses me.

We're sick, and I want to share everything with this guy, even the sickness, so he never feels alone again.

I want to kiss him for hours, days, to catch up on all the longing I've felt for him for weeks.

When I pull away, I bury my face in his neck, letting him stroke my hair, hoping that he doesn't notice the tears welling up in my eyes.

"Okay!" I pull away abruptly and walk toward the stove so he doesn't notice them. "Grits and bacon are cold. Warm-up?"

I feel better now.

He chuckles behind me, and I smile, wiping my wet cheek against my shoulder.

If I'm not ready to tell him about my feelings, at least I can feed the man who is claiming my heart.

40

JACE

I FEEL LIKE A NUCLEAR BOMB WENT OFF IN MY HEAD, LEAVING HEAT AND confusion in its wake. But I'm used to handling shit like this on my feet. A handful of cold medicine usually does the job.

Lu is wearing this plush hoodie with bunny ears, leggings, and yellow socks with red chilies.

Can any human look more adorable?

By afternoon, she's worse, her eyes sparkly with fever. But she diligently sits on a tabouret in front of the almost finished gothic portrait and paints the sky.

"I can do the background. It doesn't need much focus," she explains when I pop into her room.

I take Pushkin out and buy chicken soup and burgers from the small street joint down the street.

Lu never takes a minute to rest. "If I'm not productive, I should at least do something," she says and gives Pushkin a quick bath.

He strolls into my room with a new strawberry-patterned vest and sets his head on my bed.

"You got a bath, huh?" I pat my little dude, who smells like Lu's shampoo. "How does it feel when she washes you, huh? When she touches you?" I tease him in a jealous whisper. "You lucky bastard." I wish I were Pushkin. I could so snuggle in Lu's bed with her. "I don't think I like you right now. Go away."

And he does, leaving the trace of peach shampoo smell behind.

I think I'm gonna die from wanting Lu so much. My body is aching for her, and I don't know how to handle it. So I resort to the sure trick.

"It's movie time," I announce when it starts getting dark. "Come on, Lu."

I bring the blankets and make her cuddle with me.

"*Wasabi*," she says.

"Never heard of it."

"Jean Reno is in it, my favorite guy. He is in *The Professional*."

"I've seen *The Professional*."

"So good, right? He's a badass sniper. Lonely and charming and talented. And that girl. Ugh… I wish it had a happy ending. This one though takes place in Japan. I wanna go there someday."

But as soon as the movie is on, I start stroking her hair, and she smiles and leans into my hand.

"Jace," she whispers and raises her face to mine, her eyes dropping to my lips. "Are we actually watching a movie this time?"

I grin. "Sure. We are so good at it."

I lean in and kiss her. She scoots up and sneaks her hot palms under my shirt, and there's no fucking movie in the world that can keep my attention.

When the movie is over—I don't recall the name or the plot—Lu asks me, "Can you cuddle with me while I fall asleep?"

Fucking yes, Lu!

I do.

Who knew that my happiest would be when we are both at our lowest?

There's nothing like falling asleep with the girl of my dreams in my arms. I'm not sure I slept at all. This is the highlight of my life.

Waking up in Lu's bed still wrapped in each other? Surreal.

I feel better, sneak out of her room, and take a bunch of medicine to stay up on my feet.

An hour later, Lu texts me.

Lu: You ran away from me?

I chuckle and walk into her room with a cup of hot coffee.

"No, just woke up and took Pushkin out. And I'm bringing you coffee in bed. Tito will hate you. Especially when it comes with this—"

I lean over and kiss her.

That's right. About time we started our mornings like this. See? Roommates, friends, close friends, kissing, sharing a bed... I'm on the right track.

She cups my face, and I serve her the first taste of morning coffee on my lips and tongue.

I make breakfast for us. Look who's turning into a grits-pro! Then I make Lu come to the living room, and we spend a day watching movies. *Actually* watching movies, interrupted by occasional kissing.

"Do you think we get sicker when we do this?" she asks, wrapped around me, her lips planting little kisses on my face that make it hard to keep my body under control.

"Nah. I think it's medicine," I say, kissing her neck. "Do you feel better?"

She giggles and snakes her hands under my shirt.

In the evening, we order her favorite burgers from a small joint in Williamsburg and have dinner on the terrace.

She's in lime-green leggings and that cute plush white hoodie with bunny ears that she looks adorable in. Her nails are a wild lemon color. She loves colors. And burgers, stuffing one in her mouth in a not-so-sophisticated way.

I smile, watching her, forgetting about the burger in my hand.

"What?" She gives me a side-eye.

"You eat like Pushkin." I laugh, glancing at the mayo at the corner of her lips.

She makes a funny face with crossed eyes.

Fuck, our children would be cute as hell. I just decided that's my long-term goal.

She does feel better and cocks her pretty brow. "I'm spoiled by good food, you know. My mom is a fantastic cook."

"Is she?"

"Oh, she'll feed you like she's getting you ready for slaughter. And if you refuse to eat, she'll force-feed you. You'll like her. She's cool."

I will? Does that mean she told her mom about me?

Hey, Ma. There's this cute nerdy guy who rents a room from me. He's cool. He's an orphan, was in the service, is a former sniper, currently a bounty hunter, and is hunting your friend Reznik. Oh, and he totally shot me with a sedative the first night we met and lied his way into becoming my roommate.

That introduction would go real fucking well.

And yet, a guy can dream.

"Your dad is cool, too?" I want to know more, and not from the intel Miller gathered.

"My stepdad, yeah."

Wait, what? "Stepdad?"

"He's my dad. I only found out not long ago he wasn't my biological dad."

That's new. "You *know* your biological dad?"

She nods. "Mom told me when I was eighteen and introduced us."

"How did that go?"

Lu smiles. She's not angry, so it must not be so bad.

"He didn't know I was his. Mom decided she'd tell me when I was old enough. She was pregnant when they broke up, in fact, they weren't really together. And that's when she met my stepdad, and he took care of her and raised me like his own. Then Mom reconnected with my biological father and told him, then told me."

"How do you feel about it?"

"I was angry at first. At her." I can't picture Lu angry. "Then I thought about it and figured my mom had her reasons, and I love my dad to pieces."

That's Lu. She sees the best in people.

Miller never discovered this piece of info. I should tell him, but then I know what'll happen—we'll illegally snoop through every detail of Lu's family to find out about her biological father, and I don't want to do this to her.

Lu finishes her burger and wipes her lips, then gets up, walks to the railing, and gazes at the city for some time.

"Then I met my biological father." She exhales loudly. "I can't be mad at him, because he didn't know. Even requested a DNA test. Understandable. It's a weird scenario. My stepdad is understanding. So is my biological father."

"So, you are all good?"

Life can be a bitch and full of surprises. But Lu is the most positive person I've met.

I come over and wrap her in my arms. She sags against me, and we gaze at the setting sun for some time.

"He has an adopted son. But I'm his only biological child, and he started throwing money at me like he can buy the eighteen years back. And I can't have that. But we talk every month. We met up a bunch of times. I met his family, but I still have a hard time accepting money."

"Why?"

"Because I want to make it on my own and show my parents that I can help them. I send them money, you know. I guess, to prove that I have a talent that's worth something."

"Your biological father just wants to reconnect, Lu. I've never had a family. I would be excited to get to know them, I think, though I never got access to that info."

"I know. But… I need time. That's why I quit university. I wanted to make it big. Big dreams. Big aspirations. Look at me." She chuckles. "I live in someone else's place, renting out a room, scrambling in a small space, doing a dozen things at once."

She doesn't know how talented she is, how much I admire her and everything she does.

I let go and start stepping backward, studying her silhouette against the Manhattan skyline, the bridge, and the blazing sunset.

"It's the best view, isn't it?" She turns to look at me.

"Don't move," I murmur, taking my phone and snapping a picture of her silhouette against the orange sky, her hair blowing in the wind.

I love you, Lucy Moor.

I'm so fucking in love that I can't even breathe.

She smiles, and I snap another shot.

She laughs.

Another shot.

She is the best view I've ever had.

I come back and wrap my arms around her again, pressing my cheek against hers.

"You are doing great, Lu," I say, wanting to encourage her.

"I don't know, Jace…"

"You are. This city is already yours. Some people love you so much that they'll always be by your side no matter what."

She turns her head and meets my eyes, the blue abyss of hers so close to mine that I feel my breath hitch in my throat.

"And you? Will you be by my side?"

She's searching my face for the answer and doesn't even know that I'll trade the entire world for a minute with her.

"Anything you want, Lu," I whisper and kiss her.

My body is burning up but not from fever. *She* is my new fever, and I want to burn to ashes.

41

JACE

They drink a lot in New York City. Also meet up all the time, eat out, shop, go to parks, galleries, and try out new venues.

They say New York City is expensive. If you are young and can't sit at home—sure.

Tonight is someone's gallery opening night.

"Important," Becky says, so Lu has to attend.

The surprise? She invites me *and* Roey.

"Becky said the more people the better," Lu explains.

I have a feeling Becky is interested in Roey.

The second surprise is Roey agrees to come.

"I'm not wearing a dress shirt, Roey," I argue when he stops by the condo to pick me up.

Lu left earlier to meet up with Becky, and Roey takes his time studying my clothes like I'm auditioning for a GQ cover.

"Jace, it's black, and you look good in it."

"I don't want to overdress."

"It's called style. And you want to impress Lu."

"Do I really?"

"Maybe not her but her friends. Becky is a friend-whisperer, and trust me, if you want to get the girl, you have to do a good job with her friends."

"Becky likes me."

"I doubt she likes anyone very much except herself."

"I think I can handle it."

"Yeah? How is it going so far?"

"Good."

"On Jace Reed's scale? That means it might take half a year until you kiss Lu again?"

"Fuck off."

"I have some Ambien on me to chill you down."

I stare at Roey. "Da fuck? Dude, no!"

"You need to relax and finally make a bold move on her. Even women don't have as much patience in the sex department as you do."

"I'm not taking your shit."

Ambien pills are Roey's way out of occasional panic attacks. It has nothing to do with his confidence. Roey is a stud by any woman's definition. Red silk shirt, unbuttoned way too low, gold chain peeking over his dog tag, jeans, and sneakers.

"You are obviously dressed to impress," I comment.

"Hoping to rope in that feisty thing."

"Becky?"

"She reminds me of a black widow spider." Roey puts an unlit cigarette between his lips and pauses his gaze on me.

"Don't they kill the male after mating?"

"They're horny and initiate the mating." He chuckles. "Becky is a user, just like me. She's wild. When her mouth is preoccupied with something besides her snappy blabbering, I'll like her much better and make sure afterward that she likes me even more."

Roey is in one of his darker moods. I know all of them by now. His sleepless eyes are reddish and way too sparkly. He's taken a shower, dressed and cologned too meticulously. That's meant to disguise a two-day binge and the smell of booze. I can tell he's had a few today already. The fact that he has Ambien on him is a shitty sign.

This doesn't happen often. Usually, this means he's going through a phase, which normally ends on a light binge, sleepless nights, sometimes light drugs, always girls, more than one, who disappear as quickly as they appear. After a week or so, as if by miracle, Roey is back to normal, clean, straight-headed, a worka-holic, and a recreational drinker who has a grip on his issues.

I love when Roey is happy. But I've seen him in his lowest lows. PTSD is a bitch and can bring even the strongest men to their knees.

Women, though, really like Roey in his dark phase. He's loose, confident, playful, sharp-tongue, and hard-wired. *Hard*, period, splurging and willing to please.

And that's what he's like when we walk into the gallery in northern Brooklyn, eyes turning toward us, mainly at Roey.

I might say thank you to Roey, because Lu's eyes widen, taking me in when we approach.

But I'm pretty sure I've never seen Becky stare. She does. At Roey.

He winks at her. "She likes me," he whispers to me.

"Stay away from Lu's friends."

"Why?" he dismisses my warning. "Fuck, she's even hotter when I'm sober. That's unusual."

He's not sober. But Becky *is* hot in an orange designer jumpsuit with super-low cleavage and stiletto boots, her lush hair twisted on top of her head in a slick bun.

"Are you talking about me?" Becky saunters over, hips swaying in a seductive warning. She's clearly trying to show herself off to Roey.

We get drinks, and before I know it, Roey brings another round as we make our way through the exhibition.

I wrap my arm around Lu, which catches Becky's attention, and she gives me a tiny approving nod. That's new.

The exhibition is a maze. Red lighting, dim corridors, and some crazy installation art that doesn't make sense. That's the key these days. The less you understand something, the more trendy it gets. The shock factor is a draw.

I'm feeling really good, but this place sucks. I want different music, something more chill. I want to sit down or splay on a bed. Everything makes me smile. Lu is happy and laughs, looking amazing in her high heels and a flowery summer dress.

Just two months ago, she was a random girl who stepped into my scope vision. Now, she openly kisses me on the cheek and bats her eyelashes at me. In fucking public. Whoa. I feel like a peacock, wanting to spread my bushy tail and puff out my chest.

"This show sucks," she whispers to me, on her third cocktail already, and I laugh like a fool. We think alike.

After being sick for several days, we feel like we got reborn. So we celebrate.

Tito shows up an hour later with a guy in a suit and wearing glasses. So, Tito is into serious guys. And into glasses.

"Who's that? Another rebound?" I ask Lu.

"Actually, that's Jamie, his ex. Or current—I guess we'll find out soon enough. The one he needs a rebound from."

"Oh."

"They are in love, but Tito is a party-head, and Jamie is a little older, and still in the closet."

"Right."

I feel happy. It takes me some time to realize that I'm suspiciously way too relaxed.

Lu is tipsy too. "You look dreamy, Jace. I like it. I'm gonna go network." She says the word like she hates it.

Roey chuckles. "See? You just needed a little push."

"What push?"

He gives me puppy eyes.

Oh, no. I know that fucking look. He's up to something.

"Roey?" I warn him.

"Yes, Jace?" he mimics.

"What's up?"

"Feeling good, buddy?"

"Yeah. I'm fine. I—" Then it hits me. "You did *not*."

"I did."

"You are a fucker. You—" Spiked me! My best friend fucking slipped Ambien into my drink. "You kidding me?"

Roey's gaze scans the crowded gallery space. "It's mild. I gave you enough to relax. Give yourself another half an hour. I suggest you make it home by then. With Lu."

For a moment, anger spikes in me. "Ruined it, man, thanks," I hiss.

"You'll thank me later."

"I'll be a silly goof." I know what that shit does mixed with alcohol. Roey doesn't understand that my tolerance is not nearly as high as his. "Thanks for ruining the freaking evening. I'm leaving."

I want to be mad, except I'm lightheaded and feeling fantastic. I just need to stay away from Lu before I say some nonsense. I'll go home. I'll chill. I'll take Pushkin out. It'll wear off before Lu gets home.

Roey walks off to get another drink.

Tito is nowhere to be found, but Jamie approaches me for the first time. "So, you know Tito?"

I don't know Jamie but I like him right away because he's Tito's friend.

"Yeah. I'm Lu's roommate," I say, taking a sip of my drink and scanning the packed gallery.

It's somehow unfair to say *roommate*.

I don't like the word anymore.

I should tell him she's the love of my life.

And she writes spicy stories inspired by me.

And paints me.

And cooks for me.

And if we were in medieval times and there was a competition for her hand, I'd kick everyone's ass to marry her.

Because I'm a badass.

But she doesn't know it.

And it's okay.

And I'm a virgin.

And that's okay too.

Because I've been waiting for someone like Lu for years.

Oooooh, fuuuuuck.

I feel like talking. My thoughts are a mile a second, but they are floating and constantly changing, and I lose track of them.

Fucking Roey and his tricks.

"So, you and Tito hang out a lot?" Jamie asks, studying me up and down like he's trying to figure out whether I shagged Tito.

I wanna say that Tito is cool.

And if I were gay, I'd so shag him.

But I'm not.

And Tito is hung up on *him, Jamie.* No matter how much he tries to hide it and find a rebound.

"Sometimes," I say. "Tito is cool." I smile, though there's nothing funny about the statement.

"He probably made a move on you, huh?" Jamie takes a gulp of his drink and looks around with a sarcastic smirk. "He's like that."

I see now. They are back together. This dude is in the closet, yet he can't stand when Tito openly flaunts his sexuality and gets too much attention from others. Nor can this guy handle his jealousy.

"You know, I don't have many friends," I say. "But it'd be a privilege to have a friend like Tito. I hope one day we will be. I hope one day, you can flaunt your feelings for him as openly as he does for you."

I might've lied. Tito never talked to me about Jamie, but I've heard a lot from Lu. That's not the point. Sometimes you just need to state the obvious.

I walk off before I say that Jamie is lucky to have Tito's skillful hands at his service.

And Tito's dancing skills are top-notch.

So is his sense of humor.

And he has a dirty mouth when he's drunk.

And if Jamie really loves him, he should man up and choose Tito over other people's crappy opinions about sexuality.

Shit, I'm either waisted or... Right.

Dammit!

It's the fucking drug that makes me wanna spill my thoughts out.

"I'm going home," I tell Lu when I find her in the crowd chatting with a group of people she knows.

"Why?"

"I think I drank too much."

"Yeah, not good. You alright?" She places both her palms on my chest and leans over. "This place is boring," she whispers.

It is! And I feel fucking fantastic!

My senses are too heightened right now, and I can't stay away, so I pull her into a kiss, wanting to strip her naked, and she pulls back, giggling in surprise.

Yeeeeaah, I gotta go.

"I'm gonna bounce," I say. "You don't mind, do you? Becky wants to party tonight, so have fun. Text me later. Make sure you don't walk home alone."

Shut up, Jace.

I can't believe I'm trying to get rid of my girl, but it's better than embarrassing myself while I'm high.

"Wait a second. I'll be right back," Lu says then disappears into the crowd.

I wanted to spend time with her tonight, but the fucker—I find Roey in the crowd looks around, his gaze following Becky who strides across the gallery with exaggerated seductiveness I haven't seen in her before—catches me looking and winks.

Dick.

I should just nerd out and watch a movie or take a walk by the river. Yeah, I'll get some fresh air. That'll fix it. There are many thoughts in my head, but they are all gooey and vague. Happy, too. An image of me licking Lu's body flickers again and again in my mind.

I need to fucking *go*!

Lu smiles widely as she pushes through the crowd back to me. "Alright, all set."

"What is?"

"Oh, nothing, I just had to tell Becky a couple of things. But it's done. We can go."

I smile. "We? Go where, Lu?"

She grins. "Home! I'm so bored with this place, Jace. And I don't want to party. Unless it's with you. Let's go!"

She wraps her gentle hand around my arm, and my heart squeals like a kid on his first roller coaster ride—she chose me over everyone else.

I'm so happy.

So high.

And so, so screwed.

42

LU

"ROEY DRUGGED ME," JACE TELLS ME WHEN WE GET IN THE CAB.

"What?"

His arm slides around my waist, pulling me toward him. "It's a chill pill," he murmurs, burying his face in my hair. "It just makes one happy."

"Are you happy?"

He nuzzles my cheek. "Me?"

I try to study him, see an actual effect on his face. But his lips hitch in a smile, and he rubs his nose against mine.

"I'm always happy when I'm around you, Lu baby," he murmurs and starts kissing me softly, teasing little pecks that make me grin.

"I love when you call me that," I confess, wrapping my arms around his neck. "And the way you talk. Especially right now."

He buries his face in my neck. "You smell so good." His tongue licking my skin makes me giggle. "And taste even better."

He's a talker tonight.

Thank you, Roey.

"Your place or mine?" He chuckles against my neck.

I burst into laughter, happy like a freaking puppy.

Jace's hands sneak under my skirt.

Well, hello, Sharki.

I don't know if it's the pill or if Jace is getting comfortable with me, but I like this side of him—slightly rough, insistent, his hands so confident as they roam my body.

He pulls me into him, pulls my legs over his lap, and palms my butt, squeezing it. His body is solid and warm. It's like a magnet, drawing me in with every touch.

"I am so devouring you when we get home," he whispers.

We. Home. Devouring.

My head spins at the promise.

His lips find mine, and we sink into the back seat as our bodies twine together.

"Lu, I wanna touch you everywhere," he whispers. His velvety tongue licks into my mouth gently but insistently. "I wanna lick you. Every-fucking-where."

"Jace," I whimper against his impatient mouth. "You are making me blush."

"I'll make you blush *everywhere*, too." His hands don't stop moving over my body. "I want to touch myself, and touch you, and have you touch me, and then...yeah..."

His lips are on my neck, trailing open-mouthed kisses down to my shoulder. I melt into him, wanting to touch him everywhere too.

I'm tipsy. The cab music is soft. I don't want this to stop. But the cab halts, and I have to pull Jace off me.

"We are here," I murmur, flushed and hot, wanting to sprint up to the eleventh floor so we can carry on.

"Right here," Jace echoes, nuzzling my ear and peppering my neck with kisses.

I chuckle and pull him off of me. "Jace, we are home! Let's go!"

"Oh, right."

He ruffles his hair and looks around wildly like I pulled him out of his dream, then helps me out of the cab.

We hold hands and kiss as we hurry through the Goldsling Towers' lobby, then make out in the elevator, then stumble into the condo, kissing and grabbing at each other.

Jace gently pushes me against the wall by the door, his hands everywhere on me.

"I want to kiss you all over. Your smile"—he brushes his fingers against my lips, then licks them—"Your body"—his hands glide down my torso—"Your legs"—he slides down my body and takes off my shoes. "Your impossibly long legs," he whispers as he kisses my thighs, slowly rising, his hands following his mouth, until his face is above me and his hands are under my skirt.

Ambien can't turn you into someone you are not. It just brings out the more intense you. And Jace is a lover.

"I love when you talk like this," I murmur, burning up at his touch.

His hands leave my thighs and slide up to cup my face.

"You are a dream, Lu. You make me feel like the sun shines on me when you are around." He kisses me softly, and my heart flutters at the words. "I wanna lick that sunshine." I chuckle. "Wanna lick you like a popsicle. Head to toe."

I'm blushing.

I'm hot.

I'm grinning.

I want his hands in other places that are pulsating with need. I'll be a popsicle. Anything he wants.

He palms my butt again and picks me up, my legs instantly wrapping around his waist.

His smile is beautiful as he carries me to my bedroom. His eyes are sparkly and dilated.

"I'm gonna take you to bed, Lu, but maybe you should tell me to go away."

"Why?"

"I'll do naughty things to you."

"You should," I whisper.

"That's it, then. You are in trouble."

He kicks the door of my bedroom closed and flips the light switch.

He's so swift and smooth, and I'm so taken with his kisses that I don't register when and how he does things to me until I'm on my back on my bed and he's on top of me.

"You know what I think about when I'm in bed?" He starts kissing my shoulders.

"I don't," I whisper. *Tell me.*

He slides the straps of my dress off, kissing my chest, then starts pulling my dress down with the bra.

I hold my breath as he slowly pulls it down to my waist, baring my upper body.

"These." He kisses my breasts, soft pecks on my skin, making my body simmer with need.

"Jace," I exhale as he licks one of my nipples, then places little kisses around it.

I hold back a moan, and he does the same to the other one.

"You know what else I think about?" He glances up at me with a mischievous smile. "What color panties you wear." He kisses between my breasts. "And how often you change them when you write your spicy stories."

Wait, what?

I told him that, right?

He trails soft kisses down my stomach as his hand caresses my hip.

"I wonder what you think about when you touch yourself."

"You," I breathe out as he pushes my skirt up to my waist and kisses my thighs.

"Me," he echoes, shifts to sit back on his heels between my legs, and slowly lifts my legs onto his shoulders.

His eyes are ablaze as he takes me in, my dress and bra bunched around my waist, my panties still hiding a small part of me.

Without breaking eye contact, he turns his head and kisses my leg on his shoulder, then goes up to my ankle, then my foot.

Who taught him to kiss like this?

"I like your feet, Lu baby."

Lu baby...

I'm losing my mind.

He trails the kisses back down my calf, to my knee, and leans over, making my legs bend over his shoulders.

"Have you ever been kissed here?"

Another kiss on the inside of my thigh, his mouth dangerously close to my panties.

"No," I exhale. My ex-boyfriends weren't exactly inventive or even remotely creative in bed.

"You wanna make friends with my tongue, Lu baby?"

His hot whisper drives me insane. The words make me seep

with want and hot in those places that—yes, yes, yes—want to make friends not just with his tongue. Let's be friends!

His lips get so close to my soaked panties that a needy whimper escapes me.

His hands gently push my legs off his shoulders.

"Lu, I'm gonna take your panties off," he murmurs, and I whisper, "Yes."

Hurry up!

Slowly, he sits up and pulls them down my legs, baring me, then brings them to his nose and inhales.

This is Sharki. This is so hot, especially when he tosses them aside, then leans and kisses the insides of my thighs again, inching closer to my junction.

I feel the little licks of his tongue. Feel too exposed. Too turned on.

"My tongue likes you, Lu."

"I like it too," I whisper, holding back another whimper.

"Then open up for me." He parts my thighs. "Wider. Yeah, like this, baby. There you are, Lu."

And when he kisses me right there, where the heat burns through me, I moan.

His fingers join in, teasing me open.

His tongue licks fire into me.

Who *is* this guy?

I'm falling so fast and so deep that my thighs instinctively open for him even wider, and my mind shuts off.

The shyness of being so open for him fades away as I let him do what he wants between my thighs.

And he does. With his lips. His tongue. His fingers. Driving me over the edge so quickly that I forget to hold back as I cry out at the sudden burst of tension that explodes at his touch and surges through my body.

That's my first, I tell myself, the vague thought lost among a dozen others. That it felt fantastic. That Jace is still down there, soothing the tension with soft kisses. That I should be embarrassed. That he's an expert. That I've written scenes like this in stories dozens of times. Oral is a hot trend, but it's my first. That I should—

Jace slowly drags his tongue along my center all the way to my belly button, and I think I do blush everywhere and hold my breath when his playful eyes meet mine.

He kisses his way up my body, and I want to do the same to him —make him moan, see him unravel at my touch.

"You are beautiful, Lu," he murmurs, reaching my face and peppering it with soft kisses as I slide my fingers into his hair. "Especially when you moan for me. And open up so beautifully." I close my eyes, wanting to bottle his voice. "You taste so good. Like sunshine."

I'll come again if he keeps talking like this.

"Jace, I want to see you naked."

"Yes, ma'am."

He smiles, sits back between my legs, and slowly pulls his shirt over his head.

He's not in a hurry. His movements are slow and lazy. His eyes are unbelievably sparkly.

I take him in, his strong muscles and dark tattoos, acutely aware that I'm splayed naked in front of him.

He leans in to kiss me again.

"Jace." I gently push on him, turning him onto his back.

He lies back, grinning. "Yes, Lu?"

He cushions his head with his forearm and dreamingly studies me, his other hand reaching to stroke my hair.

I want everything all at once—to study his tattoos, kiss his body, let him kiss me in other places again, and finally be with him the way I want to. I'm so wet, I feel like I'm drowning. But I need to clean up.

"Stay right here. Don't move. I'll be right back."

I rise from the bed, push down the dress and bra, shimmying out of them, and pad to the bathroom.

The light there is too bright. My hair is a mess. My bare skin is lightly red from Jace's kisses, and I grin like a fool as I clean up real quick and give myself a last glance in the mirror.

Finally, I have him.

I walk out into the bedroom, burning with the anticipation of undressing Jace and seeing his naked body, all mine, for the entire night.

Jace is splayed on the bed just the way I left him, his eyes closed, his head turned to the side. His powerful body is a beautiful sight, the tattoos dark against my light-blue sheets, his dog tag glistening in the light of the night lamp.

But I halt at the sound that cuts off my fantasies.

Jace is snoring.

43

JACE

SHIT, SHIT, SHIT.

I wake up next to Lu. Still in my clothes.

I fucking fell asleep last night…

Lu is cuddled up to me, and I slowly move away and stumble out of her room.

It's nine in the morning. I feel dizzy like I woke up from a coma.

Shower, change of clothes, and I'm off to take Pushkin out, then spend half an hour in my room, listening to the sounds of Lu in the kitchen as she talks on the phone, arranging to meet someone.

She doesn't leave as if she's waiting for me.

I wanna lick you like a popsicle.

Embarrassment washes over me like hot lava.

Seriously? I said that?

I'll fucking kill Roey. Who the fuck spikes his own friend?

Finally, I step out of my room.

"Coffee?" Lu smiles at me.

She's dressed in ripped jeans and sandals, a yellow silk scarf around her neck in contrast with her baby-blue tank.

Color rises to her cheeks, and she looks away as I start fussing with the coffee like a dumbass.

I don't know if she's upset with me for passing out, wants to talk about it, or if she wants me around at all.

"I'm meeting up with Becky at the gallery. I'll see you later?"

Yep, she's leaving, not meeting my eyes.

"Okay." What do I say? Do I even bring up the last night?

"Alka-Seltzer is in the drawer," she says from the door. "If you have a headache."

"Yeah." I fake a laugh. "I drank too much last night."

No, I didn't. I was high. And I *did* mean everything I said. It's just I would've never dared say that if I were sober.

But I can't look at Lu, can't even look at Pushkin.

"Right." She sounds almost disappointed, then picks up her purse and keys and opens the front door.

"I really liked last night," she blurts and shuts the door behind her.

It was bad enough before, but now, there's a slideshow of explicit images in my head—my hands pulling her panties off, revealing the parts of Lu I want to see again. And kiss. And taste.

She's bare down there, with a little landing strip. Yes, it's confirmed. My body stirs to life at the memory faster than after an electric shock.

And yes, that oral scene was in her latest chapter. Except John Temple wasn't drunk or high. He was sober and confident, made Emily Aberdeen ride him afterward, and the next day gave her an encore.

Finally, I understand the idea of hormones riling up.

Heard the expression "live in the moment"? Yeah, it wasn't about my life. My teenage hormones were overridden by my desperation to get out of the hole that was the group home and find the future no one told me I could have. I didn't have the energy for girls when every day was a struggle to escape bullying.

Now I want to slow down. Since I met Lu, I want to cherish every day. She was worth the wait.

The hormones? Holy hell do I have a hard time keeping them in check.

I'm obsessively replaying the previous evening in my mind, getting hard in the process, getting anxious about her bringing it up later, and wondering if she even enjoyed it, because my memory is hazy.

My eyes stop on the closed door to Lu's room.

Don't.

I feel bad about doing any more spying, but I need to set the facts straight—the paintings mentioned in her novel. Especially after last night.

My heart starts pounding in my chest as I come up to her door and twist the door knob.

The first thing that hits me is her scent. It's so much stronger in her room. A mix of her peach shampoo and candles set up on the floor, her sweet perfume and chemicals—paint thinner, acrylics, and gesso that she primes her canvases with.

I take my time studying everything around me.

The shelf I built for her is fully stacked and a mess. My Lu is walking chaos. There are clothes on the bed and the chair.

Her light-blue panties are on the floor. I make a move to pick them up then stop myself.

There are more canvases than I remember from last time.

The almost-finished giant gothic one is against the wall. It's gorgeous and haunting, with a villainous regal couple in the center, ravens and skulls, a dark eerie sky and a castle in the background.

There's a new large canvas against the opposite wall, the blue sky and white clouds, and a stork carrying a teddy bear amidst the military jets that shower the warheads down onto the viewer.

Stacks of smaller canvases lean against the walls here and there.

I pull aside the drape that hides one of them and freeze, looking at the first one.

You don't always recognize yourself in artistic form, but Lu is too good.

Me. I'm staring at myself.

I pull it aside and look at another one.

My face. With glasses. A black hoodie over my head.

I come over to another stack leaning against the opposite wall and go through it.

Me, sleeping on the bed.

Me, with Pushkin.

Me, jogging.

Me, shirtless, a torso-long portrait with tattoos that are identical to mine but with fewer details.

When did she study them?

I pull another one from the stack, and my heart stalls.

It's me again, a full-body portrait, from the back. Naked...

When has she seen me naked? She hasn't.

But the tattoos on the canvas are unmistakably mine. My face is lifted upward, my hands rubbing my neck. I'm painted in long messy strokes, my body exactly as I see it in a mirror, my bare ass holding my gaze longer than it should. It's so... erotic.

Fuck, this painting is sex. It's lust. It's making me want to put it in the living room and, as soon as Lu gets home, confront her and do all sorts of dirty things to her.

Lick her like a popsicle head to toe.

God help me!

There's a sketchbook on Lu's nightstand. I open it and go through random sketches of hands, subway riders, the Verrazano Bridge. There's a bar scene. I recognize Tito.

Phew, so she sketches her other friends, not just me.

And then, by the end of the sketchbook, there's me again. My portraits, with glasses, without glasses, me in the kitchen with a coffee, me against the Manhattan skyline on the terrace, my back to the viewer, Pushkin next to me.

There's a sketch of my shark tattoo.

Oh, hell.

It ends at the line of my sweatpants.

Oh, Lu...

My heart expands threefold, and I feel something tugging at it so powerfully that it gets hard to breathe.

She does like me.

She does paint me.

In every. Fucking. Detail.

I didn't imagine it. I'm not a fool. I do have a chance.

Jace Reed, I tell myself, *if you don't get your shit together, you might miss the biggest chance of your life—getting your dream girl.*

44

JACE

Roey and I are off to an assignment in Ohio.

As usual, it's unexpected, Roey yanking me away like he does this on purpose.

"You need to clear your head," he says. "And it's an easy job."

The job is a runaway teenage son of a tech millionaire. Obviously, the kid has his father's brain since no private investigator could locate him.

Well, Miller is our tech guy for a reason. There's nothing he can't find. Except Reznik, apparently.

I text Lu.

Me: I'm off to Ohio. I'll be back after the weekend.

Lu: Hurry!

Me: Miss you already.

A new chapter is uploaded to Story Den.

Every new one is a clue about Lu, what she likes, or perhaps what she expects from me.

John is away on a work trip, which is obviously not accounting, but he still won't tell me what he does.

The recent attack in our apartment wasn't random, but he won't talk about it. Nor will he talk about the night we spent together. He acts like nothing happened.

Without him, the apartment feels empty. I leave the door to his room open, so it feels like he's home.

Bacon in the morning reminds me of him as I sit and eat my grits alone, with an empty plate on his side of the table. It makes me feel like he might walk in any moment.

Our puppy huffs and puffs as he walks into John's room and lies down in the middle of the floor, in front of his bed. He misses John too.

Loneliness is tangible. I never quite felt it this profoundly until him. Never understood it until I started picturing my life without him, and it felt dreadful.

Loneliness is on my skin that misses his touch. In my every cell that craves his presence. In my brain that replays the heated moments of us being together.

I try to trick my mind by keeping all the doors in the apartment open, including the one to my bathroom as I take a shower. Music echoes through the place. I close my eyes and try to conjure the sound of his footsteps through the living room.

But they are not there.

He is not there.

And my craving grows claws, scratching at my heart.

Wrapped in a towel, I walk into my room and halt.

A man's boxers are on the floor by my bed. John's.

"Oh, you..." I scold the pup and grin. "You little pervert!"

I pick them up and stare at the dark-blue fabric patterned with little pineapples. My roommate hides a gun under his pillow and wears boxers with pineapples. Cute.

I should take them to his room, but my John-obsessed mind doesn't let go. This is more than an obsession. I'm messed up. I'm falling hard and fast, about to smash into pieces.

The fabric caresses my thighs as I put John's boxers on, smiling at how wrong and yet arousing it is to have his underwear and nothing else on.

I press my hand to the fabric, trying to feel closer to him.

I'm losing my mind.

I'm slipping.

But maybe this is therapy.

And I stand in front of a canvas with a paintbrush and his boxers on, painting pineapples and John.

I.

Am.

Losing.

My.

Mind.

Those boxers. Those are *my* fucking pineapples. And those pineapples are closer to Lu than I am, touching her where I want to touch her.

Coincidence? Fuck coincidences. There are too many, and I already confirmed some of my suspicions.

I get online and order Lu flowers. No signature, just a "Thank you" note.

There are a dozen things by now that I can thank her for.

For awful grits.

For morning coffee.

For cooking me dinners.

For making me smile.

For being kind and sweet.

For her hot palms that leave invisible imprints on my body, her cute plush socks, the paint smudges that make me smile, and a hundred other things.

Lu calls in the evening.

"Thank you for the flowers," she says softly.

And pineapples, I assume, which are her new inspiration.

For the first time, we chat on the phone for over an hour. When she hangs up, I want to call her again right away. And I fucking miss her more than ever.

Roey studies me with what looks like approval. "Finally, you are using your heart instead of overthinking."

"My heart, huh?" I narrow my eyes at him. "Is this coming from you, Torres?"

"I am a heartless motherfucker, Jace. I'm not made for this

swoony stuff. But you, you finally met someone meant for you. Don't fuck it up."

"Yeah. I just need to untangle a pack of lies I created."

"Well, before you do that, let's untangle the plan of action for tomorrow."

Later, we get out of the hotel to grab dinner in a shopping plaza. We walk past a perfume shop when a girl walks out, and a smell wafts off her, a smell that triggers the longing in my heart. *Hers.*

I walk in and ask for *Euphoria.*

Roey's eyes follow my every move, but he doesn't say a word. There's no mockery in his eyes, no smirks.

"It's a present," I say.

I can bullshit Roey as much as I want, but he sees through people, just not himself.

"Tomorrow is an important day, Jace. Can you keep your head clear?"

"Yes."

Back at the hotel, I open the package and spray the perfume into the cap.

Her scent fills my nostrils.

One inhale, and my heart does a flip then clenches tightly from the need to feel Lu closer.

One spray on my pillow, and when I close my eyes at night, that's how I fall asleep—imagining Lu next to me.

It's the only way I can keep my head clear—knowing she's with me.

45

JACE

Another chapter by @MidnightLu goes live as we board the plane to JFK. Lu uploads them so quickly lately like she writes twenty-four-seven.

I swallow it in minutes.

Oh, the spice…

Miss Emily Aberdeen is painting her roommate, John Temple. Literally.

Whoa.

I reread the chapter, paying attention first to the tattoos on John's body that are identical to mine, then the spicy action.

And no, my head can't be freaking clear when the chapter ends in the hottest scene yet, with Em ordering John to strip naked then painting his tattoos with acrylics, then touching him, then letting him rub those colors on her body as he strips her naked and takes her on the floor.

New comments pile up as I read.

"She painted his Johnson!"

"Wouldn't that hurt? For her? Afterward?"

"Wait, WHAT?"

"Sharki!!! My panties dropped!"

I'm pumped about our finished job and another paycheck. But mostly, about seeing Lu.

"Welcome home!" she cheers when I arrive at Goldsling Towers in the afternoon.

I made a promise to myself that I'm finally gonna go for what I want. So I drop my bag and wrap her in a hug.

"Missed you," I say, burying my face in her hair.

Euphoria, fuck me.

Her eyes are all smiles and sparkles as she asks, "That's all I get?"

"Missed you so freaking much," I whisper. "You won't be able to fight me off."

And I kiss her with all the pent-up want of the last two days. Without interrupting the kiss, I lift her, and she wraps her legs around my waist.

In seconds, we are kissing like horny teenagers, messily and impatiently. We hold on to each other and kiss until we are breathless.

My heart is beating so wildly that her body might get a shock wave effect.

"Hungry?" she murmurs.

"For food?" I kiss her neck.

She laughs and wiggles her butt, which gets me harder by the second. Her legs are still around me, so I haul her up and spin her around to ease the pressure on my throbbing hard-on.

"I'm not, but I do need to jump in the shower and get changed."

And make my boner that strains my jeans go away.

The shower does nothing to cool me. Half an hour later, I'm still turned on and still wanting her.

The door to her room is slightly ajar, music trickling out.

This is my happy place—apartment 1101 of Goldsling Towers, Lu and me. Plus Pushkin, who I spend ten minutes goofing around with because I missed my pirate dude too.

He follows me to Lu's door, but I snap my fingers at him, and he huffs with disappointment and lies down, giving me that sad look with his furrowed eyebrows he's perfected lately.

I knock on Lu's door and walk in.

She stands facing me by the canvas set up on an easel. Lounge music is trickling from a speaker.

"What are you working on?" I ask, about to ask her if I can watch her paint or kiss her or—

"You," she says, pursing her lips to hide a smile.

"Me?" It's the first time she's admitted it, despite having a dozen of paintings of me in her room. "Can I see?"

"I only just started. But…"

And, oh, fucking hell, I sense where this is going. And I'm starting to freak out inwardly.

"But?" I hold my breath. Her latest *Sharki* episode flickers in my mind.

"Will you pose for me?"

"Will you pose for me, John?"

Her blue eyes are fire when her gaze locks with mine. I wonder if she knows I know about her writing, though she wouldn't give up her pen name no matter how many times I asked.

I know how the last chapter of *Sharki* started.

"Right now?" I swallow hard, my entire body as tense as an iron rod.

"Yes," she whispers.

Fuck me. "Sure."

I don't know what to do, how to stand, and what else to say.

"Just stay where you are for a moment," she prompts.

A moment lasts for twenty minutes.

Lu licks her lips as her eyes dart to me, then to the canvas. She changes brushes and lays thick long strokes onto the canvas. I can't see what she's doing, but it's nothing intricate. I've watched her paint before. She's doing one of her emotional impressionist paintings. I wonder if she is summoning courage.

I smile when she glances at me.

She answers with a smile, wipes her hands with a rag, then picks up a smaller brush.

"Take off your shirt, Jace," she orders finally. "I want to paint your tattoos."

My body relaxed in the short time she was painting me. Now it tenses like a string again.

"Take off your shirt, John. I want to paint your tattoos."

I just read this several hours ago. I know every detail of what's to come, and my heartbeat spikes.

I reach behind me and pull the shirt over my head.

Lu's eyes shift to my torso, studying me.

I've never been particularly proud of my tattoos. They are beautiful as per many people who comment on the beach. But art is art. Anyone can get it. Maybe, not the indigenous needle work, but enough money and you can be a walking canvas.

Now I feel like my tattoos have a purpose—to captivate her.

All yours, Lu.

She forgets herself. I can tell by the way she doesn't move, the brush motionless in her hand, her lips slightly parted, her eyes on me wide in silent awe.

But for the first time in my life, I don't feel self-conscious. I feel like I'm hypnotizing her. Confidence surges through me. Her gaze is not unnerving, it's empowering. I want her hands to slide along my tattoos like her gaze does, caressing my body.

When her eyes dip to my shark tattoo, I get hard.

She glances up at me, then her eyes move to the canvas, and she resumes painting.

"Can you...?" She trails off and licks her lips. "Can you take off your jeans? I need to see your body..."

Oooh-kaaaay.

She wants to finally see my shark tattoo.

The thought makes my head spin. My erection starts to strain against the fabric of my jeans. Sharki was much braver in that chapter. I'm not Sharki. But I don't have a choice. Not when the girl I'm madly in love with wants me to strip for her.

My hands are already pushing my jeans down, and I step out of them.

I'm in my pineapple boxers, yes, those, from another *Sharki* chapter, the ones that she wore while I was away. I wear them imagining they rubbed against her skin, and there's no stopping the madness that's happening in my head as I straighten my shoulders and give Lu a little smile, narrowing my eyes at her to project the Sharki confidence.

My heart is beating like mad, but I can't show it. I'm hard for her, and it's tenting my boxers. There's no way to hide it, and in a minute, I'll be bare for her.

She swallows hard, taking me in.

I would've blushed any other time. Except I'm so turned on and tense that I feel like my face is drained of the blood, which concentrates in my nether region as I keep my eyes on her.

She blinks away. My Lu looks nervous.

That makes both of us, Lu baby.

But I need to take the lead.

I rub myself through the fabric. I'm shameless, yes. This is the boldest I've been with a girl. But I can't help it. Lu is my fucking undoing.

Her eyes snap to my hand, and a blush creeps up her cheeks.

She bites her lip. Her chest heaves. She applies brush strokes to the canvas, her eyes going back and forth between the canvas and me, but I know she's not focused.

The revelation hits me—she's *really* nervous! Maybe even more than me, and she can't hide it at all.

That gives me more courage as I keep my eyes on her.

"I want to see that tattoo," she says quietly, her eyes on the canvas.

The notch in her throat bobs when she swallows. She blows a strand from her face too loudly and licks her lips.

"The shark one?" I know perfectly well what she wants.

Her eyes snap at me, then go back to the canvas.

Fuck. Fuck. Fuck. Calm down, Jace.

"Yes," she says quietly. "Take it all off."

Her face turns a darker shade of pink.

I hook my thumbs under the waistband of my boxers, and for a brief moment, the embarrassing memories come back. Of how in love I was at seventeen. How much I wanted that girl, Monica. How excited I was when she said she wanted to *see* me. How humiliating it was to stand naked while dozens of people laughed at me and took pictures.

But I'm not seventeen. And the girl in front of me is my dream. She wants me too, and holy hell does she obviously dream about me.

I've come a long way, and if anything can break my stupid paranoia, it's Lu.

So, I keep my confident gaze on her despite being on edge.

I'm all hers, whatever she wants to do with me.

I try to control my breathing and keep my eyes on her as I pull down my boxers, let them fall to the floor, and kick them aside.

46

LU

MY HEART IS IN MY STOMACH AT THE DARE I JUST STARTED.

Jace took it, and I think I'm about to have a heart attack.

"Take it all off," I say, not believing the words that come out of my mouth.

When his boxers drop to the floor, I steal a glance.

Jace is big, very big, and gorgeous. He's built like a God, an absolute perfection.

He's my muse. I want to paint his body, paint *on* his skin, fill in the missing colors on those black-and-white tattoos. I want to run my hands along him and feel every bulge of his muscles.

Confident, just like the time by the elevator with Chad, he stands like a warrior, magnetic and powerful.

My gaze sweeps across his body, legs, abdomen, erection, his shark tattoo that morphs into a beautiful pattern and shapes up to his chest that rises and falls slowly. His dog tag glints with past danger. His eyes are on me, making my heart beat wildly against my chest. His little smile feels like *he* is the one daring me.

I drink him in.

My hands tremble a little. I don't know how to move forward. My fiction is much wilder than I am. It's easier to be bold when no emotions are involved. Especially with sex.

Sex—that's what follows in my *Sharki* story. But this is reality.

And reality is the shark tattoo that my eyes drop down to. It disappears into the neatly trimmed dark patch around the base of his erection, his fist wrapped around it, stroking slowly up and down.

My mouth is dry. My nerves are on edge.

"Come closer," I say on an exhale, my heart ready to burst out of my chest.

Jace takes a slow step toward me.

Then another.

I'm going to touch him just like I did in my fantasy. I just need to have him next to me, kiss him, my eyes closed so I don't fall apart under his probing gaze that makes my knees weak. I'm so much braver on paper. And so much more experienced with words.

Another step.

Those feet between us are killing me.

I falter, and my fingers brush against the blue canvas.

Jace stops a foot away from me, a corner of his lips lifted in a little daring smile.

I put the paintbrush down, gazing at him, too nervous to look down at where he strokes himself.

The last step is mine.

I close the inches between us.

My hand pushes his away and wraps around his erection, velvety and warm to the touch, a rock wrapped in soft skin.

His lips part in a tiny gasp. But his hand doesn't fall off. Instead, his fingers loosely brush mine, nudging me to stroke him, like he's guiding me.

Finally, I have Jace naked in front of me. In my hand…

I rise on tiptoes, and when our lips mold in a kiss, my nervousness falls away. My other hand slides up his body, to his pectorals, the hard muscles that feel fantastic, then grazes over his hard nipple.

I want to feel him.

I *need* to. Everywhere. I wish I was naked and pressed against him.

I stroke his shaft then cup him. His soft grunt makes me smile against his lips. He bucks his hips at me just slightly, and I stroke him faster.

His hands cup my butt, squeezing gently.

I moan into his mouth, and he answers with a groan, deepening the kiss.

His one hand moves over my hip and comes to the front, then slides under my shorts and between my legs.

The room whirls around me. My core lights on fire at his touch. I'm wet and hot, and the pressure of his fingers is just right, making me moan into his mouth and stroke him harder.

Jace pulls away just a bit. His head is slightly cocked, his lips parted, his gaze, heavy with desire, searching my face like he's studying my reaction.

He kisses me softly. Then pulls away. Then kisses me again, teasing. Then pulls away.

My hand is working his hardness, the other one on his shoulder. I might collapse if I don't hold on to him. His fingers are sinking into my wet heat while his other arm is wrapped around my waist, holding me in place.

He applies more pressure between my legs, and I cup him again, and we both moan, meeting in a kiss that freezes for a long moment as we focus on how it feels to be touched so openly, to be in each other's hands.

I resume stroking him.

"Lu baby, slow down," he whispers in a low voice, rough with need.

I won't.

This is a new sound to me. That's Jace turned on. I want to see him fall apart at my touch, see him finally drop the guard that he holds like a fort. I'll breach his fort and make him crazy and—

I moan loudly when his fingers dip inside me, making me dizzy. Like he's punishing me for not obeying him.

"Slow down, baby," he whispers hoarsely.

No.

My palm cups him again, then slips to his hardness, stroking it harder.

He groans louder into my mouth, our kiss growing frantic.

He does it again, dips his fingers inside me, then slides them out and works them in circles, and I get ready for it—I always know, *feel*, when I approach the peak.

But this time it's so fast, so unexpected, *his* fingers down there, not mine, that I whimper as I tip over the edge and roll my hips against his hand, seeking out more pressure as every cell in my body explodes in a powerful climax.

I pant, losing focus on what I'm doing but stroking him feverishly like his hardness in my hand is the secret key to my own ecstasy.

Hot liquid seeps between my fingers, my palm suddenly slick as Jace groans and catches my hand with his, stopping me.

We break the kiss, panting. He bows his forehead to mine. But his hands don't stop. They tease, caressing my hips, cupping my butt. We both want so much more and so badly.

My nervousness is gone, my body pleading to shed my clothes and be naked against him.

"Lu?" he whispers.

His lips take mine in soft kisses as his hands start gently pushing my shorts down.

"Yes?" I manage.

"I'm going to—"

The doorbell rings, making us both freeze.

My phone in the living room goes off.

Then the doorbell again.

My heart starts racing, blood pounding in my ears like I got caught red-handed doing something illegal.

We are pulled out of our sex daze so abruptly, that for a second, I'm petrified.

Should I ignore it?

Should I get it?

Another buzz comes, and I do the stupidest thing and whisper, "Should I get that?" instantly realizing that I screwed up.

"Yeah," Jace whispers into my mouth, his warm gaze on mine.

Slowly, he leans and takes the rag from the paint stand. Finger after finger, he cleans my hand, the doorbell ringing insistently.

He cups my face and kisses me briefly, then nudges me to go.

It's Tito.

Argh!

I've never been more mad at him!

"Call next time, maybe?" I snap, irritated, as he sashays past me with a Starbucks in his hand like it's his house.

I need to get rid of him. He has to go. I have Jace in my room naked, waiting.

"Girl, what are you doing?" Tito confidently strolls across the living room. "I called and called."

"Painting." *And you freaking interrupted!*

"I wanna see."

Before I can stop him, he starts walking toward my room, and I stare in panic.

The door swings open, and Jace walks out, fully dressed. "Hey, man."

I might've just died a little.

Tito gives him a startled look. "You painting, too?"

"Modeling."

"Oh, yeah? Now I really want to see." Tito turns to cock a brow at me.

"Maybe not," I blurt.

"Oh, I do." Tito pushes past Jace, and Jace follows.

So do I.

There's a slight panic on Jace's face when Tito rounds the easel.

"Oh?" Tito muses.

Jace steps around to see it too.

So do I, nervously biting my nail.

"That's... very abstract," Tito says, studying the messy blue background and only several lines for the features that could be anyone. "You have great tattoos, Jace. I was hoping for a full-body painting. But it looks like Lu just started. Is it going to be a portrait?"

Tito's back is to us. He doesn't see Jace lift his hand to my face and stroke a strand of my hair with his forefinger.

"Just a portrait," Jace says with a soft smile as I blush scarlet.

47

JACE

Tito is taking Lu to a party.

"Come on, we gotta go!" he shouts as Lu closes the door to her room to get changed. "Jace, you are coming too."

"No, man, I'm good. I have stuff to do online."

No amount of Tito's persuasion can change my mind. Not even Lu's slight disappointment and the blush that doesn't go away.

She looks amazing in a dress with cherries, her face circled with a hairband. Cute red-framed sunglasses perched on her nose hide her eyes but not her blush.

I need some time alone to process what happened. Take a freaking breather.

And I need a cool shower, which I jump into when they leave the condo.

My head is on fire, and so is my heart. My dick—I stare in shock as I get under the lukewarm stream—has paint on it. I smile like an idiot as I bring my thumb to a dry blue streak on my shaft.

Lu painted my dick.

I laugh like mad, shower water sprinkling into my mouth.

It's still there when I dry myself, and I smile like a total creep as I dress.

I try to focus on my online course, but it's not working. The text notification makes me scramble for my phone.

Lu: Can you please take Pushkin out? I'll be late. Tito and B are dragging me to a gallery party. Please, save me?

Me: I'll walk Pushkin. Have fun. You need it, Lu.

I send a winking emoji, but my mood plunges below ground level.

For a change, Pushkin and I walk at a slow pace until it starts getting dark. I order Lu's favorite burgers, bring them to the terrace, and whistle to Pushkin.

"It's you and I, little guy," I say as I unwrap one burger and set it on the ground in front of him.

Pushkin has the same taste as Lu, so he stuffs his mouth right away like he starved for a week.

"No manners, dude," I say and unwrap the other burger.

Pushkin wears little shoes that look like tiger paws that Lu made for him so his claws don't click against the parquet. He looks ridiculous, but I fucking love him so much right now.

On some level, I'm relieved Lu is out partying. After our little painting session, I need a whole lot of bravery to keep a straight face. I thought I'd have a heart attack the entire time, and it took all my willpower not to show it.

Yet, everything reminds me of Lu. The night sky, the terrace, the glistening windows of the Manhattan skyscrapers, the boats slowly cruising out in the river, the police sirens—the unmistakable sounds of New York City.

I need to figure this out, *us*. I need to find a way to stay here, but first things first, I need to undo a tangle of lies that Lu might not want to deal with.

Pushkin chomps loudly on the last piece of the burger, his eye patch skewed around his ear.

"All right, dude, gotta get a bit more gentleman-like, yeah?"

I pick up the wrapper off the ground and take off his eye patch as he licks my hand, then licks the ground where the burger was.

"You wish she were here too, huh?" I say, smiling at Pushkin for no reason.

Where is she right now? What is she doing? Who is she talking to? Is she smiling? Bored? Flirty?

My phone rings—it's her—and my heart bursts into fireworks.

"Well, Tito left, so it's officially girls' night out with some of Becky's friends," Lu says, a little disappointed and without a greeting like we've just talked. "What are you doing?"

"Pushkin and I are eating burgers on the terrace."

She huffs. "I wanna come home, but Becky complains that I'm spending more time with you than her."

My heart warms at the words. "Is that bad?"

"No. But she's jealous."

"I'm jealous right now too."

"Want me to come home?"

"I do. But I don't want Becky to hate me."

We go quiet for a moment, and I close my eyes, listening to her breathing.

"So, how's dinner with Pushkin?" she asks.

"It's okay."

"Just okay?"

"Well, you are not here. And he's a lousy date. Not much of a talker."

I dissolve at the sound of her laughing.

"Hey. Do you see the stars?" Lu asks all of a sudden. "Usually, you can't see them with all the lights in the city. But I can see the Big Dipper tonight. In Russian, they call it Big Mama Bear."

Lu always notices the most random things.

I look up.

Yep, Mama Bear is there.

They say stars reflect light. Maybe, they reflect the light of her eyes. So, technically, it's like looking at her.

"I see you, Lucy Moor," I say.

"Yeah?" I can hear a smile in her voice.

"I got my eyes on you."

"Good. Keep it that way, Jace Reed."

There's a moment of silence, then there's her voice again, unusually soft and timid. "Hey, Jace?"

"Yes, Lu?"

There's obnoxious laughter in the background, and suddenly, Becky's loud voice is in my ear.

"Hey, Jace Reed? Back off! You are stealing my best friend!"

Jesus, Becky.

I know she's joking, but I want my Lu back on the phone.

"It's a girls' night out," Becky complains. "So let her go!"

I wasn't the one who called.

"Go do what you do," she adds.

"What is that?" I tease her. When Becky is tipsy, I can have the upper hand.

"Those mysterious things you call *sales.*" She's pretty lit. "With that cocky friend of yours, Rrrrroey."

Correction, she's *very* drunk.

"Cocky?" I'm so pushing her buttons.

"Yeah. With that hot-stuff attitude and those bluish-green eyes that look fake. Does he wear contacts?"

"No." I grin. "Do you always notice the different shades in people's eyes?"

"You know what—"

"I do. That's because you don't like him."

"Jace? I'm putting you on my blacklist."

"Becky?" I mimic her. "I'm sending you Roey's number."

"Jace Reed? I officially don't like you."

I stifle a laugh. "And you don't like Roey. Got it."

"Okay. Bye!"

The phone call cuts off.

No goodbye from Lu. But it's alright, as long as she's happy.

Just to mess with Becky and hoping she pours her drunk frustration on Roey, I send her Roey's number, getting a middle finger emoji in response.

I smile, lifting my eyes to Mama Bear, press my fingertips to my lips, and send an air kiss to Lu.

She's in the next borough, and it feels unbearably far away. But we're looking at the same stars, at the same time. She's not here, but she exists, and that already makes this world a beautiful place.

48

JACE

It's morning. I oversleep and wake up to Lu's upset voice in the kitchen.

"I don't want to sell myself, B! I want to do art that people enjoy!"

When I walk out, Lu, in sweatpants and a tank, stands with her palm against the fridge door, head hanging low. I've never seen her this upset.

"Yeah, I'm not a Kardashian," she snaps into the phone, her voice soft despite her obvious anger. Even her anger is subtle. "My face has nothing to do with it... So, tell him I can't! Argh! Seriously, B!"

She hangs up and exhales loudly.

"You okay?" I ask as I walk up and pull her into me.

She presses her forehead to my shoulder and rolls it, grunting.

"These clients drive me mad, Jace. First, they want a portrait. Then they want me to advertise them, the wanna-be-celebrities. That's not what they pay me for. And they didn't even pay, besides a small deposit."

I stroke her hair. "You don't have to do anything you don't want to."

"But I need money, Jace!" She lifts her beautiful eyes that have more desperation than on her saddest days. "This is my work! Tsk."

She pretends to throw her phone into the living room, then walks away without giving me a kiss.

Well, there's that.

In a minute, she's changed into a summer dress and flats, puts Pushkin on a leash, and leaves without another word.

I make myself coffee. I used to make it perfectly. Now it feels off. My coffee made by Lu tastes different.

She's gone for hours, and the only thing I can do is text.

Me: Are you okay?

Lu: I will be. Thanks, Jace.

Her mood is always contagious. I can't focus on anything, let alone my online course. So, I go to the kitchen to make lunch.

Without Lu and Pushkin, this place is a ghost town. I can handle hours of her absence, but the deadly silence without the huffing of the little pirate dude is a bad sign, making me feel like back in the day, in the group home, alone, without allies and not a single thing to latch on to for sanity.

Roey calls. I'm trying to make instant noodles, so I put him on speaker.

"We need to talk about our return to Cali and the estimated dates," he says.

I don't want to talk about Cali or go back. "What about it?"

"Are you coming?"

This is the conversation I dreaded. "I need to sort things out with Lu first. Maybe I can rent a place in New York and stay here for a bit."

"Get on it, then," Roey says surprisingly quickly.

"That's slightly complicated."

Mostly because if my conversation with her goes sideways, there might be no reason for me to stay in New York.

I always listen to Roey. He might not have good life advice when it comes to women, considering how many one-night stands are under his belt, but he gets me, always did, during the service, after, *especially* after. If it weren't for him, I'd have been stuck in the war loop for much longer.

"We might have intel on Reznik," he says, and as if he senses that I'm not in work mood, adds, "but you obviously can't think about work right now. Not until you sort out your personal stuff. Suck it up and get on it."

I burn my finger on a hot pot and hiss.

"Listen, Jace," Roey continues. "You're not like me, thank god. But you're sleeping on this one. You're lucky to have met Lu." I know it. "And you need to push harder."

"I don't need to push, Roey. That's not how it works."

The pot boils over, and I slide it to the side, irritated at everything going wrong today.

"If Lu is the one, she needs to know about what you do. Stop being someone else."

"You *made* me someone else the night I shot her," I argue. "First, you said we can't tell her anything. Now, you want me to tell her *everything*."

"I want to see you happy, Jace. Finally, I want to see you with a girl who makes the famous Shooter all starry-eyed."

"That's the problem. She might not be so hot for me when she learns what I used to be or what I do."

"You're just scared. And you're wrong. You're rooming with the hottest chick you've met, who you can't shut up about, and she thinks you are a lousy salesman. You need to break her in. The longer you wait, the harder it will be."

"I'll tell her things, but not now and at my own pace."

"*Things*?" he chuckles. "Which part are you gonna tell her first? Let me guess. That you hate grits but eat them every day because she makes them for you and you don't want to see her sad if you refuse?"

"Whatever."

"No? Oh, so you are going to confess that you served in a war zone and were a rank-A prodigy shooter with the best sniper record in your division in four years? Or that you are a bounty hunter and not a fucking salesman?"

He's so right, but it sounds so bad when it comes out of his mouth that I don't want to tell Lu anything at all.

"Or!" He pauses for emphasis, and I know what's coming. "That you are twenty-four and a fucking virgin? You might actually get away with *not* telling her that."

Blood starts boiling in my veins.

"Fuck off, Torres. Thanks for the pep talk, man."

"You need to find your balls, Jace."

"Yeah," I snap. "Gonna go look for them. I'll call you for personal advice again. I'm sure it'll be life-changing."

Irritated, I stab the "end call" button and exhale loudly in frustration, rubbing the back of my neck and slowly turning around.

It's a nightmare. I've never been a liar. Technically, secrets are not lies. Technically, I only lied about being a salesperson.

Well, and—

My heart falls as I raise my eyes.

A wave of dread washes over me. Like when you drop something precious and it shatters in a matter of seconds. Or a car accident that happens too quickly.

Lu stands in the doorway, her eyes on me bigger than quarters.

Fuck, what did she hear?

"Lu?"

Which part did she walk in on?

Her mouth opens to say something, then closes, then opens again, her eyes full of confusion, which means that she heard a lot.

Her eyebrows furrow when she says, "You hate grits?"

Fuck my life.

49

LU

My reality just collapsed.

There were plenty of signs that Jace wasn't exactly who he said he was. Becky calls them red flags. Too bad I'm an artist and love all colors.

I thought we were getting close, heading for something beyond friendship. Something much bigger that my heart still wants, but the brain says, "What else did he lie about?"

This freaking hurts.

I'm pacing back and forth across the living room. Pushkin follows me. He gives up, but I don't.

Jace's eyes follow me from the couch he's sitting on.

"I feel played," I say, lost for words.

A sniper. A bounty hunter. A virgin... The last part is irrelevant, but the rest... Oh, the rest...

"Lu, it's not like that," he says softly. "What are you upset about?"

I stop and turn to him. "You were deployed? In a war zone? Where? A sniper? Really?"

"It was a job, Lu. I was in the service, and I just so happened to be good at... shooting, yes. And yes, I served in a war zone."

"Did you have to, like, kill people?" The last two words are almost a whisper.

He flinches. "Why would you want the details about something I don't want to remember?"

"Because it's you!" My heart bleeds for him. "Because it's traumatic, exciting, horrible, or whatever—I don't know, but I *want* to know, Jace! How you feel. What you were like back then. If it bothers you. If it haunts you. Can't you see? I want to know everything about you."

It does haunt him, I know. The evenings he goes out onto the terrace and stands there in the dark suddenly make a lot more sense. Those aren't a poetic contemplation of the night city like mine. Those are dark memories chasing him. If he shared with me, I'd help him chase them away. I want to so badly. But he chose to hide it from me.

Jace ruffles his hair, not meeting my eyes.

I want him to look at me. His eyes are an open book. There are usually so many emotions in them that I should've understood all the darkness and loneliness he comes from. I just didn't know it was so much more intense. It's not just about his past or the present, but how he is with me. Like he wants me one day, and the next day he's ashamed of what happened. When he opens up one moment but omits the most important parts and pulls back like he's afraid I'll judge him.

"You kiss me one night, Jace, then don't talk about it like it's a dirty secret. Am I?"

His eyes snap at me. "What? No. Lu, it's—"

"Then we kiss again, and you do amazing things, but then you scale back like you are trying to shake it off."

"Lu, it's not like that."

"If you want us to carry on, let's talk, Jace. I want to know what's happening. If there *is* something happening." I hate how desperate I sound, but I want to sort this out. "I want to know if…" I can't spill my feelings. It's too early and unfair now that I know he was hiding so many things. "If I'm the only person here going crazy and obsessing over my roommate while you…"

I go quiet and stare at my feet, biting my lower lip so I don't show how unnerved I am.

Jace walks up to me and cups my face. "You have no idea what you do to me, Lu."

His thumbs stroke my cheeks.

No, I don't want to send him away. I want him closer, so much closer.

"What is it that I do?" I murmur with bitterness. "It must be *special* if you don't want to share the most important parts of yourself."

"Because I didn't want to scare you off. There are parts of my past and present you might not like. You *don't*, I can see that. And I so desperately want you to understand, but I'm afraid that you won't. Petrified, actually. I'm... I'm so crazy about you, Lu. You know it. How can you not?"

His forehead touches mine. Our eyes meet. His are darker but so full of warmth. That's what drew me to him in the first place. No matter what he says, does, shows, or hides, there's always this warm kindness in his eyes. It's genuine and disarming.

"All these secrets, Jace," I whisper. "I thought we were being honest with each other."

"Yes, it's just—"

"You're not a salesperson."

He shakes his head, his forehead rolling over mine.

This is crazy. I knew something was off, just not that—a bounty hunter.

"I knew it," I say. "This was the biggest bullshit. And why would you keep it from me?"

"What did you want me to do, Lu? Say, 'Hi, I'm Jace. I used to shoot people in the desert. Now I hunt people down for money. Can I move in with you?'"

"That's what you call it? Hunt?"

"Not hunt. No." He pulls away abruptly. His hands are off me and lock behind his neck. "It's a job, like policing. We don't hurt people."

"So, then why couldn't you tell me?"

Becky joked, saying I had fictophilia and am in love with my fictional character. But she doesn't know how much of Jace is in it. Or that my new novel is my diary of sorts. Turns out, even my character's secrets are Jace's. It's scary and feels like I'm losing my mind.

And here's the bitter truth.

Jace doesn't know that I blatantly use him for my writing. If I tell him, will he think I'm obsessed? Will he think I'm a stalker? A nymphomaniac? An identity thief?

In truth, I'm hiding my own secret from him.

Studying my face, Jace takes my hands in his, stroking them gently, so tenderly I want to whimper.

My anger is gone. He has this magical power to make the world fall away around us when we are next to each other.

He leans in and kisses my cheek. "I'll tell you anything you want, Lu." He kisses my brow, then my forehead, pulling me into his arms. "I just didn't want to scare you away." He places little kisses all around my face, then kisses the corner of my mouth, making my heart melt. "Is this our first fight?"

"Looks like it," I murmur, weak from his tenderness.

I want to be angry, but I don't know *how*, not with him.

"And it's about grits." He chuckles. Chuckles!

I give him a fake glare. "It's a little more than about grits, Jace Reed."

His smell makes my head spin. He makes my heart swell. Deep inside, I'm hurt he chose not to tell me things, but now that I know, I'll have to tell him about *Sharki*. And, oh, is it scary to be honest...

He keeps planting little pecks around my mouth, and I'm reeling with the need for more.

"Do you see what you are doing, Jace?" I whisper, running my hand through his hair, and he leans into it.

"Tell me," he whispers back, teasing me with his kisses.

"You are avoiding the conversation."

"I'm not."

Another soft kiss.

How can a guy be such a tease?

"You won't get off so easily, Jace. Not with these kinda kisses."

He chuckles, but his smile falls. "Lu, the night we met—"

The doorbell rings.

It's the gallery guys, sent to pick up my paintings that are already wrapped up and ready to go.

My stomach twists in a knot as they clear out my bedroom.

This is it, my big moment tomorrow, my solo exhibit. I should be happy but feel empty, looking around my room. The only artworks left are the smaller ones I worked on for myself, the ones of Jace, and the giant gothic portrait propped against the wall.

My phone rings.

"When it rains, it pours," I murmur, sensing something else is coming my way.

It's Becky.

"Hey, there," I sigh into the phone.

She tells me that my gothic portrait order was canceled, and my mind instantly flares with shock.

"What do you mean? I'm almost done! They can't do this to me, B! Talk to them!"

"They don't want it unless it's promoted, Lu. Sorry. I tried. You get to keep the deposit."

"So, that's it? I don't promote my work that was done privately, don't make *them* trendy, and they drop the commission?"

No one wants my art. They want *me*, my popularity, and the number of likes on my social media pages.

Becky tries to persuade me once again to use my social power to turn things around.

I won't. I refuse to be a glossy magazine image for someone else's sake.

My gaze lingers on Jace, who leans on the doorway, his hands in his pockets.

Was that why he didn't tell me the truth? He thought I would like a glossy version of him?

This works with people you don't care about. With him? I want to know his every dark detail. And it kills me to know that he tries to feed me the safe polished version of himself. Just like *I* do with the rest of the world.

50

JACE

My beautiful girl looks lost, like she just figured out the biggest illusion of her life, and it's slowly killing her.

The hurt in her eyes is real. I don't know if it's about me and my secrets or the shitty client that just canceled their order.

I fucked up.

I always play it safe, and Lu is not a safe person. She's spontaneous and open. She sees the best in people. So, whatever she just saw in me is a hard blow to her trust. I knew this would happen.

Lu cuts the phone call and, without another word, walks to her room.

Her bedroom is unusually empty without her art, and my heart feels the same, like we've reached the end.

Her solo exhibit is tomorrow, and I pray it goes spectacularly and she is happy enough to forgive me.

I stand by the giant living room windows, staring at sunny Manhattan and trying to gauge her emotions by the sounds from her room. The soft rustling. The tap running in her bathroom. A soft sob, or a sniffle. Then there's a muffled bang, and something rolls on the floor. Lu's, "Fuck you," whispers in the air.

It's a bad sign. I've never heard her swear before.

She walks out with a phone in her hand and a lost look in her eyes that search the living room like she needs answers.

I take a step toward her.

"Lu, don't get upset about the people who don't deserve it."

I'm talking about her clients, but it dawns on me that I might fit into that same box.

Lu cutely wrinkles her nose, trying not to cry, but her beautiful eyes are pools of tears.

She shakes her head. "You know what they said? That my work is not worth anything unless I put my face to it. Meaning, Lucy Moor is pretty but her art sucks."

"Lu, you're so wrong."

She sniffles. "I'm a failure, Jace. Everyone likes Lucy Moor with a bright smile and outrageous heels. But when I'm not trending, no one cares. Do you?" Her eyes search my face for the answer. "You feed me a bunch of lousy stories and don't want to show me the real you while the real one is so much more—"

Tears start spilling down her cheeks, and that's a sight I never wanted to see.

I rush up to her, wrapping my arms around her.

"Lu, you're the most talented person I know. Beautiful inside and out. With an amazing personality. I know all of you. My favorite is not the trending Lucy Moor but the one with messy hair and paint smudges on her hands and a soft smile and the breakfasts we have together. All of you."

I'm so in love with her that I want to find the bastards who upset her and knock the life out of them one by one.

"Is it money?" I ask, not knowing how to comfort her. "Don't be upset. I have money. Do you want me to sponsor your art project?"

She shakes her head, casting her gaze down.

Her phone starts ringing, and she picks it up, wiping away tears.

"Hi... Fine... It's not the best time... yeah... Why? In the city? I see. I'm okay. I'm fine!" She lets out a shaky exhale and wipes her cheeks with her fingers. "I understand. But I'm fine. Always was. Yes, we can meet up. I'll call you later."

She hangs up and stares around.

"You alright?" I ask.

She is not.

"I need to go for a walk," she whispers.

In a moment, she's gone.

Pushkin gives me a guilty stare like it's his fault, and when I walk into her room to see what happened, my heart sinks.

The beautiful gothic painting she's been working on is splashed with bright yellow paint, some of it dripping down, a trail of yellow leading to the bottle on the floor.

"Shit."

Pushkin sits next to me, staring at it too.

I pick up my phone and dial the one person I never thought I would.

"Hey, Becky, this is Jace Reed, Lu's roommate."

"I know your name and your voice, Jace. What's up? Is it the end of the world?"

"What?"

"Jesus, it's the first time you called me. What's happening?"

"Right. I have a question. You know art, right? How do I remove fresh acrylics from a painted canvas?"

"What, you couldn't ask Lu?" I keep silent. "Liquid?" she asks when I don't answer.

"Liquid."

"If it's not dry yet, it's easy."

And after she gives me instructions, I get to work.

51

LU

I RUINED MY WORK. RUINED! AND MADE AN ASS OF MYSELF IN FRONT OF Jace.

I circle the blocks around Goldsling Towers for the third time. Bumping into people. Aimlessly gazing around. Talking to myself.

A car honks violently as I cross the street, braking only a foot away from me.

My mind is a mess.

Quiet salesman, my ass.

Anger flares in me for a second, lacing with excitement.

I actually like the new Jace and wish I knew his secrets sooner. I wrote about them in *Sharki*, thinking that my creativity was wild. Emily, the main heroine, was turned on by John's dark past. But I'm upset about Jace keeping things from me.

That's the difference between fiction and reality. Fiction bangs it out with sex. Reality hurts.

I buy ice cream and sit on a bench at the park, overlooking the river.

A virgin... How can Jace be inexperienced? His hands were way too expert when they touched me better than mine ever did. Maybe, he perfected that part with girls. It's so strange but also so... hot.

I can't help but smile like a fool at the weirdest thought ever—I want to take Jace's virginity.

Jace Reed, you're mine.

Another thought flickers in my mind. What if he has performance issues? I should ask. Rude? Probably. But he had no issues the other day when he stroked himself in front of me. When *I* did it.

All the bits of the new info collide in my mind like a pack of flies. Deployment... Right, he said he served. I never asked what he did.

A sniper? It's a job, right? That's what soldiers do, they fight the enemy.

Orphan? I knew that and noticed how emotional he gets when I do nice things for him. I always had a family. Technically, I have two fathers. Being alone in New York occasionally makes me miserable, but back home, I have people. Jace doesn't have a *back home*. He has no one but Roey.

Tears well up in my eyes.

What's with me and crying today?

I feel conflicted and sad. I really want to be angry, but at the end of the day, I want to go home and cook Jace dinner and talk and kiss and—

That's where it always ends.

My ice cream is gone, though I don't remember eating it. I need a whole tub of ice cream to calm myself.

And here's the naked truth. I wish I was eating it with Jace. No matter what I do, I wish for him to be next to me.

And here I am, miserable and by myself while Jace, who let me in on his secrets, probably feels horrible. At home. Alone...

Going up the elevator to my condo, I feel like crap because I let Jace down. Secrets are not always a choice but a self-preservation mechanism. By the time I reach the condo, I feel guilty.

The living room is empty. The door to Jace's room is closed.

Pushkin springs to his feet and wobbles up to me.

"Hey, cutie," I murmur, kick off my boots, walk to my room, and freeze.

My painting is the way it was this morning—clean, not a trace of the mess I left behind. No yellow paint on the plastic floor. No smashed paint jar.

My chest tightens.

This is my Jace. How does he do it? How does he make my heart swell up to enormous proportions and fill it with so many emotions? It's a talent he doesn't know he has, and I should be grateful for him instead of brooding about things he didn't tell me about.

I walk out into the living room and see Jace at the kitchen island, his hands propped on the counter, eyes on me.

"Lu, I'm sorry," he says softly.

Feeling like my knees will buckle, I walk over to him.

Every day, he makes me feel more vulnerable, and I have a hard time keeping my feelings inside.

So I don't.

"*I* am sorry, Jace," I murmur as I wrap my arms around his neck and pull him in for a kiss that I probably need more than he does. "I got a little upset, but I'm not angry. I just wish you told me things instead of hiding them."

I can kiss him until he forgets the lonely places he came from. Until he feels like he finally has a home. Until he stops hiding his past, afraid that it somehow makes him less than who he is. Until he realizes that's what made him so strong. Until I know we are good.

His hands slide to the back of my thighs, and, in one swift movement, he lifts me and sits me on the counter.

Those hands can handle a sniper rifle, rude jerks, and a paint mess. They make the best bacon and touch me in a way that makes me forget how to breathe. I want those hands to be mine.

"I didn't mean to upset you, Lu," he whispers.

"It's alright."

"I only want to make you smile." He presses his forehead to mine. "And hear you sing in the shower. And see you dance to crazy music." He smiles, making my heart quiver with emotions. "And see you happy as you turn Pushkin into a brat with all his cute outfits and your attention."

We chuckle, his warm breath grazing my face. That's his magic, the goodness that seeps out of him, and I have a chance to have it all to myself.

"Your beautiful art will one day wow the world, Lu, trust me."

No one has ever talked to me like this, not even Becky who believes in me.

I palm his face. "And I want you to trust me and tell me the worst, the darkest, and the most hurtful things in your past. I want to know all of you, Jace. Please, let me."

"Lu… If you were leading me straight to death, I'd let you. I'd be like a goat heading for slaughter, happily bleeding and following you."

I laugh, and he shuts me up with a kiss, so desperate like it's our last day together.

"Truce?" he whispers.

I smile through tears. "Truce."

He kisses the tip of my nose, and I'm almost breathless from this cuteness.

"How about I make a quick dinner?" I say, sniffling.

"I'll take anything but Herring Under Fur."

We burst out in laughter.

That's Jace—my bounty hunter, sniper, grits-hater, and a joker.

Virgin…

I need to *not* think about that.

I kiss his cheek as he pulls me off the counter and gently sets me down on the floor.

His soft gaze is on me as I fix us a quick dinner.

"You know I went into the army to override my shitty child-hood," he says.

There he is, opening up again.

I make chicken cutlets, and he tells me about the deployment.

I chop up the tomato-cucumber salad as he tells me about his sniper record.

I boil rice as he talks about the bombings.

Steam fills up the kitchen, and I turn on the vent. It's humming mixes with Jace's soft voice as he tells me how his friend got blown up during a raid.

I cook.

He talks.

He tells me more about the war and how he saved Roey's life. About the year he came back and how hard it was to reconcile the Western peace and the devastation of the war zone.

"And your current job?" I ask when he stops talking.

"That's Roey's gig. He's run it for several years, and it pays great. We don't hurt people. We find them. They are just not your regular folks."

"You know how to fight," I state.

"Yeah."

"I know that." I give him a pretend side-eye. "I saw you kick Chad's ass."

He freezes, meeting my smiling gaze.

"You were so... bad-ass." My chest swells with pride for him.

"He's an asshole."

"He's gone. Thank you for that. You should've punched him right in front of everyone."

"Physical force doesn't solve everything."

Yeah, that's my Jace.

I study him at dinner on the terrace, his careful glances and soft smiles as if he's afraid to anger me.

The sun is setting, and it's him and I, always him and I that makes me the most peaceful, even after the fight we had today.

When I bring up my canceled order, Jace only smiles.

"Why are you so upset about it?" he asks, putting the leftovers away. "Listen, come here."

He leads me to my room, stopping in front of the painting he cleaned up.

"If they don't want it, sell it to someone else. It's beautiful."

I shake my head. "With other people's faces?"

"Change them." He steps behind me and wraps one arm around my waist, pointing his forefinger at the painting like he's trying to show me something I don't notice. "Paint a veil on this face. Paint a designer face mask and sunglasses over this one. It's *Modern Gothic*, right?"

"Yes, I can do that." A smile spreads on my lips at the realization.

"Yeah?"

"Yeah."

He kisses my cheek and sets his chin on my shoulder, his embrace tightening. "Maybe you can add designer fabric print and drones in the sky."

I nod. It'll only take me a day of extra work, but I can do new gothic, yes.

"Dog tags on the ground," I add, visualizing the changes I'll make.

"And"—he presses a kiss to my temple— "auction it off to your social media fans or something. You'll make way more than what your clients owe you. Rub it in their faces. Or donate it to the local community center for auction. People will love you for that. They'll spread the word."

Jace is my inspiration in everything. It's hard to grasp how a person you met only several months ago can become your closest friend, muse, and… lover. Well, not yet, but now I'm determined.

"Movie?" he asks.

"I'd love to." I turn to Pushkin, who sits in the doorway and happily stares at us. "Hey, cute muffin, wanna watch a movie?"

"Hey, Lu?"

I turn to look at Jace, and we both burst out laughing because we know the words coming next. Our smiles meet in a kiss.

"I wasn't asking Pushkin," Jace says anyway and winks.

Gosh, stop! Even his winks send me over the edge.

It's getting dark, and this moment is the one I anticipate the most lately. Not my exhibition, not the parties, not the money I get for my work. Him. Always him.

I turn on the movie as Jace splays on the couch, watching me, and beckons me with his hands. "Come here."

I'll ruin this guy tonight. He has no idea.

His lips brush against my cheek, making my skin tingle with goosebumps as I settle in his arms.

His whisper makes my skin hum. "I want to make you feel good and forget about the crappy day."

His kind eyes are only inches from mine.

"Can we touch more?" I tease. "Or is it for special occasions?"

His forefinger strokes my cheek. "Every minute with you is a special occasion, Lu. I can kiss you a hundred times a day if you let me. There are so many things I want to do to you." His whisper is better than any sex I've ever had. "I'm just afraid that one day, this will end. And when it does, it'll break my heart."

My own heart whimpers at the words. "It won't. I won't let it. Don't let it end. You are mine, Jace Reed. Can you be mine?"

"I was yours the day I met you, Lu."

"With all your dark clothes and your dark past and your tattoos. I want it all, Jace. I'm greedy like that."

"Yes, Lu." His soft chuckle grazes my lips. "That Sharki is yours too."

My pulse booms in my head.

Sharki?

I pull away and meet his eyes.

That word is not a coincidence. It's not. I can tell by the mischievous glint in his eyes.

Warmth stings my cheek, and I feel...ashamed.

"Did you read my stories online?" I whisper and hold my breath.

The sparkles in his eyes turn into little fires. And that fire starts eating me up from within.

He brushes my cheek with the back of his fingers.

"Did you?" I insist, my stomach lurching as I search his eyes for the answer.

His lips hitch in a tiny smile. "Yes, Lu. I did."

52

LU

My heart is about to jump out of my chest and leap from the eleventh floor in embarrassment.

So, Jace has read my stories…

It's humiliating. Also exciting. And I feel vulnerable. Thousands of readers—fine. Jace—and I feel like he found out my dirtiest secret. He is written all over *Sharki*. It's the first time I wrote from the heart and put myself into the story.

Smut from the heart…

"Did you like them?" I ask, looking at the TV screen to avoid Jace's eyes, feeling too exposed.

He cocks his head, trying to look into my eyes. "Yes."

I refuse to look at him, focusing on the TV.

"I wrote them thinking about you," I confess.

My heart does a flip. My breath hitches in my throat. Now I know how he felt when I learned his secrets.

"I'm not like that in real life," I say quieter as if apologizing. "I'm really not. I just write that stuff, and I kinda like it. Then you moved in, and I… I got carried away. You are always so close, and I really like you, and I…" I'm a coward, afraid to speak my mind. "No, I don't like you. You make me crazy." I keep staring at the TV, afraid to meet his eyes. "I paint you, you know. I write about you. I can't stop thinking about you, Jace."

My blood is simmering while my heart is pounding. Feelings overwhelm me, but Jace doesn't say anything.

Pushkin saves me as he comes up and nuzzles my hand.

"Hey, buddy," I whisper, stroking him behind his ear, then remove his eye patch and toss it on the table, all the while afraid to look at Jace.

Jace's hand takes mine and pulls it away from Pushkin. Then his fingers come under my chin, tipping it up for me to look at him.

I drown in the warmth of his eyes. There's a soft smile on his face, the one that always makes me weak.

"I was hoping you *were* thinking about me when you wrote those chapters," he says, his thumb brushing against my jaw. "I know you did." His smile grows bigger. "You gave yourself away, Lu baby, and wrote my name once."

I kick and scream inwardly—he's been reading all the chapters as they were coming out!

"But I don't have that much experience." There's not an ounce of shyness in his gaze. "You already know that by now," he says with confidence like he says he's never tried Herring Under Fur and would like to.

"I'm not exactly a pro either. Just on paper," I confess.

"Can we work on that?"

Abso-freaking-lutely!

We both chuckle as he leans over but pauses to brush his thumb against my bottom lip, looking at me like he's not sure I'm real.

"Can we start tonight?" I whisper in anticipation.

"We can start right now. We need more touching," he whispers back and kisses me. "Definitely more touching," he adds and cups my butt, pressing me hard against him.

Jace is a fantastic kisser. Right now, he doesn't hold back.

His kiss deepens, becomes greedy, open-mouthed, his tongue insistently stroking mine. We kiss like we need to breathe through each other's mouths. I wanted him for too long, craved this so much that my body yields to his touch and burns for more, for him being inside me.

I sneak my hand under his shirt, and all I'm focused on is his warm taut stomach under my palm. I want to feel him, touch him, other places, harder and hotter. I want to wrap around him and climb him.

He stops abruptly and gazes at me for some time.

"What's wrong?" I ask.

There's a flicker of sadness in his eyes. "I don't want this to end."

"We didn't even start yet." I stroke his skin, teasing.

"I'm talking about us, Lu. I don't want this to be a short fling. If it ends, Lu, it will hurt so bad."

"We won't let it end," I promise.

I don't need a contract to make sure I keep my word. I'm about to say just that when he speaks again.

"Lu, I love you."

My heart stops.

"I can't think straight when you are next to me. But I can't breathe when you are not around. I'm so in love with you." He takes my face between his palms. "Head over heels and up to my ears," he whispers, smiling.

In one heartbeat, his smile softly touches mine, and my heart explodes.

53

JACE

WE KISS FOR SO LONG THAT MY LIPS FEEL SWOLLEN. MY HEART HAS unfolded and is wrapping its gentle tentacles around Lu.

I want more. For the first time, I crave it so badly that my brain shuts off with its constant rationalizing.

We are a tangle of limbs. Lu is on top of me as her mouth devours mine, her hands sneaking under my shirt, setting my skin on fire.

"We can go slow," she murmurs between the kisses. "As slow as you want, Jace."

Is my girl giving me counseling while we are at it?

"Stop talking," I whisper as I take her lips again.

I know what she's doing. She heard Roey's words and probably thinks I have issues. She's being cautious.

Fuck caution.

I'm burning with need. I've always felt uneasy reaching this part. That's the reason I never sealed the deal with other girls. Call me old-fashioned, but I never wanted a meaningless fuck.

But here's the deal with Lu. She already fucked my mind, pretty much since the day I met her. She fucked my heart, and it's melting like chocolate in the sun from her being in my arms.

The big moment? I don't care what happens, but I don't feel an ounce of nervousness or fear of screwing up. Like I've been with Lu for the longest time. Like she's my best friend. My girl.

"Just touching," she murmurs, like I need reassurance.

But touching doesn't cut it anymore.

"We are not watching a movie, are we?" she whispers as if to make sure.

"We are making our own," I say. "Naked."

Maybe she doesn't want to go further, and that's fine with me.

Maybe not so much—I reconsider when her hand starts stroking my bulge straining the fabric of my jeans.

Hell, yeah, we're on the same page!

I felt butterflies in my stomach minutes ago. Now? Fuck butterflies, it's a zoo inside me, howling, clawing, grunting, as my body wants to rip through the clothes, like those werewolves during a full moon.

We are dry humping, and clothes are my enemy.

"Let's take this off," I order softly, and she shifts, letting me pull her dress over her head.

"Yours too," she murmurs as we catch greedy kisses while she helps me with my shirt.

Lu feels so much better bare against me. If it wasn't for her bra.

"This has to go." I unclasp it, my slight fumbling unnoticed as we grind against each other.

Her bare breasts are in my hands, and my mouth goes everywhere, open kisses down her neck, her shoulder, and chest, taking her nipple in my mouth.

Fuuuuuck...

The texture of it sends my mind reeling. Her moan makes me wanna moan in sync with her. I lap at it like a freaking dog while my hands start pushing her panties down.

Lu arches into my mouth, her fingers twisting into my hair as she lifts her hips, letting me push her panties down, then shimmies out of them. She pulls me away from her breasts and leans down to kiss the tattoos on my chest.

I stare wide-eyed at her naked body, splayed on top of mine. This is straight out of my fantasies. Her cute bare butt is so delicious I want to catch it between my hands and kiss the hell out of it.

Her forefinger hooks under my waistband and pauses as Lu raises her eyes at me.

"Take them off," I order softly.

I'm not shy. I want her to see me and touch me. And I eat up the view—Lu, naked, sliding my jeans down my hips, letting my erection spring free.

The self-control I've worked on for years is gone.

I don't give Lu a second to rest.

"Come here."

I grunt at the contact when her naked body presses against mine and shift us to our sides so I have more control of what I do to her. For the first time, I stop thinking and let my hands and mouth say what I can't express with words.

"I need to go get a condom," I murmur, hating the thought that I have to break this up even for a second. God, do I want to be inside her.

Her tongue is the biggest tease, sending shivers down my entire body. Her hands come second, and they will come first if they touch me where I am as hard as a steel rod.

"I'm on the pill," she murmurs, her impatient mouth catching mine.

Well, there goes my sanity. I'll be bare inside her. The thought alone is enough to make me come, but I hold back with a grunt.

She shifts, and my erection is between her legs. She presses against it and starts rolling her hips.

I'll come. If she keeps doing this, I'll blow like a teenager. In a New York second, which is the time it takes between the traffic light turning green and the cab behind you honking. Except I might beat that time. I'm a record breaker.

"Lu, baby, slow down, or I won't make it."

To where I want to be, inside her.

She's wet down there. Holy hell, she's an ocean.

"Jace," she whimpers, rubbing against me even harder. "You feel so good."

"You too."

"And so big. It might not even fit…"

Oh, hell, no. This is reverse psychology at its finest.

"It'll fit," I murmur.

"You think?"

"Yeah. Wanna check?"

We laugh into each other's mouths.

But then the little minx shifts, positioning my hardness between her legs, and starts rubbing against it. So fucking good, I moan and pull her thigh up, bringing her leg over my hips, opening her up. My hands go up to cup her face as I eat her mouth out, and she rubs against my hardness one more time until its tip is pressed against her entrance.

"I can't wait any longer," she whispers, panting.

My Lu is impatient.

I buck my hips against her, feeling myself thrust just a little in.

Fucking yes!

I can't hold back anymore either.

She starts sinking onto me in short little increments.

I thrust into her.

I *am* inside her.

She moans.

I grunt.

Good hell! Why did I wait for so long?

I cup her sweet butt, holding her tightly against me, then carefully shift on top of her and resume the gentle thrusts.

This is unbelievable.

Pleasure pulsates from where we fuse together all through my body. Amazing. But I need to focus on Lu if I want to make it good for her and last a little longer.

"Tell me what to do to make you feel good."

I slide my fingers between our bodies and down to her junction.

She's so wet.

I'm so hard.

I start stroking her, sliding my fingers down to where I can feel myself thrusting in.

Fuck, I want to sit back and watch myself slide in and out of her.

Lu's hands tighten in my hair.

"Jace," she whimpers, then moans louder. "Don't stop."

I won't. Ever.

I drive into her a little harder to prove my point.

She gasps. "Too deep."

"I'll be careful," I whisper back, easing on my thrusts, but paying more attention to my fingers on her and studying her face like it's *her* first time.

Covering all the bases. That's right.

Can I feel her orgasm?

The thought is wild. I want to rip her apart, but I hold back, thrusting with caution.

Am I too big? I'm barely halfway in, but I don't want to hurt her.

All of my senses are overwhelmed. I'm so ready, but I can't spend yet.

I can't.

I can't.

But how could I have known it would feel so good to be inside another person?

Everything is too much. Her heat I'm sinking into, the warmth of her body underneath me, her tightness around me down there, the feelings spilling over, the craving for her, the tenderness toward her, knowing I have the power to make her feel good.

One of my thrusts makes her gasp.

"I'll have to get used to you," she whispers, mewling as my fingers stroke her to the rhythm of my thrusts.

That's a promise.

"You'll get used to me, Lu baby. I'm already used to you."

This is amazing. So easy, like dancing when you catch the rhythm. I thought the first time, I'd be fixated on my own sensations. Instead, I'm fixated on her, being inside her, making her feel good.

Lu closes her eyes, her lips parting at my thrusts, her thighs falling open wider.

I smile as I kiss her cheek, neck, and shoulder.

"Tell me what feels good," I whisper.

"This," she hums back. "Just like that, Jace." She moans. "Don't you dare stop."

"I won't."

I want to say filthy things to her, go chapter by chapter and reenact everything she wrote. I'll make a list.

But not tonight.

Tonight, it's all about her feeling so good that she wants to do it a hundred more times with me.

Right now, Lu is lost completely, chasing something I can't see.

But there are signs—her little gasps, her eyes fluttering closed, a louder moan following.

I bring my mouth to hers, and her tongue plunges in, making me dizzy.

My brain is so sexually charged, I wish I had more hands, more mouths, and more fingers to fill her everywhere.

"You are so fucking beautiful," I whisper.

"Jace," she exhales, her body tensing.

She throws her head back and cries out, her fingers fisting my hair.

I don't stop. Her cries come in sync with my thrusts, and that's the last drop of my patience as I see her fall apart, her body going limp.

"Jace, I just..."

"I know, baby."

I'm so fucking proud knowing that I made her come. That's my doing—her undoing. And I'm about to follow because no one told me that holding back is harder than swimming in an army uniform against the strongest rip current.

In seconds, I come hard, spilling inside her. Without a condom—the feeling is bewildering, though I don't know any other.

I still, feeling suddenly too much love for her and slight disappointment that it's over. Wrapping my arm around her waist, I shift to her side, pulling her against me so I can see her.

We are flush against each other, skin to skin, sweaty, breathing hard. There's a satisfied daze in her luminous eyes and a little smile on her lips when she lifts her hand and strokes my face.

Dear God, when it's my time to go, I want to die just like this, next to my favorite person and feeling her touch.

"Did you like it?" I ask her.

"I should be asking *you* that. Well, considering..." Right. "Did you?" Her smile fades a little as she waits for my answer.

I kiss her mouth. "What do you think, Lu?"

I kiss her shoulder next, taking a deep inhale of her. She smells like sex, like us, like me.

"I need more practice to get the feel of it," I joke, ready to do it again.

She laughs as she buries her face in my chest, her blonde hair splayed across my tattoos.

Her breasts brush against my skin.

My skin. *Her* breasts.

I still think it's a dream.

She peeks at me from under her brows. "To get the feel of it, huh? Can we practice more right now?"

You kidding me? "I was hoping we would."

She drags her forefinger along my chest, making my skin tingle.

"Jace," she drawls, "I think that story of you not having done it before is bullshit."

I lean in to kiss her earlobe, whispering, "Oh, yeah?"

She shrugs me away with a little giggle. "Yeah. I think you are fibbing. You are too good for someone who hasn't had much practice."

Roey must've been right.

"You know what's more important than your dick, Jace? Your hands and your mouth."

"I have a manual," I say. A little kiss behind her ear makes her shiver in my arms.

"Oh, yeah?" Her fingers slide lower, teasing my shark. She has a thing for it.

I glance down. "Yeah. It's called *Sharki.*"

She hides her face in my chest again, and I can't help teasing her.

"I know all your dirty thoughts, Lu. Look at me." She peeks at me from under her eyebrows. "I'm so into them. And we are so doing all of it."

That's right.

This role reversal is bewildering. I'm ready to give her all I got, and she's shy. But I know what she thinks about me and how often. I know the feelings that soak every word in her novel. I was a fool thinking she was making it up when in reality, for weeks, she's been going through the same feelings as me.

I kiss the scarlet blush on her cheeks and let my hands trace her curves. I pull her thigh upward, resting it over my hip, opening her so I can touch her better.

Practice.

My fingers explore between her legs. I'll perfect this. Maybe I already am, because Lu mewls and presses her breasts to my chest, grinding against my hand.

Is that how addiction works?

I think Lu is my drug. I want more. Now and for hours.

"I can't get enough of you," I murmur, kissing her everywhere I can reach.

Being with Lu is effortless.

I want to explore more with her.

And, oh, we will. A to Z. Maybe the Cyrillic version of it too.

54

LU

Jace is still asleep when I wake up, snug in his arms. My body is slightly sore from all the action last night, first on the couch, then Jace's bed.

I wiggle out of his embrace, and he shifts onto his back, one arm raised above his head like he's modeling for a raunchy bed photoshoot.

My Jace.

His body is powerful. It's art. I'm still in disbelief that he is naked and next to me.

Slowly, I pull the sheet below his waist, to where it just barely covers his intimate parts, the shark tattoo ending at the fine dusting of hair.

Hello, Sharki.

I reach with my finger, wanting to trace its shape, hovering only an inch away.

A bark makes me jerk my hand away and my heart thud in panic.

My eyes snap at Jace.

There's a grin on his lips, his half-open eyes smiling at me.

"Tsk, silly." I pretend-slap him.

"You seem to really like that guy." He flicks his eyes to his abdomen, the sheet slightly tenting.

"Yeah." I laugh, burying my face in his warm chest, shy at the sign of his growing erection. "What made you get this?"

"A shark has great significance in indigenous cultures," he explains as his fingers brush against the side of my arm. "The whole pyramid of symbols was supposed to anchor on the shark and its teeth, the symbol of male and spiritual power."

"Why there?"

Jace rubs his eyes, grinning. "It wasn't supposed to go *that* low."

I hold back laughter. "You mean, it wasn't meant to lead down south?"

I bring my forefinger to his abdomen and trail it down the shark tattoo. Jace sucks in his stomach, the sheet-tent below slowly pitching higher.

"No." His eyes flicker to the tented sheet over his erection and then to me. "My indigenous tattooist might've been slightly high."

Both of us break out in laughter, and he raises his knee under the sheet to hide his hardness.

"So was I." He grins. "I'm kidding. It just… happened."

"I love it. Jace, you might be the cutest person I've met."

"Cute?" He cocks a brow. "Is that even flattering in guys?"

"It is in *you*. I think he likes me too," I whisper, trailing my finger lower to where his trimmed hair tickles my fingertip, his muscles twitching.

"He's an aggressive guy," Jace whispers. "Getting too excited already at your touch."

"So, what does it take to tame that guy?"

"Maybe a couple of kisses."

Is this even Jace?

A breath hitches in my throat.

Game on.

I pull the sheet lower, unwrapping his hardness like a gift. The sheet pulls at its tip then pops off, letting it free, and I run my fingertips along his length, studying his reaction.

If a gaze could touch, Jace's would be licking me by now and penetrating my every orifice.

I keep stroking him, but unlike the time when I was painting him, I openly study him.

He's silent. His chest rises and falls slowly, shaking just a little as if he has a hard time breathing evenly.

I break the eye contact, lean over, and press a little kiss to his hardness.

A gasp escapes him.

I look up and meet his widening eyes, then press another soft kiss to his length, then another, going lower, following my fingers that sneak between his legs and cup him.

I wrote a lot about sex—grunts and gasps. But the sexiest sound is Jace moaning.

A barely audible whimper escapes him at first. Then a louder moan comes when I gently squeeze him. It's lower, heavier, followed by a gasp, then what sounds like a curse. He lifts his hips just a little off the mattress like he's following my mouth. Another kiss, and I let my tongue out to taste him.

"Lu," he exhales.

My lips move up his length.

"Lu baby, you'll make me—"

"Yes, I will. Don't stop me," I murmur and take him in, intending to make my beautiful guy fall apart.

It only takes a moment. Like he's been edged all night. Edging—another thing I want to do to him.

I make a mental note right before he murmurs, "Lu, I'm—"

"I know," I whisper against him, pull back, and stroke him as he explodes in my hand. "Good morning," I say, biting back my smile.

He rubs his face with both hands, and when he finally looks at me, he's grinning.

He cleans my hand, then pulls the sheet over our heads, covering us head to toe.

"Hi," he whispers before kissing me.

It's dim. The sunshine seeping through the sheet casts a soft glow on his face, a naughty strand of hair falling onto his forehead.

"Turn face down, baby," he orders.

I do.

His hands run along my body, from my shoulders to my hips, like he's about to give me a massage. Then he leans over, and his lips are on me—soft kisses on my shoulders, trailing down my back, then my waist as his body shifts lower.

He nudges his knees between my legs, opening me, and kisses my butt cheeks.

Oh-oh-oh…

I don't have this in *Sharki*. Or any of my stories. This is Jace freaking Reed improvising.

He kisses one cheek, then the other. Then he runs the tip of his tongue along the crease.

"Jace," I whisper, burying my face in the pillow in slight embarrassment but lifting my butt off the mattress because it feels so good.

"I'm right here, Lu," he whispers back.

He presses a kiss just below the curve of my butt, then one closer to between my legs.

"Open wider, baby," he whispers, nudging my thighs apart, then kisses me right there, my hot center, and I shamelessly moan.

"Up," he orders, lifting my hips, and I keep my face in the pillow as I rise on my knees to give him more access.

My face burns in shame, but I want him so bad.

"Yes," he murmurs as his tongue drives me crazy.

He lets go, and in seconds, the sheet above us moves, pitching, as he rises to his knees and sheaths into me, making me cry out.

He grunts as he takes me. "Lu baby, you make me crazy."

Right away, his hand slides around my hip and between my legs.

He lied—he is a pro in bed.

"Is it true what they say?" I pant out into the pillow, chasing the high.

"What?" he exhales, thrusting deeper.

"That newbies are the most enthusiastic in bed?"

"Are they?" A soft chuckle escapes him as he rolls his hips as if to prove my point.

Every time we do it, it's a different position, like he's exploring. And nothing—*nothing*—gives away his lack of experience.

He tricked me. This confidence doesn't come from a virgin. Neither do kisses like his, open-mouthed and in the right places. Neither do the fingers that tease me open even wider for his penetration.

"Do you come every time?" he asks in a hoarse voice.

"When I do it myself? Yes." I can't believe I'm discussing this with a guy while he is inside of me.

"Will you teach me, Lu?"

He's messing with me?

"Yes," I whisper.

He rolls his hips as he thrusts deeper.

"Yes," I whimper, taking him in.

Holy crap, yes!

If he teaches me to keep it under control with him. I've never been too open with men. Nor was I ever confident in bed or a know-it-all. My writing takes a lot of research and theory. Yeah, theory...

But Jace is so shameless in the way he studies me, so enthusiastic, so greedy for my body, that I want to contort to give him every inch of me.

"Just not right now, Jace. Please," I exhale, so wanting to come. "We'll do a study group later."

He chuckles behind me. "I'll be an A-student."

His fingers between my legs apply just the right amount of pressure to prove the point, making me buck at him, wanting more.

There's a sudden bright flash of light. The sheet above us is gone, and so is the feeling of Jace inside me.

His arms wrap around me, and in a second, I'm on my back, Jace on top of me.

"Hi," he blurts with a smile, settling between my legs, and kissing me.

He's slow and careful when he's back inside me, but so intense. Too much like a book boyfriend. And too much is not enough. I want him everywhere.

"Jace..."

"Yes, baby." He keeps thrusting. Keeps touching. Keeps kissing.

"I'm so close."

"I know, baby."

I'm pushing myself into him, wanting to take him all despite him being a little too big.

More. I want more. And not just his body but the feelings, the untamable need, the intensity of his eyes as he watches me reach my climax.

My breath hitches, and everything grows together inside as I reach the peak and Jace leans over, whispering words that make my head spin. Grunting into my neck, he collapses on top of me, and I wrap my arms around him and hold him so close that I feel like we grow into one.

That's Jace and me, the ridiculous couple that we are, joking as we have sex, teasing each other with silly things.

I slide out of bed.

"Coffee?" I ask, sauntering to the door.

He cushions his head with his forearm, studying me up and down. "Sure."

For the first time, I feel totally at ease in my own skin. His eyes glide over my body with a wonder and appreciation that make me want to show off my nakedness.

The living room is littered with our clothes. I put on panties and a tank and make us coffee.

A minute later, he walks out only in his sweatpants.

It's my favorite look of his. Shirtless, his tattoos on full display, his dog tag telling the story of his past that made him into this beautiful man who took my heart captive.

He comes up behind me and kisses my neck.

My phone rings and remains unanswered, then beeps with a text message, and I pick it up.

"Right, I promised," I murmur as I read the text.

This is the wrong day and time. I have so many things on my mind. There's an exhibit tonight, which, thanks to Jace and his distraction, I haven't stressed over until this very moment.

"Jace?" I say as he steps next to me with a coffee in his hand.

His kiss on my shoulder makes me grin. I'm somehow dreading the rest of the day though I've been looking forward to it for months.

His eyes search my face like he can discern every little emotion on it. "What is it?"

"I have to meet someone before I go to the gallery. It'll be quick. Will you come with me?"

"Of course. Is everything alright?"

"Yeah. I just... I'd like you to come with me."

"Sure. Always. I can be your bodyguard." He winks.

Somehow, him being next to me makes my nervousness about what comes next go away.

55

JACE

It's hot outside and overcast, but Lu insists we take the train.

I'm not a fan of the suffocating heat in the subway. Or the stench lifting off the tunnels, the hundreds of smells of food and sweat lacing in the air. But I love observing people.

We take a ride to a little Italian cafe not far from the gallery.

Lu is quiet, like she's somewhere else.

I smile at her. She smiles back. She doesn't tell me who we are meeting, but I'd go with her anywhere. Especially when she's suddenly so unsettled when she should be reeling in excitement about her exhibition opening.

"You alright?" I ask.

She nods.

She isn't, but she won't tell me what's up, and I don't press. I'm here for her.

Her fingers intertwine with mine. She tilts her head onto my shoulder, and the Asian woman across from us glances at us and smiles at me with a soft nod.

Yes, this is us, in public, together. I want the whole world to know.

She keeps her hand in mine as we walk into a brightly lit cafe and take a front table.

Lu is nervous when I order coffee. She hasn't had breakfast but packed a bag with clothes to wear for the exhibit tonight. She'll be spending the entire day at the gallery and insisted she didn't need my help.

That's fine with me. I should give her space, though, after our night together, I want to be attached to her at the hip.

A black limo pulls up to the curb outside. A tall man in a suit steps out. Another one steps by his side—I know bodyguards when I see them.

The man in the suit walks into the cafe, and my heart sinks into my stomach.

This is a weird coincidence.

I know the man.

Fuck.

What the hell is Seth Gordon doing here?

I've never met him, but considering he is our employer, I've seen plenty of his pictures, studied his bio, his business records, his dealings with Reznik, and the crypto endeavor.

His eyes search the cafe then stop on our table, Lu, then me, narrowing as he slowly makes his way toward us.

I'm confused.

The man who is in the top hundred of US Forbes, the man who also deals with shady guys like Reznik, found me in a cafe in Brooklyn?

What's happening?

His eyes shift to Lu as he approaches the table and takes a seat across from us.

What the fuck…

Unease twists my stomach.

He's looking at Lu and starts nodding, his expression suddenly warming up and acquiring an intensity that I can't decipher.

I turn to Lu and notice her awkward smile.

"Hello," she says timidly and adds, "Father."

Mind blown.

Everything I know about Seth Gordon and Lu shifts like the information in a self-generating AI code, line by line, searching for the clues, clicking together.

"I was hoping to meet you alone," Seth Gordon says, looking at Lu with a soft smile.

I keep my eyes on him, afraid to flinch, trying to stay calm as my thoughts throw a tantrum.

How the fuck did we miss that?

She told me she had a biological father, right. I didn't tell Roey or Miller. And Roey never gave Seth Gordon the name of the new female lead we had, Lu.

"So, hey, this is Jace, my…um… friend and roommate," Lu introduces us.

I swallow hard. My heartbeat spikes so high I think I might be having a heart attack.

Seth Gordon's gaze is seemingly indifferent when he meets my eyes.

Great poker face. Fucking great. I hope mine is too.

Fuck-fuck-fuck.

And while they are having a casual chat, I think about going to the bathroom and calling Roey. Except that would be a clear giveaway. I'm a little too fucking late.

I'm trying to figure out if Seth Gordon already knew who I was before coming here. Or that I live in the same condo as his daughter. And if he didn't, what the implications are. But most importantly, why Reznik, who's scammed Gordon out of a lot of money, suddenly showed up in Lu's life.

"I'll be in the city until tomorrow," he says. "I was thinking of coming to your exhibit tonight."

Lu must've told him about it, and just the thought that Gordon and I *and* Roey will be at the same place is bewildering if not unprofessional.

"Tonight is going to be so stressful," Lu says with hesitation. "The exhibit will be open for a month. Maybe some other time? I'd love for you to see my art. It's just… Tonight is going to be chaos."

She should be proud of her exhibit, but somehow everything she does and says lately feels like she's doubting herself, and it breaks my heart.

Seth Gordon only nods, his jaw clenching, his submissiveness in contrast with his powerful build.

He's my employer and my Lu's father. Wow. That night we stalked Reznik crossed a lot of paths in the strangest way.

Soon, Seth Gordon is leaving and asks whether Lu needs a ride. *She needs a ride, not us*—he doesn't even look at me when he says goodbye and walks out. But as soon as the black limo pulls away, I get a text.

Seth Gordon: When you are alone, give me a call.

I'm fucked. I know this already, but I'm trying to focus on Lu, who exhales through her puffed lips when we walk out into the humid street.

"So, what do you think?" she asks.

"He is an impressive man," I say, my mind spinning with a dozen thoughts, the lies, the fact that this is going to be yet another blow to Lu's confidence when I tell her the truth. And I don't fucking want to ruin it for her today, but there is no other option.

We walk to an art store down the street where Lu needs to pick something up for the gallery. And while she goes inside, I stay outside and dial Seth Gordon.

The street around me pulsates in sync with the blood pumping in my head. His voice is like that of a hangman when he picks up after just one ring.

"Tell me this is the biggest coincidence and you are *not* gathering intel on my daughter for the Reznik assignment." His voice is a hundred degrees colder than at the cafe.

"It's a coincidence, sir." It's not, fuck. "But she so happens to be the new lead Roey Torres told you about. And we were—"

"You are off."

"Pardon me?"

"You are off the assignment. Our contract is off. You have nothing to do with Reznik anymore. No one from your company does. And I want you out of my daughter's life, starting today. Right now, actually."

My head starts spinning. "Sir, let me explain—"

"You heard me. I've read your portfolio. I know your history. Does she know you work for me?"

"No."

"Exactly. My daughter should not be around someone like you."

Now I am furious. It's my fault for mixing business with my

personal life. But if our business is done, as of several seconds ago, he has no right to tell me who I can be with.

"Your daughter and I—"

"Vacate the Goldsling Towers' condo today. It's a warning. Considering your record, you should be good with orders."

"Does she know what you do? Or your business with Reznik?"

"If she finds out, I'll assume it's you. And then you'll be lucky if any cell of your body is ever found."

"All due respect, sir, she's my friend. Our acquaintance was a coincidence. I'm not—"

"You are vacating the condo," he snaps, "and dropping all contact with her. Understood?"

He doesn't need to use harsher words. I know what he's capable of and what his unlimited funds can do, including making people disappear.

"I don't want her anywhere near you," he adds. "Or any of the men in your company. I see you anywhere around her, Mr. Reed, you'll be sorry. Have a good day."

56

JACE

Sweat trickles down my back, my shirt damp from it. The traffic noise makes it hard to concentrate.

I turn toward the shop to make sure Lu is still inside and dial Roey.

"Roey, I'm sorry."

I start talking, and when I'm finished, he's quiet for a moment.

"I got a call from Seth Gordon right before yours," he says. "It was brief. Yes, we are off the assignment."

And then he says the one thing I didn't expect him to say.

"Fuck Seth Gordon. He won't find a better team than us."

My breath hitches in my throat in confusion. "You are not mad at me?"

"It was a coincidence," Roey says. "I made you room with her. I was briefing him on our progress, but he cut me off when I was about to give him the details, including the name of our lead, and told me to deal with it. Miller somehow missed the connection. That's our fault, too. I understand why Gordon is mad about you being so close to his daughter. It's not professional. But the truth is, we didn't know who she was until today."

"Right," I murmur, a thousand pounds lifting off my chest at his words.

"It's entirely my fault. I didn't check her info properly. He doesn't want us on the assignment? Well, we still need to get our expenses back and pay the Eastern-European surveillance team. So we keep working on this."

"You mean—"

"We are going to find Reznik and get paid by him."

"What?!"

"Yep. The guy stole a lot of money. If we don't get paid by the first client, we find a new client. We'll get paid by Reznik for whatever he wants us to do."

"You are not serious."

"Dead serious."

"We don't make deals with criminals."

"We've made numerous deals with criminals before, Jace. We find people and get paid. We are not involved in right or wrong. And that's what we are doing. Our client is not Seth Gordon anymore. It's Anatolyi Reznik. He just doesn't know it yet."

"Roey, we can't cross Seth Gordon or go against him. I don't want enemies, and I don't want to upset Lu, considering he's her father."

I'm trying to process the info when he says. "So you are banging the former client's daughter. Your first time and a jackpot." He snorts.

"I'm not banging her."

"Yes, you are. I can fucking tell by your voice."

"That's not—"

"You know, Lucy Moor has been a strange mojo from the beginning."

"She has nothing to do with this."

"She has *everything* to do with this."

"Then that's the way it is!"

"You are fucking in love, Jace."

"Yes."

"Oh, yeah? You are not even denying it?"

"I'm not denying it, Roey. You've known it for a while. And I don't give two shits about Reznik or Gordon anymore. But I do care about her."

"Wow. First pussy, and you are ready to give up five million dollars for it. Expensive. Except Daddy just fired us and we still need to find our new client."

He sounds bitter. I am angry. But it's my fault, and it was his paycheck too, and Miller's.

"I'm sorry, Roey. I can use my savings to pay off the Eastern Europeans and the Reznik expenses."

He exhales into the phone. "It's alright. It's not your fault. And it was my idea to set you up with Lucy. So, chill. I'm glad you are not giving up on her."

"Not a chance. The rich asshole can suck it."

"Good."

"Good?"

"Yes. Good. Finally. You sorted things out then, right?"

Here's the thing with Roey. He might act like a dick, but he's supportive of Lu and me. And that's taking into account that he's a womanizer and caps his new friendships after one night.

"I'm not going back to California," I say. "Well, unless Lu throws a fit when I tell her about her father. And I will, Roey. There's no other way. Even though he threatened me."

"You've been to a war zone, Jace." Roey chuckles, his voice unusually relaxed. "You know that when you are threatened, you make sure you have a good defense."

"So, you're not mad at me for losing the assignment?"

"Jesus, we didn't lose anything yet. We are not going to cross Gordon. We are just going to get to Reznik and see what services we can provide for him."

"And get killed by him?"

"Don't be dramatic. We are businessmen. Our business is without casualties. We mostly do stuff by the book. Trust me, a man like Reznik will find our services useful. If it's any consolation, this is the most fucked up yet the most interesting assignment I've ever had. Kudos to you."

Fuck, Roey might be the most reasonable guy I've ever met. When it comes to work, not women, that is.

"Let's chat at the gallery tonight, yeah?" he asks.

"Sure. That works."

"And Jace? Honestly? I'm glad to finally see you happy. You deserve it. You just need to make this work with Lu. And Seth Gordon can fuck off."

I fucking love this guy.

"Hey!"

I turn around to see Lu smile at me. I take the bags out of her hands and do my best to smile back.

The richest man on the East Coast just told me I can't be with her and is digging a grave for me. But there's no chance in hell I'm leaving her. Reznik is dangerous. She doesn't know it. Nor does she know that the night we met wasn't a coincidence. I'm so fucking in love with this girl that I can fight an army of Seth Gordons and Rezniks as long as she lets me stay by her side.

For that, I need to unwrap one last lie.

I might ruin this with her, but if there's one thing she deserves, finally, it's the whole truth. It's also the only thing that might save us.

Her smile is finally more cheerful. "Can you help me to the gallery with all this stuff?"

"Sure." I take a deep breath. "Lu, I need to tell you something. And I need you to promise me that you will take time thinking it over and not get mad at me."

Her smile disappears. "You can't come to the exhibit?"

"I'm *absolutely* coming to the exhibit."

"Are you leaving the city?" Her eyes search my face.

"Absolutely not."

"Does it have to do with your job?"

"Yes."

"Something you didn't tell me?"

"Yes." I meet her eyes and lean over to kiss her forehead, gathering all the courage I have to make things right. "I need to tell you how I met your father."

57

LU

I'm in shock. Yes. Positively.

Or angry?

No, not angry, but I can't process what Jace just told me.

He's silent after he finishes his story about my father. His employer? And Uncle. Wanted by the FBI and my father! And the bracelet with the nerve agent. Is this even real?

I close my eyes, trying to piece together the story in my head.

The little courtyard between the residential buildings that we pulled into is empty but feels too noisy. My mind definitely is, reeling and trying to come to terms with what I just heard.

"A target," I murmur. "I was an assignment. A Brooklyn assignment, huh?"

"Lu, it started that way but soon became different."

I sit on the bench, and Jace sits on the ground across from me, his knees raised, his back against the pole of a kids' swing. His eyes are a world of emotions that mirror mine. He's so humble that I can't bring myself to say anything bitter.

"I didn't know he was your father," he says for the dozent time.

"But I was an assignment."

"At first, Lu. At first!"

"How much do you know about me?" I ask, feeling more vulnerable than when I learned he knew my SD pen name.

"Everything that was on your phone. Not me, Danny Miller, another partner of ours."

I feel so exposed. "And the bug?"

"I removed it after several days."

"My computer?"

"No."

"What else? What else, Jace? What else are you hiding from me?"

"There's a gun in your apartment."

"I know that." I feel bitter. "Thanks for telling me now."

I *want* to lash out, but the anger drowns in helplessness. There's so much I don't know about my biological father.

Should I send Jace away and tell him I don't want to see him? A second-act breakup is the rule for romance books.

But I don't have it in me. I'm in love, and I wish I didn't feel that there'll come another day with yet another lie.

"I'm sorry, Lu. It was wrong. But it was an important assignment. *Was* an assignment until..."

He rubs the back of his neck and closes his eyes like he's collecting his thoughts.

"Until?" I ask him quietly though my heart beats like a drum.

He opens his eyes and looks at me. "Until I started falling for you, and everything else wasn't relevant, because all I wanted was to be near you, with you, and not think about the fact that we met because of someone's shady deal."

His gaze is so vulnerable that I have to make an effort to take deeper breaths.

"Was Pushkin a setup too?"

His desperation-filled eyes widen in momentary shock. "What? No. No. No."

I chuckle nervously. "At least someone is not in on the lies."

Can I blame him for how we met? Not really.

"You shot me..." I say echoing my thoughts.

"Lu baby, by accident. I never miss. I... I didn't miss." He smiles vaguely.

A silly smile flickers on my lips. "Like a Cupid with an arrow, huh?"

My smile grows.

He *is* a freaking Cupid. Shot me with some potion that made me say crazy things, write sexy stuff, and have the most inappropriate fantasies about a man I barely knew. Also, cook him dinners and wear his pineapple underwear. And eventually, fall in love with him.

"I'll have to tell Becky," I say.

"What does *she* have to do with it?"

"It's just polite, you know." *Now* the bitterness comes out. "To let people know that you carry a gun license and maybe a gun and—"

"I don't carry a gun," he argues and adds quieter, "right now."

And why do I think it's so hot? Because I'm definitely messed up.

His eyes don't leave me like I'm the last thing he's allowed to look at before he dies.

"Lu?" He cocks his head like he's waiting for forgiveness. "Please, don't take this away from us."

Us. He knows how I feel. Then he should know that I won't do that. Just the thought of not having him around is painful.

My biological father threatened to bury Jace. And that's before the man who makes my heart swell officially became my boyfriend.

Not a chance in hell!

This is reality. I'm willing to deal with this. Because no one has ever made me feel like Jace.

"If you want," I say quietly, "I can call my—" Father, Jace works for my father, but I can't get myself to say the word out loud. "—your former employer and tell him to leave you alone. If he wants to have dinner, he'll listen. If he wants to keep in contact with me, he will."

"Lu, I don't want to jeopardize your relationship with your biological father."

"Well, you wouldn't have to if you didn't shoot me."

"Lu!" His gaze is so desperate that I can't hold back laughter. I laugh—how ridiculous is that?

"The strangest thing about this situation is that I know you better than him, Jace. I care about you more. I'll blackmail him. He has no right, no right to tell me what to do and who to date."

The last word just slipped out, and even though we didn't talk about it, that's what we are doing, dating, and my heart leaps at the thought. This is not the time for clarification, but my mind latches on to that word and repeats it endlessly.

Jace's gaze heats up, and he rises to his feet, comes over, and drops to his knees, then sits on his heels and takes my hands in his.

"Tonight is a big night, Lu. And I'm here for you. Always."

"I'm just afraid this exhibit will be a failure. Things are... crazy lately."

Crazy is an understatement. They are a giant swing.

"Lu, don't say this. It's all my fault. And I'm sorry that today, out of all days, you got to hear the last bit and the end of the story."

"*Is* it the end?"

"In my mind, it's the beginning. If it wasn't for that night, for Reznik, for your father, I would've never met you, Lu. It's crazy, but it's the truth, and I'm so grateful for it, even though it makes you angry."

He lifts my hands to his lips and kisses them. There is no power in the world to make me stop him, despite the hurt feelings. His touch is healing. One touch and my heart starts purring.

"I know it will sound crazy, Lu, but if I didn't shoot you that night in April, it would've been the saddest thing," Jace says quietly. "I would've never known that you existed. If I didn't have that Brooklyn assignment and move in with you, I would've never found out that there is this wonderful person who makes me dream. You. You make my heart beat so fucking hard that it aches when you are not around. I can't bear it when you are sad. And definitely not when you are hurt. Especially when I might be the reason for it."

Tears well up in my eyes. No one has ever said words like this to me. His feelings mirror mine, and I'm drowning in them.

"Love was a foreign concept when I was growing up," Jace says quietly. "Something that's thrown around so easily by many people, but I didn't understand it. I loved the way others loved each other in movies, spied on families on the streets, read about it in books. I was confused. Family is the source of love. And family is the basic unit of a society. The most common. Yet, I didn't have one. It's as if God picked me out of thousands and said, 'Nope, not this one. This one will be a lone weed.' I never thought I deserved love until I met you, Lu."

I hold my breath so sobs don't betray me as his words softly spill into the air.

I love him so much. He doesn't know it. But he so deserves it, and I need to tell him that.

"Now I know what love feels like," he continues with a soft smile. "And not an adolescent attraction driven by hormones, but a profound feeling of knowing that someone is more important to you than the entire universe. It's magical, really. You are magic, Lu. Given a choice, I would've spent my twenty-four years in misery again if only I was promised a chance to meet you. You were so worth the wait, Lu."

I bite my bottom lip so hard that I might break the skin.

"I love you, Lu," he says quietly. "I love you so much that there is no threat that can possibly make me step back and let you go. I won't."

My chest shakes as I suppress the sob. "I thought my father threatened you," I say, trying to hold back tears and emotions and a silly smile because this man is willing to fight for me and no one has ever fought for me before.

He chuckles. "Lu, you know I don't like to fight, but I don't like threats and bullying. And I'm great at disarming attackers."

He's so much more powerful when he takes pride in his past.

"I have my own ways," he continues. "I'll do whatever it takes to make up for this mess. I'll be patient and give you space if you need to think about us. But I won't let you go. This, I won't do. I'm a freaking Brooklynite now. And Brooklynites are unapologetic and strong-headed as fuck."

A laugh escapes me.

No, this is not Sharki. Sharki didn't get to this point in my book yet. Jace is taking the lead, *has* been since the beginning, and he's everything I ever wanted.

I just need to take a deep breath. Get my thoughts together. Tuck my feelings under my sleeve for the day so I can focus on my exhibition. Because when I'm around Jace, my feelings are this giant balloon, waiting to be popped and spill over.

Jace leans over and kisses me softly on the lips. He seriously needs to go away, because my thoughts are not about the exhibition anymore.

"Lu baby, I'll do anything you want," he whispers against my lips. "I'll clean, I'll cook breakfasts, lunches, and dinners, serve them to you in bed, on the terrace, on the moon, on dead stars. I'll make Mama Bear shine every night. I'll be on my best behavior. I'll pose for your paintings, practice with you chapters seven, nine, and ten—"

"Jace!" I throw my head back and blush.

"I'll even help you write more chapters. You have no idea. Your fictional men are so—"

"Staaahp." I roll my eyes.

"I'll be the best—what's the word—groveler you've ever seen."

I burst out laughing, and Jace gets up and sweeps me in his arms.

Swooning? Check.

"Just don't be mad at me, beautiful girl. I'm gonna make you so happy." He kisses my cheek. "I promise." He kisses the other and sets me back down on my feet.

I give him a playful suspicious stare, but my heart is already swirling in a dance, reaching out to his like a fated mate.

"I love you, Jace," I say quietly, blinking away tears. "I love you so much."

I'm about to break into tears, but I can't have that right now.

"You'd better show up tonight," I murmur, fist his shirt, and pull him in for another brief kiss so I can shut up and collect myself.

With all that's happening, I hope the gallery night doesn't turn into mayhem.

58

JACE

I WEAR MY FANCY SUIT ONLY WHEN WE MEET WITH IMPORTANT CLIENTS.

Considering Lu and her gallery night are the most important things in my life right now, and I promised to be on my best behavior, Roey forces me to dress up. He's as always stylish, in a slick gray suit over a white T-shirt.

Have you been to a gallery opening?

This fucking intensity. Suits. Attitude. Watch your words—anything can be a trigger.

There are only a dozen people in the gallery on Broad Street. The giant canvases cover the walls. Smaller ones are on pedestals. One is mounted on the ceiling—a stork carrying a teddy bear in a cloth bundle dangling off its beak, and the blue sky is dotted with military airplanes, showering bombs onto the viewer.

I've seen them all before, but Lu's talent still takes my breath away.

"The stork is safe, and so is the teddy bear. But the future? That remains a grim mystery. That's our children, born into the uncertainty of the current political dichotomy," a guy in bohemian clothes explains to his friend as they stand in the center of the gallery, their faces lifted to the ceiling.

There's a bar stand and a caterer in the corner, but barely any people to serve.

I feel overdressed. The place looks empty. My heart falls at the sight—this is not the exhibit opening Lu was hoping for.

Seth Gordon's warning spins in my head. But when I look at Lu, I know I will never give her up. And I definitely won't stay away on the most important night when she might need me the most.

"I love you, Jace."

I feel like I can fly every time I remember her words.

My phone dings with a message.

Amon/ Brexton Recovery: Losers gonna lose. Reznik is ours.

I clench my jaw and raise my eyes to Roey. "I guess Brexton Recovery got the Reznik job again."

Roey takes a sip of his rum and coke and swills it in his mouth before swallowing, his eyes on Becky.

He's brooding. Not getting lucky with Becky is not helping. And now our rivals have the biggest assignment again.

Lu and Becky talk to the visitors, and we don't interrupt, waiting, just being here for the support, until they both walk up.

"Gentlemen," Becky says with exaggerated diplomacy. "Did you leave your weapons at the door?"

Lu purses her lips as she casts her eyes down—of course, she told Becky everything.

And Becky won't let go. "Maybe we should set up a bin at the entrance, like an umbrella one but for guns and rifles."

Roey only smiles at her. "I'm saving my biggest weapon for you."

Lu looks so humble tonight. Wide pants, tight tank, bracelets, necklaces. She has an artsy hippy vibe with her hair curled and let loose.

And she's on the verge of tears.

Shit.

Her smile is big. So big. She's trying so hard to keep her spirits up. But her beautiful eyes are filled with desperation.

"Your art is beautiful," says a girl in a neon cardigan, finishing her third glass of wine. "I like the social context."

Lu smiles politely as the girl heads for the exit.

Becky checks her phone, and her face falls.

"There's a flash mob dance in Central Park, secretly organized by the local theatre." Her jaw actually drops. "Several movie celebrities were spotted. It's hitting the news right now. Everyone's heading there. Shit, shit, shit."

She raises her eyes at Lu, who bites her lower lip.

"The whole world is there, Lu." Becky has the most pitiful expression I've ever seen.

I can't tear my eyes off Lu, studying every little change in her face as she nods repeatedly, and that beautiful light in her eyes is at once extinguished.

Roey tries to comfort her. "Hey, easy. It's no one's fault. It'll pick up."

Becky sends him a murderous glare. "At least we have bounty hunters for security. That's reassuring. Fuck!"

Ouch.

Lu sadly looks around the almost empty gallery.

"Even Tito is not here," she murmurs. "He was whisked away by Jamie and promised to stop later. But I have a feeling he won't."

I pull my phone out and send him a text.

Me: Better get your ass to Lu's exhibition, traitor.

"It's alright," Becky tries to cheer her. "I'll take pictures. We'll put it on social media. That guy from the *Juxtapoz* is coming to do a feature spread. We'll be alright, Lu. It's not the end of the world."

Lu nods meekly. "It's not."

Look at me, I silently ask her.

She does. I smile at her. She needs to know that I'm here for her. All of us are.

She steps closer to me. Her hands absently fix her clothes until they touch me, and I pull her into me.

"Hey, you. It'll be fine," I reassure her.

She smiles, tilting her head to rest it on my shoulder. "Just promise you'll stick with me till the end of this. As long as you do, Jace, I'll be fine."

I bring my lips to her ear so that Roey and Becky can't hear what I say. "Lu, I'll stick with you till you are old and wrinkly and do crazy art and your hair is bleach white from age and I'll be broken and still madly in love with you and your biggest fan."

My Lu laughs, and her eyes light up. "Scout's honor?"

There you are, baby.

"Scout's honor."

A group of young people walk in, and Lu and Becky hurry away to greet them and offer wine and walk them through.

I can't look at the sight of my beautiful talented girl being so discouraged.

"Roey, what do I do?"

"What are you supposed to do?" he asks, his eyes on Becky.

"I should call Mrs. Kubinsky from La Jolla."

He turns his confused gaze to me.

"She's a gallerist," I explain. "Maybe, she can do something."

"Go for it. Gotta save your girl here."

"I'll be outside," I tell him, already having found Mrs. Kubinsky's number in my phone.

"I'm coming with you. Need a smoke."

We walk out through the back office room and the door into the dark back alley, lined with dumpsters and piles of trash bags.

Mrs. Kubinsky picks up but doesn't recognize me. She's patient when I explain who I am.

"That's right, Mr. Reed, how could I forget?" She laughs.

I tell her about the exhibit. She says there's a flash mob in Central Park that's gone viral online and gathered a lot of people. We know that already. But she has a friend who reports for the *Art Weekly*, so she says she'll try to send her to Broad Street to check out Lu's exhibit.

Mrs. Kubinsky is brief but polite, and when she hangs up, I exhale in relief. It's something.

Roey leans on the wall of the building, puffing out smoke. "You're a good guy, Jace. Just not quick with women."

"Fuck off."

"The girl you fall head over heels with"—he cackles, and I can't help grinning—"turns out to be the daughter of your employer. Just a reminder, you shot her, too."

Stress gets the best of me, and I rub my face with both hands but can't hold back laughter.

"The prodigy sniper, the youngest member of an elite sniper club," Roey taunts me, "missed for the first time in years and shot the future love of his life. That should be a movie."

It's ridiculous, I know.

"It's just a slight complication," I say. "Her father, I mean." And a promise to be buried.

"Jace." Roey's voice is low and etched with warning, and I turn to follow his gaze.

Five guys are walking from the dark end of the alley toward us. Their attire is a giveaway—black boots, black clothes, and baseball hats.

They are staring at us as they approach fast.

"Jace?" Roey warns again, pushing off the wall and flicking away the cigarette.

One of them nods at me, his eyes drilling into me like he knows who I am. "You had clear instructions to stay away."

And he whips out a knife.

59

LU

"Something is happening in the back alley behind the gallery," one of the caterers says as he rushes back from the office.

Becky and I exchange confused glances.

"With those two guys who were here. I think there's a fight going on."

"Oh, shit," Becky murmurs.

We dart to the office and throw the back door open.

"What is—"

Becky's words cut off abruptly as we spill outside and halt.

The dim back door light casts a glow on Roey and Jace who throw punches at several guys.

I've seen people fighting only a few times in my life. Extreme violence makes me nauseous. And this is nothing like the scene by the elevator.

Jace and Roey kick and punch the dark shadows with methodical precision. I think I hear a bone crack.

Four? Five other guys?

I can't even count, frozen in shock.

"Stop!" Becky shouts, the thudding of the fists against hard bodies resonating with the blood pumping in my head.

But I can't look away. This is just like the scene from my book when Emily and John were attacked.

I can't take my eyes off Jace, his kicks and punches, the elegant danger in the way he moves and knocks the guys around.

"Freeze! Or I'll shoot!" one of the guys barks.

The distinct sound of a trigger being cocked echoes against the buildings.

Jace and Roey freeze in their spots.

My head spins as I see three of the guys back off, spitting and cursing. The other two are trying to get up off the ground.

Another one pulls out a gun.

No-no-no-no-no.

He points it at Jace as he steps closer to him, sniffling, blood running from his smashed nose down his chin.

"Mr. Gordon sends a warning," he hisses. "Next time, you'll end up six feet underground."

My stomach turns at the mention.

"Mr. Gordon?" Becky whispers to me. "Isn't that your biological dad?"

Yes, and now I know what's happening.

Just then the guy swings his hand and strikes Jace on the side of the face with his gun, sending him stumbling backward.

"Jace!" I scream, lunging toward him.

"Let's go!" the guy orders, and the group of them take off running into the darkness of the alley.

I run up to Jace, who touches his face with his fingers, looks at the blood on them, and sends a murderous stare in the direction of the shadows.

Roey spits on the ground, his hands on his hips as he studies Jace.

"Well, that's a not-so-surprising turn of events," he says and spits again, a smirk on his lips.

"The safety was off," Jace says in a gruff voice. "They weren't fucking around."

"I know," Roey responds.

"Inside, now!" Becky orders.

In the bright light of the office room, I cup Jace's face and study his split cheek.

"I'm fine," he says quietly.

"You are not. I'll bring ice."

Becky glances at Roey. "Your lip is bruised. You need ice, too."

He only smirks. "I know better remedies for my lips."

The guy never gives up.

As I open the mini fridge and get a cup full of ice, I hear Jace's sigh behind me. "I probably shouldn't show up at the gallery with a bloodied face."

"No, you shouldn't," I say and point for him to take a seat.

Biting back tears, I wrap ice in a cloth and press it to Jace's bruised face, registering his bloodied collar.

Everything is wrong today.

My solo show is a complete fail.

Now this, a bruise on Jace's face and the threats.

I just want this day to be over.

"Let's go home," I say to him. "I'll take care of it at home."

"Lu," he says, raising his hand and stroking my cheek, "it's your big night."

"It's an epic fail, Jace."

"We'll stay till the end," he insists. "I'll stay here, in the office, so I don't scare away people with my face."

"I don't want to stay!" I snap, swallowing tears, then press my forehead to his and run my fingers through his hair.

Roey clears his throat. Becky's heels click against the floor as she shifts.

I don't care for the audience. Jace calms me. But if I don't get out of here, I'll break down crying.

Becky looks defeated. This is possibly the worst exhibition she's ever organized. But she's supportive. "I got this, Lu. If you wanna leave, go. It's nine o'clock. There are only a dozen people. I'll manage."

Becky will go out onto the street and drag people inside the gallery if needed. She never gives up. Definitely not when she has another pair of eyes on her, Roey's.

Roey shrugs. "I'll stay, help close down. You and Jace bounce. We'll handle this."

He glances at Becky, who meets his eyes and nods.

Frustration blocks my throat with a giant lump. I tried so hard for the last year to prove that I can make it in New York as an artist. And look at me, I can't even keep my boyfriend safe.

I whip out my phone and type my father a text message.

Me: I thought you were a decent human. But considering you send thugs to beat my friend and try to curate my life, I don't think I want to get to know you. I've seen enough. You touch Jace, and I'll never speak to you again.

Seconds after I press send, he calls.
I cut the call.
He calls again, then texts.

Father #2: Sweetheart, let's talk.

Me: I don't want to talk to you. Leave Jace and me alone.

Father #2: It's for your own good, sweetie. You don't know what that man is.

Me: I do. He told me. As of today, I also know what YOU do. Maybe there was a reason my mom never told me about you. You don't get to come into my life and take charge. Thanks for making my exhibition opening unforgettable.

Father #2: Let's talk, Lucy. I'll explain. Please.

I've had enough explanations.

"Lu?" Jace cocks his head, studying me.

"Let's go, Jace."

Becky nods, and Roey motions to her. "Let's get to work, beautiful."

Jace and I get a cab, and as we ride, he intertwines his fingers with mine.

"I'm sorry, Jace. For everything," I murmur.

"Lu, don't apologize."

"He's an asshole."

"He is a father," Jace argues and squeezes my hand in his tighter. "As to the exhibition, don't get upset. It's only the first day. Your art is great. It'll get noticed, believe me."

I turn to study his face, lit up by the flickers of the passing cars.

"Where do you get all this optimism, Jace?"

There's this kind smile on his face like everything is a blessing.

"Because I have you," he says. "What's there to complain about?"

"You got hurt because of that."

"You know, even if they crippled me, I wouldn't give up on you."

"Don't you dare."

"Not a chance. The question is, do you want a crippled roommate?"

"He won't touch you. I won't let him."

"Lu baby, look at me, please." He takes my chin between his fingers. "I'm not going back to California. That is, if you are willing to deal with me."

"Two hundred percent," I whisper.

"That's a lot."

"A hundred percent from me and a hundred from Pushkin."

He laughs softly. "I'm all for being a Brooklynite."

"But you'll have to stop hiding things from me."

"There is nothing left to hide. You even got to the bottom of the shark's den."

I burst out in laughter, then pull his dog tag out and kiss it, thanking the universe for keeping him alive for me.

60

JACE

Lu laughs at my silly jokes as we get back to the condo, and I kiss her smile, wincing in pain when I move.

But who cares about pain when the hottest girl in the universe wraps her beautiful legs around my waist as I carry her to my bedroom?

Weeks ago, I wouldn't dare touch her. Now I whisper all kinds of dirty things into her ear.

I'll be her Sharki, Moby-Dick, whatever she wants. I'm not a pro and have so much to learn. But one thing I know for sure—women like being touched, and they have a soft spot for a tongue.

I'm good with touching and using my tongue. I need to distract her.

We learned this at war. Psychological trauma can be overshadowed, at least temporarily, by physical work. That's why we work out so much even after leaving the army. That's why I go for jogs when I try to forget. That's why some of us fight, especially intoxicated, especially in dark moments—not to lash out but to purge.

I'll override Lu's sadness.

"You want me, Lu?" I ask.

"Yes," she whispers, her little tongue licking at my neck as she kisses it.

"Then have me tonight any way you want."

I'll make her forget the shitty day, if only for an hour or two or a night.

Sometimes luck doesn't work in your favor, and it has nothing to do with your talent or hard work. Life is a strong current you can't swim against even when you know it's carrying you in the wrong direction. Sometimes, you just have to let go.

Her phone starts beeping in the living room. It's a reminder of tonight.

"Don't worry about it," I murmur, distracting her with my kisses.

I undress her, lay her on my bed, then take her hand in mine and slide it between her legs.

"Open wider," I whisper. I am persistent and a good student, disciplined above all. *"Opening my aching flesh for his gaze,"* I quote her words from *Sharki*, making her gasp in shock. "Did you do it, Lu? In front of my portrait?"

She nods timidly.

"Show me what you did. Teach me how to touch you," I ask softly, though I've made her come before by doing just that.

"Down there…"

"I'm not good at guessing yet. Show me, Lu," I tease her.

She opens her legs wider in front of me and slides her hand between them.

I can't take my eyes off her bare in front of me, pleasing herself. I reach for her, and my fingers brush against hers, catching the rhythm, skimming the spots they linger over.

"Two pairs of hands are better than one," she says quietly.

Holy hell, she just quoted my words from the day I came to rent the room. She remembers. Every fucking word.

I push her hand away and take over, doing exactly what she did, gauging my success by the little sounds that escape her.

She's so soft down there that my hand feels like a paw. But I have man's greatest weapon, a tongue.

The next ten minutes, it's me practicing Oral 101. Tongue and fingers. Occasionally teeth—there's a certain technique I learned, in theory, and a whole lot of gentle pressure. I'm great at implementing theory into practice.

"Right there," she whispers timidly.

"Good?"

"Faster," she demands, panting.

"You like my fingers here? Like this?"

"Oh, God!"

"Is that a yes?"

"Yes!"

"How about this?" I change the strokes.

"'Jace…"

"I'm right here, Lu baby."

I want to learn her every sensitive spot. I want to know how fast she can come. What makes her roll her hips in that delicious way of hers.

When she mewls under my tongue and finally cries out in ecstasy, I feel like a Superman.

Her phone won't stop beeping in the living room.

"Should I check it?" she gasps under my weight when I shift on top of her.

Good try. She looks delicious in her post-climax high, licking her lips, swollen from my kisses, her pupils dilated.

"Not a chance," I murmur. "The world can go to hell."

"Come here, you."

She pushes me onto my back and pulls my jeans down until I'm naked, too, and she wraps her delicate hand around my hardness.

"My turn," she says, her face flushed, her eyes blazing with determination as she leans over and kisses me down there.

There are many shades of kissing, I find out, as Lu works on covering the real estate down there with her mouth. She's so eager that I'm approaching the peak too fast.

"Lu…"

"Shh," she shuts me up amidst whatever witchery she's doing down there.

I can't think. Can't argue. All I do is feel with my fingers laced into my favorite blonde mess.

And when I'm so ready that I can't hold back anymore, she doesn't listen to my barely audible pleas to let go and takes all of me, everything I have, down to the last drop.

I lie empty in utter amazement as her naked body slides up and presses against mine. Her eyes are full of mischief and pride as she licks her swollen lips.

"Another round?" she whispers.

That's my sexy minx.

How did I get so lucky? Right, the Cupid shot. Turns out my mistake was the best shot of my life.

I flip her onto her back and latch onto my favorite mouth.

Sex has a taste and a scent. Hers. Mine. Both of them mixing together.

"Prepare for a swift invasion," I warn her, making her shake in laughter that dies out when my mouth goes to work.

Screw the *Sharki* chapters. We reenacted four of them in the last two days. I want to do my own thing.

I feel like I'm high, but I'm not. Not even drunk.

Shame? What's that?

I lean over and run my hands down Lu's body, feeling the texture of her smooth warm skin, then plant kisses on it, then slide my hand to her abdomen, my lips following.

I want to learn every inch of her body, every sensitive spot, the ones that make her giggle or gasp or her breath hitch in her throat— yeah, that one, when I place my hands on her hips like she's an offering and trail little kisses down to her junction.

Her breathing grows louder as I nibble at her skin. Her legs inch apart as I descend into my favorite spot between them and let my tongue do the work until she is spread-eagle, wanting more.

"Jace, please…"

Please?

I play with her until she's thrashing in my arms in ecstasy again.

Sex has so many sounds…

61

JACE

"I SHOULD CHECK MY PHONE TO MAKE SURE BECKY DIDN'T MURDER Roey out of frustration," Lu says as we lie naked on top of the sheets.

I love the way she looks stretched out on my bed, her legs slightly parted, her arms over her head.

Heaven definitely has a face, hers, with her lips curved in a little smile and a dreamy gaze I drown in.

I get up and walk to the living room, then come back with her phone, enjoying Lu's gaze sweeping over my naked body.

All yours, Lu.

She checks her phone, and her expression changes to one of shock.

"Oh, my god..." Her eyes dart over the screen. "Jace," she whispers.

My heart does a warning thud as I lean over and read Becky's texts.

10:40

Becky: Wait, wait, wait. This collector from LA, Eleanor Kubinsky, just called.

10:57

Becky: She just purchased a painting! The ceiling one! Woot-woot!

Thank you, Mrs. Kubinsky!
11:05

Becky: She tweeted about the opening and put it on her social media. Several people just came in. We are closing soon, but we might get some quick action.

11:55

Becky: LUUUUUUU! Come back!!!!! There are like a hundred people here, following the tweet!

12:20

Becky: It's madness! Lu! Our opening failed, but this is an epic after-party!

12:40

Becky: Tito and Jamie showed up. They and Roey are at the door, stopping people from coming in. Four paintings are sold. That lady's tweet was retweeted forty-five times.

12:50

Becky: The reporters from *Art Weekly* just showed up druuuuuunk AF. They want an interview with you! You should be here! Luuuuuu! I hate you! I love you! Where the fuck are you????

There's a picture from the gallery. It's packed. There's no room to stand.
I gape at it in shock.

Becky: We sold half of the paintings and had to lock the door. It's madness! The publicity will be insane! You owe me, babe. What the hell are you doing with Jace? Byyyyye. Muah!

Lu meets my eyes in disbelief. "Jace, what's happening?"

I smile, pulling her naked body into mine. "It's you, Lu. You are talented, and you deserve it. You trust people so easily. You should learn to trust life. It always works out in the end."

"Does it?"

Her dreamy eyes are on me as she traces my nose and eyebrows with her forefinger like she's painting a portrait.

I close my eyes, smiling at her touch.

"And tell Becky to thank Roey," I murmur, then open my eyes. "I have a feeling Roey might've redeemed himself tonight. Knowing Roey, I have an idea what kind of thank you he'll want."

Lu laughs, grabs her phone, and types something real quick. "Knowing B, she might just feel grateful enough to go with it."

She tosses her phone aside and comes back into my arms.

"You missed your big night because of me," I say, cuddling with her.

"*You* are my big night, Jace. I get excited about nights with you more than anything else. And evenings. And mornings."

"You'll be famous one day, and I'll be your bodyguard."

Lu throws her head back in laughter. "Deal. You know what happens in all bodyguard romance stories, right?" She wiggles her eyebrows.

I kiss her nose. "Let me guess. HEA?"

She bursts into another fit of laughter, nuzzling my neck. "You are so sneaky, Jace Reed."

"Lu?" I palm her face. "I'm so crazy in love with you."

That's not the right word. It's so banal that in no way can it explain the way I'm falling. No, not like a rock. Like a feather carried by the wind, with all the powerful pulls and tugs, stronger and weaker, up and down, left with no thoughts, just this—feeling. Her. Her closeness.

My love is like a bullet ripping through the air, shooting for its destination, finally lodging a fatal shot in the heart. Hers.

I *am* a motherfucking Cupid.

"Me too." She kisses me so happily that the bullet explodes like a grenade. With fireworks. "I love you, Jace," she whispers. "But you already know that. You've read about it."

My hands have a mind of their own and already paw her again, wanting to consummate this confession.

"Hey, Lu?"

"Yes," she hums, not paying attention, because her attention is on my harder parts.

"Did you actually do what you wrote you did with my pineapple boxers?"

She presses her forehead to my chest, and I hear a little chuckle escape her as she whispers, "Yes."

Fuck, yes!

Her hands sneak dangerously low, making me hard with want again. And my hands start stroking her exactly where she was pressing those pineapples, while wearing my boxers and thinking about me.

How much can one want another person?

I'm pretty sure I can live being buried in Lu at all times.

What's the expression in her novel? Yep, to the hilt.

62

JACE

I HOPE TO WAKE UP LIKE THIS EVERY DAY FOR THE REST OF MY LIFE, WITH Lu still asleep, her body pressed against mine, her arm over my chest.

I can't torture my girl anymore, despite me having morning wood that won't go away because my mind has our shenanigans on constant replay. I can't even count how many times we went at it last night.

It's almost noon when we finally get out of bed, though I could spend a day with her between the sheets.

Lu puts on her bra and panties with little kitties.

That's my Lu at home. Everyone knows Lucy Moor as the Brooklyn "it girl," with ironed blonde hair, furs, and high heels. Only I know her like this—with no makeup, messy hair, hello-kitty panties that get stuck between her butt cheeks when she walks to the kitchen, and she wiggles her butt, pulling them out.

She checks her phone. "Look what the *Art Weekly* posted!"

The Hottest Exhibit With a Chippendales Bouncer.
Art Turns VIP.
Everything You Need to Know About the Hot Young Artist Lucy Moor Who Doesn't Show Up For her Solo Exhibit.

"Noooooo!" Lu throws her head back and palms her face. "I

can't believe it," she says as she goes back to reading the online article.

"They should've added, 'an underwear thief and a pineapple deviant,'" I joke, nuzzling her neck as she sticks her tongue out at me.

I want her again. Maybe I'm a sex addict after all.

She puts aside her phone when I press myself into her from behind, sneaks her hand between us, and strokes me through my shorts.

"Lu," I murmur into her hair.

"Yes, Jace?" she echoes, pushing into me.

"I like your smell." She smells like me.

Her insistent hand pushes my sweatpants down, just enough to let my hardness out, and I slide my hands up her torso, under her shirt, and cup her breasts.

We moan in sync.

Change of plans. I'll torture her just a little more.

"Shower before coffee?" I ask, thrusting into her hand.

"Go for it," she murmurs.

Tease.

"With you?"

"Yes," she whispers.

I hope she survives all my excitement because I'm hard and horny again as I pick her up and carry her to my bedroom.

"I love when you do this," she murmurs, nibbling at my earlobe. "When you carry me in your arms."

"I'll do it every day, baby. You don't have to walk. I'll carry you around Brooklyn like a princess."

I love carrying her in my arms, or with her legs wrapped around my waist, or throwing her over my shoulder. When she doesn't touch the ground, I'm her only gravity.

We fumble out of the few clothes we have on as our mouths fuse together, burning with the need to repeat the feeling of being closer to each other than we've been to anyone else.

Our hands greedily explore each other like we didn't just go at it all night.

Lips, tongues, hands, skin to skin, and after five minutes in the shower, she murmurs, "Turn on the water, maybe?"

Right, we forgot that part.

She laughs into my mouth, then squeals when I spray her with water, turn her around, and take her against the wall.

"Chapter number eleven," I whisper into her ear as I enter her.

We go at it slowly and for the longest time, reaching our climax when we can barely stand on shaking legs.

"I think I found my happy place," I say, panting into her neck.

"Shower?"

"Being inside you."

She laughs as I slide out of her and tease her with kisses as we actually shower.

I can wash off the paint and the sweat, even the sweet tiredness of being with her numerous times in the last twelve hours. But the shower won't wash off the feelings etched in my heart that cut deeper every day. She's finally mine.

"Coffee? Breakfast?" she asks, putting her panties and shirt on.

I throw her over my shoulder and carry her to the kitchen.

She squeals. "How are you so strong?"

"Practiced for years to impress you."

She laughs and slaps my ass. "Jace!"

Her hands slide inside my sweatpants and palm my ass cheeks, squeezing them.

"You want another round, Lu baby? You won't be able to walk. Just a warning."

I shake her off my shoulder and hold her butt as she slides down and wraps her legs around my waist.

"You are my superhero," she murmurs, kissing me.

"You got it." I can hold her like this for days. This is nothing. "I'm good at multitasking."

"Oh, yeah? What else?"

"Stick around and find out."

I'm getting cocky. It's hormones. I feel high just on the thought that she is mine.

With one hand, all the while holding her in my arms, I pour us coffee. She tries to wiggle out—no way, ma'am. I can go through the whole day with this cute monkey wrapped around me.

The creamer carton in the fridge is empty, and I finally sit her down on the counter.

"We are out of creamer," I say. "I'll run downstairs and get some."

"No, rest." She jumps off. "I'll take Pushkin for a quick walk and be back in the blink of an eye."

Skipping like a kid, she disappears into her bedroom to get dressed, then puts Pushkin on a leash, humming a song as she leaves.

I'm lost in my dreams about her, what we can do, what's next for us.

I want to take Lu to Thailand. She might not want to actually move there. That's fine. I can be anywhere as long as she's with me. We'll move out of Goldsling Towers and get our own place. Somewhere in the East Village. Something cute, whatever Lu picks. I'll build a studio for her and keep working for Roey.

My phone rings with the number from the Goldsling Towers' concierge.

"Mr. Reed?"

"Yes."

"Your dog is roaming around outside the building."

I frown. "What?"

"Jim just brought him in. I have him. Is he lost?"

My insides twist. "I'll be downstairs in a sec."

I frantically dial Lu.

What happened? Pushkin never runs away.

Her phone rings once, and she picks up.

"Lu, what happened?" I ask right away.

"Hello, Mr. Reed." The voice that answers is low and cold.

"Who is this?" My guts turn because I recognize it.

"Anatolyi Reznik. I have something you want, Mr. Reed. *Someone*, to be exact."

63

JACE

I'M FREAKING OUT.

I *never* freak out. Not since boot camp. But I'm freaking out.

Reznik has Lu. He wants truce with Seth Gordon and ten million dollars on top in retribution.

Fuck!

Like there's any chance in the world Gordon will go for it.

I hurriedly dress as I dial Roey.

"Jace, buddy, it's the wrong time to call."

"Where are you?" I snap and hear a familiar female voice in the background. "Who's that?"

"That's B."

"B as in…"

"Becky."

"And you are?"

"At her place. Spent the night here. Listen, what's up?"

"We have a situation, Roey."

I tell him about Lu and Reznik, then tell him to meet me at our Sheepshead Bay apartment.

Jim brings Pushkin, and in a minute, I sprint downstairs, catch a cab, and call Seth Gordon.

He doesn't pick up.

I call again.

Then again.

Before he blocks me, I send a text.

Me: Reznik has your daughter. He wants immunity and money.

Gordon calls back right away.

"I swear, Mr. Reed, I will destroy you—"

"Her being taken by Reznik has nothing to do with me."

I can hear his angry huff. "First you get between my daughter and me, then—"

"To be fair, sir, if you didn't have a falling out with Reznik, he wouldn't have stalked your daughter and we would've never have run into her. You never let me explain, but the evening we met Lucy, we were shadowing Reznik, who just so happened to have a meeting with her. Odd? Yes. And then he came over to her place when he thought I was out of town. Bad sign? Yes. But we didn't know she was in any way connected to you. And you have powerful enemies who know you very well, sir. So, tell me, if he hadn't shown up in her life for years and in the last three months met up with her twice, what does he want?"

Gordon is silent.

"Right." I know I am. "So, here's the thing. I love your daughter, and I'm getting her back. What I need from you is to have the money ready."

"When does he want to meet?"

"Tonight."

"I'm in Vermont. It's a little complicated, you see."

"Complicated?" I snap, shocked at his wording. "Complicated to negotiate with your rival? Or complicated to give up certain things to save your daughter?"

"Do you know how much money that is, Mr. Reed?"

"We need it for the initial negotiation. *Do* we have your support?"

"You want me to pay the guy who stole a fortune from me when your fucking job was to bring *him* to me?"

"The circumstances changed."

"I'm not giving ten million to the fucking criminal who—"

I cut the call.

Fuck Seth Gordon.

Asshole.

I'll deal with this by myself.

Adrenalin spikes in my blood as the cab approaches Sheepshead Bay. I try to swallow the bitterness at Gordon's unwillingness to ransom his daughter. Pride is a powerful thing until it becomes a weakness.

He calls me. I cut the call, then block him.

Roey is already at the apartment when I walk in.

He and Miller raise their eyes at me.

"Gordon called me," Roey says.

"Of course, he did."

"He got a picture from Reznik of Lu in some dingy place."

I grind my teeth.

"He says it'll take a while to get the money."

"He told me he won't pay," I blurt. "Fuck him."

"Jace?" Roey's voice is a warning. "We need that money for the meeting."

"He told me no, Roey, and I'm not begging. We can deal without money or Gordon. I'm getting Lu back. I hope that you are with me even if Gordon is not."

Roey narrows his eyes at me, his lips hitching in a smile.

A fucking smile?

Right now?

"I like seeing you like this, Jace," he says, sucking his teeth. "All riled up, determined. There's the old Jace, the Shooter. Welcome back."

I shake my head in annoyance.

Roey nods toward the couch. "All right. I'm with you, Jace. Let's sit down and figure this out. Miller has some good ideas."

64

JACE

Reznik calls again with instructions, using a ghost VPN Miller can't track.

Of course, there can be no phone or trackers or anyone following me when I meet him tonight, at a location yet to be disclosed. Just money.

We don't have money, fuck, but we'll deal with that when I meet Reznik. Roey has a negotiation plan in mind.

Seth Gordon calls Roey.

"I'm not giving Reznik another penny," Gordon says sharply on speaker. "Nor do I trust you with handling this operation well. But I want my daughter back. You do that, you get paid. You want to handle this properly? Accept help."

"Help?" Roey exchanges glares with me and Miller.

"Brexton Recovery will call you shortly. You need to cooperate with them."

When he hangs up, Roey jams a cigarette between his lips and stalks to the open window to smoke.

"Motherfuckers," he mouthes. "They're arriving in two hours. They must've had an assignment nearby."

"Gordon gave them Reznik yesterday," I remind him.

"Oh, right. Fuckers."

We have several hours before the meeting, so we sit down to discuss the plan of action.

Roey calls Kolchak and requests a few guys on standby in Brighton.

"Inconspicuously," Roey says, but you don't need to explain that to ex-military guys.

When the doorbell rings, Roey lifts his eyes to me with a smirk on his lips. "Ready for them to rub horse shit in our faces?"

Amon's the first one to come in. Jeans, a t-shirt, shoulder-long blond hair like he's going surfing in a moment—he's wearing a wig —and a mustache.

"Da fuck?" I murmur.

Roey snorts. "At least you were smart enough to wear a disguise."

Amon pulls the wig off.

"Fucking hot," he says, throwing himself onto the couch next to me. "My other guy is helping a girl with a stroller downstairs not to be obvious. Another one is a pizza delivery guy. In case your place is being watched. You are slipping, Torres. We should've met elsewhere."

Amon turns to grin at me. Actually *grins*, fucker. "Got yourself into a pickle, Shooter?" He nudges me with his shoulder.

Roey has a beef with the Brexton guys. Me, I understand the rivalry but actually like Amon. He's only in his thirties but has a brutal and deserved reputation in the bounty-hunting business.

His other guys come in shortly.

Two hours later, it's six o'clock, and we've mapped out the plan of action. We have the Kolchak guys on standby, expecting the meeting to be in Brighton Beach but ready to send them anywhere. Brighton is Reznik's home turf, and the city is much easier for him to get lost in if something goes wrong.

Miller installed a tracker inside one of my shoe soles. Unless Reznik uses a metal detector, he won't find it, but Miller will know where I am at all times so our guys don't have to follow me and take a chance of being spotted.

"There's your backpack for when Reznik's guys check you on the street, as I'm sure they will," Roey says as Amon stuffs it with bundles of fake money. They came prepared.

Amon stares me down. "Nervous, Shooter?"

I don't answer. I wouldn't be if Lu's life wasn't in jeopardy.

"We'll track you. Don't worry." Amon winks at me.

"Reznik has my girlfriend. It's not a game," I murmur.

He rolls his eyes. "Relax. I saw her photo. Did you show off your sniper skills or something to rope her in?"

He has no idea.

My phone rings with an unknown number.

"That's Reznik," I say, taking a deep breath before I pick up.

"Get out of your Sheepshead Bay den," he says. Fuck—I meet Roey's eyes—Reznik knows where we are. "Alone. No phone or anything else. Just the money."

"How do I talk to you without a phone?"

"Don't worry about it. Start walking toward Brighton Beach Avenue."

He hangs up.

I look at Roey. "He has his eyes on us."

"No shit," Roey grinds out. "I'm calling Kolchak. Amon, you and your guys get out through the basement. I unlocked the door that connects it to the next building and leads out into the backyard of a convenience store at the end of the street. Don't go out all at once. Head to Brighton, it's a little over a mile away. I'm sure Reznik knows your faces by heart. So besides your lame disguises, use baseball hats, food in your hands, shopping bags, whatever."

We nod, my heartbeat spiking as I get up and put the backpack on.

The walk to Brighton seems like forever.

That's what Einstein once said. Being on a date with a dream girl for an hour might seem like a minute. Sitting on a hot cinder for a minute might seem like an hour. Or something like this. That's the theory of relativity for you.

Brighton is a Soviet museum, an ode to the '80s.

My eyes dart around as I walk the main avenue, knowing there will be someone to give me instructions.

Sure thing, a guy in his sixties with a mustache and a dog motions with his finger to me. "Come here."

I do because he's not a regular stranger. No one is tonight.

He pulls me onto the side street.

"Hold still," he says in a friendly voice as he does a pat down. "Make a right on the next street, then a left."

He starts cooing to his dog as he walks away, bowing to a group of old ladies sitting on a bench.

Three minutes later, as I'm walking along one of the back streets, a buff guy next to a car with an open hood whistles and summons me to him.

"Get in," he orders.

Another guy in the back seat blindfolds me.

The whole thing is so well-oiled and without any abuse of power that, for a moment, I admire Reznik.

The car drives for about fifteen minutes. I count turns, gauge the speed, the time it takes, and I know that we didn't leave Brighton. This is just a distraction.

The car finally pulls to a stop, I'm dragged outside, and there it is, the unmistakable rumble of the train on the elevated subway tracks only several blocks away. Anywhere in New York City, subway trains are a giveaway.

"Move," the man says, pushing me forward and through a door held by another man.

Inside, it's cool, and when my blindfold is lifted, I find myself in a dim hallway to a small warehouse with high ceilings, stacks of pallets, and a warning sign on the door in front of me. *Temperature controlled.*

"No tricks," one of the guys tells me as he roughly grabs me by the shoulder, opens the door, and pushes me inside.

65

LU

"And here we are," says Diadia Tolia when I take a seat on a folding chair at the far end of the warehouse he brought me to.

I shiver. It's cold here and dim.

Pallets stacked with boxes line one wall. The other one has double-high racks of fur coats. I'm used to thrift store clothes, but I know good stuff when I see it—minks, sables, chinchillas, most in breathable clear bags.

There's a long table piled with loose fur pieces. I wonder if there's a sewing shop somewhere here.

At the front of the warehouse is a short row of stand-alone chambers with glass doors—fur storage vaults.

Brighton doesn't get more cliche than this—we are in a fur coat warehouse.

Uncle lights a cigarette and exhales heavily, squinting at me through the smoke.

All the years I've known him, thinking he's family, can't erase the anger simmering in my blood. At how one of his goons snatched me off the street by Goldsling Towers into a van, so roughly like I was a doll, Pushkin's whimper when he was kicked away, Uncle's evil, "Finally," as he studied me during the ride while I thrashed and demanded answers but he talked to his men instead, ignoring me. How malicious his laughter was when I said Jace will find him and hurt him.

His posture is confident, his blinking slow as if he's bored. He's never been so hostile with me. Nor would he ever let anyone hurt me.

Wrong.

Seven rough guys with guns tucked into their belts stand around and chatter in whispers.

I'm collateral. I know this. But I don't know if I should be more angry at him or my biological father. Considering I'm kidnapped, no one's hands are clean.

"What do you want?" I ask, trying to calm my trembling hands. And legs. And my fast-beating heart. My whole body is on edge.

"I want to finally have a say in what happens next."

"Finally?" I latch on to the word.

"*Ты много чего не знаешь, солнце.*[1]"

It bothers me that he calls me "sun," though he's called me that since I can remember.

"Speak English," I snap. "Since we are not on friendly terms anymore."

"You were never important," he says gruffly. "Not since your mother married that tool, Mike."

I stare in shock. He was always a polite man until now.

"Don't look at me like this," he says with a sneer. "I would've adopted you, you know. I would have. And I would've loved you like my own and we would've never ended up in a situation like this," he says, confusing me.

He wanted to be with my mother? That's news.

"Your mother would've been happy with me. I would've made her a millionaire. She would've bathed in gold, worn diamonds, and never had to work a day in her life."

But he was just a friend, wasn't he? "A *dear* friend," Mom always said.

"But no." His gaze acquires a hint of spite. "The bitch married that fucker."

I gasp at the words.

"Met him in Virginia, and before I even got a chance to see her after she left New York, she was already married."

He crumples the still-burning cigarette between his fingers, his jaw tightening.

"I loved her, you know." He raises his hard stare at me. "I fucking worshiped your mother since the day I met her. Offered her the world when she still lived in New York. When she got knocked up by that Seth Gordon, fuck, I contemplated killing him. But you know what she said? 'He's nothing. It was a mistake. But I'm keeping my baby.'"

He sucks his teeth as I listen without interrupting.

Life is strange. Mine is a mess. And not just because I got shot with a sedative one fine Brooklyn night or fell for my shooter.

This—my entire life or how I came about—was never revealed to me in so many details, not even by my mom. Instead, I get bits and pieces from an international criminal wanted by the government.

"Seth Gordon wasn't nothing," Uncle continues. "He was already wealthy back then. Your mother didn't tell him about you. And, oh, did I want to break every one of his fucking bones just for getting lucky with her. That's how young and stupid I was. And I would've still married her and taken care of you!"

His low chuckle is edged with slight madness. He could be unstable. I never spent enough time with him to get to know him.

"But then," he continues, his jaw tightening. "Right, fucking Mike. When I learned she chose him over me, even though she barely knew him, I saw red. I knew, I fucking knew she wasn't worth it. And still, still!" His expression changes to rage. "Fucking still!" he roars, then grunts and exhales heavily, his mouth twitching in a smirk.

I sink into the seat in dread.

He looks dangerous. Could be a psychopath. He's not over it.

His goons hush their chatter, the warehouse a silent vacuum.

Uncle licks his lips. "I've been plotting revenge against Seth Gordon for years. Not your mom, no. I could've destroyed her in a second, but I wanted her to see how high I can climb. I was preparing a surprise for her. And you, sweetie, were gonna be the cherry on top. I was planning on kidnapping you the night we met in Dumbo. Then in Brighton when you were shopping. Then at your condo. But that fucking sniper kid"—Uncle's lips curl in an ugly smirk—"he was everywhere you were, messing up my every plan."

There's spite in his stare, but I feel pride for Jace.

"So today," Uncle continues, taking a step closer to me, hands in his pockets. "Today I will finally get what I want."

"Which is?" I say in a whisper.

"Seth Gordon and your mother on their knees, begging me to let you go."

"My mother?" My heart stills.

"Oh, she got the picture of her little Lu all sad. Just like Gordon."

Asshole.

I wish I was a fictional character. Brave like Emily Aberdeen, who shot a gun and set buildings on fire when John Temple was in danger.

I'm not. There's nothing I can do against the seven goons who carry guns.

Uncle checks his phone and sucks his teeth. "Alright. The show is on." He takes out his gun and motions to his men. "Get in position. This guy might have some tricks up his sleeve."

This guy?

Uncle scowls at me. "Your sniper boyfriend is here."

The front door opens, and Jace is pushed in by another goon.

If only we knew back then is the most overused phrase. Usually, etched with sadness or regret.

But my heart aches at the thought when I see Jace. *My* Jace.

He didn't need to lie to me when we met. He's my hero, and I admire him for his past and what it made him into.

My heart flutters with worry and glee at seeing him.

Uncle turns to him and spreads his arms. "Welcome to our humble gathering, Mr. Reed."

Jace's worried eyes find me across the warehouse, and Uncle right away snaps his fingers at me.

"Сидеть. И ни звука²," he hisses. "Mr. Reed," he says loudly. "What do you have for me?"

The goon behind Jace rips the backpack off his shoulders and dumps the contents onto the floor. He rummages through what looks like wads of bills, then curses.

"Fuck, boss, these are fake."

Uncle cocks his head. "You have the audacity to play games right now?" He raises his gun at Jace.

My heart thuds in my chest.

Jace takes a step forward, standing tall and strong. "We have a proposal." His voice is soft but with an edge.

"A proposal?" Uncle snorts. "That wasn't the deal." His voice is a notch harsher.

Jace raises his palms, asking for attention. "Gordon terminated our contract. He refused to pay the money. Refused the negotiation. But Roey Torres, my employer, has an offer."

"Piece of shit," Uncle hisses.

My heart falls.

My father refused to pay for me? Not that I know him well, but what father wouldn't agree to make a deal to get his daughter back?

"I figured he'd be smarter than that," Uncle murmurs only for me to hear.

He's simmering. His chest rises and falls. His fingers around the gun tighten. He moves his head slowly side to side like he's cracking his neck, and I can't see his face but I pray Jace knows how to handle this. Something is coming his way.

My eyes snap to Jace on the other side of the warehouse.

"Roey Torres offers his services—" Jace starts saying when Uncle shifts, and a shot echoes through the warehouse.

I scream as I duck in panic.

Across the warehouse Jace stumbles backward, his hand flying up to his shoulder.

"Jace!" I shout.

The goon behind Jace catches him and pushes him forward, but Jace twists and slams into him.

Uncle's hand with the gun moves, following them, as Jace knees the guy and elbows him in the face, sending him onto the floor.

"Jace!" I scream as another guy charges at him.

Jace ducks and punches him in the gut.

Face punch. Elbow cut. Knee cut. He grabs the guy and twists him like a puppet, then uses him as a human shield.

The other goons cock their guns.

"You are making it complicated," Uncle hisses and fires the gun.

I flinch, deafened by the shot, watching the guy Jace uses as a shield slide down onto the floor.

"Get him!" Uncle roars, his gun still pointing at Jace.

Uncle will shoot again!

My heart is hammering in my chest, blood pumping in my head.

Uncle cocks the gun, and I don't hesitate even for a second as I dart out of my chair and tackle him, sending us both to the floor.

There's a loud bang as the door is smashed open.

Another shot echoes.

Then another, the loud sound assaulting my eardrums.

A punch in my chest leaves me choking for a moment as Uncle pushes me off him.

I gasp feverishly, fighting the sharp pain and trying to get my breath back.

The shots start firing everywhere.

Jace doesn't have a gun. Where's this coming from?

A bullet grazes the floor next to me, and I scream, covering my head, panic rising in my chest.

"Get down, assholes!" someone yells.

Several men file through the front door into the warehouse and behind the storage vaults. These guys don't belong here. I can't see Jace and frantically search for him.

A hand jerks me by my scruff to my feet, and Uncle hisses, "Your boy fucked up. Let's move," sending shivers down my spine as he drags me toward the very back of the warehouse.

Guns start firing everywhere, gunshots booming through the small space.

"Fucking morons. They'll pay," Uncle rasps.

I try to fight, but he sticks the cold gun barrel into my neck. "Either follow me or I'll shoot your pretty head off. I won't hesitate. It'll be a nice souvenir for your mother."

He drags me toward the exit sign above the back door, and I scramble, following.

Right before he yanks me out of the door, I scream, "Jace!"

And dread fills me at the thought that I might never see him again.

---

1. *"Ты много чего не знаешь, солнце."* — (Russian) "There's a lot you don't know, sunshine."

2. *"Сидеть. И ни звука."* — (Russian) "Sit. And not a peep."

66

JACE

Lu's fading scream pierces me with sharper pain than the bullet. My eyes dart in the direction of the back door Reznik just dragged her out of.

I lean back on the wall behind a storage vault and pant, my mind reeling.

Another shot goes off. Then another echoes through the warehouse.

One of Brexton's guys ten feet away from me gives me a smirk like we are playing laser tag.

"You," I mouth to him. "Cover me."

Without waiting for a response, I start crouching along the perimeter of the building.

"Put your guns down!" another guy shouts, impossible to tell if he's ours or Reznik's.

"There's a backup team outside!"

So, Kolchak's men are here. Good.

The shots start firing again from all directions.

I run behind a coat rack, and a bullet swishes through the coats, sending a cloud of fur into the air.

One of Reznik's guys is crouching behind the next rack, repeatedly popping above it to shoot toward the front end of the warehouse.

I lunge at him with a vicious blow to his face, sending him flying through the fur coats as his gun slides across the floor to the center of the warehouse—fuck!

I move quickly.

I don't have much time.

Bullets zip above me.

Moans echo from the opposite side—someone got hurt.

But I don't stop, don't look, my eyes on the back door as the warehouse turns into a shootout.

In a minute, I'm out the door, shielding my eyes from the blinding outside light.

A red sedan storms with screeching acceleration toward the main avenue. I can't see who's driving, but the blonde hair that I spot through the back window is *hers*.

Lu!

I dart after it, reaching the main street—yes, we are still in the Soviet fucking Motherland.

For once, there's something else I love about Brighton besides food—double parking and traffic. Reznik could've run the red light, but when some asshole double-parks, blocking one of the two lanes, and a bus blocks the second lane, the red sedan behind it has nowhere to go.

The pain in my shoulder sharpens as I run as fast as I can after Reznik's car.

I want to snatch someone's phone and call Roey but have to keep my eyes on the car. Hopefully, Miller is following the tracker in my shoe.

I almost reach Reznik's car when the light switches to green, and as soon as the second lane is free, the sedan passes the bus and vrooms forward.

Fuck!

I sprint like I'm trying to catch a Formula 1 racer.

The same scenario repeats one light after another. The sedan turns onto Corbin Place and gets stuck a hundred feet ahead of me in traffic.

My wound hurts like a bitch, bleeding through my shirt. Sweat rolls down my face as I sprint across the road and along the sidewalk. My lungs burn but I can run like this for blocks. Except I don't know where Reznik is heading, and I pray Roey keeps an eye on my tracker and sends more guys.

The sedan turns a couple of times on the smaller streets and veers onto Emmons Avenue which runs along the bay, lined with boats and charters.

I run past the pedestrians, panting, knowing that if Reznik is heading for the highway, I'll lose him, and if Roey doesn't send a car after him, Reznik will get away.

Roey! Where the fuck are you?

My lungs scream as they burn with oxygen. Blood pounds in my brain. Sweat leaks into my eyes as I try to keep them on the red sedan ahead that's getting farther and farther away.

Until it stops abruptly about three hundred feet ahead, and Reznik darts out.

What's he doing?

I push myself forward.

Reznik drags Lu out and toward the bay.

Where's he going?

When I reach his car, I dart toward the open gates, the packed parking lot, and the railing that fences off the marina behind it.

A speedboat veers away from the dock.

Shit!

I lean with my hands on my knees, panting, but in a moment, I gather my remaining strength and go up the steps to the crowded restaurant deck that gives a much better view of the marina.

A big party is going on. Pushing past people, I run up to the railing of the terrace that overlooks the bay.

Reznik's boat is veering out of the bay, and, fuck, if I don't feel like Lu is slipping through my fingers.

That's it! We lost them!

My heart pounding, I look around wildly.

Barons of Brighton, the sign on the building says. It's a boat club with a restaurant, and it's a Saturday, still daylight, but the party at the club is in full swing.

A crowd of dressed-up women and men smoke outside. Others lounge around the patio tables. Music is trickling from inside the restaurant through the open terrace doors.

There are plenty of people who look rough and weathered—

boaters and yachters, I assume. I don't stick out with my sweaty bloodied shirt.

I feel up my wound—it's a through one, thank God.

A group of guys stands by the railing not far from me, chatting in Russian, I assume, smoking and sizing me up.

I shift and wince at the pain in my shoulder, dizzy for a moment, leaning over the railing with my eyes closed.

"Эээээ, чел, ты норм?[1]"

A tall guy steps toward me. The other two stare me down. Those unintentionally angry stares are definitely Slavic. So are jeans, dress shirts, several-day stubble, and fuck-all attitude.

"I don't speak Russian," I grit through my teeth.

"You okay?" he asks.

"Fine, thanks. Hey, can I use your phone?" I ask, and before he gets suspicious, I add, "Some asshole stole my phone and I need to get help."

Pity-fuck, see? People always go for a charity case over an emergency one.

It works.

I dial Roey.

"Reznik is on a boat," I blurt when he picks up after one ring. "I don't know where he's heading, but he just took off from the Barons of Brighton marina."

"I see you on the map. Guys I sent to follow you got stuck in traffic." Of course. Fucking Brooklyn. "What kind of boat?"

"I didn't catch what boat it was."

"Donzi 22 called Flyer, purple and white," the guy next to me says as his eyes slowly slide up and down my body and fix on the dark bloodied stain on my shoulder.

"You hear that?" I ask Roey.

"Yes. Miller is starting the drone. We're on it. Brexton and Kolchak's guys got Reznik's men. I'm sending the teams to the marina."

More people pour out of the restaurant, laughing. The music gets louder.

I pass the phone back to the guy and lean over the railing of the deck, scanning the rows of boats and yachts, moored and decked. Halyard ropes beat against the tall sailboat masts out in the water, producing a ringing noise.

Think, think, think, Jace.

This is a boat club, right? People gotta have boats I can hire, even on a Saturday.

"What help you need?" the same guy asks, not taking his eyes off me.

"My girl."

He snorts, puffing out a cloud of smoke. "She ran away?"

The other guys chuckle and spit on the ground.

"She got kidnapped," I answer.

I don't know why I explain myself, but I learned at war that sometimes help comes in unexpected forms. These guys might know how to get a boat.

"Kidnapped? You serious?" The guy leans with his palms on the railing next to me, a cigarette hanging from his mouth as he squints at me through the smoke.

"Yeah."

He nods toward the bay. "Blonde girl and old guy on the Flyer?"

I meet his eyes. He must be a boater if he casually smokes during a party but notices every boat that comes in or out.

I nod, keeping his stare.

Next, his heavy paw is on my shoulder, shaking me with what apparently is reassurance. "We can get her, man."

I want to laugh in his face, but he seems friendly in his own brutally awkward Eastern European way. His tipsy eyes squint at me like he's trying to figure out if I'm up for whatever crazy idea just triggered his brain.

"Эй!²" He turns to his friends, says something in his language, and they circle me.

"Let's go get her," one of them says as he flicks what looks like a joint in his hand with his finger.

I wonder if they are drunk. It's hard to say. The Eastern European gauge for booze is a unicorn with three eyes.

"I'm Alex," the tall guy says slowly like we are making friends at a banquet, and stretches his hand for a shake.

"Jace."

"Dzima, Misha," he introduces the others.

They shake my hand with caution like we are striking a deal but they are wondering if I'm tricking them.

"You know where to get a boat around here right now? A fast one?" I ask.

"You fucking with us?" Alex chuckles, exchanging mocking glances with his friends.

"I can pay."

"Where do you think you are?"

It's a boat club, I'm not dumb. But a lot of random people probably come to drink here.

The guy named Dzima turns to his bud. "Bro, there's cognac on the boat. And I need air." His English is great.

"I need to fuck," the guy called Misha murmurs and looks in the direction of the girls who chill at a distance.

"Okay, let's go." Alex swings his forefinger in the air.

"Go where?" I ask, my heart giving out an excited thud, because I'm ready to chase Reznik and my Lu as far as the Caribbean.

"What you mean where? Get cognac and get your girl."

I hope I'm not making a mistake when I follow them to the stairs that lead down to the marina pier.

"*Дим! Куда, блин?*³" a gorgeous girl in a mini dress shouts at him from the terrace doors.

Dzima turns around toward her without stopping. "*Лен, ща вернемся! Человека спасать идем!*⁴" he yells as he motions toward the bay.

"What kind of boat do you have?" I ask, my heart fluttering with hope as we pass all sorts of watercraft docked at the pier. "A sailboat won't cut it. It's too slow. The guy just took off in a speed boat."

Alex glares at me. "Don't insult me. You pay for gas, by the way."

He halts by a fancy yellow speed boat. "Dzima, get the cognac! Misha, ropes!" Then he turns to me. "Hop in. You need legal backup?"

I stall. "What does that mean?"

"The college across the bay"—he nods in that direction—"has their own water patrol. I know a guy."

"Not yet."

"Dzima," Alex barks, turning on the engine, my nerves

humming in sync with its loud rumbling. "Fucking cognac! Let's roll!"

These guys treat this like a party because Dzima comes out of the cabin with a bottle and aluminum shots in his hands.

Misha unties the docking lines. "Got it!" he shouts, hopping into the boat.

"Watch the beams," Alex commands and starts veering the boat away from the dock while Dzima pours the shots and balances as the boat backs left, then slowly straightens out.

Alex throws back a shot, a proud smile on his lips. "Okay! *Погнали?*[5]"

We veer past the moored boats toward the opening out of Sheepshead Bay, and I ask for their phone so I can call Roey again.

Misha offers me a shot, but I decline. "You guys really do drink a lot, huh?"

Dzima shrugs. "Man, we drink, do crazy shit, and embrace it. You Americans drink, cry about it, and go to AA meetings."

"Now hold on!" Alex interrupts him and revs up the motor. "Saturday. Let's rrrrrrride!" he roars with an accent that's sharper than the motor sound.

These are crazy people, I realize, and I just put my life into their hands.

---

1. *"Эээээ, чел, ты норм?"* — (Russian) "Hey, dude, you all right?"
2. *"Эй!"* — (Russian) "Hey!"
3. *"Дим! Куда, блин?"* — (Russian) "Dzim! Where the hell you going?"
4. *"Лен, ща вернемся! Человека спасать идем!"* — (Russian) "Len, we'll be right back. Gonna go save a person."
5. *"Погнали?"* — (Russian) "Let's roll?"

67

JACE

I DIAL ROEY.

"Jace, Reznik is heading toward the Lower Bay," Roey says right away. "I'm driving. Miller's next to me. We are heading east, toward Rockaway. Miller has a drone following Reznik's boat, but we're not sure where he's going. The Brexton Recovery assholes are on the move, too, determined to help out. *Help out*, my fucking ass. They are heading west, toward Staten Island, in case that's where Reznik is going. Gordon is on the way to a helipad."

"Helipad? In Brooklyn?"

"It's the local high school's athletic field. He got NYPD clearance. Asshole has connections everywhere."

"*Now* he's worried," I grind out.

"Jace, we're in fucking traffic. You need to find a boat. Maybe you can—"

"I'm *on* a boat." If he hadn't interrupted me, I'd have told him earlier.

"That was fast. With a captain?"

"The whole crew."

"You're an ace! Okay, so head toward the Lower Bay. Reznik is only a mile away. Stay on the phone with me."

I do. Dzima pours another shot of cognac for Alex and himself.

"You want?" he asks me.

I down one. Sure helps with the pain that's burning my shoulder.

He notices me wincing as I touch it. "Man, you hurt, huh? Want medicine?"

He raises the bottle in his hand, and somehow I feel like that's the only medicine he has.

Roey is back on the phone. "All right, Jace, Reznik's boat is turning around Breezy Point and is heading toward Rockaway Beach and into the Atlantic Ocean. How far are you?"

"Head to Rockaway," I yell to Alex. "How far are we from the Breezy Point?"

"A minute or so."

"Can you go faster?"

Alex shifts his sharp gaze at me and revs up the motor. "Hold on!"

The boat zooms between the land strips, the breeze cooling my face.

Honestly, I didn't even know they had so many yachts, sailboats, and speedboats in Sheepshead Bay. Let alone the charter boats and party cruises. There's my ignorance. Brooklyn is surrounded by water.

These Eastern-European guys are off the hook. Not sure if they fully realize the meaning of kidnapping, but they look like they're ready to cross the Atlantic.

"How much gas do you have?" I ask Alex at the helm.

A smirk curls his lips, a cigarette bobbing between them. "Don't worry, man."

"I'll pay for that."

"You will." He doesn't look at me but squints at the distance.

Maybe these guys enjoy adventure. Maybe they *are* crazy. Or just party heads.

It's Saturday, and the open waters ahead are sprinkled with dozens of boats.

Alex laughs at something Dzima says in Russian as he pours him another shot. Then one for himself. Then offers me one. Alex has another cigarette between his lips, squinting ahead, sparks flying from the wind, smoke puffing from his mouth. Only sailors know how to keep their cigarettes burning in the wind going at high speed. Only sailors can fucking stand on their feet and drink as the boat zooms at sixty miles an hour, the water spraying in their faces.

"Where's Misha?" I ask, wondering if he fell out of the boat with the speed we are going, crashing through the waves.

Dzima shrugs. "In the cabin, on the phone with a client. He does IT. Probably fixing someone's firewall."

We should hire these guys. That's an idea.

"Jace, what's the update?" Roey's voice is in my ear. I forgot he's still on the phone with me.

"Alex?" I look at our Slavic captain.

He nods ahead. "That boat, see?"

"Wait," I say. "Roey," I blurt into the phone. "Does the drone show a yellow speed boat about three hundred yards behind Reznik's?"

"Wait," he says. "Yes. Is that you?"

"Yes. Alex!" I get up, widening my stance for balance. "Follow it, try to get close. Now careful, the guy might be armed."

He cuts me a glare. "You didn't say armed."

"Like guns?" Dzima asks, turning to study the boat ahead that we are approaching fast.

"Roey, what do we do?" I ask.

That very moment, the boat catches a wave bump and slams hard, sending me and Dzima toppling over onto the seats.

"Блять, че за хрень, Саш?¹" comes from the cabin, and I look in and see Misha scrambling on his knees on the floor, looking for something.

But my eyes latch onto one thing next to him—a flare gun.

"Alex!" I bark against the wind and the loud roaring of the motor. "That flare gun works?"

"Of course works."

Perfect.

I go down and grab it. "You have another one?"

"No!" he shouts against the wind.

Fuck. Then I have one shot, one opportunity, as one great rapper said.

"Get closer!" I order. "Not too close right now."

He is.

"Binoculars?" I ask.

Dzima fetches them in a flash of a second, and I get a closer view of Reznik standing at the helm.

And Lu...

My heart gives out a howl.

She's in the front seat next to him, looking back at our boat. And I fucking wave, even though Reznik might do something stupid. She needs to know I'm on it.

Hold on tight, Lu. I got you, baby.

I have an idea and shout into the phone, "Roey! We need a distraction!"

And then there's a shot.

Our boat swerves sharply, sending me onto the floor.

"*Сука!*[2]" Alex hisses. "Fuck, man! He shoot at us!"

I scramble back onto the seat. "Avoid the direct course!"

"He shoot my boat, you pay," Alex grunts. But there's new determination in his eyes. "You know what you doing, love boy?"

"I do. Roey!" I shout into the phone. "Where's your drone?"

Another shot comes, but Alex is driving in a wavy trajectory, hunching like he's in the Venture Cup racing competition. He's soaked with the salt spray, his face wet, but his eyes are sparkling with excitement as he murmurs something in Russian.

"I have the drone, Jace. I see you," Roey snaps into the phone.

"I don't need you to see me. Right now, I need you to get very close to Reznik and distract him."

"Distract how?"

"Distract so he doesn't shoot at us or look back."

"He'll shoot the drone."

"I don't care about the drone! This is our only chance, Roey. I have one shot. I can't miss it. If I do, we have nothing. Do your best!"

Another shot rips the air, and I pray to God our boat is not shot and sinking, because then I lose Lu for sure.

I press the binoculars to my eyes and see the drone keeping up with Reznik's boat. The drone costs over ten grand, but Miller has several and is proficient with them.

"Alex! Get closer!" I shout. "As close as you can on the driver's side!"

"He will shoot my boat."

"Don't worry about the boat. Get fucking close!"

His momentary glance in my direction is angry but full of determination. He's either an adrenalin junkie or senses that I'm not an average boat rider. Or he might be carelessly drunk. His boat probably costs close to a hundred grand, but he's too enthusiastic about the chase.

There's a freshly lit cigarette bobbing between his lips. I don't even notice when he lights them, or how, with both hands on the helm, wind blasting, the boat slamming against the waves, and sea spray showering us head to toe.

"Roey! Now! Get close and distract him!" I shout into the phone, the boat bumping, but I drop the phone and grab the flare gun.

My eyes are on the drone that starts descending onto Reznik's boat. He looks up, distracted, his boat swerving slightly as he holds the helm with one hand, the other pointing the gun in the air.

Lu is looking back at our boat, and I wave for her to get away from Reznik. She scoots all the way to the left.

"Alex! Now pull up to their side and try to keep steady!" I shout.

"Got it."

The drone is hovering lower, and Reznik shoots at it, but the drone swerves to the side, ditching the shot. Reznik's boat swerves toward ours, and Alex swerves away, making me wobble.

But I steady myself and widen my stance.

There have been a few times in my life when I wasn't sure if I could handle my task. The first sniper assignment. The first person I had to shoot at. The first bounty hunt when I was nervous about using my rifle on the mainland.

There's no way to sync my heart with the target right now like I do when my eye is in the scope.

I don't have a proper gun.

The boat is unsteady.

The wind blasts in my face.

But I absolutely *cannot* fucking miss! This is my only chance. *She* is my only chance. So this flare gun? It better work.

I point it at Reznik, who's only forty or so feet away, both boats bumping the waves.

Reznik shoots at the drone again.

I counted his bullets. The gun he had at the warehouse had

twelve rounds with a full clip. He's used eight so far. I just need him to shoot four more times so he doesn't get a chance to shoot at us at close proximity.

Reznik fires another shot at the drone that flies erratically in circles above him, making him spin around.

One.

He turns toward our boat, raising his gun at us when the drone gets even closer, above his head, and he jerks his gun up and shoots again.

Two.

The drone swerves, avoiding being hit, then lunges at him and sweeps only a foot above his head.

Reznik's boat swerves to the side, and he shoots, aimlessly, obviously angry.

Three.

"Keep up!" I shout at Alex, my eyes on Reznik.

Reznik leans on the helm, holding it with his belly, and I fucking pray I wasn't mistaken about the number of shots he took. This *has* to be the last one.

Reznik steadies himself, points upward toward the drone, and shoots.

The drone explodes into pieces ten feet above him in the air.

That was his last bullet.

My turn.

And I shoot.

Bang!

It's my only shot. And when the flare zooms with smoke toward Reznik, for a second—one brief motherfucking second—my heart stalls.

Then Reznik spins, so fast that it's unmistakable—I hit him, though I don't know where.

He topples over, his gun flying out of his hand, and I wave at Lu and roar, "Jump!"

---

1. *"Блять, че за хрень, Саш?"* — (Russian) "Shit, what the hell, Sash?"
2. *"Сука!"* — (Russian) "Bitch!"

68

JACE

"Jump!" I shout to Lu and wave like a mad lifeguard. "Jump!"

And there's my Lu, the girl who walks in high heels like they are her feet extensions and dances like a ballerina. The soft-spoken sunshine with a gentle touch, who, without hesitation, goes over the railing like a freaking American Ninja Warrior and dives into the water.

"Stop!" I shout to Alex.

No need. He's a fucking pro. I want to kiss the man who makes a U-turn like you only see in cop-chase movies and cuts the gear to neutral.

I don't wait. Reznik's boat keeps going forward, speeding away in an erratic trajectory, as I dive overboard.

Cold, hot, excited, and anxious, I swing my arms like crazy when I reach the surface and locate Lu.

I don't know if she can swim, I never asked. But when I reach her, she's floating, panting, spitting the salty water out.

"Lu!" I pull her toward me, and we both go under. I push us back out and try to hold her to keep her above water. "Can you swim?"

"Yes," she pants.

The ocean is cold, but my heart is so fucking hot, because I got her, and Reznik is nowhere near. But Alex's boat is. Thank God for the crazy Slavs!

Alex idles the boat toward us and throws out a life ring.

In a minute, we are pulled into the boat.

"*Ого!*[1]" he blurts out, scanning Lu up and down.

I cup her face. "You alright? I'm so sorry, baby. I didn't know what else to do. I didn't know that would happen. I thought he—"

"Jace, Jace, Jace. Baby, slow down," she whispers, slightly trembling but with a reassuring smile on her face.

Baby... Fuck me sideways. It sounds so freaking cute.

She cups my face too and strokes my cheeks with her thumbs. Then she kisses me, and the world is suddenly calm and cool and full of emotions and the guys' whistles and chuckles and a subtle, "*Во как*[2]."

"I got you, Lu," I murmur between the kisses. "You okay? You got scared?"

"I saw you wave," she says, panting, "and I jumped in the water like a dolphin to get to you."

We laugh, hugging.

When she pulls away, she looks at Alex and smiles.

"Are you Russian?" she asks.

"Belarusian," he says.

"My mom is Belarusian."

His face lights up. "*Ааааа. Ну, здравствуйте.*[3]" He cackles, a cigarette between his lips. "Ours!" He winks at me. "Good choice, man."

I know.

Alex passes her a shot. "*Пей.*[4]"

She throws it back, wiping her mouth with the back of her hand.

"You hurt?" I ask.

She shakes her head with a smile. "No."

I don't care about Reznik, but the motherfucker stole my girlfriend and unleashed a band of goons on me. There's nothing I want more besides taking my girl home than to roast his crypto-thieving ass.

I turn to Alex. "You think you can catch up with that guy?"

Alex exhales the cigarette smoke into the air.

Dzima chuckles.

Misha, who sat through the chase and bullet shots with an IT client, is up on the deck and pours shots like I just asked if we can take a sunset tour. Which is an option, the sun *is* setting over the beautiful sparkling blue water.

"You care about the guy?" Alex throws back a shot that Dzima passes him and exhales through his lips.

"Wanna make some cash?" I tempt him.

"How much we talking? My wife will kill me. We almost out of cognac, too."

"If we catch him? Twenty grand."

His narrowed gaze drills into me. "You high?"

"Yes or no?

Misha whistles. "Yes."

Alex is suspicious. "And get killed?"

"He doesn't have any more bullets," I reassure him. "Or at least I don't think so. But I don't know how to catch him. It's probably a no-go at this point. He's too good."

I'm baiting Alex. Oh, fuck yes, I am.

His jaw sets. "You know where you are? We from Brighton. You want action? We got action."

A piece of advice? Never challenge Eastern Europeans with crazy dares, unless that's your goal. They don't have brakes. Nor do they have a notion of red flags. And the sea? True sea devils seem to have no limits, and Alex definitely doesn't.

"Sit tight," he grinds out.

I sit Lu down on the bench.

She's shivering, soaked but smiling at me. I smile back, my heartbeat spiking at the sight of her safe as I run into the cabin and grab a dry towel for her.

"Lu, baby, did Reznik have any other guns on him?"

She looks at me with the desperation of wanting to help but bites her lip. "Not that I saw, no."

"Alex." I turn to him. "The guy shouldn't have a gun anymore. But I don't know how to stop him so we can get him."

Alex nods to Dzima. "A shot." He does one, then cracks his neck and jams a cigarette into his mouth. "I got it."

The motor roars again. We swerve, making a U-turn, and we are back in the chase.

I pick up the phone and hug shivering Lu with one arm as I dial Roey. "What's the update?"

"The drone is shot, Jace. We parked and need a moment to start another one."

"I got Lu."

"You got her?"

"Yes."

"You *got* her? You mean *with* you?"

"Yes! Yes! *With* me!" I kiss her wet head and tighten my arm around her. "I got her. But we are chasing Reznik again."

"Be careful. He has a gun."

"And no bullets. Plus, he's injured."

"Good. Remember he has the bracelet. You have to figure out the way to get him."

In several minutes, Alex catches up with Reznik and turns to his friends. "The safety raft! Blow it up! Quick! Now!" he barks.

Misha and Dzima dart to the cabin.

"Jace, baby, you got hurt."

Baby...

Say it again, Lu.

Her hand is on the dark spot on my shoulder.

"I'll be fine for now," I reassure her. "You okay?"

She nods fast.

Misha and Dzima come out with a bale that they flatten out and pull a rope. It's an emergency raft. I've seen those before. We had first aid stretchers like this in the service. You pull the rope, and the capsule pumps the air. Smart. These guys are prepared.

"Got him!" Alex shouts.

My eyes catch the boat in the distance that's going much slower now.

Alex is on the hunt. He goes to the right, then approaches Reznik's boat which swerves to the left.

"Yes, motherfucker," Alex growls in a sharp accent. I feel like he learned his English words from movies. "Go that way..."

His eyes dart to the depth sensor on his helm then back at Reznik, and he swerves his boat toward Reznik's.

"What are you doing?" I rise up from the seat.

"Going to run him off. He good with boats?"

"I don't know."

He swerves our boat into Reznik's again, and Reznik zooms

toward the coastal area and the beach. But Alex doesn't chase after him. He stays parallel to the beach, a mysterious grin splitting his face.

And then something happens that makes us all gasp.

Reznik's boat suddenly halts, so abruptly that Reznik's body surges forward, over the windshield, onto the bow, then topples overboard.

"Rockaway Beach, motherfucker," Alex growls. "He hit land. Don't know shit about depth."

I grab the binoculars and watch Reznik on his feet struggle through the shallow water as he grapples toward the beach. His boat is tilted sideways, immobile, stuck in the shallow waters.

"What now?" Alex asks. "Chase him?" He turns to Misha and Dzima in question.

I exhale, trying to concentrate.

"Here's the deal. We can't get him barehanded. He might have a bracelet with a nerve agent. And if you get close and get stabbed— you'll be as good as dead."

The three of them take their eyes off the emergency raft that now takes up half of the deck and stare at me.

"Seriously?" Alex asks. "You didn't say about nerve agent. Who's he?"

I shrug. "Eastern European."

He snorts.

I wait for their decision. "What do you think?"

Alex spits overboard. "You know what Jay-Z said? It's New York. Nothing you *can't* do." He nods to his friends. "Boat on the water. Jace, you with us. Dzima, get rope and fishing net. Misha, you stay with pretty girl." He winks at Lu. "That okay?" he asks me.

I look at Lu. She nods.

"Let's go!" Alex orders.

In a moment, Dzima, Alex, and I are on the raft until we anchor on the beach, the binoculars never leaving my face. "He's heading toward a residential street in the distance."

"We have to move!" Alex orders.

We run, chasing after Reznik, me barehanded because I still have no idea what's happening, Dzima with a rope, Alex with a fishing net.

We are faster than him. I must've injured him pretty badly with the flare gun.

I've tracked people so many times back in Yemen. But you are never prepared for a chase in a Long Island beach neighborhood, tracking a guy who might be more dangerous than a bomb. And not with two crazy Eastern European guys who've had more cognac than I do before I pass out.

Humankind is amazing. You learn this at war of all places.

Apparently, this also happens on a calm evening in Brooklyn when some random guys decide to help you rescue your girl and catch a criminal and do that with a flimsy promise of a reward, just hoping that things will turn out good. Some people believe in goodness and love and helping others and yes, in the motherfucking happily ever afters.

Alex, you are a badass!

We are only forty feet away from Reznik, who limps badly, reaching the end of the beach line.

Alex raises his joined hands at him, mimicking a gun.

"Hold!" he shouts. "I'll shoot!"

Is he fucking serious?

But Reznik halts, not even looking back as he raises his hands in the air.

"Dzima, rope! Fast!" Alex orders.

You think you know people? Think twice. Tito was right—never assume things.

Who knows when Dzima crafted a lasso, but it swings above his head as he runs toward Reznik, then throws the loop around him and yanks him off his feet.

"You kidding me?" I mumble, startled.

I've seen many things overseas. Most of it had to do with guns and heavy explosives.

Lassos? That's for Western moves.

Or New York. Because Reznik wiggles like a worm on the sand, and Dzima tugs at the rope attached to him then walks up to him and sends a punch to his face.

Alex gives a backward nod in their direction. "Boxing State Champion of Belarus, 2015."

"Don't touch him," I warn. "There might be poison on him."

Alex only hums. "Want to strip him naked?"

"Let others handle it when we deliver him. We just need to figure out—"

"Hold up. Now, watch, American," Alex says, walking up to a cursing Reznik.

Alex shakes the fishing net out and throws it like a cast, covering the ten square feet on top of Reznik, then tugs, closing him in.

I'm freaking speechless.

"*Сука,*[5]" comes from Reznik.

"*А, да?*[6]" Alex laughs grudgingly. "*Нехер стрелять куда попало.*[7]"

And just like that, Dzima has a lasso around Reznik, Alex—a fishing net.

"What now?" I ask them.

"Now we go back." Alex shrugs and turns to Dzima. "We have more cognac?"

These guys have no sense of danger.

I gawk in amazement as they drag the cursing Reznik across the sand. I swear, you give them a good cause, and they can take on an army barehanded.

Half an hour later, Reznik, wrapped in a fishing net, is bobbing on a blow-up dingy attached by a rope to our boat that's heading to Sheepshead Bay.

And I'm in my happy place next to Lu.

She smiles at me, then touches my bloodied shirt. "Jace, we need to look into that."

Of course, Alex has superglue on his boat.

I pull the wet shirt over my head and pass the glue to Lu. "You are an artist." I smile. "Do your best."

She grips my wound with her fingers and squeezes it tightly as she draws a super-glue line. My pain is stuck between my teeth and in my gut and her fingers as I hold her gaze while she smiles.

"You are so…" she murmurs, gazing at me.

"What?" I whisper.

"I love you," she says.

That's it. That's the right answer.

"Fuck, man…" That's Alex.

He's staring at my tattoos. "That"—he gives me a backward nod —"*the* eye tattoo?"

He's referring to my elite sniper club eye tattoo that has a reticle instead of a pupil. How would he even know?

He cocks his brow as his eyes rise to my dog tag. He passes the helm to Misha, then pours two shots and gives me one.

"*За нас и за спецназ.*[8]" He winks and throws it back.

So do I. "What did he say?" I ask Lu.

She smiles. "Cheers to us and special forces."

Close.

"I read a blog about you guys." His eyes drop to my tattoo again. "Wow," he whispers. "My respect." Then turns his gaze to Lu. "*Крутой чел.*[9]"

I melt when she cups my face and kisses my jaw, my cheeks, my eyes, and brows. Right in front of fucking everyone.

"You are amazing, Jace Reed," she purrs.

"*Любовь и голуби*[10]," Alex says, staring.

I brush my lips against hers, shaking my head at this little Eastern-European exchange. "What did he say?"

Lu laughs, high-fiving Alex. "A reference to a movie. Love and doves."

Love and doves? How about love and bullets and a missed sedative shot that spun our lives out of control and gifted me with Lu?

"Lu, you are..."

With all the emotions flooding me, I can't even finish the sentence.

"You are my Cupid," she murmurs, "with a gun," and kisses me again.

---

1. "*Ого!*" — (*Russian*) "Wow!"
2. "*Во как.*" — (*Russian*) "Look at that."
3. "*Ааааа. Ну, здравствуйте.*" — (*Russian*) "Aaah. Well, hello."
4. "*Пей.*" — (*Russian*) "Drink."
5. "*Сука.*" — (*Russian*) "Bitch."
6. "*А, да?*" — (*Russian*) "Oh, yeah?"
7. "*Нехер стрелять куда попало.*" — (*Russian*) "Don't be fucking shooting at others."
8. "*За нас и за спецназ.*" — (*Russian*) "To us and special forces."
9. "*Крутой чел.*" — (*Russian*) "Tough dude."
10. "*Любовь и голуби.*" — (*Russian*) "Love and doves."

69

LU

WHEN YOU SURVIVE A KIDNAPPING, A GUN TO YOUR FACE FROM A MAN you've known since childhood, a boat chase, and the man of your dreams saving you, well, you know the universe aced it.

Oh, and my biological father.

His gaze is tense when he meets us at the marina, three black cars parked at the gates.

"Lucy, I need to explain," he says without looking at anyone but me.

"It's alright," I blurt and scoot closer to Jace. "Maybe tomorrow."

There's hurt in his eyes. But I am yet to find out the details of the story that got me kidnapped.

Jace's arm around my shoulders tightens. "Want a minute with your father?"

"No." I shake my head. "Let's go home."

There are several other guys standing around in bulletproof vests and duty belts. I don't know who they are, but I know my Jace is stronger than a legion of them. He didn't even have a gun when he saved me.

Jace nods to them. "Reznik is in the emergency raft, tied up. Alex will show you."

One of the guys gives Jace a smirk that's almost half-playful as he walks by, and Jace whispers to him, "Suck it, Amon."

A pickup truck pulls up to the curb with a screech. Roey jumps out of it, in a bullet proof vest—whoa, Becky would love the sight of this—and hurries up to Jace. Not me, not my father—Jace. His eyes scan Jace's body and pause on his bloodied shirt.

"What you got here, brother? Let me see."

"I'm fine." Jace tries to fight him off, but Roey won't have it. "Hold fucking still, Shooter."

He tugs Jace's shirt down and inspects his shoulder. "Through wound? Superglue? Good."

Roey *is* the best friend, and I would've never guessed when I first met him in a slick suit and with a cocky attitude at the bar in Williamsburg that he's capable of genuine concern. You rarely get to know a person in a bar. But you do when he makes sure his friend is taken care of after an injury.

"Any other wounds?" he asks.

"No."

"You need to go to the hospital."

"No hospital," Jace argues.

Roey turns to me like I'm Jace's supervisor. "Treat the wound with alcohol and an antibiotic cream when you get home and watch his temperature overnight."

I chuckle. "Oh, I'll watch him overnight."

"Tomorrow, I'll send a doctor to your condo, one of Kolchak's connections. He'll do a thorough exam."

My father clears his throat. "We need to discuss business." He looks at Jace, who says, "You can discuss it with my boss," and nods toward Roey. "Alex and the guys from the boat need to get paid."

"I'll call you," Roey says as Jace is already leading me away.

"Mr. Reed!" My father catches up with us. "My driver will take you. Considering…" He vaguely motions at us—we look like we are coming back from a messy beach party.

"Thank you," I say. I'll take that.

"Here." He passes his phone to me, and it's my mom's desperate voice on the other end as she talks a mile a second in Russian.

"Mom, Mom," I say, trying to stop her. "Jace got me. I'm alright. We are fine."

"I need to meet him. I'm flying in tomorrow."

"No! Mom, please, let's just talk tomorrow. You want to talk to" —I raise my eyes to my biological father—"Seth?"

"I'll fly in tomorrow to snap his neck!"

I laugh, hanging up. My mom would deliver on her promise, too.

"Lucy?" my father says, suddenly looking very small despite his guards and chauffeurs and his fancy suit. I don't know him well, but I suppose a few scenarios can make a powerful man humble. This is one of them. "Can we please talk tomorrow?"

I don't answer.

"Please. The three of us, if you want. I owe Mr. Reed an apology, and I need to explain certain things."

I nod. We'll figure it out. Tomorrow or the day after.

Tonight, I just need my Jace.

I need to tell him how much he means to me, how much I love him. Even better—I'll show him.

70

JACE

My first reward after the chaotic day is Ibuprofen and a warm shower. With Lu. Inside Lu. We claw at each other with so much greed that I'd go through another boat chase and get shot just to see my Lu on her knees, working me like she just found the most delicious popsicle.

That word again.

My brain is off. My senses are on. And next, I'm on my knees, my tongue on my Lu like I'm trying to lick all the ocean salt off her body. That little landing strip on her pelvis is the cutest thing ever.

"You should turn it into a shape," I murmur, teasing it with the tip of my tongue. "Maybe a pineapple since you like them down there."

"Jace!" She covers her face with both hands, grinning, but I pull them away and keep working on her, making sure she watches every flick of my tongue.

Our interactions are limited to the words, "Right there," "Yes," "More," "One more."

Lu's fictional men are pros, and I used to be envious.

Nah, the learning stage is hot as hell. Especially as I find new ways to get my pretty girl so mindlessly needy for me.

I'm a good student. This? I'll have a summa cum laude degree.

Lu gets so intense that she scratches me while I'm on her.

When we finally do get to cleaning up, Lu takes a sponge out of my hand and starts carefully soaping the skin around my wound that I almost forgot about while getting rowdy in the splash zone.

"We need to clean it properly," she says, cocking her head as she cleans me. "Jace," she whispers, studying the scratch on my skin from her nails. "I hurt you."

"Yep. You are my little animal. Wanna do it again?" I grin. "The first time I saw you, I thought you were so sweet and innocent."

Lu bites her lower lip. "And I wanted to strip you naked."

This is unreal. I let her clean me. She gives me playful glances, then locks eyes with me as she cleans me *down fucking there.*

I'm gonna die.

I get hard. She licks her lips, blushes, and whispers, "One more?"

She's definitely not concerned about my wound right now.

I grunt. "One more it is."

And the shower takes for freaking ever, the most amazing shower I've had in my life.

Afterward, we order takeout and have dinner on the terrace. Lu, me, Pushkin, and Mama Bear.

Roey calls. "Chilling?"

"Yeah," I say. "It's been… a lot."

"A lot of fucking money, Jace. Ten mil."

"What?"

"Yep. That's the amount Reznik wanted, and you hung up on Gordon, so he's giving us ten. Me, to be exact."

"What's that supposed to mean?"

"You don't need money. You did it for love, right?"

"Asshole," I murmur as he laughs into the phone.

"I'm kidding. But we have to pay the Brexton guys out of that."

"Right. And double the promised amount for Alex and his guys. It's all their doing."

"That works. We got our target *and* our boss's daughter. Double whammy. Jace, seriously, that beats all the jobs before. And you? You did it."

"I just wanted Lu back."

"Well, we hit the jackpot. We are going to Thailand. Take Lu. Take your creepy pirate dog. Let's celebrate."

"I am. With Lu. Right now."

"I hear you. I need to blow off steam, too."

"Call Becky." I chuckle.

"On my way to meet her, buddy."

"Oh? That's two nights. I thought you don't double-dip." Those are Roey's words, cringy as hell, but, hey, that's my best friend.

"Just one more time. The chick is batshit crazy in bed. By the way, the piece of info she spilled last night? Wanna guess?"

"No. Spill."

"That Goldsling Towers condo you're staying at? Owned by Seth Gordon."

"No way." I glance at Lu, who plays with Pushkin.

"Yeah, he purchased it after Lucy moved there to house-sit. Becky found out when the previous owners called and asked her to keep it hush-hush at the new owner's request."

Seth Gordon does have a soft spot for his daughter and, conveniently, bags of money. And Lu would've moved, out of pride, if she knew. And I wouldn't have met her. Maybe. Maybe not. There are so many variables, some I don't like, including Seth Gordon, but...

I'll tell her tomorrow. There'll be a lot of talking tomorrow. No one else will take my time from her tonight.

"Thanks for the update, Roey," I say. "And listen. Be nice to Becky. She's my girlfriend's bestie."

"Nice is my middle name. With women. Hey, I'm curious about something."

I don't answer, because knowing Roey, I kind of know what's coming.

"Did Lucy make a closer acquaintance with the shark?"

He barks out a laugh, and I stifle a grin. "They are best friends."

"That's my guy! Cheers."

Roey hangs up, and Lu and I move to the bedroom.

I thought the shower was the highlight of our sex practice so far. Nah. Nope. Not even close.

For the next hour, we can't keep our hands off each other.

Clothes? What clothes?

Later, Lu rests naked on my lap, worn out from our lovemaking. My hands don't stop moving. Neither do hers, gliding over my skin like she's touching another human for the first time and is trying to learn textures.

I trail kisses down her neck, making her laugh through the nose and gasp, those little sounds of hers driving me insane.

Where did shame go? Mine was lost in the ocean when I thought I might lose her.

Before we practice yet another sex position, I have some questions.

"Three questions," I clarify, chuckling at the sight of her. My little minx is not much focused on my words but more on sneaking her hand up my bare thigh. "Lu baby, look at me."

"Huh?"

She finally raises her eyes at me, her cheeks flushed, her pupils dilated, lips swollen from my kisses, hair a blonde mess. She's so sexed up that I can't hold back laughter at how ridiculously happy I am right now.

"Questions, yes." She smiles, nudging my nose with hers.

"I want to be your boyfriend. Will you date me?"

"Yes!" she exclaims, making my heart swell, and her arms wrap around my neck. "I mean that's what we were doing lately, right?"

"I just needed to make it official."

"And guess what?"

"Guess what?" I cock my head at her.

"You don't even have to move in. Because we live in the same place."

Right. I kiss the tip of her nose.

"Next question. Will you go to Thailand with me and Roey?"

"When?"

"Soon."

She stalls.

My heart stalls.

"What if I can't go?" She squints at me with a sneaky smile. She's messing with me, and that's alright. She can.

"Then I'll stay."

"Really?" She's testing me, and that's okay too.

"Yeah. Roey will be sending me beautiful pictures from the paradise beaches, but I'll suck it up and stay in New York because you like it so much. I'll be wherever you are, Lu."

She rubs her nose against my cheek like a kitten. "How did I get so lucky?" she whispers.

"I shot you, that's how."

She throws her head back in laughter.

"I wanna go," she says. "But can we decide on the date later? I told Mom and Dad"—she rolls her eyes—"my Dad-Dad in Virginia that I'll bring you home for the Fourth of July."

Whoa.

That feeling in my chest? It's a mix of anticipation and dread, similar to when I was supposed to be taken in by a foster family years ago.

"Sure," I say.

"Is that okay? They really want to meet you."

She told them about me, then. "Meeting your parents, huh? That's quick."

She laughs. "Yeah. You already met one of them. I have a handful."

True. Most of us have one father. Some of us have none. The lucky ones have two, occasionally in the same household.

I can't stop looking at her, wanting to snap pictures of her laughing.

My beautiful Lucy Moor.

Lu baby.

Lu.

The girl of my dreams. In sweatpants, stretched-out sweaters, in my boxers, though I'm yet to make her wear them as I play with her. And of course, she's mesmerizing when she's all dolled up in her minidresses and impossibly high stilettos, everyone's eyes always on her.

Konstantin, who always said to Eva, "Cover up that body. I don't want anyone to look at what's mine," wouldn't approve. But he's fictional and he's wrong.

Lu is mine, and she doesn't look at any other man but me.

I want to flaunt her, boast about her. I want the whole world to admire my Lu. She's a star, and not one that reflects others' light. Her own light can illuminate the whole universe. She wrote once that power is contagious. Next to her, I feel like I can conquer the world and lay it at her feet.

Lu baby, you are a marvel, and I'll love you till the end of my days, I want to tell her, but she knows that, and I'll make sure she never forgets.

I still don't know what went wrong in the universe that said, "Let this guy have the most amazing girl in the world."

Her bare feet rub against my shins, and I can't stop looking at them. I might be that five percent who develop a foot fetish.

"What's the third question?" she asks, her fingers playing with the hair on the back of my head.

"Chapter twenty of *Beautiful Vice.*"

"Oh." She's flustered. "I don't remember."

"Fibber."

"That's... the bathtub scene?"

"Yeah, the bathtub. I thought you don't remember."

She hides her face in my neck, then pulls away, scarlet up to the tips of her ears.

Holy hell, how is my Lu shyer than me?

"Should I install a detachable shower head?" I tease her.

"Stop," she whispers, shaking her head.

"You are blushing, Lu baby." I chuckle. "No, no, no, you are the color of Santa Clause's robe."

I duck my head, trying to catch her gaze, but she bats me off, huffing.

"And pineapples, Lu. You need to write a scene with actual pineapples. We can reenact it for credibility. Pineapples down there—"

"Jace!" she shouts and covers my mouth with her palm that I lick, making her laugh and wiggle on my lap, which makes me hard again.

I finally catch her mouth with mine in a gentle kiss and wrap my arms around her tighter.

"I want to learn every inch of you, Lu. So that you never want anyone else's hands on you but mine."

"I won't."

"Promise?"

"Promise," she whispers. "I love you, Jace. You are the best thing that ever happened to me."

My heart can't handle all this cuteness the universe is pouring on me.

There's a whimper behind the door that's slightly ajar. Pushkin sticks his head in, panting, the tip of his tongue out like he's teasing.

He's jealous and feels neglected, but he can bug off tonight. He already gets the attention of the entire Dumbo neighborhood, plus the social media account Lu created just for him.

"That's right, shithead, Lu is mine. Thanks," I say and wink at him.

His pirate patch is off. The lamp light reflects in his good eye, and it looks like he winks back at me.

Just like then. The night I shot the girl of my dreams.

EPILOGUE

LU

Six months later...

Chok Dee Villa,
Ko Pha-ngan Island,
Thailand

I REREAD THE LAST CHAPTER OF *SHARKI* AND TRY TO HOLD BACK TEARS.

Emily Aberdeen and John Temple fell madly in love with each other. She got to know his secrets and his connection to her past. He found out that nothing in the world, not even the job he was so dedicated to, was more important than her.

But in the end, when the undercover operation went down, Em thought he died in the warehouse explosion. She grieved for weeks, hoping to hear from him, waiting for him to come home.

On a dark lonely night when she couldn't help her aching heart, she set up the painting of him in the center of her bedroom and poured her heart out. She thought it was a farewell and confessed her love to the dead man.

But John Temple survived. He was in hiding. And when the enemy was taken down, he finally made it home.

The night Em was standing in front of the painting, confessing her feelings, was the night he walked into their apartment and stood in the doorway to her room, his eyes closed, listening to the woman he fell in love with confess her feelings to his portrait.

The most emotional chapter in my book was the easiest to write. It was a dedication to my Jace.

Now that I stare at the proof paperback copy in my hands, the feelings come back. How I fell for Jace. The crazy things I did. The first kiss. His confession. What we went through.

Most importantly, every day, he makes me feel like the luckiest girl in the world.

Even Mom is in love with him.

"Jace, baby, you tell me if Lu treats you wrong. I'll handle her," she told him when we were leaving for Thailand.

My heart swells at the vulnerable shift in his eyes when my dad calls him, "Son."

"Lu?"

I turn around.

There he is, the man who makes my heart smile.

Jace leans on the doorframe of our bedroom. His smile is so big, always is, like he's the happiest person on earth.

We rented a cute little villa in the jungles of Ko Pha-ngan in Thailand. Jace is taking a break from work. He found a plot of land so he can build his dream resort. I write random things and take a break from art and everything else, trying to spend as much time with him as I can. Roey is in and out, mostly working in Bangkok, relentlessly tracking some ghost man.

The only thing missing is our Pushkin. For now, he's with Mom and Dad in Virginia.

"Is everything okay?" Jace asks, coming up to me.

He's in swim shorts, my half-naked god, my Cupid who on a random night in Brooklyn shot me and changed my life.

This feels like a dream.

He *is* a dream.

Happiness is tangible. It's on his fingertips that gently stroke my hair. On his lips that softly kiss my shoulder. In his gaze that makes my skin tingle with love every breathing second.

"Please, sit," I tell him.

He takes a seat on the edge of our bed, and his eyes drop to the book in my hands. "Will you read it to me?"

He's read the final version of the book, of course. But I want to read the epilogue because it was written for him.

And I read.

I have to.

It's my confession, and this time, I do it in person and let the love of my life know how much he means to me.

"The world is colors, shades, and tones," I read from the last page of my book though I know the words by heart. "There are opaque colors. And there are translucent ones. And then there are vibrant ones. No, not neon. Those scream and are too straightforward. Vibrant are the ones that don't blind you but capture you, hold your breath, then take it away. They hypnotize, magnetic in their nature, like a Cupid's arrow that slowly infuses love into your heart."

Jace's smile grows bigger.

"That's how I started seeing the world when I met you. The world was always in color, but you made them burst."

I take a deep breath, my heart squeezing so tight, it hurts.

"Fate is a roulette," I continue. "The ball always falls into a slot. Occasionally, it's a win. Rarely, it's a jackpot. Once in a lifetime, it's a life-changing shot. Yours was forty-forty, the perfect sniper's score. Perfect, like you."

I raise my eyes to his. What I'm about to say is not in the book.

"Down the road, love, you would've met many women who would've tripped over themselves to make you happy. You deserve it. You are amazing. You make people want to do good things and be good. Many women would've fallen head over heels in love with you if you let them. But your Cupid's arrow hit me hard. And I fell first. Head over heels and up to my ears."

A soft chuckle escapes Jace, but his eyes are full of endless love he gifts me with every day.

"If you hadn't come back to ask about the room for rent, we would've met again. In my heart, I know it. And now all those what-ifs don't matter because I'm never letting you go. You are my best friend. My lover. My muse. You are the fire I never saw coming. The most beautiful human being. My favorite color. My favorite poem. You are it. Don't you ever forget it, baby."

I smile, wanting to hug the world. Him. *He* is my world.

"I love you, Jace Reed. Thank you for being you. Thank you for being."

Slowly, he gets up and steps up to me, placing his hands on my hips.

"I have something for you," I say and pull a little box out of my pocket and pass it to him.

His eyes flicker to the box, then to me, then back to the box as he opens it.

"An arrow?"

"Yes." It's a golden arrow on a chain. "I have the matching piece." I tug at the gold chain around my neck, showing him the red heart with an indentation. "Look." I take his arrow and snap it into place against the heart. "It's one piece, see?"

Jace lets me put the chain on him, his eyes never leaving mine.

I chuckle, nervous at what I am about to say. This isn't the traditional way. Maybe it's not romantic, but I've made up my mind, though I don't have the rings.

"Jace, I want to ask you something," I say quietly, summoning the courage. Not because I'm afraid to hear the wrong answer but because it's emotional, and girls don't usually do this. He's mine, and this is just a little legal step to seal it. Mom and Dad were ecstatic about the idea.

I take a deep breath and meet Jace's eyes, saying the words that I've practiced in front of the mirror so many times.

"Will you marry me?"

I'm startled right away because the words echo off his lips. The moment the words leave my mouth, Jace asks me the same thing.

We both realize it and start grinning, nodding.

"Yes," I say at the same time Jace says, "Absolutely."

And we laugh.

He wraps his arms around my waist and lifts me up.

I bury my face in his neck, inhaling my favorite scent, him, and kiss him, kiss him, kiss him, then palm his face and kiss the hell out of those beautiful lips.

"You are mine forever, Jace," I whisper.

"You'll be my wife," he murmurs, and it sounds sexy as hell. "Roey will demand an engagement party."

I chuckle through tears. "So will Becky. But after what happened that night between them, they might kill each other and everyone at the party."

"Maybe Tito and Jamie will be the mediators."

"Unless they get into a fight again."

"I'll save you." He grins. "When are we getting married?"

"Whenever you want." I can't wait to call him my husband.

"Tomorrow?"

I laugh. "Silly." But he's not joking. He's not, I can see it in his face. "Jace?"

He shrugs with that sneaky smile that means he's up for any crazy idea. "Let's celebrate?"

"Yes!"

"Champagne and pineapples and chapter thirty-seven of *Sharki*."

"Jace Reed!" I wail and pretend slap him as he throws me over his shoulder. "You'll never forget those pineapples, will you?"

"Your future husband demands proof that his future wife tastes better than pineapples."

He laughs and carries me to the bedroom.

To read a bonus epilogue,
Please, sign up to Lexi Ray's newsletter:
WWW.AUTHORLEXIRAY.COM

ALSO BY THIS AUTHOR:

RUTHLESS PARADISE SERIES:

BOOK 1: **OUTCAST**
BOOK 1.5: **ANGEL, MINE** (NOVELLA)
BOOK 2: **PETAL**
BOOK 3: **CHANCELLOR**
BOOK 4: **WILD THING**
BOOK 5: **RAVEN**

STANDALONE NOVELS:

BROOKLYN CUPID

Printed in Great Britain
by Amazon

37682083R00219